The Architect Who Couldn't Sing

By J.D. ALT

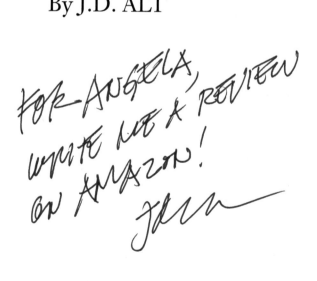

FOR ANGELA,
WRITE ME A REVIEW
ON AMAZON!

Cover Design by J.D. ALT
Editing by Lynn Schwartz Writer's Wordhouse

First published by Dog Ear Publishing
4010 W. 86th Street, Ste H
Indianapolis, IN 46268
www.dogearpublishing.net

ISBN: 978-145750-720-5

This book is printed on acid-free paper.

Printed in the United States of America

TABLE OF CONTENTS

PART I

The Fish Camp

1

IT'S SAFE NOW, I THINK, to tell my father's story—or at least as much of it as I know. It's really my story too: I only knew him for seventeen months, but that was long enough to change the course and trajectory and purpose of my life.

The story begins on my eighteenth birthday, a few weeks before I graduated from high school. That morning my grandmother, Gramella, led me with her painful limp out to the detached, two-car garage behind our white, clapboard house and pointed with the rubber tip of her cane up into the rafters.

"There Charlie," she said. "That's your birthday present."

The cane couldn't point long because it had to quickly resume its role of supporting Gramella's arthritic hip. But it pointed long enough for me to see what I'd never noticed all the years I'd been going in and out of that garage: Pushed back in a corner of the open ceiling joists, partly covered by a dusty folded tarpaulin, was a small black steamer trunk with brass corner guards.

At my inquisitive look Gramella simply gave an upward nod in the direction of the trunk. "It was your mother's," she said.

Until that moment I'd led the sheltered and almost reclusive life of an only child raised by his maternal grandmother in a small, North Carolina house filled with grandmotherly furniture and photos, crocheted doilies and knitted comforters, glass vases filled with perfumed flower petals, artfully arranged porcelain figurines—mementos that, with a single exception, included no physical reference whatsoever to the fact I might have had a mother or a father. Of great aunts and uncles and cousins, there was clear evidence in the small, framed photos on the fireplace mantle and dining room sideboard. But it seemed an entire generation—the one between my grandmother and me—had been skipped over by the facts of historical evidence.

Inquiries about my parents had always been answered by Gramella with light, sunny mantras: "Your mother was as beautiful as they come," she would intone. "She sang like God's favorite angel. Laurie loved you so much, Charlie." And then, shaking her head and wringing the dishtowel she seemed always to have in her hands: "It was such a tragedy…."

About my father: "He was as tall as he was handsome, Charlie. Your mother named you after him! He was an architect—had just graduated with all kinds of big awards when he went off to Vietnam. They were college sweethearts. Just like Romeo and Juliet!"

The fact that Gramella had some literary confusion about the educational circumstances of Shakespeare's characters did not diminish the effect of her sentiment. In the fourth grade, I doted on the imagined images of my mother and father dressed in Elizabethan gowns and stockings, speaking in the high-sounding "thees" and "thous" of the play our school was putting on. I had a minor role and was warmed by the feeling I was somehow connecting with my mysteriously dead and missing parents.

When I was ten this kind of imagining was put to an end when Gramella opened her black, pebbly-textured bible one day and extracted a browned newspaper clipping announcing my mother's fatality. She had drowned in a swimming accident on the French Broad River. It was at a music festival in Asheville. "Performer Feared Lost in the French Broad," the headline said. Her band and a group of "revelers" had gone swimming after a late night performance. Authorities were still searching for her body. For a long time this revelation gave me nightmares, dark watery dreams having to do with the search for my mother's body. I began the habit of sleeping with a small night-light in the corner of my room—just enough illumination to outline the hard, dry reality of my closet door.

But the pebbly surfaced bible contained nothing about my father. At my inquiries Gramella was always quick to extol some virtue: "He was so talented, Charlie. He could draw a line as straight as an arrow without even using a ruler!"

About his demise, however, all she ever said was that he never came back from Vietnam. "He never really came back, Charlie. There were lots of young boys that never came back."

When I was thirteen, my seventh grade civics class went on a field trip to Washington, D.C. Among other places, we visited the Vietnam War Memorial. I told my classmates that my father's name was on it somewhere, but I didn't know the date. Avoiding the easy way of looking in the directory, my classmates spread out along the length of the wall looking for the name "Charles Robert" inscribed in the shiny black marble.

After fifteen minutes or so the teacher, Miss Westerbeke, asked me, "Charlie, are you sure?"

I remember the rising shame that clamped hold of my face and chest. Miss Westerbeke put her arm around my shoulder and guided me off to the side.

"There's a lot of names, Charlie," she said. "We have to be at the Smithsonian in a few minutes. We can always come back when there's more time and check the directory."

But I didn't need to go back. I had realized in that panicked moment what a strange way Gramella had always phrased it: "He never really came back," she'd said.

For me, the rest of that field trip was the teetering realization of the possibility that my father was not mysteriously dead at all, but somehow, somewhere, even more mysteriously, alive.

I never confronted Gramella with this suspicion. Instinctively I knew she did not want to go there. I always steered away from anything that would kindle her strong emotions for the simple reason they kindled strong emotions in me that I neither enjoyed nor understood. There was something about my mother and father, I could sense, that Gramella had hidden away, and was never going to bring out for me to see.

The lack of proper role models, I suppose, was what instilled in me a profound shyness that first took hold in junior high—in the fall of that same seventh-grade year, to be exact—when the boys and girls of my class, to my surprise and puzzlement, first began pairing up in quiet, darkened-room basement parties.

I might never have discovered my own sexuality had it not been for a big, red-headed boy named Nick who began telling me how he "jaggered-off" every night, and how incredible a thing it was to feel. At first I did not believe him. I tried a few times on my own, late after I was sure Gramella was asleep, but nothing like he described took place or could be felt. Then one night it happened all by itself, while I was asleep, dreaming I was pulling a thorn from the foot of Mary Evans, a brown haired girl who lived down the street and never wore shoes during the summer. After that, I took great pains to make sure Gramella had no idea what I knew about, being absolutely certain, somehow, that such activities would be strongly disapproved of.

But in terms of boy-girl love, I was already behind the curve. I was not athletic, and as sports and manliness rose in the social protocol, I withdrew to a world of literary pursuit. I could not imagine how to approach a girl in a romantic way, and so I became the editor of the school newspaper and approached them intellectually, on paper. Even though I grew six inches in my senior year—surpassing most of the popular "studs" in the hall-ways—my interior self remained the short, spindly kid I'd grown accustomed to being in the seventh grade. It takes a long time, I discovered, to grow into your body.

I attended my senior prom with the cheerleader girlfriend of the basketball team's all-conference point guard. I didn't have a girl to take, of course, and she had inconveniently broken off with the team hero a few weeks before the big event. Our date was arranged by a group of her girlfriends who accosted me with bubbly enthusiasm in the office of the school paper. I rented a tuxedo and Gramella tied my bow-tie while I looked down at the part in her shiny grey hair. I drove Gramella's big Buick, and the cheerleader's parents, with ridiculously cheerful smiles and encouragements, took our photo when I picked her up.

The cheerleader, beautiful as any creature I'd ever been close to, was politely talkative when we first got in the car, but by the time we got to the extravagantly crepe-papered school gym, she'd grown quiet and apprehensive. She was immediately surrounded by her girlfriends when we got inside, and I quickly realized—though of course I'd known it from the beginning—that I was merely serving the purpose of legitimately delivering her to the event and, having accomplished this task, my role for the evening was essentially over. I suppose I'd imagined there might be other possibilities—that we might end up dancing the night away, that we might fall in love, that we might kiss tenderly and then have sex in the back seat of the big Buick.

But the cheerleader and her estranged boyfriend made up half-way through the first slow dance, with the lights dimmed low and the big mirrored ball scattering shards of colored light over the clinging, mesmerized couples as they drifted back and forth across the free-throw circles.

For me, the rest of the prom consisted of watching a full moon rise over the practice baseball diamond behind the gym, listening to the muffled swell and fall of the music from inside. Eventually, I started thinking about the little black steamer trunk Gramella had pointed at with her cane just a few days earlier: It had been surprisingly lighter than I'd expected when I pulled it down from the garage rafters. It hefted easily on my shoulder and plopped lightly on my bedspread barely making a dent or wrinkle.

When I'd popped the brass latch and swung up the lid, the first thing I'd seen had been a yellowing envelope addressed to me, Charles Robert Cadwell (my Mother's surname) in a bold, slanting, all-capitals handwriting.

Inside the envelope was a single, deeply creased page with the same bold, print-like script:

Dear Charles,
I have just found out that, miraculously somehow, you exist! There's nothing I want more than to come and see you. But sadly I can't. Please believe me when I say that someday I will come and meet you, and make things right. I promise. But in the meantime, your Grandmother Ella is a beautiful and wonderful person, and I know she'll always give you more love than a person could ever need. I loved your mother very much, and I'll think about you every day....
Your father, Charles Robert

I'd quickly searched the trunk to see if there were more letters. But there was only the one. I read it a dozen times, trying to decipher its meaning, trying to recognize some connection with the bold, slanted handwriting, trying to listen to someone talking to me who I couldn't hear. The fact that my father was alive—or at least had been during some of my youth—was no longer surprising. The fact that he had actually been thinking about me was a revelation.

The trunk contained only a few other items: A dark blue knitted sweater. A pearl-handled hairbrush and comb. A pair of white leather baby-shoes (mine?). A well-worn baseball cap emblazoned: "Meet me at Woodstock". A red and white cotton bandana. Not much at all.

The next day I'd asked Gramella what happened to the rest of my mother's things.

"I don't know," she answered. "That's all there was. Maybe Kurtz took it."

"Kurtz?"

Gramella winced, as if she hadn't meant to say this name.

"He was in your mother's band. It was a long time ago, Charlie. They traveled all around in a bus. I never saw them much."

"What about my father? There was a letter from him."

"I know."

"What happened to him?"

"No one knows, Charlie. We never heard from him again."

Spare as it was, the trunk did contain a few treasures. Three items had been carefully folded in the blue knit sweater: a fat leather-bound diary, zipped closed; an old-fashioned plastic reel of brown, metallic-looking tape, labeled: "Charleston Peace Rally"; and a framed 5X7 black and white glossy photo.

Thick as it was, the diary was sparsely populated. Only the first 50 pages or so had been used, and there were long periods between the dates, as if my mother had only written in it when something in life compelled being recorded. The first entry began with her cryptic, backwards date symbol—year first, month, then day:

72-6-2

I'm moving in with Charlie! He has six months special training in Charleston, and we decided we have to be together. My mother is appalled—"crushed" is the word she used. We're just not ready to get married, I told her. In truth, she loves him as much as I do. I'm so excited! We're going to find a carriage-house downtown. He's going to make the furniture! And I've found a band there looking for a singer…. If it wasn't for Vietnam, life would be absolutely perfect.

The photo was the most immediately compelling thing. It was of a young man and woman. They were leaning on either side of the grille of an old Mercedes Benz. The grille was vertical rather than horizontal—an old model I'd never seen before.

The young man, dressed in a navy officer's uniform with the coat thrown open, is tall and thin. His short-billed Officer's hat is pushed back on a high forehead, and a pair of John Lennon wire framed glasses perches at the midpoint of a straight, eagle thin nose. Most striking was his smile: big and wide with a noticeable gap between his two front teeth. He's laughing big at something that's just happened or been said.

The young woman (she has a striking resemblance to the cheerleader I'd just delivered to the prom) leans with competitive nonchalance on the opposite side of the Mercedes grille, her mouth shaped into something she's saying, apparently to the cameraman, something that's elicited the big smile on the young lieutenant. She is slender and delicate, every feature painted by the sunlight with great affection. She is wearing—in stark contrast to the officer's uniform—ragged edged cut-off jeans, unlaced high-top tennis shoes, and a T-shirt emblazoned with the faded image of the Vietnam Peace Symbol.

Until that moment, the only image I'd ever seen of my mother was the photo Gramella kept on the upright piano in the parlor: a touched up studio portrait that must have been her high school graduation picture. It had always seemed unreal to me, like the photo of a plaster statue someone had applied rouge to. But here in this new photo, captured miniature and alive in my hands, was my real mother. And a man I'd never before laid eyes on— who I instantly recognized was my father.

I drove home before the last dance of the prom had been sounded, and went up to my room and opened the steamer trunk, and took all these things out and looked at them again.

2

I WENT ON TO MAJOR in English at the University of North Carolina where I eventually dated several girls, one who took me to bed and showed me with great patience, detail, and participation, how to make love to her. But the relationships did not take hold. I discovered, to my surprise, that sexual gratification—while it kept my attention—was not, after all, the central thing I was longing for.

I spent one semester, as part of a course on investigative journalism, researching and trying to track down my father. He'd majored in architecture at Clemson, where he met my mother, and—just as Gramella had said—he'd won several regional competitions—not for designing buildings, but for designing cities. I even found a micro-flitch in the school archives that included one of his drawings—a complex network of lines and shaded boxes titled "Urban Study II". His fitness reports from the navy's Officer Candidate School in Newport were unremarkable. His tour of duty in Vietnam was classified. And after he was discharged at the San Diego Naval Base in the spring of 1972, he vanished, apparently, from the face of the earth.

Gramella died two months before I graduated, unable to hang on to see me in cap and gown. What I got from the sale of her house and furniture was not considerable, but I was determined to live on it long enough to write my first novel. I rented an old, partially furnished, paint-peeling farmhouse off a gravel road outside of Chapel Hill, and moved in with my portable typewriter and five reams of paper.

The novel I tried to write was an imagined version of my parent's courtship, woven around the sparse and cryptic entries in my mother's diary. In truth, I had no idea what I was doing, or even why I was doing it. I got up every morning and sat at my typewriter and wrote about these characters that, really, I didn't understand at all, hoping, I suppose, that if I could make sense out of them, I could make sense out of my own life as well. But it was an exercise in futility.

I worked on this for about three months, and then one morning, instead of sitting down at my typewriter, I walked outside and down the muddy, two-track driveway to the mail-box. I never got any mail of course—there was nobody to send me anything except for my electric bill, so I rarely even looked. But that morning, for some reason, I was drawn to that rusted mailbox as if it had an aura around it. I pulled down the squeaky hatch and stared with numb shock at an envelope lying there in the semi-circular shadow. My first thought was, "How did it get out here?" Because I knew it was still in the steamer trunk at the foot of my bed.

I carried the letter up the muddy driveway, holding it lightly in my palms as if jiggling or squeezing might cause an explosion, noting that it was new and white, that it had a post mark only two days before. A bomb. A landmine that's been found and must be carefully handled and managed.

I put the envelope on the round kitchen table and made a pot of tea. As the tea-leaves steeped, I walked round and round the table shooting secret glances at the strange yet familiar all-caps handwriting. Finally, with the tea steaming in my nostrils, my heart racing, I sat down and sliced the envelope open with a paring knife. Folded papers. More all-caps, block lettering:

> Dear Charles,
> You have my permission, my understanding, should you choose to crumple up this letter and throw it in the trash with your junk mail and banana peels. I cannot claim any right to your attention. How could I? And yet I feel time and circumstances have finally created a situation...how can I put it?...that makes it right for me to contact you. (In case you are wondering how I know your address, I have always managed to keep track of you.)
> You know how many empty pages there are to be explained. Perhaps can never be explained. But if you will come, as soon as

possible, to the location provided on the attached, I will do my best at explaining everything I know.

Your father.

P.S. It would be important to keep this letter confidential. It would be best not to share where you are going with anyone. I'll explain when you get here—if you come. I hope, with all my heart, that you do.

There was no phone number, not even an address, just a hand-drawn map beginning two thousand miles to the west of Chapel Hill in Port Townsend, Washington. An annotation on the map said: "I figure you can find your way to Port Townsend. It's a good place to spend the night. Recommend breakfast at the Blue Moose Café."

It took me only a day to pack everything I owned under the camper top of my Toyota pick-up. The last thing in was the little black steamer trunk I'd been carrying around since my 18th birthday. The night before I left, I opened the trunk again for the first time since Gramella had died. I laid the second addressed envelope next to the first, momentarily comparing the slanted block lettering on each. Then, unfolding the blue sweater, I found what I had suddenly wanted to see again: the black and white photo.

There they were, perpetually leaning on either side of the old Mercedes grille. I studied closely the face of the young man. The John Lennon glasses. The big-energy, gapped-tooth smile. I tried to imagine what he would look like now; tried to imagine those hands, thumbed behind his navy belt buckle, being real hands that I could see and touch, wondering what it was going to be like to actually meet him.

3

THREE DAYS LATER I WAS sitting at the window of a near-empty restaurant in Seattle. Below was a waterfront of warehouse buildings on piers, converted now to shops and bars and seafood cafes. The ferry terminal, which I knew I would be utilizing the next day to complete my journey, was just visible to the left. Beyond the bustle of cars and buses and pedestrians stretched the wide, sparkling expanse of Puget Sound, the hazy shoulders of distant islands and, faint as a water-color wash hanging in the sky, the jagged-white brush-strokes of far away mountains.

I was sipping a beer, feeling the body-buzz of my non-stop drive slowly dissolve to numbness. After three days on the road, with only brief naps under the Toyota camper top, I had reached what seemed a jumping off point. I was beginning to fill up with doubts and apprehensions—about exactly what, I wasn't sure. The most troubling thing was that I didn't know what I really felt about this person with the slanting, all-caps handwriting— whether I was angry with him, or whether I even should be angry. The harder I tried to imagine our meeting, what we would say, how we would shake hands, or whatever we would do, the less I understood how I felt or what I expected—or what I wanted.

Soon, the after-work crowd began to arrive and invade my sanctuary by the window. I huddled closer to the glass and slid out from my day-pack my mother's black zippered diary. There were some entries I wanted to read again before I caught the ferry the next morning.

73-2-14.

Valentine's Day. How I wish Charlie was here! Yet, now, what would I say or do if he was? I slept with Kurtz last night. I didn't mean to Charlie! And it didn't mean anything either—I didn't feel anything. But I'm just so lonely and I did it. I just let it happen. And now I'm afraid things have changed. Charlie, you seem so far away—as far away as we used to be close. I don't understand why it has to be this way! There's a protest march tomorrow. They've asked us to perform at the rally place. Kurtz said that Father Berigan might be there to speak! Kurtz wants to start out with Woodstock then do all Dylan. He's put them in his own special order. He thinks when you order Dylan right, there's a secret message. Oh, Charlie! I'M SORRY! I'll sing them all for you! I promise.

The restaurant was filling rapidly now with couples and four-somes, waiters and waitresses, clinking plates, disjointed conversations, fragments of laughter. I thumbed through the diary, looking for the entry I especially wanted to read, dated almost a year later.

74-1-15.

I told Kurtz tonight that I'm pregnant. He said it was a child of war. Oh God! What am I going to do? How could we have been so STUPID!? We'd already said our goodbyes. We'd already said, face-to-face, that it was over, sitting there in that freezing Japanese hostel. And that was so hard. So incredibly hard. I couldn't breathe when it came time to say it. Dear Charlie: I'll always love you, but I can't love you anymore. We've evolved into separate worlds. And your world, to me, is evil incarnate.

The sadness of his body was overwhelming. He cried—not outwardly, but inwardly. He didn't even know he was crying until the tears started dripping from his chin.

And God please explain to me what happened next. All the way back from Japan I was in a stupor. But my body knew—even then—what had happened. My body knew.

So what does it mean? A child of war, said Kurtz. I don't want a child of this FUCKING war! I screamed it. Kurtz was gentle. He held me and rocked me. Then he said I could get rid of it, and I slapped him and beat on him, and then he held me and rocked me again and said he was sorry. I can't get rid of it! I can't!—But oh god: how, or when or CAN I ever I tell Charlie Robert?

I looked out the window. The sky was losing light rapidly while the water, in some inverse relationship, was gaining it,

growing thick and syrupy with the sky's light, as if glowing photons were draining from the air into the sea. A big, green and
white ferry, its lights already sparkling, was laboriously pulling a
long, watery V away from the city, towing it slow and silver out
towards the dark island shapes on the horizon. I watched the
ferry's silent efforts, trying to imagine what had happened, all that
time ago, in Japan, trying to imagine if I could remember being
there, being conceived there, coming into existence in a freezing
Japanese hostel in my mother's womb. Hard as I tried, though, I
couldn't make it seem real.

4

THE NEXT MORNING I CAUGHT the first ferry to Bainbridge Island and from there drove on to Port Townsend. As my father's instructions suggested, I had breakfast at the Blue Moose Café. I found it in a sprawling complex of work-sheds and dry-docked boats with sea-gulls screeching and swooping among the masts. The tiny café building was filled with local boatyard-workers: scruffy beards and ponytails, thick, square hands out-lined with working grime. I sat at a small counter.

Thinking I might stumble on some clue, I said to the waitress: "I think you might know my father. Charles Robert? Does he come here often?"

A blank but friendly stare.

"No. I don't think so. That name isn't familiar. Sorry."

After breakfast I acquired a map of the Olympic Peninsula at a store selling backpacking and mountain climbing equipment. The clerk was a guy about my age, with a wispy beard and curly yellow hair. As I paid for the map, I said: "My father lives around here somewhere. Charles Robert. Ever hear of him? He may be into mountain climbing I think."

"I don't do much climbing," the clerk replied. "I mostly kayak. Headed up to the park?"

"I guess so."

"Well, you'll love it up there, man." An eager smile. "It's incredible—especially this time of year."

Back in the Toyota, I consulted the newly acquired map, com-paring it with my father's hand-drawn instructions. As the store clerk had guessed, I could see I was headed to the Olympic National Park (which the store-bought map referred to as the

"Emerald Wilderness.") The route would take me first through Port Angeles, then the small town of Forks, and finally to a secondary road (which on the store-bought map was a pink, dashed line) that seemed to have no particular destination, but simply meandered to an end at the park boundary. I calculated it would be a three or four hour drive.

Having spent my whole life in North Carolina, I was unprepared for the scale of the landscape I was about to encounter. Near Chapel Hill, where I grew up, the land had been owned and domesticated for generations—hardly a tree grew that hadn't been planted by someone for some purpose, shade or wind-break or fruit, hardly a square foot of soil that wasn't tilled or mowed or paved over or fenced in. There were animals, of course, but the land was clearly owned and managed by people. Even the mountains in the western part of the state, which I'd visited several times, seemed to have been worn down by the continuous occupation of human endeavors. At first, the Pacific Northwest didn't strike me that much different; bigger, of course, a deeper and different shade of green, larger expanses of water, but still very much a place where man was the primary resident. This was about to change.

After Port Angeles the highway began to climb, the trees grew thick and taller, and suddenly, around a curve, the world was transformed into a scale of natural beauty that caught me by surprise: white, chiseled, snow-packed mountains jutted with enormous force into the blue sky, their upward push made even larger by their perfect downward reflection in a pristine lake whose long shore-line seemed to extend as far as I could see. The asphalt ribbon of road followed this shore, held against the edge of the water by a wall of enormous trees. Of human habitation, there was not a sign: there were no boats on the lake, no buildings or houses in the trees, no gas stations or convenience stores anywhere to be seen. I drove slow and cautious: It seemed like I had entered another universe—a place inhabited by gods.

Half an hour later, the big lake was behind me—a shimmering spot through the trees in my rear view mirror—when, abruptly, I drove into total devastation: An entire mountainside had been denuded of trees as if by an atomic blast. The land on either side of the road was a graveyard of giant stumps and the chunked, mud-brown mulch of chewed, broken tree parts, ripped topsoil, and smoky, smoldering slash. Further on, the stumps were hidden by short stubby pine trees. Every couple of miles, small, rectangular signs began to appear along the road-side: "Olympic Timber Company— Trees Harvested 3226, Trees Planted 3372." Then another: "Olympic Timber Company— The beginning of a new forest is logging." If there were gods here, they seemed helpless in defending their territory.

This alternating cadence of grandeur and total devastation continued all the way to the one-street town of Forks, which reminded me of an old, western cowboy town where the horses had been replaced with pick-up trucks, the livery stable with a Sunoco Station. A big Safeway grocery seemed to have landed on the outskirts like something from another planet, and a string of motels and truck cafés jostled for highway frontage. Big logging trucks were everywhere, their enormous loads precariously balanced in steel cradles with wheels. Beyond Forks, the highway crossed a wide river and was enveloped, once again, in the wilderness.

I turned onto the secondary road, which soon became only one lane wide, with pull-offs every half-mile or so to facilitate passing. The trees became even larger, with prehistoric shaggy bark and sagging, horizontal branches festooned with yellow mosses. The forest was enormous and ageless, rooted in the jagged fragments of rocky boulders, cluttered with bouquets of fern and spilling hedges of rhododendron. Sunlight penetrated the green canopy with bright shafts animated by a rising mist that seemed to hang everywhere. The road wound and turned as it climbed higher, frequently crossing steep cascading creeks and, occasionally, revealing glimpses through the trees of a wider, rocky river. Half an hour out of Forks, the pavement ended and I followed a graveled two-track until it came to a one-lane wooden bridge over the big river. I crossed slowly, looking down through the open rail at white-water surging around large rocks and boulders. On the other side of the bridge the gravel quickly petered out into a dirt-packed road with grasses springing up in the middle.

I stopped and studied the written directions on the hand-drawn map. I was getting close. My heart began thumping annoyingly under my windbreaker. If this man was really my father, I was about to meet him. I needed to calm down. I got out of the Toyota and peed off the side of the road. The air was tangy with moist, woody fragrances. Out of sight, the sound of the river thrummed incessantly, like the engine of some great machine, yet overhanging everything was an empty and immense silence.

Back in the Toyota, I took some deep breaths and started off again. Following the hand-written directions, I turned right between a big rock someone had painted light blue and the shaggy-moss bark of an enormous fir tree. The two-track descended steeply beneath dense overhanging branches then abruptly leveled out into an open meadow. The meadow was occupied by a scattering of large rounded boulders and, at its furthest edge, like a glittering out-of-scale jewel, a chaotic group of silver, slanting roofs glinting bright and angular in the sunlight.

I came upon this scene so unexpectedly my foot instinctively hit the brake.

I sat for a moment taking it in. I'd never taken much notice of buildings as aesthetic objects, but there was something unusual here. The metal roofs jutted and sloped in different directions, springing apart and colliding together, each silver plane catching the sunlight in a different way. The affect was startling and energetic, yet peaceful at the same time: It seemed like some great flurry of movement had just come to rest.

I rolled slowly forward, following a gravelly drive across the rocky meadow, studying the group of buildings as I approached. I stopped in a parking area next to what seemed a main entrance: a wide sheltering roof supported on heavy timber columns, raised above the ground on stone piers. Opening the door of the Toyota, the rushing sound of the river greeted me unseen on the other side of the buildings.

A wooden walkway sloped up to a pair of thick, glass-paned doors. A small sign on the shingled wall beside the doors stated simply: "Fish Camp".

I hesitated to go in. The sudden prospect of being face to face with my father froze me to the spot. I looked around to see if there was an alternative approach or someone, maybe, to inquire with, who could be an intermediary. My heart started racing again as I stared at my broken reflection in the glass door panes.

"Oh! I thought you was Maggie," came a voice.

Startled, I looked to my left.

Framed in an open side door was a small woman with grey-white hair pulled back in a ponytail.

She studied me a moment.

"You look a bit thunderstruck," she said. "You need some help?"

"Actually, I'm here looking for my father," I answered.

"What's his name?"

"Charles Robert."

"Aint nobody here by that name, I don't think," she said. "I'll have to check the register. Go on in. I'll come around and meet you inside." She disappeared behind the closing side door.

I pushed back a swell of rising panic. What was happening? How could I be at the wrong place?

The big wood-framed doors opened into a long gallery space that stretched off to the left. Straight ahead, a few steps across the floor, was a matching set of glass-paned doors that opened onto a large outdoor deck, partially shaded with a slanting roof. Beyond the deck was an emptiness which I knew must be the space above the river.

"Let's see, what was that name again?"

The petite, grey-haired woman popped into the long gallery with a bustle of energy and came walking toward me holding an open register book.

"Charles Robert." I said.

"Nope. I don't see it. We only have four guests right now. I didn't think I remembered that name."

"I don't understand," I said. "I have this map, drawn by my father, telling me how to get here, telling me to come. How could he not be here?" As I spilled this rambling declaration, I pulled the hand-drawn map from my pocket, unfolded it, and pushed it out at her.

She put the register book under her arm and held the unfolded piece of paper in front of her for a moment. Then she looked up, studying me again, like she had outside the front doors.

"Sweet Jesus," she said. The register book slipped from under her arm and fell to the floor.

I knelt, picked it up, and held it out to her. But she paid no attention.

"What's the matter?" I asked.

"Let's go sit," she said.

I followed her down the gallery. Heavy wood ceiling beams crossed above us. On the right, the gallery opened into a large dining room with an enormous round table canopied by an iron-work chandelier.

We walked around the big table, past a stone fireplace, toward a wall of windows that leaned outward from the floor. We sat at one of the smaller tables next to the window-wall and I could see now, for the first time, the river below.

"I think I need a drink of water," the little woman said, immediately standing up again. "Do you want one? Or anything? How long you been driving? You want a beer?"

"A beer would be great. But what about—"

"I'll just be a second," she said.

I studied the room while she was gone. There were ten or twelve ladder-back chairs around the big table. The wide chandelier hovering over it was welded and hammered into patterns that included fish.

"So here's a beer for you. It's our own brew."

She handed me a dark bottle labeled with the hand-printed silhouette of a fish, then sat down with her glass of water, studying me again with dark, quick eyes.

"I can see it, but I can't believe it," she said.

"Can't believe what?"

"So you're CM's son."

"But I thought you said…"

"There ain't no Charles Robert here," she said. "Your father's name isn't 'Robert'. It's McCormick. Charles McCormick. Everyone calls him CM."

"It can't be the same person, then," I said.

"It's the same person who drew that map. I can vouch for that," she declared.

"But who is he?"

"Charles McCormick? This is his fish camp. His and Maggie's. Actually, I guess it's Maggie's—inherited from her father, Randolph Scott. But CM's the one that mostly built it. He's an architect. Maggie guides the guests fly-fishing. Along with Gus— he's my husband."

I took a slow, extended swallow of the cold beer. Confusing as it was, I finally knew this was the right place. Things were beginning to feel more solid.

"And who are you?" I asked.

"Me? Why I'm Louise," and she held out her hand with a shy smile. "I and my husband Gus more or less run things. I handle the kitchen stuff and the garden. Gus takes the fishermen out, arranges for the drift boats and guides. He's out with 'em now. Maggie is usually out too, though she don't do drift boats. It's against her religion, she says. So what's your name?"

"Charlie Cadwell. It was my mother's name, Cadwell."

"Sweet Jesus", said Louise under her breath, her eyes searching my face again. "It's just hard to believe. CM said a while back you might be coming. But I don't think none of us really believed it."

Eventually Louise settled me in a sitting room on the other side of the stone fireplace, shooing me into a big leather easy chair with a second beer. She pushed an ottoman up under my feet.

"You rest here awhile, Mr. Charlie," she said. "CM's been gone to Seattle the past three days. He's supposed to be back this afternoon. I'm always the last to know what the schedule is though. Everyone goes on their merry ways, and leaves me here to figure out what's going on."

She pulled a side table a bit closer so I'd have a place to set my beer.

"The guests will be back in a few hours, so I need to start the dinner stuff. You just rest up and enjoy the view. If you need anything, give a holler."

I finished the second beer and closed my eyes, sinking deeper into the leather chair, on guard for any sound that might announce my father's arrival. Soon though, the sound of the river was the only thing I was hearing.

Much later I was awakened by voices intruding vaguely from another room: one rising, the other shushing. A door opens and closes. Footsteps approach softly. A movement in the air above my closed eyes. I'm suddenly terrified to look up and pretend sleep. Someone is standing there, looking down at me, looking down at my eyes closed too tight, watching my falsely shallow breath.

Then the footsteps retreat. The space is empty again. Blood is throbbing in my ears, and my face is hot with the absurdity of what had just taken place.

The sound of the door opens again, this time with intentional loudness. The footsteps approach again, this time boldly.

I stand immediately and turn, trying to prepare myself as I rotate.

A young woman is marching toward me with theatrical determination, like a German storm-trooper.

Halfway across the room she breaks into a spontaneous smile, and her Gestapo marching movements soften into an energetic, but graceful, walk.

"I'm Maggie," she says, holding out her hand as she approaches. "And you, I can see, are Mr. Charles himself!"

This girl was not what I'd expected and I was struggling to process her, dimly recalling Louise's earlier comments about someone named "Maggie", realizing I had assumed her to be my father's— what? Wife, lover? Someone maybe the same age as Louise.

But this Maggie is no older than me. She's about chin height, slim and boyish. Her hair is chopped short into sun-bleached chunks and cowlicks. She's wearing jeans, sandals, and a loose, army-green tank-top with the same black silhouette of a fish as the beer label. Under the tank-top, the visible straps of a string bikini-top. Her nose and cheeks are peppered with freckles.

She steps back and looks me over, as if I'm an artifact of great wonder. Louise has come up behind her, wringing a dishtowel in her hands.

"Well," Maggie says, "I imagine you guys will recognize each other, that's for sure."

"Oh Lord," said Louise. "Didn't I tell you?"

"Yep," said Maggie, giving me another once-over. She stepped forward and grabbed my hand again—still stupidly out-stretched, I realized—in both of hers. She squeezed.

"Don't look so dumbfounded, Charlie! Say something!"

"Hi," I said.

Maggie laughed. "You have no idea how happy we are to see you! CM was hoping against hope you'd come….And here you are!"

"Lord Almighty," said Louise. "I knew it was a miracle when that truck drove up. Didn't I tell you?"

Now there was a brief conference between Maggie and Louise about how the afternoon and evening should unfold. My father, I came to understand, would not be returning from Seattle until late the following afternoon. Since they were floating a different river that day, Maggie guessed that Gus would stop with the guests for dinner in Forks.

"There's a case of wine in the Cherokee for tomorrow night," said Maggie.

"Let me help," I said.

Both women stopped talking and looked at me, startled.

Then Maggie laughed. "Okay, Charlie. And then I'll give you a tour."

5

I DON'T KNOW WHICH HAD more surprises in store—
the fish camp, or my tour guide. Maggie was filled with a bright
energy that animated her even when she was standing still. She
didn't walk; she marched—as if the song playing in her head was
by John Phillip Sousa. But her eyes were her most expressive feature, wide apart, deeply green, often sparkling with a hidden
laughter.

"You're already familiar with the cigar parlor," she says, nodding in the direction of the chair she'd first found me sleeping in.
"That's what we call it, though there's no smoking permitted. If
you have to smoke you're required to adjourn to the back garden...."

"Here's the dining room where we eat." A graceful referral
with her left arm as we walk past. "And out here is the main
place." She leads me through the double glass doors out onto the
big deck I'd observed earlier. "This is where we cook." She
strokes the rough, flat surface of a large river-stone island with a
flag-stone counter-top. Embedded in the center of the island is a
fire-pit with grates over it. The island is sheltered under an open,
slanting roof supported by timber columns. Beyond the cooking
island, the deck railing has weathered wooden chairs and low
tables arranged for viewing the river.

"We all cook dinner together on the fire," she says. "It's our
signature tradition." But now she's already moving on. "Stairs
down to the river." She gestures to a switchback stairway that
springs from the far left corner of the deck. "And here's the
veranda"—

"What're those?" I ask, and we come to a stop.

Opposite the stair going down to the water, the deck connects to a long veranda that follows the edge of the high river bank. This veranda is composed with a series of straight sections that, following the river, form a gentle curve. Each section has its own silver roof, and at the junctures where these roofs meet, jutting out toward the river, is a large, stylized metal fish-head: gaping fish-mouth pooching slightly upward, steel rods pushed through metal cheeks like stiff whiskers, torch-cut slits for gills, welded washer eye-balls staring empty at the sky.

Maggie sees where I'm looking. "That's Zarathustra," she says. "My father made them. Each one is connected to the rain catchment for one of the units."

"Your father?"

"Yes, Charlie!" She looks at me with surprise, and I notice for the first time there are brown freckles in her green irises. "This was my dad's fish camp. His students built it."

"But how did my father…?" I struggled to phrase my confusion.

Maggie looks back up at the fish-heads, as if she's remembering something now she'd forgotten.

"It's a long story," she said. "Come on, I'll show you the units first."

The veranda was fifteen feet or so above the river and the rush of the water below reinforced a dramatic sensation of being suspended in the air. At the juncture of each straight section, a short bridge connected to a guest unit. These units were separate "buildings"—but at the same time they formed a connected, contiguous structure for which the veranda served as a kind of front porch. Rising above the sloping metal roofs of each unit was a river-stone chimney and, attached to the side of each chimney, a two-legged tower with black solar panels glinting in the sunlight.

"Those are for hot water," Maggie informed me. "We have a water turbine up-river that generates our electricity. Not much, but enough for basic necessities: refrigeration, reading lights, music…"

Most interesting was the fact that on first impression each unit seemed quite similar—dramatic, metal roof slabs being the dominant feature—but in actual experience each was unique. The short bridges and front entries were configured differently, and inside the spaces were always surprising, ceilings and floors angling and stepping in different ways. Yet each seemed related, similar somehow, like different interpretations of the same song, and they connected together as if they'd been orchestrated.

In the third unit Maggie leaned against a thick, wood column and said, "So do you notice anything happening over and over again?"

We were standing in a small kitchen area. With her prompt I realized the stone counter, stainless steel sink, two-burner cook-top, and the steel-framed glass cabinets and under-counter refrig-erator, were identical in each unit. In each case, too, the wide countertop island grew out from the side of a big stone fireplace with a raised hearth you could sit on.

"The kitchens and fireplaces are all identical," I said, "but everything else is…different?"

Maggie smiles at my observation. "That was part of the exper-iment," she says. "It took eight years to build all this. When we started, I was ten years old."

Now I was doing mental calculations: ten plus eight, but when did they finish building? A year ago? Three? Maggie was the last thing I'd expected to encounter here. I watched her striding ahead of me now down the next section of veranda, her long ath-letic arms swinging gracefully. Her body was girlish and slim, yet something about her seemed older than any of the girls I'd dated in college. Surreptitiously, following along behind, I checked the feel of the whiskers on my chin. I'd only begun to shave the year before—and now only once every three or four days. Even though I'd attained my credible height of six feet three, and filled out that frame with a reasonable bulk of muscularity, I was still a complete failure at what I considered to be the fundamental badge of manhood.

The last veranda section had a short stair at its end that led down to another unit that was separate from, and slightly lower than, the others.

"Your father's studio," Maggie said, nodding at the two silver roof-slabs that hinged apart like giant butterfly wings. I could glimpse large, sloping glass windows beneath one of the over-hanging roofs. The small entry deck was flanked on either side by tall, stone walls. I tried to imagine someone laying all those stones.

"That's a lot of stones," I commented.

"It was!" Maggie agreed. "I helped carry the rocks up for all the foundations. They were slip formed, two feet at a time. My father said, 'Miggs, you carry the little ones because they're the most important: they connect the big ones together.'"

She looked back down at the stone walls, remembering again.

"So how did my father get involved in this?" I said. "And why did he change his name?"

Maggie looked up, surprised. "Changed his name?"

"His name is supposed to be Charles Robert. Why would he change it?"

She looked at me for a moment, perplexed. Then she looks down at the river. "I never knew that," she says quietly. "That's so strange."

"Can you tell me what you do know?" I asked, feeling a small desperate urge in my voice. "Look, I can't even guess why I'm here. Why this man decides, all of a sudden, after twenty-two years, after never having seen me ever—ever even trying to see me—why does he all of a sudden want to see me now?"

Maggie hesitates, trying to decide something.

"Let's go sit," she says, finally. "I'll tell you what I know. But I don't think it's going to answer your questions."

6

WE SAT IN THE GUEST unit nearest my father's studio, in deep cushioned chairs with a wide ottoman in between. Maggie slipped off her sandals, wiggled her toes for a moment and folded her legs up under her on the chair cushion.

"This unit was built by Ben Sprague," she says, looking up at the sloping ceiling beams. "It was the last one we built."

There was an odd, low window extending all the way to the floor next to us, and framed in the window, fifteen feet below, a section of the river slides fast around a large grey boulder. Sunlight is reflecting off the water, bouncing through the low window into our little sitting space like a laser show.

"Who's Ben Sprague?" I asked.

Maggie gave me a quick look, as if the question caught her off guard.

"One of my father's students," she said. She looked down through the low window, rubbing her cheek thoughtfully. "I guess I should start at the beginning."

The beginning, as Maggie told it, was when she was seven years old and her mother died. Her father, Randolph Scott, was a professor in the architecture department at the University of Oregon. But he wasn't an architect. He was an ecologist with two obsessions: The first was something called the Olduvai Theorem which postulated the time line on which post-industrial society would begin to run out of fossil fuels; it was with this theorem that he challenged his students to rethink what kind of architecture the world was going to be needing as it proceeded down that timeline.

His second obsession was with a fish called steelhead—an endangered species of rainbow trout that, like salmon, spawn in the wilderness rivers and then swim out to sea for their adult lives, swimming in some cases as far as Japan before returning, fat and wild, to their birth-river for the spawning cycle. Somehow, in Randolph Scott's mind, these two obsessions were linked—the measurable, progressive demise of the wild fish as its spawning habitat was degraded and destroyed, and the burning of the fossil fuels that ran the machines that did the destruction. When Maggie's mother died he used her life insurance payout to purchase the land on which the fish camp was now situated, ten acres in all.

"We're going to be forward observers," he told Maggie. "We're going to make a wilderness observation post."

Maggie was eight when they spent their first summer on the river, living in an old Winnebago camper with a big awning stretching out toward the river. Randolph Scott taught her how to fly-fish for the steelhead, and by the end of the summer of her ninth birthday, she knew the pools and rapids within walking distance of their camper like the back of her hand.

That was the year my father mysteriously arrived. Randolph Scott had met him by chance at a used bookstore in Port Townsend. They were both looking for the same architecture book and struck up a conversation.

Maggie was backpacking that week-end with another family up in the Olympic Park. When they dropped her back at the camper, Randolph Scott and Charles McCormick were sitting in canvas folding chairs under the awning, still deep in conversation.

Charles McCormick slept under the awning that night in a blanket provided by Randolph Scott. The next morning, Mr. McCormick borrowed their "summer vehicle", an old Dodge pick-up, returning in the afternoon with a large green tent which he soon pitched a few hundred feet down river from their camper.

He never left again.

When Maggie and her father returned to Eugene for the fall teaching semester and Maggie's fifth grade, Charles McCormick (they had begun to call him "CM") stayed and moved into their camper for the winter. Maggie asked her father why CM was staying.

"He has something important to do, and this is the only place he can do it. We're going to collaborate with him, Miggs. You'll see," Randolph Scott promised, "our summers are going to get a lot more interesting now."

And indeed they did. The next summer, when Maggie turned ten, three architecture students—young handsome men—came to the river and put up a little camp of tents to sleep in. CM moved back into his tent. Maggie and Randolph Scott reoccupied the camper. And work began on what was to become the fish camp.

Maggie watched as odd, wooden frames were pounded into the ground and a complex web of bright green and orange strings stretched between them. CM, Randolph Scott, and the students adjusted the strings many times, peered through a telescope-like instrument as if they were taking pictures of each other, called out feet and inches above the incessant rushing sound of the river, pounded more stakes and frames into the ground, and pulled more strings.

Next to CM's green tent a big grey tarpaulin had been pulled over a wooden framework CM had built during the winter. In the center of this pavilion was a large wooden table—also built by CM—covered with CM's drawings on large pieces of white paper. Round river-stones kept the drawings from blowing away when the breeze came up. The "construction committee", as they called themselves, spent considerable time in this tented pavilion, consulting the drawings, gesturing and conversing. This is also where they had lunch each day. Maggie's job was to make the sandwiches in the camper and bring them to the table pavilion exactly at noon.

The young architecture students doted on Maggie. They pretended to be competing for her affection. (When Maggie told me this, I wanted to protest, 'they *were* competing for your affection!' But I didn't.) In their spare time Maggie taught each of the students to fly-fish in the pools and rapids within walking distance of the camp. They were amazed at her knowledge of the river and her skill with the fish. This honest admiration, combined with their playful courtship, pumped her self-confidence to the point where, as she put it, she was convinced she could make any man do almost anything she wanted.

Maggie interrupted her story to make us something to eat. She slid out of her chair and padded barefoot into the little kitchen. I watched her opening cabinets and drawers.

"We generally keep the units pretty well stocked," she said. "You like smoked oysters?"

"Sure. Can I help?"

"It's not going to be anything fancy. You want a beer?"

I got up and stood on the opposite side of the stone counter watching. She was slicing cheese wedges on a plate of crackers. Her fingers were strong and slender, the tops of her hands browned and freckled.

She opened a tin of smoked oysters and put them on the plate with the cheese and crackers. I carried the plate down and set it on the ottoman between our chairs. Maggie handed me a beer and we sat again, leaning forward now, eating from the plate. After a few moments of chewing, Maggie picked up the story again.

That summer of her tenth year they built what is now the veranda. By itself, it was simply an open pavilion, on timber legs, following the edge of the river bank. It made little sense to Maggie. But she enjoyed running along the sections of boardwalk, looking down at the rushing water. She especially liked to sit with her legs dangling over the edge, her chin on the lowest rail, and spy fish hiding behind the rocks below. What you could see, she said, were not the fish themselves but their shadows.

When that August came to an end, Randolph Scott, the students, and Maggie went back to Eugene for the beginning of school and CM, as before, moved into the camper for the winter.

The next summer Maggie turned eleven and a new set of architecture students—again, all young men—came to the river. This time there were five of them. And they competed with great enthusiasm for Maggie's attention and affection. They also brought a gasoline powered cement mixer that forced Maggie to put her fingers in her ears when they started it up. It ran most of the days, and the construction team built six fire-places and chimneys on the river bank, each aligned with the center of one of the veranda segments. They also built a series of low stone walls and piers that created a mysterious, repeating pattern along the river bank.

The winter after the chimneys and piers were built Randolph Scott did something unusual in his architecture class at the university: He held a competition. Maggie remembered vividly the evening he brought home a large cardboard box and proceeded to unpack from it a series of small, model buildings made of grey chipboard and balsa wood. He set them out on the dining room table where she was doing her homework. Each of them had been designed and built by a different student.

"I need you to help me judge, Miggs," he said.

She watched with curiosity as he arranged the models on the table. Then he reached into the box one more time and pulled out another, larger model.

"But that's the fish camp!" Maggie exclaimed. "That's the veranda along the river!"

The model sat on a large, cardboard base that included the river (blue paper with little round rocks glued to it simulating boulders) the high river bank, and a portion of the flat meadow where their camper was set up. The curving veranda had six little bridges connecting to the edge of the high bank, and a stone-colored chimney aligned with the center of each veranda segment—exactly like the real veranda, now on the real river.

"That's right, Miggs. Now watch…"

One by one, Randolph Scott took the little cardboard models and slid them over the chimneys. The effect was startling. Before her eyes a compact little village assembled itself along the top of the riverbank, with the curving veranda becoming a common front porch connecting them all together.

"Pretty neat, huh?" said Randolph Scott. "This is CM's experiment: He wants to come up with a way to make it easier for people to build their own housing."

But there were still models left over. "What about those?" Maggie asked.

"Let's try!" said Randolph Scott. They spent half an hour arbitrarily placing the different models over the chimneys. The effect was always new, but always the same: A compact little village with the curved veranda front porch.

"It's interesting, isn't it? And it fits so perfect with the Olduvai Theorem, Miggs. The world is going to need something like this. But the question we have to answer now is which one do you think we should build next summer?"

So they looked at them again, one by one, sliding them over the chimneys, putting their chins down on the table to peer at them from "ground level", and they selected the one they both agreed was best of all.

"But what about the others?" Maggie asked. "I like them too."

"So do I Miggs," said Randolph Scott. "But this is the process we've decided on. One at a time."

When they arrived back at the river the following spring, CM had built something strange around one of the stone chimneys: a large rectangular box, taller than a person, six feet wide, twelve feet long, wrapped tight in white, water-proof building paper, all secured together with metal packing straps, like a giant present with steel ribbons. CM called it a "chimney-box".

"It's your birthday present," he kidded Maggie. "But you can't open it yet."

When the summer students arrived a few days later, Maggie was surprised to see that one was a girl. She had long black hair and white skin without a single freckle. Maggie was instantly jealous. The summer dynamics she'd grown so accustomed to instantly changed. The little model that Maggie had helped her father choose that previous winter had been designed and built by this flawlessly skinned girl. To make matters worse, it soon became apparent the boys were all in love with her.

In spite of Maggie's subtle schemes to undermine the success of this unexpected nemesis, the team of students spent the summer building around the white box that was her "birthday present" a structure that (Maggie had to admit) was exactly as beautiful as the little model she'd helped her father select. In fact, she was secretly envious of their daily accomplishment and camaraderie, and confused and frustrated by the emotions that kept her apart from them. She fished mostly by herself, and swam in the river, and brooded and schemed about ways to get rid of the black-haired girl.

In late August, when the students' structure was nearly complete there was a christening celebration. Maggie was pouting down by the river, throwing stones in the water, refusing to participate. CM and Randolph Scott came down and sweet-talked her into coming to the celebration. When she entered the nearly finished structure, walking across the short bridge from the veranda, the whole group was standing inside waiting, gathered around the white strapped box that now occupied the central space of the interior.

What the students had built were a series of light, angular, airy spaces around and over the wrapped box. There were sloped ceilings with wood beams and tall windows looking out over the veranda and river.

Then, to her surprise, CM formally presented Maggie with a pair of tin snips. "Open your present," he said, nodding at the steel straps wrapping around the white box.

Maggie snipped the straps and they fell away, twanging. Box cutters came out and the students slashed the white building paper, wadding and rolling it into chunks they pushed out through one of the back windows. The white box had become a plywood box. Then CM reached for the edge of one of the plywood walls and pulled it away. The students stepped up, grabbed it, and carried it out the front door. The other walls of the box followed.

What remained behind—what was inside the box—was at first a surprise, but quickly attached and integrated itself into the reality of the living spaces the students had built: a complete kitchen with stone counter, two-burner cook-top, stainless sink and under-counter refrigerator—all built into an extension of the river-stone fireplace. Suspended above the counter were steel-framed glass cabinets—already filled, she could see, with cups and plates and sparkling glasses. CM had not only spent the previous winter building all this, he'd completely supplied it as well, with utensils and canned-goods: knives and forks were neatly arranged in a small drawer under the counter, a dish-towel hung from a bar beside the sink. On the other side of the chimney from the kitchen counter, he'd built a small, finished bathroom, with a white porcelain sink and a stone-walled shower. There were even plump, white towels hanging from iron bars on the wall—and toilet paper on a roll next to the john! All had been sitting secretly inside the white waterproof box all summer, waiting for this moment. In a micro-second, the students' empty architectural spaces had been transformed into a cozy, complete little house.

Randolph Scott now stepped forward and gave Maggie another, smaller package tied with a green ribbon. Inside was a small plaque with a carved, gold-embossed inscription: "Maggie's Unit".

"Miggs," he said, "No matter what happens this will always be your personal fish camp."

What flustered Maggie most was that the dark-haired girl, her arch-rival whose unblemished complexion had hogged the affection of the boys all summer, came up to her and looked her in the eyes and said: "Maggie. I hope you like it." And Maggie had seen something honest in her eyes, something kinship-like, that made her instantly doubt the antagonisms she'd felt all summer.

This seemed to be the end of Maggie's story. We sat in silence for a few moments, listening to the river. The sun had finally settled below the tree-line on the other side of the water, and the room was growing dark.

"I've never told it like that before," Maggie said, looking down through the low window, her hand slowly rubbing her cheek. The telling of the story had somehow subdued her energy.

"So, the rest of the units got built the same way?" I asked.

She nodded. "My dad had paid for the first unit—my unit. After that, the students' parents paid for what they built—it was structured as an investment. They still own the units their kids built and get a percentage of the revenues we produce each year."

"And my father? He stayed here the whole time?"

"CM became like my second dad. Every winter he'd stay here and build a new chimney-box. And my dad would have his little design competition at the school. And we'd select a winner. And the team of students would come the following summer...."

"And what about Ben Sprague?" I asked, eyeballing around the space we were sitting in.

"What about him?"

"You said this was the last unit. How old were you when he was the one...."

"When he was the one what?"

Maggie was looking at me, steadily now, holding my eyes.

"When he was the one who was in love with you," I wanted to say. But I didn't say that. What I said was: "So how long ago did all this get finished?"

"I was eighteen," she said, answering the question I hadn't asked. Her eyes were challenging me to go further. The energy field in the room had altered in some way.

"Did you teach him to fly-fish?" I asked.

Maggie continued her evaluation of my facial twitches, which I could feel coming on as I tried innocently to hold her gaze. She looked away, down through the window at the river. "Yes," she said.

Then she stood up, the momentary spell broken.

"This, by the way, is where you're supposed to stay." She looked around at the ceiling beams, as if something about them was still nagging at her memory. "CM left specific instructions that you should stay in this unit if you showed up."

This caught me by surprise. "I can stay in my truck," I said. "I've been sleeping there fine the last four days. I don't want to..."

"You don't want to what?"

"I don't want to barge in...like this."

Maggie looked at me with an amused smile.

"Okay," she said. "If you'd be more comfortable in your truck. There's no locks on the doors, though, or burglar alarms. Breakfast starts at eight."

She suddenly held out her hand, awkwardly. "I'm glad you're here, Charlie."

"Me too," I said, and shook her hand up and down with equal awkwardness.

"Good night, then. Maybe I'll see you in the morning."

I watched her walk down the darkening veranda, her hair dimly catching the reflections of a silvery light that hung in the air. Then I went out to the Toyota, got the old laundry bag I kept my clothes and toothbrush in, and took them back to Ben Sprague's guest unit.

I got another beer out of the under-counter fridge and sat for a while, looking down at the darkening water slip and swirl around the shadowy boulder. After living my whole life without any information at all, it seemed I was suddenly confronting an avalanche of it.

Little did I know how big the avalanche was about to become.

7

THE NEXT MORNING I AWOKE disoriented, searching for something familiar in the strange shapes of the room: the steeply angled wood-beam ceilings, the stone chimney with bright patches of sunlight from an unseen high window, the steady river sound churning outside.

So it was here, I slowly began considering, that somehow my father had been all along while I was writing stories for the school paper, while I was looking for his name on the Vietnam War memorial, while I was wondering how he could have disappeared. There was a numbness to these thoughts. Something I could push on but not feel.

I pulled on my jeans and t-shirt, brushed my teeth, tried to flush the toilet again, discovering for the third or fourth time since I'd arrived it was a composting unit that didn't flush. Finally I walked out onto the veranda. The river swept by just below, sparkling and tumbling around its obstacle course of grey and white rocks. The sun was already high, the bank of trees on the opposite side of the river shimmering a bright iridescent green.

I was sure I'd missed breakfast. The cooking deck was empty. Peering through the heavy, wood and glass doors of the camp house, the dining room looked empty as well. Stepping inside, I stopped for a moment and listened to the silence.

Then I noticed on the big round table a single place-setting: A royal blue placemat, white linen napkin folded, shiny silverware on top. Most interesting, however, slung over the back of the chair in front of this place-setting was a pair of floppy, rubber-looking pants, olive colored, with socks sewn onto the ends—like an oversized version of the pajamas Gramella dressed me in when I was a kid.

I was holding these rubbery boots up, noting the suspenders attached to the waist opening, when I sensed someone watching.

"Do you think they'll fit?"

Maggie was standing in the large framed opening to the gallery. She was holding a silver coffee carafe.

"What are they?" I asked.

"They're waders. Most people wear them fishing around here."

"They look a bit slippery," I said, looking doubtfully at the rubbery socks.

"That's why you wear boots over them—or tennis shoes, in a pinch."

She walked up with the silver carafe.

"Do you want some coffee? Louise is bringing breakfast in a minute."

"She is?"

"Of course she is. What did you expect? We've been waiting all morning for you to wake up."

Then she laughed, apparently at the expression on my face. "Sit down, Charlie. You're home now, right? Louise has been fussing all morning wondering what to make for your first breakfast."

I slung the hip-boots over another chair and sat down at the place-setting. Maggie poured me a cup of coffee. She set the carafe on an oversized lazy-susan that occupied the center of the big table. She sat down, leaving an empty chair between us. She planted her bare elbows on the table, laced her fingers into a support for her chin, and regarded me with her wide, green eyes.

I gave the lazy-susan a push, sending the coffee carafe on a long merry-go-round ride around the table.

"Pretty neat," I said.

"Did you sleep good?" Maggie asked.

"Yeah! I slept fine."

Looking up, I noticed the metal fish in the iron chandelier were set at angles so they appeared to be jumping and diving.

"So, did you sleep in the guest unit—or in your truck?"

I glanced at her. She was trying to hold a straight face, her cheeks puffed up, squinting her eyes.

"Did I what?"

Her laugh slipped out. "You said you generally slept in your truck. You don't remember?"

"And so here's your breakfast, Mr. Charlie. Welcome up!" Louise bustled suddenly into the dining room carrying a big white plate with rising steam.

"Don't you look handsome," she said, setting the plate on my blue placemat.

"Jeez. Thanks Louise."

"I hope you like grits," she said, pulling a dishtowel from the band of her apron. "I read somewhere that's what they breakfast on in North Carolina. 'Course, I added a crab omelet. Just so you'd understand the possibilities up here on the peninsula."

"Wow," I said with emphasis. "This is really great, Louise." I smiled up at her. "That's the most perfect omelet I've ever seen!"

She stared at me a moment, judging my sincerity. Then she snapped the dishtowel lightly at my face.

"You go on, Mr. Charlie," she said, and twirled back in the direction of the kitchen.

Maggie laughed. "I think you've overwhelmed Louise with your charm," she said.

"With my what?"

"Your charm," she said—and I sensed, or thought I sensed, an irony in her voice that tilted me off balance.

I ate my omelet, Maggie watching.

"What size shoes do you wear?" she asked while I was chewing.

I gave her a quizzical look.

"For the waders," she said. "I thought we might do some fishing. CM's not due back till dinner tonight."

"Actually, I've only fished a couple of times," I said.

"That's perfect," Maggie said, her eyes animating with delight. "I like beginners. Beginners are my favorite clients."

When the omelet and grits were gone, I followed Maggie out onto the cooking veranda. She opened a latticed storage closet, pulled out a pair of low, canvas boots and handed them to me. Olive colored canvas. Big eyelets. Oversized laces.

"Try these," she said.

I started to put them on.

"No. Over the hip boots."

I started to pull on the hip-boots.

"You might want to take off your jeans first. You'll get too hot this time of year."

"Take off my jeans?"

"I'll turn around," she said. "There's nobody watching."

I glanced down the curving veranda at the fronts of the units.

"Maybe I'll just go down to my room and change," I said. "I have to brush my teeth, anyway."

"Okay," she said, "I'll get the other stuff and meet you back here in a couple minutes."

After futile minutes in front of the bathroom mirror trying to devise suggestions for something to do other than fishing, I clomped back down the veranda feeling like I was wearing a rubber grocery bag with suspenders. The canvas shoes seemed a size too big, with soft felt soles that sounded muffled on the floor boards.

Out on the open deck again, the sun was bright, almost directly overhead. The air had warmed. Maggie was waiting, streamlined sunglasses pushed up in her cowlick hair. Surprisingly, she'd now added a thick stripe of eye-black on each of her upper cheek bones, like an NFL wide receiver. She was wearing baggy, khaki-colored nylon pants and the same army-green tank-top with black fish silhouette. Around her sun-freckled neck she had strung a wire-loop with large cork beads interspersed with what looked like miscellaneous surgeon's instruments. On each cork bead was a fluffy or prickly looking shape of colored feathers and hairs. Fishing flies, I decided, noticing the tiny glint of the hooks imbedded in the cork. Altogether, she looked like a blonde aborigine with war-paint.

"You're not wearing waders too?" I said, noticing how unencumbered she appeared. "What happened to your eyes?"

Maggie laughed. "This time of year I don't wear waders," she said. "Water's only chilly, not frigid. But I'm used to it. I just need these…" she lifted one foot, showing me an ankle-high sneaker-looking bootlet with the same grey-felt sole as mine.

"But what about your eyes? Do you scare the fish into submission?"

"It's just a vanity thing," she said. "I always try to look as attractive as I can when I'm out on the river."

She gave me a faux smile and picked up a brown paper bag and a long fishing pole with an old-fashioned looking reel clamped on a cork handle.

"Are we ready? You bring the lunch." She handed me the paper bag.

I followed her across the deck, and we descended the stairs to a wooden landing then stepped off onto a narrow beach of round smooth stones. The river slid by, close to our left, the sound brighter now—the water clean and clear.

We walked along the stone beach, under the cantilevering edge of the veranda. We continued down the narrowing beach for a way, then climbed the bank to a path just inside the forest.

I found myself pushing hard to keep up with her. The path, defined on either side with high, sweeping ferns, was a soft mix of pine-needles and spongy rotted wood, but it was often crossed with fallen trees, mossy and slick, and some of these old, weathered trunks were as high as my waist. Maggie floated over these obstacles like a young doe, without hesitation or effort, balancing on them with one hand for just an instant, the long fishing rod held in the other over her head as she sprang into flight. Restricted by the awkward waders, I mounted the massive trunks as if they were horses, dismounting on the other side like a city-boy at a dude ranch.

Sometimes Maggie would stop and wait and watch my efforts, but she stayed far enough ahead that I could never make out her expression. I began to suspect she was evaluating me, comparing me to probably a thousand guys she'd taken along this same path.

The more I thought about this the more determined I became to achieve some kind of style and grace in spite of the clunky boots and waders, an effort which made me feel all the more foolish.

Then I began to suspect Maggie had dressed me in this ridiculous outfit as a kind of test. Eventually, I began to consider the fact that just five days earlier neither Maggie or these giant trees, or this thrumming river, for me, had even existed, and how easy and pleasant it would be to simply go back to my Toyota and drive back to North Carolina where everything was normal and familiar.

Finally, I decided the only tactic available for preserving any dignity at all was rebellion. Straddling the summit of a particularly large windfall, I stretched backward on its mossy back, my hands behind my head for a pillow, the paper lunch bag balanced on my stomach, and closed my eyes, resolved to go no further.

I did not have to wait long.

"Have you given up, Charlie?" Maggie was standing next to me.

"Nope. Haven't given up."

"What are you doing then?"

"I'm contemplating. Trying to understand, actually, why I never thought this fishing thing was any fun, when obviously it's one of the most fun experiences I've ever encountered."

Silence.

I kept my eyes closed.

Something twitched on the edge of my nostril, an insect. Then it twitched again and tried to crawl up inside my nose. I opened my eyes and Maggie jumped back, laughing. I sat up quick, swatting at unseen swarming insects.

"If you lie on a log up here, things'll crawl in your nose," Maggie said.

"What's that you're hiding behind your back?"

"This?" She held up a long, snaking tip of a fern frond, waving it at my face. "It's a thing." She poked it at me again, laughing.

I slithered off the log, batting at the fern frond.

"And people actually pay you for this experience?" I said. "They fly from all over the world, drive hours and hours, spend the day climbing over soggy logs, and then they pay you?"

"Of course they do!" Maggie tossed the frond and picked up the lunch sack which had fallen down by my feet. She handed it back to me. "We're almost there, Charlie. Come on. It's just a little ways now."

She slowed down her walk and stayed beside me, talking.

"Most people who come up here to fish go in drift boats," she said. "They just float down the river and cast out to either side. But I like to sight-fish and stalk. It's how I learned. It's more interesting that way, too. You feel more like an animal, like a part of nature. You feel like a panther on the hunt. Do you see the difference?"

"Do you eat the fish raw on the spot? When you kill 'em?"

"I don't kill the fish, Charlie," she said firmly. I could tell I'd touched now on a topic that was not to be made light of.

"So what do you do with them when you catch them?"

"We let them go. We also crimp the barbs off our hooks, so we can release them without any damage. We don't let any of our guests kill a fish. Ever. Unless, of course, it's a hatchery fish."

"Hatchery fish?"

"You can keep a hatchery fish if you want. They can always make more of those. And pretty soon, that's all the fish there'll be, and then it won't matter anymore if you kill them or not."

We reached a place where there was an opening in the trees; a relatively shallow embankment sloped down from the path to the river.

"Wedge the lunch sack up on that branch there." Maggie said. "Here's a nice spot to do some practice casts."

I followed her down the embankment and out onto a wide beach of round, sun-baked, river-stones, about the size of grapefruits and oranges, all shades of grey and white. We walked to the edge of the water, clear as gin, a slightly rust-tinted color, the stone bottom starkly visible under the current. It didn't look deep. A few large boulders jutted up through the surface, the water pushing white and frothy around their bleached grey hulks.

The sun was intense and hot, and Maggie pulled her sunglasses down on her nose. She pulled one of the fluffy flies out of her necklace, looked at it carefully and pinched at it with her fingers. It was purple and brown with a distinctly sharp looking hook sticking out. She balanced the long rod against her bare shoulder and tied the bright piece of fluff to the end of a nearly invisible, translucent thread dangling from its tip. This thread, I could see, was attached to a thicker, chartreuse colored line rolled rather loosely on the metal reel.

It was an odd looking setup from my perspective. The only time I could recall having fished before, the reel had looked like the silver nose-cone of a rocket, with a hole in the end where the line came out. There was, I remembered, a big black button on the back of the nose-cone that you pushed in synchronization with your cast to release the fishing lure.

As I watched Maggie pull an invisible knot tight with her teeth, I was also remembering how I'd actually been pretty good at casting with that nose-cone reel. A school friend's dad had taken us fishing and showed me how to make the cast. "You've really got a knack for that, Charlie," the father had said. "You must be a baseball pitcher or something."

"No. He don't play baseball," my friend had said.

"Okay", Maggie said, stepping out into the shallow edge of the water so the cuffs of her nylon pants got wet. "See that rock over there with the white birthmark on its cheek? Try to put your fly about five feet above it. Do you see where I mean?"

I suddenly felt a swell of confidence. The rock, with its white "birthmark", was only about fifteen feet from where we stood on the river bank. I could almost reach out with the long, cork-handled rod she'd handed me and touch the spot with its tip.

"First you have to strip some line off the reel," Maggie said, "so you have some to shoot with." She reached over and pulled green line from the reel, letting it fall in the shallow water at my feet.

I dropped the rod back and, careful not to overpower since the target was so close, cast the fly at the swirling river water above the rock.

Immediately I knew something was wrong. After a disconnected moment searching the water ahead for my cast, the line began to descend from above, tangling onto my head and shoulders like a stringy, green bird dropping. Instinctively I froze, remembering the bright hook attached to its end.

An awkward silence fell with the last loops of the green line.

"Not a bad cast," Maggie said.

She stepped around facing me, working hard to control her expression, her sunglasses reflecting my face for a moment. She began picking and gathering the sprawl of fishing line from around my shoulders, telling a story as she worked.

"My dad told me about a fellow, on this very river," she was saying, "who strangled himself with a big roll-cast and fell over in the water. He got caught by the current and swung down the rapids he'd been fishing. It was three days before they found him. But when they did, there was a fifteen pound Coho on the end of his tippet."

I remained still, certain I could feel the feathery hook somewhere down the back of my neck.

"So, what he always said," she was searching now for the hook, "there's really no such thing as a bad cast....You see what I mean?"

With a wide, open-arm gesture she dropped a neatly coiled pile of green line into the water. The clear tippet, as she called it, with the purple-feathered fly on the end, she dropped off to one side.

"The bad news is," she said with mock seriousness, "I think you've inherited your father's fly-casting technique."

"Look, I've never done this before," I said, trying to keep a rising peevishness out of my voice. "You could have warned me or something."

"Charlie! I'm just kidding! We'll have you fly-fishing like a pro in no time. Even your father eventually got the hang of it. Sort of. You want a quick lesson?"

She pushed up her sunglasses and looked at me with concern. I was surprised to be suddenly staring into the deep black holes of her pupils. Her eyes looked strangely upside down above the dark slashes on her cheek bones.

"What do you say? I won't even charge you for it."

She stepped back and I could put her face in perspective again, could see all of it instead of just the parts, the sun-burnt hair, the upside down eyes.

I must have nodded, because she immediately commenced a quick demonstration. With a nearly motionless flick of the rod she tossed the line coiled near my feet out into water where it floated and began to meander down river on the edge of the current.

"Flies don't weigh anything," she said. "It's like trying to throw a feather. It doesn't go anywhere no matter how hard you throw it. So the trick," she said, lifting the long tip of the rod and pulling a big section of the floating line out of the water, "is to load the rod so it throws the line. To make it shoot the line is how we call it, and the fly will go along for the ride."

She flicked the rod up and back, the line whizzing over her head.

"You stop the back stroke suddenly, about one o'clock," she said. "And that loads the rod….Watch the line….Then, you stop the forward stroke right about here. See? The rod does all the work. It's like shooting an arrow with a bow."

Effortlessly, the line shot from the tip of the rod as if it really were being pulled by an invisible arrow, shooting out straight nearly parallel to the water's surface.

After a dozen tries I began to get the hang of it. Maggie was patient. We had walked deeper into the river, and her nylon pants were wet up to the knee. The sun, reflecting off the rocks and water, seemed to grow in intensity. I rolled up my shirt sleeves. The under-water rocks were jumbled and uneven, slippery as ice. I nearly fell each time I tried to reposition myself for another cast. I could see the river bottom clearly under the water, but the rocks and small boulders weren't where they appeared. More than once, Maggie reached out and steadied me, her hand tight on my upper arm.

It was hard to tell which effort occupied more of my brain processors—the effort of staying upright on the slippery, bumpy river-bottom, or the effort of remembering to stop my back-cast at one o:clock, because if I didn't, the line would end up all around me instead of out in the water where it was supposed to go.

Finally I made a cast that actually shot the line.

"That's great, Charlie!" Maggie shouted, applauding enthusiastically.

Then she did something unexpected: she walked a few steps into shallower water, leaned down, and the next thing I knew she was unzipping the inseams of her nylon pants—ziiiiiipppp—all the way up to the crotch, first one, then the other. She was talking to me while she did this: "I think you've got the hang of it now, Charlie. Reel that in, and we'll go down the river a bit...." But I'm not reeling, I'm watching the bizarre transformation occurring a few steps away. One after the other, she rolled the pant cuffs up her bare smooth legs to her hips, where she tied them off tight with drawstrings that appeared from inside.

Most arresting of all, however, was this: a dark tattoo encircled her left upper thigh, like the band of an old-fashioned silk stocking, a ribbon, about four inches wide, of blue-green fish scales.

Having thus revealed and transformed herself, she stalked gracefully over to the rocky beach, white bare legs descending from the bunched up nylon around her waist, ankle-high booted feet, like an exotic water-bird. She turned to check my progress in retrieving the line, which I had neglected to even begin doing.

"What are you looking at?" she said, lifting her sunglasses.

"I'm looking at those rocks over there," I said. "Those are pretty interesting rocks over by the trees."

"You're supposed to be reeling in that line." Then she nods down river. "Reel that up, Charlie, and I'll meet you down that way. I'm going to reconnoiter."

And she stalked off again, her strides even longer and lighter now, as if she were partially weightless, as if she were about to take off and fly.

The fly line had gotten tangled on something down stream, and it took me a while, pulling on it and walking toward the snag, reeling it in, then pulling some more and walking toward it again, to get it loose. I nearly went down, stepping out deeper than I intended, feeling for the first time the cold pressure of the current pushing against the rubbery fabric around my knees. Cautiously I moved back to the shallow water and the white-rock beach.

Maggie had disappeared around a bend, and the view of the beach downstream was blocked by a thick growth of white-barked trees and shrubs. I found a path into this thicket, but struggled to keep the fly-rod, which was pointing out in front of me, from snagging on the branches.

When I finally caught up with her, she was crouching behind what remained of a mammoth-sized tree that had washed down river, apparently eons before. Her back to me, she was peering over its bleached hulk, the breeze lifting her hair into little rooster-tails.

As I approached, she turned and held two fingers to her lips. I attempted, without success, to cover the remaining distance through the shallow, rocky water in silence. When I reached the tree trunk, she pushed me down into a crouch beside her.

"See there?" she whispered.

"Where?"

"Under that overhang over there."

Just beyond our fallen-tree hideout the river sluiced down three or four feet into a crescent shaped pool that curved sharply to the right. On the far side of this pool, about thirty feet from where we crouched, the bank rose steeply. The current had cut away under this bank, leaving a moss-covered section drooping out over the water.

"What are we looking at?" I said.

"Underneath the bank," she whispered. "Look underneath".

Sunlight penetrated the undulating water in places, illuminating rocks and boulders and casting shadows from the rippling surface.

"Do you see it?" Maggie whispered.

"I see rocks."

"You're looking for a fish," she whispered. "It's about one o'clock from that big boulder under the water with the sunlight on its face. Do you see it?"

"I see a boulder."

"I have to get over there to cast to him." She nodded to our right, toward the far end of the pool, where the river turned again around a bend. But there's an obstacle—the rocky beach is blocked by the impenetrable looking tangle of a tree that's fallen from the edge of the forest. "You stay here and watch. I have to get on the other side of that somehow….But stay down. He's right there in front of you. They're very wise to what's happening above the water, right? They spook easily. You see what I'm saying?"

She took the fly-rod from me and quickly twisted it apart into four pieces, lashing them together with some loops of the line. With this shortened package in one hand, she used the other to support a low, stealthy, crouching walk across the beach to the tangled windfall. She stepped carefully into its twisted embrace, ducking under a large, scraggly branch, and immediately the hem of her tank top gets snagged. She backs out carefully, hefts up the hem and ties it in a tight knot just under the modest shape of her breasts, her bare mid-rift now shining in the sunlight, and I'm getting the strange impression that fly-fishing is really about the slow and erotic act of incrementally disrobing.

She re-entered the windfall and worked her way slowly through it. On the other side, she puts the rod back together, organizes the line, and examines the fly closely, rearranging some of the feathers with her finger tips. Then she steps away from the windfall, crouching low, and slowly enters the water.

She sets herself in a mid-rift-deep spot, the knot of her tank-top just touching the surface, and begins to work the fly-rod. She shoots the line directly toward me, it seems, but it arcs slightly away and I watch the fly flip over at the end and drop, with surprising delicateness, on the water.

I glance over at Maggie. She is leaning forward intently, her mouth open just slightly, the fly-rod pointed straight away from her, one hand holding a loose tangle of the green line, her sun-

glasses reflecting shards of sunlight. I was just imagining she'd
been turned to stone when she springs suddenly upward, throwing a bright spray of water into the air, the rod lifting and bend-
ing sharply. The iridescent green line stretches out straight and
taut like a laser beam.

Now the rigid, line begins to move mysteriously. First it slices
the surface back toward the overhanging bank, then over towards
me, then abruptly changes direction again.

Suddenly the water breaks in a frothy explosion and there,
wriggling in the air, its tail kicking the surface, is a silvery, ocean-
sized torpedo flashing bright with a smudge of neon red. It jumps
and tail-beats the water twice more, heading for the downriver
side of the pool while Maggie is coming the other way, stripping
line in as fast as she can, the rod held high, bent nearly double.
Then she is up again in the shallower part on my side, still backing, still holding the arched rod high, its tip pumping like something alive.

The water is high on her bare thighs, just touching the dark
band of her tattoo like a depth marker. She begins to alternate
pulling back on the rod, then reeling in line as she eases it forward. Pull back… ease forward and reel—the rigid line digging
through the river surface in front of her, first one direction then
the other.

Then she's just holding the arching rod high in one hand,
looking down into the water.

"Come here, Mr. Charlie," she calls. "You need to see this."

Invited, I slithered over the wide tree trunk.

Maggie is crouching in the water now, still holding high the
arching rod. The line is nearly vertical into the undulating, reflective surface in front of her. I slip momentarily, making a splash.

"Don't scare him Charlie," she says in a hushed voice.

I approach carefully. As I step up beside her the fish suddenly
materializes beneath the watery reflections. It is directly in front
of Maggie, fins and tail barely moving, facing into the current.

Maggie reaches out and grasped the taut vertical line with her
free hand and slides her fingers down it into the water. Her elbow
makes a small twisting motion.

"Hold this," she says quietly, handing back the draggled, purple fly. "Take the rod too."

Surprisingly the fish does not bolt. Maggie reaches around and grasps just in front of its tail with one hand, the other under its belly, and pulls it gently towards her, lifting its heavy, sleek body up toward the surface. Just for a moment, its head comes into the atmosphere of air and its fish-eye regards us with an expression of wonder: a curious, round black pupil in an ochre disk.

"This is a wild steelhead," Maggie whispers. "My dad called them disciples."

She lowers the sleek, silver prize back into the water and gently pushes it back and forth, like you might awaken a sleeping child. Back and forth.

Its tail wakes first, wagging gently. Then, there is an explosion in the water and for no reason I can explain, I'm down, the cold water suddenly enveloping my head and hair in a slew of loud, rushing bubbles. The hard, slimy rocks are pushing against my hands and back, my feet are flailing, trying to get a hold of something, the waders full of air at first, holding my legs up, forcing my head down, then filling fast and heavy with the cold, the current starting to pull me. Then I'm being pulled the other way, forcefully, and my head comes out of the water, and Maggie is dragging me into the shallow rocks close to the beach.

"Jeeze Charlie," she says, looking down at me, the sunglasses pushed up into her hair, her eyes wide with amazement. "I thought we'd lost you!"

8

I MANAGED TO CLAMBER UP the rocky beach to the big wind-fall we'd been hiding behind, and Maggie told me to lie on my back there, and helped lift my legs up on its round saddle to drain the water out of the waders. I lay there, eyes closed, trying to remember the exact events that led me to this upside down position with the cold river-water dribbling out onto the rocks under my back.

"I have to ask you a question," Maggie said.

I opened my eyes. She was leaning against the ancient log, looking down at me.

"What?"

She was watching me with a thoughtful but hesitant concern.

"It's kind of personal."

"What?"

"On a scale of one to ten, how presentable is your underwear?"

"Presentable?"

"I mean is it regular underwear, or is it something bizarre, like a thong or something."

I lay there looking at her for a minute, trying to remember my underwear, the gist of where she was going with this line of questioning starting to dawn on me.

"Actually, it's Tommy Hilfiger," I said, recalling my purchase at the Chapel Hill Mall just a few days earlier—recalling, as well, in a sudden rush of images, my preparations to drive across country, recalling the letter from my father, recalling the black steamer trunk and the quilt of Gramella's that I used as a cushion for naps in the back of the Toyota camper. These flashing memories seemed strange and distant and it felt odd to think I was actually wearing, at this very moment, a piece of that disconnected reality.

Maggie looked down at me, working to hold a straight-face. "Tommy Hilfiger," she said thoughtfully, as if she was testing the acceptability of this information. Then she puffed out a short laugh: "Tommy Hilfiger is perfect!" she said. "Come on. Let's get you dried out."

We walked back up the river and retrieved the lunch sack. Then Maggie led me up into the forest path again, which we followed a short way, then down to the river again at a steep place along the bank. There was no beach here, but jutting out into the deep flow of water was an enormous flat rock, broad as a pier, its surface slightly tilted down to the water. We stepped onto this slab of rock and Maggie sat me down. The rock was warm—almost too hot, from the baking sun. Like a gentleman's valet, she knelt down and untied one of my big, felt soled boots. I untied the other. We pulled them off. Then she grabbed the rubbery sock-feet of the waders and, stepping backwards, pulled them off my white, wet legs. She was very professional about it. She turned the waders inside out and spread them on the rock.

"Let's have your shirt," she said. And she spread that out too, next to the waders.

"What about you?" I said.

"Everything I have is fast-dry. I plan on getting wet."

She sat down behind me and off to the side, and put the lunch sack between us. I watched her untie the bundles of khaki nylon at her waist and unroll the legs of her pants, spreading them out next to, but away from, her real legs, so she appeared to have two sets of walking appendages. She pulled her tank top over her head revealing the black bikini top. Then she opened the paper sack and extracted a thick sandwich and handed it to me.

"Louise's smoked salmon special," she said.

She took another sandwich out of the bag, and put the bag under her hip, so it wouldn't blow away.

So here I am, I'm thinking to myself—taking a big bite of the sandwich and realizing how desperately hungry I am—sitting on a baking rock in my underwear, eating a salmon sandwich which

I would never even consider as something you'd put between two slices of bread, situated next to a beautiful girl whose eyes are upside down, and whose got four legs, one of which is partially covered with a band of fish-scales, and who knows my father, has known my father all the years that I've never known him, and I'm looking out at a sparkling river who's relentless, churning sound has become a background noise in my brain, and I've felt the strange sensation of shooting a fly into that water, and I've seen a wild fish called a disciple, as long as my arm, look me in the eye, and I don't even know who I am anymore.

We ate our sandwiches in silence, the river slapping and smooching at the edge of our rock pier, the deep water a complex weaving of translucent blues and turquoise. Like the day before, the afternoon sun hung in the slot above the river as if it were stuck there.

Maggie broke the silence. "It's a great place to go swimming," she said.

I looked at the swift, deep water with a sudden apprehension. What was she suggesting?

"You can dive right in there…it's deep," she said. "The current is strong, but if you just go with it, it's like a circus ride. Before the bend down there, you just angle over to the edge, and the current disappears. Then you can swim back and do it all over again. It's how the fish travel."

"I think I'm going to concentrate on getting dry," I said as evenly as I could.

Maggie laid back on the rock, a four legged girl sunbathing at the beach.

In truth, I'd never learned to swim properly. Deep water, if I looked into it, gave me vertigo and reminded me of the dark dreams about my mother. I took the slow, deep breaths I'd taught myself to use when these feelings started to come. Then I laid back too, the stone smooth and warm under my back, and closed my eyes. The sun became a hot mask on my face. I began trying to sort things out.

"So how many years," I said, "have you guys been living here on this river?"

"Since I was eight." Maggie's lying-down voice came from up-rock to my left, but close. "That was the first summer my father brought me here."

Yes, I remembered that detail now.

"And my father," I said, "when was it again that he came?"

"When I was nine. That was the summer CM showed up."

"And he never left? Ever?"

"Not really. He'd go into Forks on occasion. Sometimes to Seattle. But never for long. He always stayed here during the winters. He never visited us in Eugene. My father said he had work to do."

"What I don't understand," I said, "is why he didn't come and get me, why he didn't bring me out here, if he was here all that time. I could have just come for a visit, right? I could have learned fly-fishing when I was eight, just like you, right? Why do you suppose…"

"I don't know, Charlie. I didn't really think about it. After a couple of years, I guess I realized CM was hiding from something, but I never knew what, and we never talked about it."

When she said this, I felt the blood rush suddenly into my face, flushing my cheeks and eyes hot with shame beneath the sun mask. I knew what he was hiding from. He was hiding from me, of course. He was hiding from the fact that I existed. What other explanation could there be?

But why did he send the letter?

"You okay, Charlie?"

"Yeah, I'm fine."

"We didn't know you existed until a year ago. You're the mystery boy."

"Yup."

"One night at dinner, when it was just family night, no guests, he told us he had a son, and he was thinking of inviting you to come out here. We were amazed, of course! Gus looked at him and said, 'Why'd you wait so long?' And CM just stared back at Gus, stared him down, till Gus got up to check on the drift boats….That was after…."

She faltered here, and stopped.

"After what?"

"After I came back."

"You went someplace?"

"There was two years I wasn't here."

"College?"

"It was definitely a learning experience."

"Where'd you go, then?"

"Why am I telling you this?"

"Don't tell me then."

"I ran away with Ben Sprague." She says it in a flat voice. "We went to Mexico. I was going to marry him."

"And what happened?"

"My father, of course, objected. He—objected strongly. He wanted me to go to college. 'I can go to college anytime,' I said to him. He said I didn't know what I was doing. That Ben Sprague was too old for me. We had a big—argument, a big falling out."

"And so you ran away?"

"We left in the middle of the night. My father was packing everything to come up here, just like we always did. The living room was stacked with supplies and clothes. He insisted I was coming too, like always. He'd positioned himself in a chair by the door to our apartment to keep me from leaving. I stood there and looked at all that stuff, stacked and organized like it had been every year since I could remember, and my dad sound asleep in the chair. Then Ben rolled into the driveway with his lights off. He'd just graduated from architecture school in Eugene. It was the year after he'd been up here building the last guest unit. The one you're staying in. It was after…that summer."

"What do you mean that summer?"

At first I thought she hadn't heard this last question, but then she gave me her revelation: "The first time I had sex," she said, "was right here, on this rock."

I squirmed, imperceptibly, then noticeably.

"I guess I shouldn't tell you things like that."

"Not right at the moment," I said.

I lay there, trying hard now to visualize something other than Maggie naked and engaged in sex on this very rock, her white legs and arms wrapped around this Ben Sprague fellow, whatever he looked like, entwined and impassioned under this same hot sun that was baking us now, but I was having difficulty not visualizing it, and it was starting to have an inevitable and disconcerting impact. I sat up and pulled my knees against my chest.

"Ben was very—persuasive. After that we started having sex almost every night, up on the sleep loft he was building in the guest unit, even before there was a roof over it. We did it in total silence so no one could hear. We hid the rubbers in his nail pouch. I remember staring at the stars between the open rafters....zillions of them."

"I think I'm going to put my waders back on," I said. "They look pretty dry."

Keeping my back to her, I scooched down the rock.

"You need some help?"

"Nope, I got it." I pulled the rubbery fabric outside-out, first one leg then the other, then, still keeping my back to her, got my legs inside and scooched into them, pulling the suspenders up over my bare shoulders.

"What is it about you, Charlie, that makes me want to talk? I've never told this stuff to anybody."

"I don't know. I guess I'm just a good listener."

"Maybe you should say something."

"What should I say?"

I turn around now, standing on the rock in the stocking-foot waders, looking down at her. She's sitting upright, her two real legs, beautiful and bare, pulled up against her chest, her arms wrapped around them, her chin on the delicate knees, her sunglasses perched in her burnt tussle of hair. She's staring past me with her upside down eyes, out at the stretch of rippling-sounding water behind me.

"So why'd you come back?" I said.

"Because my father died."

She stared hard at the river, and the scope of what she was feeling at that moment washed over me like a big wave at the beach that rises up higher suddenly than you expect.

9

THE PATH BACK TO THE fish camp seemed familiar to me now. When we reached the big windfall where I'd staged my rebellion, I slithered over it without much difficulty. Maggie waited for me, the fly rod balanced over her shoulder, and we walked side-by-side. It seemed shorter going back.

"So when did you say my father was going to get here?"

"He probably already is," she said. "Likely, they'll be starting the cocktail hour by now."

This slowed my steps. My chest began to tighten up.

"You mean you think he's already there, waiting?"

"Charlie, relax," Maggie said. She put her arm through mine and gave it a shake, laughing. "You and CM are going to get along just fine. He's a pretty easy guy to know....He's a lot like you."

"I don't know how this is going to work," I said. In spite of Maggie's encouragement the feeling of dread was spreading to my shoulders and down my arms. My feet were walking but I wasn't aware of it.

"Look, I'll make the introductions," she said. She squeezed my arm against her side. "Just be your charming self."

"Do you think Louise will have told him I'm here?"

"What do you think?"

The path ahead curved down out of the trees to the rocky beach and the first buildings of the fish camp came in view. Maggie didn't let go of my arm. In a moment, it seemed, we were standing at the bottom of the steps leading up to the veranda.

She looked up.

"So here we are," she said, quietly.

I followed her gaze toward the edge of the cooking deck above us. A man stood there, leaning on the railing, looking out at the river. He hadn't yet seen us.

My heart began to race. Maggie unlaced her arm from mine and closed her hand around my elbow. She squeezed, then squeezed again, hard, sensing my rising panic.

"Come on, Charlie," she said without looking back or giving me time to reflect. "You two need to get this over with."

She started up the stairs, calling up loud as she went: "Look here, CM! Look who I found down by the river!"

He turned, looking almost straight down on us, leaning out over the rail. His head and shoulders silhouetted against the afternoon sky, his features in shadow. Curly hair, fussing in the breeze. A glint of glasses.

As we climbed the stairs Maggie still held my arm, as if I were a recalcitrant child being returned for punishment. At the last landing we turned and stopped, and she let go.

My father stood just a few steps above me, the light now fully on his face.

I was nearly numb. We looked at each other. I struggled to organize his features into somebody I knew. My first impressions were fragmented. He was tall. He had broad shoulders, slightly stooped. His round-lensed glasses sat midway on the bridge of his nose. His mouth was pulled in a tight, straight line. His fluffy, curly hair was grey.

Maggie grabbed my arm again and pulled me up the remaining steps. My father stood back making room for us. I was shocked to find that I was taller. He looked up at me. His mouth pulled into an even tighter smile. I tried to find him; tried to see him all at once. But I could only see pieces—a small scar on his cheek, red sunburn on the bony ridge of his nose. He shrank slightly as I stood looking at him. I saw that the corners of his eyes were deeply wrinkled and they were blinking rapidly against the afternoon sunlight behind my head.

Then something shifted, and he stood taller, nearly looking me in the eye. "Charlie?" he said. "Do you go by Charlie?"

The actual sound of his voice caught me by surprise. It was softer than I expected. I realized I couldn't answer. So I nodded.

Then his straight mouth relaxed a bit and the corners turned up in a smile. His mouth, I could tell, had a broad flexibility.

"Well Charlie," he said, holding out his hand. "Welcome to the fish camp."

"Thanks."

His grip was at first tentative, then strong. He held my hand just a moment longer than a handshake. I don't remember letting go…but then we were looking at each other again.

"And was the map…?

"Perfect," I said.

"And you've met Maggie?" he said, as if about to introduce us.

"Heaven's sake, CM!" said Maggie. "Can you begin to talk sense? Didn't you just see us walk up from a day's fishing?"

He gave a little laugh, glancing at Maggie. "And how was it?"

"Well, I think Charlie's got great potential," she said. "Except he seems to have inherited a few of your casting techniques."

My father wagged his head in amusement. "Don't let Maggie lay any trips on you," he said. "There's other things than fly-fishing we think about up here.'

"I like the…place," I volunteered. "This is all so—unexpected." I cast my gaze around, indicating the roofs and verandas.

"I'm glad you like it!" he said. "When we have a chance, later on—but there's a lot to talk about, isn't there?" He looked at me, tentatively. "I always imagined I'd give you a hug," he said. "But now that you're here…"

"Why don't you guys just shake hands again, for now," Maggie said. "We're ignoring the guests. Which as I recall is not allowed here." She glanced behind my father at the group of people talking near the cooking grill.

His face brightened. "Okay, Charlie," he said with a sudden enthusiasm. "Let me introduce you!"

He turned and led the way. I watched him walk ahead. Long strides. He was perfectly straight until his shoulders, which were oddly out of balance, one slightly higher than the other.

I followed in a daze, oblivious to the fact I was still wearing the rubber waders and boots that clunked along the decking. I sensed Maggie staying close by, oddly protective—of whom, I couldn't tell: me or CM.

There were, as Louise had told me earlier, four guests: two men and two women, presumably couples in one way or another. Two, I managed to discern, were much older than the others, so I pieced them together—but forgot their names the instant we were introduced.

The younger woman was startlingly beautiful. For whatever reason she engaged me immediately: "So Charlie! You look like you've just come up from the river! How did you do? Isn't it spectacular here? Did you catch anything?"

"I'd guess he caught at least something if he went with Maggie." A voice off to the side. I glanced toward it and a round, grinning, gray-whiskered face beamed up at me.

"This is Gus," my father said.

Gus stepped forward and grasped my hand with surprising affection. He was only five feet tall, maybe shorter—just below my shoulders.

"If you aren't a sight, Charlie," he said. "This is a blessing if I ever saw it!"

"What is this?" asked the beautiful woman.

"This is CM's son," said Maggie from the side. "He's been away for awhile. It's… sort of a homecoming."

"Oh really! How wonderful! Let's celebrate!" The beautiful woman was suddenly in a partying mood. She poked her assumed husband in the ribs.

"Welcome back!" he toasted me with his wine glass.

"Thanks," I said. "It's great to be…back."

"So where've you been?" asked the older husband behind thick, tortoise-shelled glasses.

"I've been in North Carolina."

"Great state," he said. "The mountain golf courses are sublime. Do you play golf?"

"Actually, I'm a writer," I said inexplicably.

"A writer?" said the older woman. "Lady Brenda, did you hear that?"

The beautiful woman's eyes looked me over for a moment. Then she smiled warmly. "I love writers," she said.

And I'm wondering: is she a countess or some kind of royalty?

"So here's the entrées," Louise announces, coming up behind us. She was pushing a stainless steel cart topped with plates of meat: fish filets, bright red cuts of steak and what appeared to be small game-hens, split and opened flat. The meats were powdered over with flakes of green spices and white-flaked chopped onions. A tall, wooden pepper mill stood at one corner of the gurney, and a decanter of what I assumed was cooking oil at the other. A stainless bowl with four or five wooden handled basting brushes. One steel handle of the cart had white towels folded over it.

Louise stood by the gurney while the guests crowded around. "Here's black cod filets," she pointed. "And the grass-fed beef. And these are Montana quail tonight."

"We missed the cook-out last night!" said the older man behind his thick glasses. "That restaurant in Forks doesn't hold a candle to this."

My father lifted an iron poker that was leaning against the stone wall of the grill. He drove it into the coals. Sparks shot up under the sloping metal roof.

"Just a few minutes," he said. "Louise, what about that bottle of champagne we've been saving?"

"Champagne?"

"That one the French Ambassador left. For our most special occasion. Remember?"

"But it isn't cold," said Louise. "It's been in the cellar for nearly a year….Maybe even the varmints took it."

"See if you can find it," my father said. "I can chill it if you can bring a big bowl of ice."

"The ambassador of France?" asked Lady Brenda as Louise headed for the kitchen.

"He was here a year ago," my father said. "He caught a— what?" He looked at Maggie. "A twenty pound steelhead?"

"It was a wild fish ," Maggie explained. "He wanted to take it back and hang it in his throne room. I told him even ambassadors sometimes drowned in white-water rivers."

"You what?" asked the younger husband.

"I threatened him with death," said Maggie. "I held the tip of my fly-rod just between his eyes and asked him which eyeball he'd like me to cast to the next steelhead that might be hungry…"

"Bravo!" said tortoise-shelled glasses. "Some people want to buy everything. Good for you, Maggie! Some things aren't for sale, eh?"

My father poked at the fire again, sending sparks twirling upward.

"So, I found the Ambassador's champagne," said Louise, pushing a smaller gurney toward the cooking grill. In the gurney's center was a large wooden bowl filled with cubes of ice. A dark green champagne bottle lay on its side in a white towel, next to the bowl.

"Excellent!" my father exclaimed. "And glasses, Louise?"

"So they're under the counter, of course! What do you think? I don't know you need glasses?"

"No, no! Louise! For heaven's sake!"

My father reached under the gurney's stainless top and began to extract crystal champagne glasses which he placed on the stone slab counter next to the grill.

"Beautiful, Louise", he said. "The fire's ready too, I expect."

"I'm focusing on the champagne," said Lady Brenda. She had stepped close to my father and looked up at him expectantly. Her hair was black and silky and organized in a thick, straight swirl against her slender neck. "How do you instantly chill a hot bottle of Champagne?"

"It's an old trick I learned in Vietnam," he answered.

"You were in Vietnam?"

"Just briefly….a couple of months. But I learned this…." He was suddenly flustered.

"So were you in the war?" She seemed genuinely interested in this question. She was looking up at my father with an intent expectation. "My big brother was there too," she said.

CM glanced at her, then rearranged his position—planted his feet just a tad further apart, preparing—I realize now—for a Tsunami to overwhelm his position.

"I was just talking to him last week," she went on, "before we flew out to Seattle. He still talks about it. He's still amazed we let them…."

"I was there just long enough to learn this little trick," my father said, forcefully changing the topic. He lifted the champagne bottle from the white towel and, with mock drama, laid it in the bowl of ice. Then he began spinning the bottle against the ice. It quickly melted a groove in the shape of the bottle.

"How long does it take?" Lady Brenda asked, watching intently.

"With Champagne, I'm not sure," my father answered. "We were doing this with aluminum beer cans. That took about sixty seconds per beer. I imagine a glass bottle will take a bit longer. I'll let you test it."

"I'm honored," she said playfully. "I like champagne really crisp, don't you? Otherwise it's too sweet."

"Yes, crisp is essential."

The coals in the grill flared suddenly as Louise wiped the oil over the grate.

"Grill's ready," she announced.

"I'll get the veggies," Maggie announced.

"Charlie?" my father looked over his shoulder and caught my eye. "Go get out of those waders and we'll have this ready by the time you get back." He kept spinning the champagne bottle.

I clumped off to my guest unit and quickly extracted myself from the waders. I found what I thought might be a cleaner pair of jeans and a polo shirt in the bottom of my clothes bag. I took a quick look in the mirror—a dazed looking reflection—and tried to flatten down a couple of odd pieces of hair. Things seemed to be unfolding like a rock-slide must begin…a few tiny pebbles losing their grip.

When I got back to the cooking deck the grilling was just finishing up. The two husbands were flipping and testing the meats with silver spatulas, transferring the done pieces to a wooden tray on the dolly. Maggie was turning thick slices of potatoes, sprin-kling them with oil and salt. I could see she'd already finished a bowl of grilled tomatoes. The bottle of champagne was standing upright-unopened, deep in its bowl of ice.

"Charlie!" My father said with great enthusiasm. "Just in time!"

He grabbed the champagne bottle from the ice.

"A little celebration here! You folks ready?"

"Give us a minute, CM." Maggie looked up and caught my eye.

The grilled food was quickly organized on the gurney, and my father commenced working on the champagne cap. A loud pop! Lady Brenda squeals. Bubbly foam erupts from the bottle in my father's hands. He quickly pours from the foaming bottle, not stopping between the glasses lined in a row along the stone counter. Some of the spilling champagne falls into the fire, send-ing up sizzling puffs of steam.

My father handed round the glasses, then held his up high, clearing his throat theatrically, starting to toast in the jocular mood of the moment. But nothing came out. His throat seemed to have tied itself in a knot. His eyes darted around for help, almost as if he couldn't breathe.

"Here's to Charlie's homecoming," Maggie said, stepping for-ward and raising her glass.

"Here, here!" agreed the tortoise-shelled glasses.

We all drank down the champagne. But my father was momentarily deflated. As everyone walked into the dining room, Louise pushing the dolly of food in the lead, he angled over to me.

"Sorry about all the to-do," he said. "The guests get a bit car-ried away sometimes, you know?"

"It's okay," I said.

"But will you come and talk to me later? After dinner? There's nothing I want more than to have a long talk."

"I'd like that too," I said.

"I'm in the last unit at the end. After dinner then?"

"Sure," I said. Then added: "Actually, I have something to give to you…"

But Lady Brenda had grabbed CM's arm and was pulling him toward the big round table.

Louise had cut the meats into bite-sized pieces on a side-bar and combined them on serving plates. These she placed on the lazy-susan. The outer perimeter of the table was set with white napkins, silverware, iced water goblets and wine glasses sparkling in the early evening light.

Before sitting down we filled wooden bowls with salad from the adjacent buffet. After we were seated, Gus appeared wearing over his fishing jeans a white serving jacket with black bow-tie held in place with an elastic band, a white towel folded across his arm, and a bottle of wine in each hand. Around the table he went. Red? White? Madame? Suddenly I realized there was music: A slow jazz trumpet up in the ceiling rafters.

10

MY FATHER EXCUSED US FROM the table conversation after dessert was served, telling the guests we had some catching up to do, and I followed him out onto the cooking deck, a knot of apprehension tightening in my chest.

"Give me fifteen minutes, Charlie," he said when we got outside. "To straighten up a bit. okay? I've been away and can't remember exactly the size of the mess I left."

I pulled a deck chair over close to the railing and sat down. Dusk had finally gathered around the river. I looked out across the darkening open space above the rush of water. The spiking tips of fir trees were black silhouettes pointing at big, floating stars. The air was barely cool. Other than the river sound, it was perfectly silent.

To my left, through windows looking into the river-room, I could see the foursome pulling chairs up to a card table. Tortoise-shelled glasses began to shuffle and deal. Lady Brenda pulled her thick, straight hair back so it fell freely behind her neck. Her husband was pouring into a glass from a decanter. There was a bird call. An owl, I was guessing. I remembered the screech owls in North Carolina, in the dark woods around the old farm house. I'd awaken, adrenaline pumping, thinking someone was being murdered....

I suddenly panicked, realizing I'd lost track of the time. Fifteen minutes, he'd said. How long ago was that? It was somehow completely dark all of a sudden. The lights from the camp-house spilled across the cooking deck. It had to have been at least fifteen minutes.... But what were we going to talk about? What was he going to say? What was I going to say? The knot in my chest tightened harder.

Then a soft whistle came from half-way down the veranda, and I saw his silhouette waving at me.

The studio space I stepped into was warm and tall. Anchored in the middle was the now familiar stone fireplace, extending to become a stone-topped kitchen counter. Three deep reading chairs clustered around a large leather ottoman next to the burn-stained hearth. Two side tables held iron lamps with dim, glowing shades. The side tables were stacked high with books.

"Come in. Come in!" my father turned and gestured with his hands, drawing me out of the doorway vestibule.

"I'd give you a tour," he said, "except this is it!" He swung his gaze around. "The spaces in the back are just a bathroom and sleeping alcove. The studio is on the other side of the fireplace….

"But let's sit," he said. "I can show you that later. Tell me about your trip. How long did you take?"

We sat on opposite sides of the big, leather ottoman.

"I drove it in three days," I said. (His eyebrows went up.) "Just slept off and on in the back of the camper. Drove straight through, more or less."

"I didn't expect you to get here so quickly," he said.

What did you expect, I wondered. The knot turned into a little curl of emotion in my ribs. All that evening, when he wasn't looking in my direction, I'd been studying him. I'd been looking for some connection, some familiarity. But I couldn't find it. His face was interesting but flat, like the face of a stranger you'd seen in the newspaper.

"I was…curious, of course," I said. "So I more or less drove straight through…"

The corners of his mouth turned up in a tight, wry smile.

"Yes, I'm sure you were."

"I've been wondering a long time," I said "…you know, basically: why?"

Surprised I'd put it out so directly I waited, my heart momentarily pumping fast.

His eyes searched over my face, gauging something.

"That's a legitimate question," he said. He put his hands together, prayer-like, and pressed them against his lips. "It's complicated I'm afraid. Do you have a few minutes?"

"I guess I do."

The ironic smile again…. Or was it a painful smile?

"I guess we have to start with Vietnam," he said. "What do you know about the war in Vietnam?"

"I know my mother thought it was evil. I know you volunteered to go there. I know…you didn't come back." I didn't trust him yet with what I did know.

He nodded, thoughtfully. "But what about the war itself? I mean, what is your understanding of what the war was about?"

I started to wing something conversational but stopped and said, "Sorry. I wasn't focused on that part of it. I don't really know what it was about—except 'communism'".

Another tight, wry smile. He turned and reached for a bottle of red wine and two glasses from the raised stone hearth.

"As I remember it, Charlie, that's exactly right. It seems to me you have a pretty clear picture." He lifted the bottle in my direction but I waived it off.

"Would you rather have a beer?" he asked.

"I'm fine."

"Eventually," he said, pouring himself a glass, "you'll find wine is more conducive to philosophical and spiritual insight. Beer just makes you want to whack baseballs and hump girls."

"Is that supposed to be fatherly advice?" My tone surprised me. The curl of emotion twisted again under my ribs.

My father waved his hand abruptly in the air.

"Charlie, let's start over. I'm sorry. I'm not doing this right. I waited a long time to have this conversation. And now I've started it about as badly as I could. I apologize. I should have been better prepared for this."

He shook his head as if to reorganize his thoughts.

"Let's start again like this: Tell me how you feel."

"How I feel?"

"Yes. I mean you've got to be angry…you've got to feel something pretty bad about me, right? If we can, I'd like to get over that first." He looked at me with an open searching gaze, honestly, I sensed, trying to gauge and understand my feelings.

I hesitated. The twist of emotion kicked again at my diaphragm.

"Okay," I said. "I guess I'll start with a beer."

When I said this something extraordinary happened: My father's face softened, and expanded suddenly into a wide, spontaneous smile with a noticeable gap between his two front teeth. It was the exact same smile I'd studied so many times in the black and white photo in my mother's steamer trunk. And all at once I made the connection I'd been unable to make since I'd first seen him leaning on the deck railing that afternoon. It was the connection I couldn't make all through dinner as well, watching and listening to him bantering back and forth with the guests.

But he'd never given the guests—not even the beautiful Lady Brenda— that big, black and white photo smile. And when at last he gave it to me, reality shifted.

I watched now, in amazement, his tall stooped shoulders as he stepped up into the small kitchen area and opened the under-counter fridge. I watched the downlights reflect on a balding spot in the middle of his curly grey hair as he leaned down to pull out a beer. I watched the slender fingers of his big square hand hold the bottle out to me. And his wide, gap-toothed smile, again, as I took it.

This was him, I suddenly understood. This was actually the mystery of my father materialized in front of me. I began to feel something sliding away in my chest.

He settled back in his chair and picked up his wine glass. He lifted it in the gesture of a toast. I lifted my beer in return.

It was a new beginning. We exchanged self-conscious smiles.

"So," he said, "I believe you were telling me how you feel."

My answer jumped out like it had been sitting in the back of my throat for 22 years: "I feel like I have amnesia," I said.

I was completely surprised by these words. His eyebrows went up, too.

"It's like there's a part of my life I can't remember. It makes me feel...disconnected...." For a clear moment I felt my disconnectedness, realizing for the first time what it was. "I've felt it ever since I can remember, especially when Gramella talked about my mother…and you."

He closed his eyes.

"Until I was fourteen," I said, "I thought you were dead. Did you know that? Did you have any idea?"

His eyes were still closed, hands clasped against his chin.

"When I figured out otherwise, I never told Gramella. Actually, I always thought she thought you were dead too…so it felt like I was protecting her in a way."

He nodded, eyes still closed.

"Tell me about growing up," he said.

So I told him. About grade school and middle school and high school. About the field trip to Washington D.C. and the war memorial. I told him about my senior prom. About my eighteenth birthday and the steamer trunk in the garage. I told about college and the girl who'd finally taken me to bed, and about how Gramella died. Then I told about living in the old farm house outside of Chapel Hill, and starting to write a novel—and burning it.

He alternated between eyes-closed concentration and a steady, grey-eyed gaze throughout my story. His eyebrows and the corners of his mouth giving a sign-language commentary of his reactions.

"So then your letter came," I said. "Your second letter."

He grimaced, closing his eyes again.

"So I guess the mystery is what was it all about?" I said. "Why didn't Gramella tell me about you? Why didn't you come back? …And now that I think about it, why is your name McCormick?"

He tried a big smile again. "McCormick! It's got a ring to it, don't you think? Do you think I can pass for Irish?"

But the smile collapsed.

"Not funny," he said. "I'm sorry."

He looked down into his wine glass.

"The straight-out answer to your question, Charlie, is that I gave myself the name McCormick because I'm a fugitive from the law."

I laughed, involuntarily. "Please! Can't we be serious here, just long enough…"

"But I am serious," he said. "Look at me, Charlie: I couldn't go back to Charleston, or North Carolina, or anyplace else after the war, because I had to go into hiding to escape going to prison. That's the simplest part of the answer to your question."

He gazed at me steadily, forcing this to sink in.

"But it's also a lot more complicated than that. For one thing, I didn't even know you existed. Laurie never told me. I didn't find out until after…."

My father's square hands suddenly covered his face. Pushed and kneaded his forehead, making his curly forelocks bounce.

"Look, I can see this is going to be harder than I thought."

He stood abruptly and stepped over to the windows next to the stone hearth.

From my vantage the glass window panes were a faceted mirror, throwing back fragmented soft-lit images of our sitting space. But my father, his forehead leaning against the glass, was looking into the outer darkness. His hands were pushed stiffly into the front pockets of his jeans, hunching up his shoulders.

"The last time I ever saw your mother," he said, still looking out in the darkness, "was in Osaka, Japan."

He turned and looked at me. Then came and sat again. He leaned forward and looked down into his big open palms, as if he were holding something for me to see.

"I had a three day R&R," he explained. "Everyone went to Japan for the whores…for the Geishas. But I had something better to look forward to: Laurie had agreed to meet me there—in Japan! She flew all the way from Charleston, Charlie.

"I don't know if you can understand the state I was in. We won't even talk about Vietnam. Even without that shit I was crazy being away from Laurie. I dreamed about her. I fantasized about her until I was nearly crazy.

I was looking down at his open palms too, listening, visualizing the young woman in my black and white photo— cut-off jeans, sparkling eyes, leaning against the Mercedes grille.

"Our timing was off," he continued. "I don't remember why. It turned out we only had one night together. It was a bizarre night. It was winter. We were staying at a country inn—an old Japanese farmhouse. A big, heavy timber-framed place that smelled like wood-smoke. We had a little room with a futon on the floor and a big window that looked out over a snowy field. There was a full moon and the light bouncing off the snow lit up the room. Filled it with cold light and cold shadows. We didn't even have a candle. The mama-san kept bringing us hot-sake in little white pitchers. We sat on the futon with a down quilt around our shoulders and drank hot-sake and talked.

"She told me she was going on tour. There was a base guitar player named Kurtz. I knew Kurtz from college. I didn't like him. I didn't trust him either. 'Look', I remember she said, 'don't make a big deal of it. I just can't love you right now.'"

"We watched the moon for a long time floating over the cold white field, and then, I'll admit to you, I began to cry. I didn't even know it. My next sip of sake tasted like salt. Then Laurie sensed what was happening and she leaned her shoulder in against me, pushing against me, like trying to prop me up.

"I was scared shitless of both ends of my life. In less than 12 hours I was going back to Nam, to a disconnected nightmare I couldn't even talk about with anyone. And she was going back to Charleston, to the anti-war movement and a sleazy, base guitar player with long slender fingers. That was the last night I was ever in love with anyone, Charlie....So you should feel good about that, at least."

I didn't answer. I was thinking about my mother's diary. A twinge of guilt was growing as I realized he was being completely honest—that I was the one holding back information.

"I can't explain what happened that night," he went on. "One minute our shoulders were touching, Laurie propping me up, and the next a huge passion overwhelmed us. Before it was over we must have made love at least a half a dozen times. We got so hot we pushed out the big casement window and let the moonlight and cold mountain air blow over us. In the morning, the down quilt we'd finally buried under to sleep was covered with a powder of snow. It was like we'd died and gone to heaven."

He stared a few moments more at his open palms. He closed them into fists. Then reached for the wine bottle.

"You want another beer?"

"I'll get it," I said.

When I returned my father was lounging back, eyes closed behind his round glasses. I plopped into the chair and they opened. He looked surprised, for a moment, to see me there.

"Laurie and I said goodbye at the Osaka airport. I never saw her or heard from her again. She flew back to Charleston. I flew back to Da Nang. I've always been an optimist. But that flight to Da Nang was my flight into Hell.

"You say I volunteered for Vietnam. But that's not exactly the case. The case was I was going in any event. I was either going to get drafted or I was going to get myself into officer candidate school and try to stay off the front lines. There were a whole lot of us who were going in any event. The difference was some of us thought it was sensible to go off and do battle to defeat the Communists. There're probably a lot of people who still do. If you know anything about how the communists twisted an ideal about social and economic fairness into a new kind of human slavery, you might be one of them.

"What turned out to be so wrong in Vietnam, though, was that the reality of the war had no connection with defeating communism—or any other useful goal any of us could begin to see or comprehend. It began to feel like we were just killing Vietnamese as part of a business venture…Are you with me Charlie?"

"I'm here," I said, partly holding back now, instinctively apprehensive at his tone.

"I don't need to go into details," he said. "The details, in a way, aren't even important. The military 'business leaders' came up with a new idea about how to sell their product. And wanted to test it in the marketplace. There were even industry representatives there—civilian advisors from Dow Chemical. I was part of the testing team. And because I was their Tester, I was responsible for something unbearably cruel. Something that shocked me numb when I saw it happen. Something I knew, immediately, I was not going to be able to live with...."

Suddenly I was frightened. My legs stood me up, surprising me.

My father looked up, startled.

"I don't want to know." I said.

"I'm not going to tell you," he answered quietly. His hands gestured for me to sit again, but I remained on my feet.

"I've learned to live with it after all," he said after a moment. "In fact, I think I've turned it into something positive...maybe. I'm sorry I had to tell you this much. But otherwise none of the rest of what I have to say will make any sense at all."

He took a swallow of wine and looked down into the glass.

"Let's take a break," he said, standing impulsively, just as I was about to sit down again. "Let's go see what Louise put out for midnight snack."

11

THE COOL RIVER AIR FANNED over us as we walked along the dark veranda.

The camp house was silent, dimly lit with just a few spots in the gallery. On a side table in the river room a low lamp illuminated a white plate of cookies. On the same table were a water carafe and a cut-glass decanter with amber contents.

"It's a tradition," my father smiled. "Louise's oatmeal cookies will chase away the most persistent nightmare. If it's cold-sweat nightmares a glass of ice-water is best. If it's an intellectual nightmare—one of those problems you can't stop your brain from gnawing on—then a snifter of brandy is what's prescribed." He smiled big. "I invariably require the brandy...."

We sat in the semi-darkness, near the leaning window wall. Deep leather chairs with a side table in between holding the transported plate of cookies. The mosaic of glass windowpanes reflected the lamp behind us. Beyond these reflections, the white water of the river glimmered like a flickering ghost. We sipped our brandies in silence for a moment. Then my father took up his story again:

"There's no reason to make this part longer than it needs to be," he said. "There are other things—more important, believe it or not—we need eventually to get to. But for those things to make sense you need to understand what happened after Vietnam. Are you still with me here, Charlie?"

"I'm here," I said, wondering with a fleeting apprehension what 'the other things' were going to be.

CM set his brandy on the side table and leaned forward, hands under his chin.

"Things changed catastrophically for me after Japan," he said. "I was unscratched. Not a single bullet or shrapnel hole in my body. But my mind was filled with anger, Charlie—like shards of broken glass cutting away. If I'd been burned, crippled, maimed—if I'd been suffering from some slow-mending wound—things might have been different. What seemed so evil though, when my tour was over and they sent me back to the States, was that I was untouched, as if I'd made a deal with them. It felt like everyone could see that I'd made a deal, that I'd been spared because I'd gone along with what they wanted. I felt guilty, Charlie, ashamed I hadn't stood up to them. I felt dirty. I felt I needed…to get clean, is the best way I can describe what I did…"

"Did?" I asked. "What did you do?"

He fell silent for a moment.

"Have you ever heard of napalm?" he asked.

"It was a fire-bomb, or something."

"That's right. Odd name, don't you think? The most insidious thing about napalm was that they experimented with how to make it sticky. In the beginning the VC were just rubbing it off. But at 2000 degrees a little blob of sticky napalm, they decided, would burn a hole—but never mind that. I wasn't going to go into that. Sorry."

I shifted and the leather chair creaked. I crossed my legs tightly.

"Napalm was manufactured by Dow Chemical in Torrance, California," he went on. "It was a big sprawling chemical plant surrounded by a sixteen foot chain-link fence with razor-wire at the top. A total waste of razor-wire, Charlie. Why they thought anyone would try climbing over the top of that fence is beyond me. We cut through the bottom in less than five minutes."

"What do you mean?" I protested. The room began to feel like it was tilting. "Where are you going with this, for chris-sakes?"

"This is what I'm trying to tell you, Charlie," my father said, leaning toward me for emphasis. "This is why my name is McCormick. This is why…everything went wrong."

I looked out the glass windowpanes, trying to focus on the river.

"There were three of us," he continued. "We'd become acquainted at a cellar bar in Berkeley where Nam vets read poetry and political pieces about the war. There were guys there without legs reading from spiral notebooks like they'd carried around in high school just a year before.

"The other two had both been trained in explosives. We agreed that night not to know each other's names. That's how the conversation started actually: 'I'm not going to tell you my name.' It started out as a conversational joke. But then we realized that, underneath, we were all serious in the same way, about the same thing.

"We called each other 'one', 'two', and 'three'. I was 'two'. 'One' knew how to get the explosives. 'Three' knew how to make a timed fuse. I was given the task of finding the safest part of the Torrance perimeter and figuring out how to get through it."

A door clunked quietly out in the gallery. Footsteps padded across the floor behind us. Before she spoke I knew it was Maggie.

"I figured you guys would eat all the cookies," she said.

"Hey, Miggs," my father said. "The plate's over here. We saved one for you, of course! So, was it a cold sweat or a hot dream?"

"Shush up, CM," she said.

I heard her select the water carafe and pour herself what sounded like half a glass.

"Come join us, Miggs," my father said. "We were just talking about you".

"I think you've got other things to be talking about," she said.

I wanted to turn around in my chair and look at her. What did she wear wandering around for a midnight snack? Her dimly lit reflection was broken into multiple facets in the window glass in front of me. I could see her arm lifting the water glass to drink. The rest of her body, fragmented into the other panes, was impossible to decipher.

"Charlie?" she said, startling me.

"Yup?"

"Don't let CM tell you any fish stories."

In the soft reflection of the lamplight off the window glass, I saw my father's face break into his big gap-toothed smile, and suddenly the room was bathed in a complex pleasure I'd never experienced before.

"Good night, Miggs," my father said.

"Good night guys." The soft footsteps padded away leaving a palpable silence.

"You'll come to understand," my father said, "Maggie's main interest in things is whether they're right or wrong. She inherited it from her father, I think. Randolph Scott liked to take things, anything—even picking a color for something—and work it through some process of logic until he could arrive at a point of right or wrong. I saw him do it over and over with students…. So what color do you think is the fact we bombed the Dow Chemical plant in Torrance?"

"What color?" I was trying to grasp the implications of the word 'bombed' .

"I've come to realize, of course," my father said, "right or wrong about it doesn't even matter. Right or wrong, it was an incredibly naïve and ineffective way to try to change anything. Right or wrong it was unimaginative and unintelligent. I can't believe I did it—what desperate frame of mind I must have been in.

"There wasn't supposed to be anyone in the building, of course, where we set the explosives. We timed everything specifically for that not to happen. But for some reason someone was there….They got injured—pretty bad."

CM shifted uncomfortably in his chair, the leather creaking.

"I can see so clearly now how futile it is to pound and whack away against a machine. The best you can do, by setting off explosions in its face, is simply to get its attention. And then it starts to look for you—not someone like you, which it does every day as a matter of course—but you personally. And when it finds you…." He waved his hand. "I realized all that way too late, Charlie."

Distracted, he poured himself another glass of brandy.

"What I realize now," he said, holding the glass under his chin, "is that to change a machine, you've got to get inside the machinery. But I can't do that, Charlie. They've got guards posted now with my picture in their back pockets. Do you see what I mean?"

"Number three was caught at the scene," he went on. "There was an FBI case-officer named Pikeman. Abe Pikeman. He tracked down number one four months later. I read about it in the paper. I was living in a weekly rental in Boise, Idaho, working at a gas station. I was desperate and lonely. I took a chance and wrote a letter to Laurie's mother, to see if I could find out where she was. Two weeks later there was a knock on my door. It was Kurtz, the guy from her band. He told me about Laurie's accident—and about you. That's how I found out...."

He stopped, looking at me, letting this fact settle in. Then he continued:

"Two days later, there was another knock on my door, this time at four o:clock in the morning. It was Pikeman, flashing a badge in a flip-open wallet. He was a short guy with a military crew-cut, but wide and stocky, like an army drill sergeant."

"What—did he arrest you?"

"No. He didn't have anything concrete. But I knew right away he knew I was number two. He just knew it somehow. It was like he was a dog that could sniff you out by the smell of your socks. But there was no direct connection he'd made yet.

"He tried to scare me; tried to bluff me into saying the wrong things. He ordered me down to the FBI office in Boise and took my deposition: Where I was on such and such a date. All that stuff. Then I walked out. He leaned against the door as I was going down the stairs, and he said: 'Go hide somewhere, Mr. Fuckhead Traitor. We'll find you when the time comes.' I'll never forget the expression on his face.

"I got out of Boise fast, Charlie, but before I left, I sent you a letter. Did Ella ever show it to you?"

The image of the black steamer-trunk, and the folded yellow paper with the slanted, all-caps lettering, flashed in my head, puzzle pieces slipping into place. "Yes," I said. "I got it."

THE ARCHITECT WHO COULDN'T SING

"I knew they were following me so I invented the most screwed up, circuitous, fragmented route to nowhere I could imagine. I rode every form of transportation available, including a ten-day hike through a corner of Yellowstone park. Then I got to Seattle and, just by chance, I ran into Frederique."

"Who?"

"He was a gay Frenchman, an attaché I knew in Vietnam. I'd done him a favor there—a big favor, actually. I'd saved his life."

"How did you do that?"

"We won't go into that Charlie. But now he saved mine in return. He got me a new identity and driver's license. It was Frederique who came up with the name McCormick. He said he always thought I looked like an Irishman. Then he got me to Port Townsend and arranged a job in the boat yard there.

"It felt safe in Port Townsend. I could move around, drive to Seattle on occasion, as long as I was careful. I worked on the boats for a couple of years. I couldn't contact you, or write you, or go and visit you because I was afraid they were waiting for me to do that. Do you see? I'd realized the reason Pikeman had showed up in Idaho so soon after Kurtz. Somehow they'd made the connection. That's why…I never contacted you."

I was remembering my birthdays and Christmases and baseball games, and trying to visualize my father in Port Townsend, working on boats, while all those things were going on.

"Then, out of the blue," he said, "I met Randolph Scott."

"Maggie told me that part of the story," I said.

"She did?"

"Last night. She gave me a tour and…sort of a history."

My father smiled. I sensed the tension in his posture relaxing. He sat back in the chair, the leather creaking again.

"So I guess you understand, for me Randolph Scott was like a gift from God. Not only did he give me a place to hide, he gave me the chance to redeem myself."

"Redeem yourself?"

My father leaned forward, energized in a new way.

"The day we met, I told Randolph about an architectural idea that I'd started thinking about while I was in Vietnam. About how architecture could happen in a way that empowered people, little people, poor people.

"We talked about it. Randolph got enthusiastic because he had a parallel idea, one he'd been pursuing for entirely different reasons. And then he said, 'I know exactly where we can experiment with building something like that.'

"So that's why he invited me to come up to the river here: to build the fish camp using our experimental process. I had to tell him about Torrance. He's the only person I ever told. Lots of people have helped me, Charlie. But Maggie's father gave me the greatest gift of all. He gave me the chance to build something.

"We were getting close to what he called 'publication'. 'We're getting close to publication' he'd say, each time we finished a guest unit.

"By 'publication' he meant that we'd open a firm in Seattle and take on international projects. We'd talked about it a lot. For me it was a dream. He'd be the front man. But I'd be more or less out of hiding. I wouldn't be in the public eye but I'd be doing something good....Something to make up for what I did in Vietnam. I fantasized that maybe it might be possible...."

My father leaned back in his chair again. He sipped some brandy and set the glass on the side table.

"Then Randolph Scott got sick one day and died within a week. It happened while Maggie was away. We didn't even know where she was.... It took Gus a month to track her down."

I let this hang there, not knowing how much CM really knew, amazed that I might actually know more than he did.

We sat in silence for a minute, contemplating, I thought, the disappearance of Maggie. But my father's thinking had proceeded to other topics.

"So there's only one thing more I guess we should cover before we call it a night," he said.

He seemed suddenly uncomfortable. He adjusted his position, making the leather chair squeak in protest.

"You want some water or something?" he asked.

"What is it we need to cover?"

"Well, I guess it's the fact that I signed you up."

"Signed me up?"

He broke into his big grin. "I signed you up, Charlie, as a member of the Team."

"What team?"

"Well…it's a competition I entered. An architectural competition. I had to enter it as a matter of fact. It was like the world was asking, 'Hey, Charlie Robert, what was your life supposed to have been about, anyway?' So I entered it. It seemed like maybe it was going to be my last chance. You know what I mean?"

"Last chance for what?"

"To redeem myself," he said. "Of course it never occurred to me.…It was a national design competition. The prize money was significant. I knew there were big powers behind it, big names would be in the ring. So it was a lark, you know? There was no way.…"

"And what happened?"

"Well, the great shock is I got short listed."

"Meaning what?"

"Meaning when there's an architectural competition like this, there's hundreds of entries and the first thing they do is narrow it down to a few—a short list. Usually it's five. This time it's three."

"So out of hundreds of entries in this competition, you're one of the three in contention?"

"That's essentially the facts."

"So, what am I missing? That's great, isn't it?"

"It's amazing actually.… But it presents a kind of problem, don't you see, Charlie?"

"I'm not sure. You get a chance to design something…what? What is the competition about?"

"I knew you'd ask me that, so I came prepared!" With a sudden flurry of enthusiastic movement, he extracted from his shirt pocket a folded piece of paper. He handed it to me. "Don't read it now," he said. "The light's not good. It's getting late anyway.…"

I laid the folded paper in my lap.

"Okay," I said. "But why is there a problem?"

My father fidgeted in his chair again, re-crossed his legs.

"It's only a problem because the short-listed people are required to make a presentation of their final design—a personal presentation—this coming November, to the evaluating jury."

A small kernel of understanding, of premonition, began to swell in my imagination. My father was leaning forward now, trying to read my face.

"You can't make the presentation, can you?"

"I didn't expect that I'd actually win, Charlie.... I don't know what I thought. That maybe they'd just print the runner-ups—that somehow the ideas I'd been working on for so long would get published or something. I didn't think I'd be in a position of actually having to make a public presentation."

My father nervously poured another brandy. "Just a short one," he said with a quick smile.

"So what are you going to do?" I asked.

"Like I said, Charlie. I've created a Team. You know: The McCormick Planning Group. Mr. McCormick has been taken ill suddenly. Gall bladder surgery. So the Team, naturally, will make the presentation in his absence."

"And who's on the Team?"

"Well, it's you...and Maggie. I decided Gus and Louise would probably not be much use." The big gap-toothed smile stretched across his face.

I looked at him in disbelief.

"Me and Maggie?"

He nodded, still smiling with genuine excitement.

"Are you nuts?" I said. The implications of what he was suggesting were now blossoming rapidly in my mind.

"Are you crazy?" I repeated. "How can I pretend to be some architectural genius? I don't even know how to draw a straight line!"

I suddenly had a vivid memory of Gramella saying to me: "He could draw a line straight as an arrow..." Emotions started sliding up into my throat. I leaned forward in the deep leather chair and put my weight in my feet, ready to spring up and run.

"Okay, Charlie! Relax," my father said. His big hands waved me back into the chair. "Don't go overboard about this, please.

It's enough that you're here! That's amazing, don't you think? I'm sorry you might believe now I had ulterior motives. But it's not that, I swear. I mean it's really not that."

"Aren't you afraid they followed me out here?"

He regarded me a moment, searching my face.

"I don't think they did, Charlie. Assuming you didn't say anything to anybody."

"I didn't."

"And anyway," he said. "I decided it was time. It was worth the risk."

I stared at him.

"I'm sorry I laid this on you so suddenly," he went on quickly. "The competition is not the most important thing to me. Worst case we just withdraw. Charles McCormick regretfully withdraws due to health problems.... So what? But let's sleep on it, Charlie. Okay?....Let's get some sleep."

The folded piece of paper he'd given me fell to the floor. I reached down and picked it up.

"Don't worry about that. Just stick it in your pocket for now. We can talk some more tomorrow." He stood up. "I'm going to turn in."

"Look," I said, "I don't want you to think...."

"Just sleep on it," he said. "I shouldn't have laid this on you so fast. It was my mistake. Maybe it will seem different in the morning. When I can explain it better. Nothing's poured in concrete here. It's just an idea...for contemplation."

We walked out onto the cooking deck. A half-moon had risen above the trees behind the river, casting black shadows. The secret conversation of the flowing water rose up from below our feet.

When we got to the short bridge to my unit we stopped.

"I brought something with me," I said. "Actually, it's yours."

"Mine?"

"Yeah. It's something my mother made for you."

"Oh, Jesus."

"Wait a second and I'll get it."

I ducked across the short bridge. I'd long ago re-recorded my mother's reel tape onto a cassette, and I'd laid out a copy of it when I'd changed my clothes before dinner. I was back in a moment.

"It was in her trunk," I explained, holding it out. His hands seemed reluctant to take it. "I think it's self-explanatory."

"Thanks, Charlie," he said. He hesitated, looking at me.

"Just listen to it," I said. "I have my own copy. Do you have a tape player?"

He nodded. "Okay, Charlie," he said. "See you tomorrow."

He turned away, holding the tape cassette in both hands, peering down at it.

"CM?" I said.

"What?" Turning back.

"I was just trying out what to call you."

"That'll do perfect, Charlie." And he flashed, one more time, the gap-toothed smile.

12

WHEN I OPENED MY EYES the next morning, it took me a moment to understand—again—where I was. I sat on the edge of the bed, looking out into the angular room, remembering fragments of the day before. As I pieced things together, my attention focused on a folded paper next to my pile of clothes on the floor, and the last bit of conversation with my father came rushing back.

I still have that folded paper. It's a semi-gloss magazine page carefully torn from the June 1994 issue of Architectural Record. It is folded once in half with a bold, black headline facing out: "Call for Entries".

The call must have attracted the attention of virtually every subscriber, for under the headline a black banner announced in bold, white block letters: "$100,000 First Prize!" ("The prize is substantial," my father had said.)

If you unfold this page, you can read the pertinent details of the competition:

Open to any architect or urban designer in North America.
$100 entry fee due no later than August 10th.
Preliminary Design Concepts to be submitted no later than December 10th.
Jury selected "short-list" to be announced March 16th, 1995
Short-list entries to receive $25,000 each to complete their Town Plans.
Short-listed entrants to make formal presentation of their completed designs at the Buchanan County, Iowa Courthouse the first week of November, 1995.
Final winner to be announced December 1st.
Contract for Construction Documents to be awarded by March 1st, 1996.
Fast-Track Construction to begin September 1st.

Most eye-catching and mysterious, however, is that all these pertinent details are printed over a surreal, monochromatic mud-green photo of building roofs, church spires, and cupolas projecting above a heavy, glinting flow of dull, borderless water. (Identified in fine print at the page bottom: "The Great Midwestern Flood of 1993".)

The bottom quarter of the page—again dropped out letters from a stark black rectangle—is the following background explanation:

> Having experienced catastrophic floods every decade since its founding on the northern bank of the Wapsiconicon River, the town of Hope, Iowa has determined to abandon its 200 year old foundations and rebuild itself on the higher, southern bank as a visionary example of the future of the American small town. The object of the Architectural/Urban Design Competition is to design this visionary future—the new town of New Hope, Iowa.

I skimmed all this quickly, standing in the little kitchen space while coffee percolated and filtered into the small stainless serving carafe. Coffee mug in hand, I sat in the same chair I'd occupied two evenings before, listening to Maggie's story about the building of the fish camp. I glanced briefly out and down at the river. Sunlight was warm on the now-familiar boulder, the water gliding clean and swift around each side of it.

Sipping the coffee, I read the slick magazine page again, trying to focus on the reality of what it was actually saying.

So this was the competition my father had entered—had been short-listed on. Only he and two others were now in contention to design, from scratch, a completely "new town for three thousand inhabitants". To visualize a "new future for man's habitation on the Earth". To create an example that was "to inspire world architecture for the 21st century". Nothing less.

I began to wonder what he could have submitted to have been chosen one of the three finalists. Even more, as the scope and complexity of the challenge unfolded in my imagination, I found myself wondering about his sanity. How he could possibly think I could make such a presentation? For me, explaining a building design was obviously impossible—but an entire city? How could he be that unstable?

Finishing the coffee, I realized I dreaded leaving the safe, quiet nook where I was sitting to confront someone who was probably delusional. He'd seemed reasonably normal the night before—in spite of the bizarre story he told—but he couldn't possibly be in his right mind. Even worse: that I was going to have to tell him I couldn't help. I was dismayed and disoriented by the absurdity of his plans. I'd be much better off to politely extricate myself and get back to North Carolina. I was sure I could get a high school teaching job. Perhaps in a year or so start another novel.

In the shower I rehearsed what I was going to say. By the time I stepped out of the stony enclosure my confidence was rock solid. The compassionate logic of my argument was irrefutable: I held him in the highest regard. I would assist him in any way I usefully could. But simple reality dictated that I couldn't possibly, conceivably, make the presentation of his design for a futuristic new town in Iowa.

Both the sun and my spirits were high when I finally stepped out onto the veranda. I wasn't sure if it actually still qualified as morning: my watch read 10:15—yet the sun seemed almost directly overhead. The river shooting under me seemed especially exuberant and playful.

I turned and walked along the veranda toward the camp house. As I stepped onto the cooking deck I saw CM sitting over by the railing in a deck chair. He was writing in a little black book, a wide-brimmed straw hat shading his face.

I hesitated. Then I called out a Good Morning as aggressively as I could.

He turned, startled. Then his big smile.

"Charlie! Up at last! I guess yesterday wore you out. Wore me out too, I think. I only just got up here myself. Louise is doing some scrambled eggs…"

He closed the little black book and clipped his pen over the edge of its cover. I took a step to join him, but he quickly unfolded himself from the deck chair and walked in my direction.

"How'd you sleep?" he asked, holding out a big square hand. His energy projected like palpable photons.

"Good."

"Come-on, let's eat." He pulled open a door to the dining room. "We seem to be on the same schedule today!"

We sat next to each other at the round table. The dining room was crisscrossed with bright shafts of sunlight and wafting, iridescent dust particles. CM reached out and set the lazy-susan in motion, then stopped it when the silver coffee carafe arrived in front of me.

"Landsakes," said Louise behind us. "You folks multiply faster than fruit-flies. Good thing I cooked some extra."

She reached between us and placed a big plate of eggs and sausages on the lazy-susan. "You need some fresh fruit, Mr. Charlie?"

"That'd be great, Louise. Thanks!"

I was suddenly trying to generate some energy of my own. I could feel the confidence I'd built up in the shower beginning to deflate.

CM handed me the serving spoon. "You first," he said.

Louise returned with a bowl of sliced peaches and plums. She patted me lightly on the shoulder.

"Maggie said to tell you good morning," she said. "She's off with Lady Brenda, down the river."

We ate mostly in an awkward silence. When the eggs and sausages were gone, we took our coffee mugs out on the cooking deck and sat in the deck chairs. Awkward silence again. Only the river sound below.

I puffed up my courage and plunged: "Look, I've been thinking about what you said last night..." Having started, my mind raced backwards to find the phrases from my morning shower. "I know this is important to you. And I honestly want to help. I'm honestly intrigued, you know? But I don't think this is going to work."

"Why wouldn't it work?" His voice was calm. He crossed the legs of his faded jeans and looked at me over the tops of his round glasses.

"Well, first of all, I know zip about architecture," I said. "How can I possibly learn enough in this short a time to be able to pull something like that off? I mean, they'd see right through me....They'd be asking questions, right? It's not like I can memorize some presentation...memorize some structural formula about how buildings stand up."

"It's not about how buildings stand up." CM said patiently. "The world is full of very competent engineers who can figure out how to make buildings stand up. You don't have to have a competition to figure that out."

"But look," my voice rising, "I'm a twenty-two year old English major for chrissakes!" My coherent shower monologue had collapsed that quickly.

CM nodded his head, acknowledging this piece of information.

"It's true the jury will realize you're not an architect," he said. "But that's not a problem. I'm not asking you to pretend to be an architect. What you'll be presenting isn't actually architecture anyway...it's something else."

"But I read that magazine page you gave me last night. You've designed a city! That's got to have some architecture in it somewhere."

"You'd think so, wouldn't you?" he said with a smile. His eyes were flashy now and full of enthusiasm. "But that's just it, Charlie. You'll see. What we're presenting isn't architecture, it's a way to help people make architecture happen."

I sat looking at him, part of my mind still searching back in the shower stall for the arguments that would make me safe.

"Come on," he said standing up. "Let's go down to the studio and I'll show you."

Without understanding how or why, I found myself following this tall, slightly stooped but broad-shouldered man down the veranda. My arguments against his plan, whatever it might turn out to be, seemed to have evaporated into the crisp air above the river.

13

STEPPING INTO MY FATHER'S STUDIO in the day-light was like entering a wood and glass prism: light and sun-beams bounced from every direction. On the opposite side of the fireplace sitting area, where we'd talked the night before, was the studio space itself: a large, angular room with a bank of outward sloping windows looking out and down at a section of the river. Against these windows stretched a long work table. Two of the windows were tilted open, letting in the sliding sound of the water.

The work table was divided into three sections with different heights. The center section was at desk height with a wooden chair pulled up to it. The chair was on rollers and had a faded red cushion. An old black typewriter with fat mechanical keys occu-pied the middle of the desk space. Next to it three or four little black notebooks lay open, face down on top of each other. A ream of typing paper stacked in front of the window, held down by a smooth grey river-rock. Next to it, under another rock, was a shorter stack of typed pages.

"I didn't know they made these anymore," I said looking at the typewriter.

CM laughed. "I don't think they do," he said.

To the right of the typing area was a sloped drawing board with a parallel bar that had worn dirty tracks along the edges of a light green, rubbery drawing surface. Little wooden boxes filled with pencils and pens and colored markers were organized neatly to the side. A large drafting lamp with grab-handles hung out over the drawing board on a long articulated arm. The slanted board was covered with layers of white and yellow tracing paper, different sizes, corners taped down, creating overlapping layers of pencil and ink lines and notations.

To the left of the typewriter the work table stepped up to a height you could stand at. This was the longest section. A tall stool was pulled up to it. This part of the table was covered with a jumbled array of small, white and grey cardboard and balsa-wood models of buildings and building parts. The entire working surface was a thick cardboard mat cut with thousands of sliced scribes and nicks. A large bottle of white glue and a series of cutting knives and tweezers sat in a shallow wooden organizer.

"This is what I wanted to show you," CM said, heading for the scramble of models. He lifted a larger model with a rectangular cardboard base from the far end of the table.

"Let's take it into the sitting room," he said.

We walked back around the fireplace and he set the model on the big leather ottoman. We pulled the easy chairs up closer and sat down.

To my surprise, I immediately recognized what we were looking at: It was the model Maggie had described to me two nights earlier. The model of the fish camp.

"Maggie told me about this model the first night I was here," I said.

CM's eyebrows went up in surprise. "What else did she tell you?"

"About her father. About how you came here. Her recollection of it all."

CM studied me for a moment, the corners of his mouth playing with a smile.

"I didn't realize she'd gone into so much detail," he said. "Maggie isn't usually that forthcoming. You must have really charmed her."

"I don't think that's exactly what happened," I said. "I don't know what I did...she just told me the story. She told me about the model. About the architecture students. About the summers. About the girl student who built her unit. She told me she taught you how to fly-fish."

CM laughed and smiled his big smile with pleasure. "You have been blessed, Charlie," he said, shaking his head slowly. "I don't expect Maggie has ever told that story to anyone—ever. Not even to herself!"

"Well, she told me," I said, wondering about it, now—trying to recall what exactly precipitated the telling.

"I'm grateful she did," said CM. "It saves me a lot of telling myself. What's more to the point, though, you understand how the fish camp was built?"

"I understand how," I said. "I mean I understand that each guest unit had a different author—was built as a separate project by a different group of students. But I don't understand why—or why that's even important."

"Excellent!" CM said. "This is really excellent! We're way ahead of the game here! Look:"

He reached out and started removing pieces—units actually—from the model. One by one he lifted them away and set them carefully on the floor. Finally, all that remained were the sections of the veranda, angling along the edge of the cardboard river bank, each section with its short, perpendicular bridge connecting to a series of grey "stone" piers. Opposite each veranda section, and centered, more or less, within the pattern of stone piers, was a vertical chipboard chimney with its tiny hearth and kitchen counter, and a connected box-space that I knew was the bathroom.

"Okay. So this is what we started with," he said, "except each kitchen-fireplace-bath core was enclosed in a temporary weatherproof box."

"Yeah, Maggie told me about that."

He reached down and picked up one of the little models and slid it over a chimney into its place. "This is what we built first."

I recognized Maggie's unit—the one adjacent to the cooking deck.

"The cooking deck was added later," CM said, "when we built the dining room and kitchen." He reached down and picked up those pieces and put them in place. "This was the next guest unit," he said, reaching down for another piece of the model. He carefully slid it over another chimney, fitting it snug against the end of its tiny bridge. Then he reached down for the next one.

While I'd understood from Maggie's description that the units of the Fish Camp were built one at a time over consecutive summers, watching this sequence build upon itself in the model held a surprising fascination. Before setting them in place, CM held each individual project in the palm of his hand and pointed out some interesting feature. "This one split the sitting space in two, creating a little eating nook. You can see how the main roof is split, making a glass clerestory here...."

The tiny models were each a different thing in the wide flat palm of CM's hand. What was fascinating to watch was how, when each was attached to the curving veranda, it became a part of the fish camp as a whole—its uniqueness somehow absorbed and yet expressed at the same time.

In turn, CM added the camp house and the studio, leaving only a single gap remaining.

"This was the last one we built." CM placed a small replica of Ben Sprague's unit, filling in the gap.

"It's finished," I said, surprised at a subtle inner feeling of satisfaction to see the model reassembled.

"Not quite." CM said.

I glanced up and found him grinning at me.

He reached and picked up a couple of books from the stack next to his chair. He used these to prop up the back of the model so it was canted in my direction. "So you can see the whole thing better," he explained.

"So what's not finished?" I asked.

He pointed to the upper left corner of the model. The layers of the cardboard base were built up here, creating a large hill rising above and off to the side of the fish camp. This hill was covered thickly with skinny, dark-green triangles glued vertically into the cardboard, representing—with surprising effectiveness—a forest of trees. In the middle of this little forest was a clearing, and in the clearing was a small white box penetrated by a chipboard chimney.

"So that looks like another chimney-box," I said.

"That's right."

"Maggie didn't show me that unit."

"She was gone," CM said. "Randolph Scott and I put this up here just before he got sick two years ago. Then…it sort of got forgotten."

"So what is it?" I asked. "I mean, why is it way up there away from everything else?"

"It's the last guest unit," CM adjusted his glasses and folded his hands under his chin, leaning forward, staring intently at the model. "I've always thought of it as a retreat—a hideaway. The place a guest would stay if they wanted to be secluded from the rest of the Camp—like say, they were on a honeymoon or something."

"So has anyone stayed there?"

"It hasn't been built yet—only the Enabling Structure."

"Enabling Structure?"

"That's what the chimney-box and the pier system are. That's what we call it. It's what each unit starts out with."

"So why hasn't it been built?"

"Well…." CM pulled on his chin. "We were sort of waiting for the right person to come along to build it."

"What happened to the architecture students?"

"I'm still working with a few students, but on other things—on the competition model. That's why I go down to Seattle every couple of weeks. The student connections are more difficult now that Randolph Scott is gone….But he and I had already decided it was important that this last unit be built by a neophyte, so to speak. Someone who wasn't self-consciously trained to think about creating 'architecture.'" (He scribed quotation marks in the air with his fingers.) "We decided it would help with the development of the theory. With the experiment."

"So this is all an experiment?" I asked. Hard as it is to believe, I was still clueless where he was going with this conversation.

"That's right."

"And this experiment has something to do with the competition?"

"That's right too. Although, of course, the experiment started a long time ago—way before the competition came along. The experiment started when I met Maggie's father in Port Townsend."

"So what's the experiment about?"

CM smiled brightly. "It's about organizing chaos. About enabling things to happen chaotically, but ending up with something highly ordered."

"And this last unit....When are you...?"

CM was looking at me with amused intensity.

I stared back at him feeling my face going numb.

"You're crazy," I said.

"Charlie, that's the same thing Randolph Scott said to me over our first beer in Port Townsend. But by the time we'd finished our third beer he'd invited me to come up here—and look what we've done." He lifted his hands indicating the room we were sitting in.

"But me? What makes you think I could build one of these units?"

"Because you're a person."

"But I've never built anything in my life!"

"Unfortunately that's true of most people, Charlie. But so what?"

I stood up, throwing my arms out in exasperation.

"You are crazy," I said. "You know that? When I got up this morning and remembered what you'd been talking about last night—I was afraid you might be crazy....But now...!"

CM's smile radiated.

"There's no need to get riled up, Charlie," he said. "We're not trying to make decisions now...commitments. We're just talking possibilities, right? Reality is full of possibilities. Some will happen. Some won't. But we each get to choose our own. Don't think I don't believe that. In fact, it's a central premise of the experiment."

"But this is nuts," I said.

"If you decide that's true, Charlie, that's fine. Right? I'm not trying to force you into anything."

He stood up as well, his smile still beaming.

"Let's take a break," he said. "You ever had one of Louise's sandwiches?"

14

WHEN WE WALKED INTO THE dining room I was surprised to see Maggie and Lady Brenda sitting at one of the small tables by the window, sandwich plates and tall glasses of iced-tea in front of them.

"Ladies!" CM exclaimed. "What a pleasant surprise."

"We've had a delightful morning," Lady Brenda said. "Maggie here is the most charming guide I've ever known. Why do you keep her such a secret?"

"Well, she's not exactly a secret," CM laughed. "It's just that most often people want to go in the drift boats...."

"And Maggie doesn't do drift boats!" Lady Brenda said with delight. "She's told me her whole philosophy!"

"So how did you do?" CM asked.

"Brenda caught three nice cut-throats," Maggie said. "She has a beautiful roll cast."

"But you came up for lunch?"

"I was telling her about my secret stretch of Spruce-berry Creek. So we decided to try that this afternoon."

"Why don't you and Charlie join us?" said Lady Brenda.

"A nice idea," said CM. "But I'm afraid we have some important errands to run."

"So where are you boys going to sit?" came Louise's voice from behind us. She was standing next to the big table wiping her hands with a dishtowel.

"Louise! I was just coming to find you," said CM. "Charlie, why don't you join the ladies. I'll be back in a couple minutes."

Lady Brenda pushed out the chair next to her. "Come sit Charlie."

She was wearing a pink, multi-pocketed fishing shirt with the sleeves rolled up above her elbows.

"Thanks." I glanced at Maggie as I sat down. She was wearing the same green tank-top with the fish silhouette, black stripes painted under her eyes.

Maggie reached across the table and gave my wrist a friendly squeeze. "So you're getting acclimated to being back?" she asked, catching my eye.

"Yes. Yes! I think so." I glanced at Lady Brenda. "It's been a while," I said.

"Charlie's gotten a bit rusty on his fishing," Maggie said.

"Please do come with us tomorrow," Lady Brenda said. "It would be especially fun to have you with us." I was startled by an accompanying squeeze of my knee under the table.

"...I'm not sure what CM has planned. I'll have to see." I looked at Maggie for help. But she simply raised her eyebrows and adjusted the sunglasses nestling in the tussle of her hair.

"Well, it would be pleasant to have some sensitive male companionship," Lady Brenda went on. "The big boys are such bores when they're fishing. There's no intellectual discussion at all. What do you write about, Charlie?" She took a bite of sandwich and wiped a crumb from the corner of her red lips.

"No topic in particular," I said. "...I'm more of a journalist."

"Oh! And what do you like to report?"

"I haven't actually reported anything yet.... I started a novel, but it got burned in a fire."

"How tragic!" she exclaimed, genuinely alarmed.

"Actually, I threw it in the fire myself."

Maggie laughed. "Please, Charlie!"

"But I'm serious," I said.

"Here's sandwiches," CM announces, arriving with two plates. Louise followed with two bottles of beer, frosted glasses inverted over their necks.

He pulled out the chair next to Maggie. "It is a pleasure finding you ladies up here for lunch. I assume you've tried to lure Charlie down to the river for a little fishing?"

"We did," said Maggie. "But he seems to think you have other plans for him."

CM looked at me over the tops of his round glasses.

"I was thinking I might," he said.

The good-natured energy radiating from this expression was almost reassuring.

15

WHEN WE STEPPED OUT ON the cooking deck after wishing the "ladies" good luck, CM said: "I usually take a little nap after lunch. Do you want to come down to the studio in about forty-five minutes? There's something else I want you to see."

I felt a sudden relief at the unexpected chance to organize my thoughts—to possibly think of some way out of what was beginning to feel like an inevitable, unfolding disaster.

Inside the guest unit I quickly wrote down whatever arguments I could think of.

> CAN'T DO IT BECAUSE I NEED TO GET A JOB. CAN'T LIVE ON THE MONEY FROM GRAMELLA'S HOUSE FOREVER.

Then I wrote:

> CAN ONLY STAY TWO MORE WEEKS. HAVE TO BE IN NORTH CAROLINA FOR JOB INTERVIEW.

I stared out the window, grasping for ideas.
Then I wrote:

> COULD GET JOB SOMEWHERE AROUND HERE...PORT TOWNSEND NEWSPAPER? COULD HELP BUILD UNIT ON WEEKENDS. NEED TO FOCUS ON MY CAREER!

I stared out the window again. Claiming to need a job seemed my only legitimate argument. In truth, the money from Gramella's estate was almost gone. It was stupid to continue using it for living expenses. I had to get somewhere and begin structuring my life.

How could I possibly build a guest unit? I tried to remember something I'd built with my own hands.

Teaching. I could get a job teaching. Maybe in Port Townsend.

Bookends. Fourth grade shop class. Wooden bookends that didn't even match because one turned out slightly taller than the other. That was the only thing I could remember ever building.

I had to get control of this situation. Why did it seem I had so little control? Everyone else seemed in control of what they were doing. Even Louise was in control of her pots and pans! She didn't get up in the morning wondering what she was going to do, wondering if someone was going make her build a roof or give a presentation to a room full of people.

I laid on the bed and closed my eyes, taking deep breaths.

Knocking on the wall. No, on the door.

Another knock.

"Charlie? You in there?"

CM is leaning against the railing of the bridge, hands in his pockets, smiling at me.

"The first gift I'm going give you, I can see, is going to be an alarm clock."

"Sorry," I said. "I just sort of lost track."

CM laughed. "Up here keeping track of time isn't that important. This may be your natural element."

I started to say something, then stopped and just looked at him.

He laughed again. "Come on," he said. "There's something I want you to see."

I followed him down the steps toward his studio. Instead of turning left into the doorway, however, he continued down another set of steps to the stone beach. He walked along the back side of the studio and then veered off to the right, up the bank away from the water.

"CM," I said, hanging back. "I think we need to talk."

He kept going. "Okay," he said, stepping up into an opening in the trees. "I'm listening."

The opening angled a short way through a thick grove of slender, white-barked Alders. I followed CM through the trunks and branches and we soon were on a small path leading up through the big vertical pillars of the fir trees. The forest floor became soft, and thick with ferns. Straight shafts of sunlight knifed down through the high green canopy.

"What I've been thinking," I said, walking just behind him now, "is that I really need to get a job. I can't keep living on the money from Gramella's estate. That doesn't make sense."

"That's very clear thinking, Charlie."

He continued striding up the steep path. It seemed now like a door had closed behind us. The sound of the river hushed.

"So I was thinking what made sense was that I'd get a job in Port Townsend, you know, not far away, and then I could come here on week-ends maybe and help."

"What kind of job were thinking about getting?"

This answer gave me encouragement. The soft path did a switchback in the ferns and started off on an opposite tack up the hill, weaving through the tree trunks.

"I could apply with the newspaper, get a job as a reporter. I could also get on the roster to do substitute teaching...."

"Those would be good jobs," said CM.

The path does another switchback and suddenly opens out into a high-grass clearing sloping gently uphill. We hadn't been walking more than ten minutes from the studio, yet it seemed we'd entered an entirely new world.

The first thing I saw at the top of the clearing was a wide river-stone chimney with its attached, two-legged tower of solar collectors. Around it, about eight feet high, six feet wide, and twice that long was a box wrapped with white building paper and metal strapping. The box rested on river-stone foundation piers which poked out beneath the four corners.

The churning of the river had long disappeared behind us, but as we approached the chimney-box, the clearing had its own water sound—smaller and brighter. Following the edge of the trees, a small stream tumbled over the outcroppings of mossy rocks.

Off to one side, under a sloping roof shelter, was a large stack of lumber, neatly organized according to thickness and width. I immediately avoided looking at it.

CM sat on one of the stone piers that poked up through the grass around the chimney box. "Makes my knees hurt, climbing that hill," he said. "So, back to what you were saying—how much do you figure a newspaper reporting job would pay?"

"Well, of course it's nothing great," I said, warming to the direction I now had things moving in. "But my expenses aren't big. It's just a place to start—you know?"

"That makes sense," he said. "But how much do you think it would be?"

"Well, in North Carolina a starting out reporter probably gets twelve dollars an hour. I wouldn't need any more than that."

"I'll pay you fifteen," he said.

"Excuse me?"

"I'll pay you fifteen dollars an hour."

"For what?" Panic flapped up in my chest.

"For working for me. That's what people get paid for, right?"

"But I mean...for doing what?"

CM laughed. "Don't look so stricken, Charlie! You'd be working for the McCormick Planning Group. You're already listed, in fact, as an associate. You'd be doing what we talked about this morning. Like I said, I need someone just like you for the team anyway. Why not...." He suddenly faltered.

"Why not what?" I asked.

He looked away, across the clearing. "Why not keep it in the family—is what I was going to say. I guess I don't have the right to say that though, do I?"

I studied him a moment, sitting on his rock pier, staring off into the trees.

"I don't want to disappoint you," I said, realizing the truth as I said it. "But I can't do this."

He turned back to me with a tight smile.

"Just doing it is doing it, Charlie. It's not a question of success or failure. It's just a question of doing."

"But CM, think! The only thing I've ever built with my hands was a pair of book-ends in fourth grade shop. And they weren't even even!"

His smile relaxed and broadened.

"But you built them right? They held the books together, right? Who told you they were supposed to be even? When you're making something, the thing participates. Maybe the bookends wanted to be uneven. Ever think of that?"

"But CM! Look at the other guest units. They're beautiful! They're perfect. I could never build something like that...I wouldn't even know where to begin!"

"You haven't looked at them closely, Charlie. They're full of mistakes, flaws, imperfect wood cuts, missed measurements, last minute fixes of unforeseen participations by the 'thing'. Part of the experiment is how we respond to that participation. How we adapt to mistakes. How we make something full of mistakes feel in its own way...perfect."

"Look, we're talking abstractions here," I said. "What I'm talking about is that stack of wood over there," I nodded toward it without looking at it. "I assume the idea is for that stack of wood to be reorganized over here somehow to become a guest unit. I don't have a clue how to go about doing that CM. This is what I'm trying to get you to understand for chrissakes!"

His face suddenly brightened. "But I can show you that, Charlie! It's really way simpler than you think."

He stood up. "Come on, I'll show you right now."

"What do you mean right now?"

CM was already walking toward the wood stack, talking over his shoulder. "Come on. It's a free architecture lesson," he was saying. "No commitment required. You can think about the job offer for a couple days if you want. Crumple it up and sleep on it. But for now, let me just introduce you to this stack of wood. It's nice stuff. All recycled. Randolph Scott bought an old textile mill that was going to be demolished. The whole fish camp is a reincarnation."

I had to follow him just so I could hear the last part of what he said.

16

THE PASLODE NAIL GUN, I think, is what got me hooked.

It was a big, bright orange, ray-gun-looking thing with a pistol handle and trigger. It used gas cartridges to shoot nails that you loaded in the handle like clips of bullets. CM pulled it out of a big tool-compartment built into one side of the wood-shed. Also in the tool-compartment, neatly arranged and hung on its side walls, or placed on a row of shelves across the back, were framing squares, pencils, measuring tapes, hammers, a crowbar, a long and a short carpenter's level, two chalk lines—one red and one blue—a battery powered electric drill with boxes of bits and driver heads, a line level, a plumb-bob, a cats-paw, a transit on a folded tripod, one electric circular saw, a long, thick yellow power chord coiled like a cowboy's lasso. On the floor were boxes of nails and screws. CM took each tool out in turn and told me what it was, and what it was for, and gave a quick demonstration of how to use it, what its personal idiosyncrasies were, its hidden dangers. The tools were well used and loved and, somehow, intriguing and beautiful to me. They were like a secret treasure, hidden in a non-descript wood-slab compartment with a nail and piece of wire to hold the door shut.

But the most remarkable tool of all was the Paslode nail-gun. CM took it out last.

"You don't know how lucky you are," he said, showing me how to load a nail clip. "When we started out building here, everyone was still using a hammer."

He pushed the nose of the gun against one of the columns of the wood-shed. BANG! And there was a bright nail head flush against the weathered flesh of the wood. He handed the gun to me. It was much lighter than it looked, and well balanced. I pushed the nose against the wood-shed column and squeezed the trigger. BANG! And there was another bright nail head just below the one CM had shot. A little spurt of adrenaline coursed through my chest, a spark of power I'd never experienced before.

Electricity for the circular saw was provided by a small, water turbine positioned between two concrete pads under a short, natural fall in the stream. The silver and black saw whined bright and sharp, and kicked in your hand when you pulled the trigger—and it cut through two inch thick wood planks like butter. CM demonstrated how to adjust its depth, and how to cut through the heavier timbers with two or three cuts.

Before I understood what was happening, we were building a floor next to the white-wrapped chimney-box, hauling boards from the wood-shed, setting them up on saw-horses, measuring along their length with the bright yellow tape measure, scribing a cut-line with the framing square, buzzing them to length with the circular saw. CM was directing and holding, and I was measuring and cutting. Then I was nailing with the nail-gun— BANG! BANG-BANG-BANG!—adrenaline rushing through me as if I were in a fire-fight on a marine patrol.

Four hours later we were sitting on the edge of the completed section of floor deck, legs dangling in the grass, looking out at the big shadow that was starting to inch across the open field from the green wall of the forest.

"Not a bad afternoon's work," CM commented.

He handed me the bottle of water we'd been sharing—filled from the stream just above the water-turbine.

"What do you think, Charlie?"

"I'm thinking," I said. In spite of the big, warm feeling that now enveloped my whole awareness, committing to this was still too threatening to contemplate.

I looked over my shoulder and sighted down the straight floor planks I'd just nailed into place—a twelve foot by eighteen foot floor deck, level and straight and square, stretching alongside the white chimney-box, where just earlier, I could still clearly remember, there'd been nothing but grass—and stone piers—which turned out not to be randomly arranged at all, but precisely positioned and leveled to support floor beams and joists.

"The only thing you have to do now," said CM, "is imagine how you're going to use this floor."

"What does that mean?"

"Well, I mean are you going to put a table and chairs up here for eating, or a sofa for watching the fire, or deck chairs for watching the sunset—or maybe this is a place to sleep—probably not, but it's possible—or maybe a study for writing novels?"

"I sort of like it just the way it is," I said.

CM enjoyed this. He laughed and looked at me with his big smile.

"I like that, Charlie!" he said, delighted. "You've got a very good instinct for this. Most buildings are ugly, in fact, because people decided first what's going to happen inside them, then they wrap those bubbles of activities with wood and concrete and drywall, and stick a window here and there where they need some daylight. In fact, architecture students are actually taught to think that way: 'Form follows Function' is the famous adage…."

"So how do you do it?"

"Just like you said: I make a beautiful structure—logical and beautiful in its own right. Then I figure out how to live in it."

The shadow had moved perceptibly further into the open field.

CM scooted off the edge of the deck and stood in the grass, stretching his long arms over his head.

"I'll bet it's almost cocktail hour," he said.

17

WALKING BACK DOWN TO THE fish camp I found what I was now anticipating the most, what I was starting to play over and over in my imagination, was the expression on Maggie's face when I told her that I might be building the last guest unit. What would she think? What would she say? What would her green irises register as she looked back at me....You're What?

I showered and rummaged through my laundry bag to find my cleanest pair of jeans and a collared shirt. Then I stepped out onto the veranda to find her.

There were three new guests standing in a group next to the stone grill, but no Maggie. I supposed she was back in the kitchen. I decided to wait for her to come out, to let the topic come up casually. What were you and CM doing all afternoon? Who us? I pulled a beer out of the ice bucket and turned to look out at the river.

"There you are, Charlie!"

Lady Brenda stepped from the veranda onto the cooking deck with a warm smile. She'd changed out of her fishing clothes and was wearing a tight pair of jeans and loose sweatshirt blazoned with DKNY.

"Will you pour me a Pinot Gris? I was hoping I'd find you."

I handed her the glass of wine and she immediately took hold of my hand and led me over to the far side of the deck, next to the railing.

"I so wanted to talk to you," she said. "Did you and CM get your errands accomplished?"

"Well, sort of," I said.

"Good! I'm glad. But Charlie, you have to tell me your secret."

"My secret?"

"Why did you burn your novel? I'm fascinated! Can you tell me? Or is that sharing too much? I'm good at keeping secrets, you know...."

I kept glancing over my shoulder, hoping to see Maggie coming through the wood and glass doors. Gus had appeared in his white coat and black bow-tie. He was adding wine bottles to the stone counter. But Lady Brenda's soft voice insisted on my attention.

She was exotic. Big hooped earrings hung from the black wave of her hair. She had to be in her thirties. Her eyes were a fiery, crystal blue.

"You're shy, aren't you?" she said. "A lot of the artists I know are shy."

"It's not that I'm shy," I said, eyeing down into my beer for some unknown reason. "I'm just not a big fan of crowds."

She glanced around, dramatizing the obvious fact that we weren't exactly standing in a crowd. But the wry comment I expected to follow didn't come.

"I know exactly how you feel," she said. "I used to be petrified of crowds!"

"You did?"

"Petrified," she repeated.

"So how did you become so..."

"So what, Charlie?" She cocked her head.

"So...outgoing, I guess." I glanced down into the bottle again.

"I worked at it."

"Worked at it?"

"Yes!" She was smiling at me now. "And you know why? I'll tell you my secret first, Charlie, if you'll tell me yours."

She leaned slightly toward me. "I worked at it because I decided I wanted every handsome boy I ever met to make love to me."

"I see," The cooking deck began to tilt slightly. "And...that worked?"

"It worked wonders."

"Well. I can certainly see how that might...have an effect."

She laughed lightly. "Now you have to tell me your secret," she said. "But you need another beer!"

"Actually, I guess I do!" I spied once more down into the green bottle, grasping at the sudden chance to escape.

"Will you bring me back another Pinot Gris?" She held out her wine glass.

There was an odd numbness to things as I walked now across the cooking deck. My hearing seemed unbalanced. The sound of the river momentarily rushed louder. I set Lady Brenda's glass on the stone counter and examined the wine bottles lined up in a row, looking for the Pinot Gris.

"I'd get her a fresh glass, Charlie."

Maggie was suddenly standing beside me holding a big plate of sliced tomatoes and onions, densely speckled with black pepper. A nice smile.

"I'd get Lady Brenda a fresh glass," she said again, nodding at the used one which had a smear of lipstick on one side of the rim. "Ladies appreciate that."

Saying this, Maggie turned and carried the plate of tomatoes and onions over to the grill. Oohs and aahs as she arrived. Everyone had gathered round Louise's cart discussing the meats.

"Maggie's grilled tomatoes!" someone said.

Lady Brenda was staring down at the river when I returned. I set her wine glass on the wood railing. She looked up.

"Thank you, Charlie!" she said. "I was just watching the water." She looked back over the railing.

"Do you like fishing?" I asked, hoping to steer the conversation in some neutral direction. "Maggie said you were quite good...."

She turned and leaned back against the railing, facing me.

"Your Maggie is quite something," she said.

"My Maggie?"

She cocked her head and took a sip of wine.

"I think she's quite taken with you."

"Taken?"

She laughed softly.

"There is a moment about it I like." It took me a second to realize she was back to my previous question. "When the fish pulls really hard. That desperate pulling...it gives me a great pleasure."

She sipped her wine, looking at me over the rim of the glass.

"They're about to put on the meat," I said. "Tell me what you want and I'll...."

"I already told you what I want," she said.

"Elk steaks? I think I heard Louise say that. Have you ever had Elk?"

"I'll have whatever you want," she said.

"Where are your friends?" I blurted. "Where's your husband?" I looked around the cooking deck.

"The Ericksons went back to Seattle this afternoon. Richard had to go to Tacoma for a video-conference. He'll be back in the morning. He promised."

"Ah!" I said. "So an Elk steak sounds pretty good then? Like, medium, or what?"

"Rare," she said.

"I'll go put in the order!"

These traipses across the tilted cooking veranda were becoming absurd. Why was I ordering Lady Brenda's dinner? Why wasn't I mixing and conversing with the other guests? Why wasn't I standing over there next to Maggie, flipping tomatoes and onions on the grill...helping her set them out on the plate? I'd put in the order, I decided, and then just give Lady Brenda a thumbs-up.

CM had now arrived and was having a conversation with Gus. I stepped in between them for a moment, as if it were a hiding place.

"So he made us wait till the other boat came down," Gus was saying. "Then he makes a big show of checking the licenses, and have we filled out the catch reports too."

"This was warden Jonesford?" said CM, giving me a quick smile and a wink. He stepped to the side a little to include me in the conversation space.

"No. It was that new fellow," said Gus. "The one with the little black mustache. So then he says, 'You got a license for that fish camp?'"

"A license for the camp?" CM's eyebrows arched up in surprise. "There's never been anything like that."

"I know," said Gus. "But that's what he said. He said we'd better get down to Olympia and fill out the application because he wants to see it next time he stops us."

"That's a bunch of crap," said CM. "Sounds like he's just hassling us for some reason. Why do you suppose he's doing that?"

Gus looked down at his boots. Then he looked up

"My opinion is it's the Miggs," he said.

I'd only been half listening to this exchange, peeking off and on around CM's shoulder at Lady Brenda sipping her wine on the far side of the veranda. Now my attention veered abruptly to what they were discussing.

"Maggie?" said CM. "She's been sassing the wardens forever. They just think she's eccentric."

"Not no more, I don't think," said Gus. "She's starting to get on everyone's nerves with that petition. I've heard a lot of grumbling."

"But I don't think anyone's actually ever signed the petition," said CM. "What harm is she doing?"

"I'm not sure they're seeing it that way anymore," said Gus.

"What petition is that?" I interjected.

CM shook his head with slow amusement.

"Maggie's decided to close down the hatcheries," he said. "And until then, make the wardens stand guard at their traps to make sure they don't accidentally kill any wild fish."

Gus chuckled ruefully. "Damned if she didn't give Jonesford a piece of her mind last fall down below the bridge. Told him the only thing he'd find in the direction he was looking was his own ass."

"Meats going on!" Louise announced loudly.

Attentions diverted. Gus jumped to resume his duty keeping the wine glasses filled. CM stepped over to engage one of the new guests in conversation.

"I need two steaks rare, please," I whispered in Louise's ear.

She gave me a sideways look. "I'm watching you, Charlie," she said. She eyed me meaningfully.

I knew, of course, this admonition had to do with my conversation with Lady Brenda. What? Had everyone been watching us? I mean, we'd just been talking. I couldn't help it she wanted to stay over in the corner like that. I didn't really even want to be talking to her. I glanced at Maggie as she wielded a big silver spatula over the cooking grill, sending clouds of steam and smoke swirling. Then back at Lady Brenda who had turned again, looking out over the railing.

I couldn't just ignore her. I couldn't be that impolite.

"So the orders are in," I said, walking up behind her, preparing to leave a soon as this information had been conveyed.

But she didn't turn around.

"Will you give everyone my apologies about dinner?" she said. "I think I'm just going to rest for a while…."

"Sure! But… I mean, are you okay?"

"I'm fine, Charlie." Then: "Will you bring me a dessert after you eat? I'm in unit two. Anything that looks sweet."

When I entered the dining room, the chairs on both sides of Maggie were occupied with new guests—middle-aged men who were listening attentively as she demonstrated some fly-casting technique with her fork. I tried to catch her eye. Even though dinner was the same long and lively conversation it had been the previous evening, I never succeeded once in catching her attention. Not even when she picked up my dinner plate and carried it back to the kitchen.

18

AFTER THE PLATES HAD BEEN cleared, the guests dispersed into the river room, cajoling CM, Gus and I to join them. I bowed out, thinking I might go help Maggie and Louise back in the kitchen. But I hesitated at the kitchen door, and decided against that plan. I wandered out onto the cooking deck and looked down the dark veranda. I could see a light on in unit number two. As I got near it, I rose up on my toes and sneaked past as silently as I could. There was no way I was going back for dessert for Lady Brenda. No way I was going to go up and knock on that door. When I got to my unit I left the lights off. I got a beer and sat for a long time in the dark.

It seemed like a year had passed since I'd stepped out on the veranda—the very morning of this actual same day—armed with all the confident arguments I'd practiced in the shower about why it was literally impossible to imagine I'd be presenting the plan for some utopian town to a competition jury. It still seemed literally impossible and absurd. But this unreality was overlaid with something else now, something strange and warm. In the fingers and palm of my right hand I could feel the nail gun firing into the soft wood floor-boards, and the soles of my feet contained the hard, rigid feeling of the nailed structure under my weight. And thoroughly mixed with these sensations were two other ingredients: CM's gap-toothed smile and the green, speckled eyes of Maggie Scott.

The room was pitch-black when I dropped my clothes on the floor and crawled into the bed. I pulled the comforter around my torso and stared up into the grainy, river sounding darkness. Before I fell asleep a sliver of moonlight had found its way through a high window, setting the ceiling beams and rafters into a crossed pattern of stark shadows.

I didn't hear the door open. Normally I have acute reflexes: On many occasions I've grappled—instantly pumping adrenaline—with demons that descended upon me in dreams. I've broken lamps and side-tables in defense of my dream-self.

My response to this dark hovering shape, however, was dream-like itself. The silent form materialized in silhouette against the moonlit room, grew suddenly large above me with arm-like movements, lifting shadows and dropping them on the floor. Then it touched me lightly on the lips, a finger pushing my raised head back down into the pillows.

The shadow spread over me and I was enjoined, within the twisting folds of the comforter, by a hot, soft body, wet lips and mouth, snaking-tongue, fingers delicate and exploring. In my dream, I slowly began to participate, until I was awake and realizing this was happening, and that I was far beyond having any choice about it.

Afterwards, the uncoupling occurred slowly in the floating moonlight, slowly with only the sound of breathing.

Then she separated and rolled away. Hovering over me again like a shadow, she pushed the comforter around my torso, molding it to my legs and groin and chest, as if she were re-arranging something she'd messed up. Trying to put it right again.

Then the shadow was gone, as silent as it had come.

I continued dreaming this dream. There was something about it I needed to dream again. Something I need to remember about it. Something important.

I awoke with sudden clarity.

A sweet perfume still emanated from the pillow. I shoved it onto the floor and propped up on my elbow. Grey light is seeping into the shapes of the windows and skylights. I kicked at the covers and gathered a warmer portion of the comforter around my legs and shoulders. I stared through the dim silent space of the sitting room, making a mental note of the river-sound. Its pre-dawn conversation was subtly different than its day or night pronunciations. It seemed crankier, as if it, too, had awakened too early in the cold.

Inexplicably, my mind fixated on retrieving my box of books and typewriter from the back of the Toyota. I wanted suddenly to get them out and set them up on the small empty desk built into the wall behind the sitting area. It was like I'd awakened on a boat realizing I'd forgotten to put out an anchor.

I pulled on my jeans, but couldn't find where I'd kicked off my tennis shoes. The air on the veranda was cool, but I could go without shoes—or a shirt. It would only take a minute. I felt a shivery sensual rush over my bare chest and back as I walked quickly along the veranda through a foggy mist rising off the river. I crossed the cold, wet boards of the cooking deck and ducked quickly through the gallery out to the front porch and parking area.

There were more cars now, sitting silent in the early dawn. An old blue pick-up that I knew was CM's. A couple of white vans that Gus used to taxi the fisherman back and forth. The Toyota was next the old red Cherokee that Maggie drove.

As I stepped up to the back of the Toyota I was surprised by a sudden movement. The Cherokee's rear hatch slammed shut—a crisp cherchunk!—and I was looking into Maggie's wide, astonished eyes.

"Jeez!" I said. "You scared me! What are you doing here?"

"I live here," she said. She was dressed for something other than fishing: blue-jeans and an olive green wind-breaker. Sunglasses pushed up on her head. Her eyes did a quick search of my bare torso and crumpled jeans, stopping momentarily on my hair—which I realized must be standing in the odd angles I usually observed when first looking into the morning mirror.

The air was suddenly colder than I had thought. My chest skin began to contract into goose-bumps. I wrapped my arms around my ribs.

"What are you doing here?" she said.

"I came to get my books," I answered. It's strange how the truth, the absolute truth, often sounds like the most made-up lie imaginable.

"Your books?"

"From my truck," I explained. "And my typewriter."

Her eyes made another tour of my arm-wrapped torso, and my jeans, and stopped again at the top of my head. I wanted to reach up and smooth back my hair, but instinctively knew this would only make matters worse.

"Did you sleep well?" she asked.

"Yes!" I said. "Guess that's why I'm up so early!"

Her freckled nostrils expanded, and the brown specks in her irises began to animate, clicking around, taking measurements. Her pupils seemed to be observing, recording everything that happened in my bed a few hours earlier. I felt like I was helplessly broadcasting it, and she was like a radio receiver, the darting specks in her eyes doing the fine-tuning.

"So, you're having quite a first week here, aren't you Mr. Cadwell?"

"Yes! I mean…I've decided to stay."

She arched her eyebrows. "Turned out to be more exciting than you thought?"

"Look, Maggie," I said, beginning to bounce my weight from one bare foot to another, "I've decided to stay and help CM."

"That will please him," she said without emotion.

"I'm going to build the last unit."

Her eyebrows arched up again. "The last unit?"

"The one up on the hill," I gestured with my head. "The one up there."

Maggie's eyes looked up at the forest rising on the big shoulder of land next to the fish camp. Then they came back to me.

"What are you talking about?" she said, slowly.

"It's the last guest unit. CM and I started it yesterday. That's what we were doing."

Maggie looked up again, then back at me.

"Oh-kay," she said, spreading the word out doubtfully.

"Maybe you could help me some."

She turned up the collar of her windbreaker as if a cold breeze had suddenly touched her neck. I squeezed tighter around my exposed ribs.

"Sure. If there's time. It's a busy season. There might not be much opportunity." She was no longer looking at me. Her eyes were focused inward, the specks in her irises quiet.

"I'll probably need a lot of help," I added. "A lot more than the others."

"The others?"

"You know…the architecture students. I mean, I really don't even know how to start."

"I'm running into town for a couple of hours," she said, as if reporting an itinerary. "Then I'm taking Lady Brenda back to the creek mid-morning. They're leaving this afternoon."

She looked me over again, her eyes calculating and distrustful.

"You look cold, Mr. Cadwell. You should dress more appropriately, I think, for the climate."

She walked briskly around and got in the Cherokee and cranked the engine. She backed out a ways, put it in drive and spun the wheels on the gravel, heading out across the meadow toward the big Douglas firs that defined the edge of the road.

PART II

The World-City Project

19

I WATCHED THE RED CHEROKEE until it disappeared into the trees. The sound of tires on gravel continued and I caught a red glimpse through the nearly solid wall of heavy trunks and branches as it turned onto the two-track above the meadow.

I watched in a daze. How had this gotten so messed up? And I hadn't even moved in yet. Leaving was obviously the best option. Just get the hell out of here if it was going to be like this. All my stuff was still in the truck.

I clambered with spastic anger into the Toyota. The cold vinyl seat shocked my bare back. I didn't have the key. I sat there and stared out the windshield at the sloping silver roofs in front of me. I needed to get my clothes too.

I climbed out and headed back to the guest unit. I could call CM from Bainbridge Island and explain. This just wasn't going to work out. I'd come back and visit in a few months, after I'd settled into a job somewhere. What could he expect, after all? I had my life to live! Why was he trying to push me into something? And what was Maggie's problem? Why was she judging me? What did I really do, after all?

In the guest unit I started throwing stuff into my laundry bag. I heaved a tennis shoe, too hard, and it bounced into one of the low window panes. I held my breath, stunned, steeling myself for a shattering of glass. The window vibrated and rattled but then held together, calming itself back to silence.

I sat on the edge of the bed holding the tennis shoe's mate in my hand.

I didn't want to leave. More than anything I'd ever felt, I allowed myself to realize, I wanted to belong here.

I found my shirt and went back out to the Toyota and retrieved my box of books and portable typewriter. I set the typewriter up on the small desk behind the sitting space. Above the desk, in the same wall niche, were two bookshelves. I placed the books on the lower shelf, one by one. These were my core books—the ones that through high-school and college had become my adopted family. Their spines and titles were like the friendly faces of aunts and uncles—though I seldom visited them anymore.

Next to the typewriter I placed a thick stack of clean paper. On the top shelf I put my mother's zipped black diary. I was beginning to feel the anchor catching, beginning to feel myself swinging around in the current and holding fast, looking upstream now at where it was all coming from.

I rolled a fresh paper into the typewriter and sat down. "The Fish Camp" I tapped out. It was the beginning of the notes I'm working from now.

Eventually I found myself describing the active brown specks in Maggie's green eyes, and admitting that somehow I'd betrayed her. Jesus—what did she think had actually happened? "The Betrayal" A small short-story. Maybe I would give it to her to read—ask her to proof it for me. Maybe that way she'd know I was really innocent. I typed away a good long time before I knew this was not going to work.

I yanked the paper from the typewriter, crumpled it, and sat back, rubbing my nose in frustration, startled by the sudden sweet smell of Lady Brenda's perfume. It hit me then: That's how Maggie had known. That's what had so fired her imagination out in the parking lot. In less than a minute I was up, stripped naked and stepping into the shower, not even waiting for the hot water, scrubbing hard all over with the thick white bar of soap.

20

WHEN I VENTURED OUT TO the veranda again it was mid-morning. CM was on the cooking deck in the same chair he'd occupied several light-years earlier on the previous day. He was writing again in his little black book.

"Morning," I said, startling him as before.

"Charlie! On the same schedule again! You haven't had breakfast have you?"

"No. I was up earlier but...just getting organized."

"Well, come on," he said, standing abruptly. "I'll bet Louise already figured you'd be joining me."

She had of course. We no more than walked through the dining room door when she emerged from the kitchen with two big plates of eggs and sausage. She added a silver carafe of coffee to the lazy-susan. Everything was seeming okay again. Maybe everything was going to be fine. Maybe I'd over-imagined things.

"You probably need some orange juice, don't you Charlie?" she asked.

I was hesitant to look her in the eye. I studied the eggs and sausage as if they were some new discovery. "Thanks Louise," I said, head down.

CM and I poured ourselves coffee.

"So, how'd you sleep?" CM asked, normal, chatty.

"Fine," I said.

"It takes some people a few days to get used to the river sound."

"I like it, actually," I said.

"There you go, Charlie!" said Louise, putting a tall glass of orange juice next to my plate.

"Thanks, Louise."

"Landsakes! Don't I get a smile this morning?"

I looked up at her with apprehension.

She simply beamed at me with big soft eyes and grabbed the dishtowel from her apron pocket.

"Aren't you handsome with your hair pulled back like that!" she said. "Look at him, CM. Don't he look like some movie-star?"

CM shook his head with slow amusement. "Just because you went and married an old scraggly goat like Gus doesn't mean you should fawn about over Charlie and mess up his mind, Louise."

"You just mind your own business," she said, snapping her dishtowel lightly at his face. CM watched her until she disappeared into the kitchen. Then he poured more coffee and turned his attention to me.

"I have to go down to Seattle this afternoon," he said, reaching for more eggs. "Have to meet with the students who're making the model for the competition. So I'm thinking –"

"I have a question," I interrupted.

CM raised his eyebrows, waiting.

"What is it I'm supposed to be building next?"

I was wanting, I realized, to grab on here, to insert myself now into all of this, wanting to tie these people and their energy around me like a safety strap. I was wanting not to fall off the earth—and I understood, suddenly, just how desperately I'd been holding on.

CM's face brightened and he took a big bite of sausage, chewing it and smiling at the same time. "That's exactly what I wanted to discuss," he said.

After we took our dishes to the kitchen, I followed him out across the cooking deck and down the veranda to his studio. He sat me on the stool in front of the high portion of his work table. One of the balsa-wood and cardboard models was sitting there.

"You recognize it?" CM asked.

I saw then it was a model of the unit we'd started the day before. A blue ribbon of paper was the stream curving past the small, white chimney-box. Grey chunks of cardboard were the stone piers spaced around it. The floor we'd built—the one I'd shot a hundred or more times with the Paslode nail gun—was represented by a white rectangle of cardboard, sitting across six of the little grey piers. It was all there in miniature.

"You can figure it out here before you actually build it." CM said. "It's easier to visualize when its small like this. And of course it only takes a minute to try something out, see if you like it. And if you don't—just pick it up, turn it around, see if you like it that way better."

He was demonstrating this with another white cardboard rectangle, his long square fingers gingerly setting it in onto the small grey piers, trying different positions.

"Keep it simple," he said. "That's our mantra here. The fish camp may look complex, but it's actually just a series of simple sheds. Build your floor decks first. After you get the floor decks built, we add the columns and beams that will support the roofs." He was now holding the rectangle of cardboard in various roof positions. "We use shed roofs here because they're the simplest and easiest to build. You can slope them any direction you want, and that allows you to control where you're putting the rainwater."

All of it was there, laid out and ready, the stack of random sized white cardboard, the pile of balsa-wood sticks, the old, much-used and refilled bottle of white glue, the sharp little scalpel knife and metal ruler for cutting straight. How many hours, how many years had he been sitting at this table, doing this?

"But my real question," I said, hesitating, searching for a way to say it, "is how do I even know how to begin here? I mean, what am I trying to do?"

This stumped CM's energy for a moment. He walked around in a small circle, then pulled out the swivel chair by the typewriter and sat in it, looking up at me.

"Let's try this," he said. His eyes were starting to sparkle. "This is supposed to be the honeymoon cottage, right? So I guess what you're trying to do is get a beautiful woman to take her clothes off, get her into bed and make love to her. I guess what you're trying to do is encourage—set the stage for—an erotic seduction...."

I stared at him, my cheek-bones going numb.

"Imagine it like this," he was leaning forward now, excited. "Imagine you're writing a play about the romance between this guy and this beautiful stand-offish woman, and he somehow manages to seduce her, wins her into bed. You could write a play like that, as a writer, right?"

I was still staring, my expression frozen oddly across my upper lip.

"You could, right?"

"I suppose I could do that...."

His big smile flashed in triumph, as if everything had been solved. "So then just imagine what you're building here is the stage for your play. The place where the actors are going to act out the scenes you're going to create, where they're going to talk the dialog you're going to give them to say. What you're building, what you're imagining, is a stage for your play, and this"—he gestured into the air above and river outside—"is your theater."

To this day I don't really know how serious CM was when he gave me this little speech. But it definitely succeeded in getting my attention.

21

AFTER CM DEPARTED, SAYING HE'D be back the next afternoon to give me a hand if I needed it, I fiddled with the model just long enough to decide where I was going to build the next section of floor deck. I wanted to get up on the hill and get started. I wanted to make an impression. I wanted Maggie to see me up there working. I wanted CM, when he returned, to find that I'd taken the initiative and done something—hadn't just been sitting around waiting for him to help me.

But first I made a detour to the kitchen. Louise immediately offered to make me a salmon sandwich. She was full of encouragement when I told here what I was going to be doing.

"Oh you can do it Charlie!" she said. "I expect you know as much about it as those students who built the others. They didn't seem to have a lot of expertise themselves."

"They didn't?"

"The last folks, especially, that group seemed all thumbs to me. Plus the boys got in a big fight over Maggie. One of 'em left early and went back to Portland. In the end, even me and Gus was nailing up boards to help them get finished. That was a crazy summer."

"So Maggie…. Did you see her this morning?"

"Saw her when she got back from Forks. You want mustard or mayonnaise?"

"Did she seem…upset about anything."

Louise eyed me curiously, and I glanced casually out the door again, avoiding her look.

"Maggie don't get upset about much except the hatcheries and tree loggers. Here, I gave you a little of each." She handed me the sandwich wrapped in white butcher's paper. "She's gone now with Lady Brenda up to some creek. That whole crew's leaving this afternoon. I was getting kind of tired of 'em personally."

Louise gave me a friendly pat on the shoulder. "You're going to do just fine, Mr. Charlie. I got confidence!" She even reached up and pinched my cheek.

When I got up to the clearing, I sat on the floor deck CM and I had built the day before and ate the sandwich. I sat on the end of the deck that faced the stream, watching its water tumble and search its way through the rocks and outcroppings of boulder. This was where I'd decided to build the next floor deck, to build it as a bridge from where I sat, across the stream to the stone piers poking up there in the ferns on the other side. I could see now that whoever had built those piers had thought of that as a possibility. What I was imagining, chewing away at the salmon sandwich, was the scene where Maggie came up to help me, and we would sit on this bridge for lunch, and she'd unzip the inseams of her khaki fishing pants, and roll them up to her hips, and dangle her white legs into the cold water, the fish-scale tattoo blue-green and irridescent in the sunlight.

I finished the sandwich and got out the tools and set the saw horses up again where CM had put them the day before. I took some measurements. Each stone pier had a thick metal strap sticking out its top, drilled with three holes. The heavy beams would bridge from pier to pier first, and these would be pushed snug up against the straps and bolted through the holes. To my surprise, I found I could manhandle the beams fairly easily by tying a short rope around one end, hefting it over my shoulder, and dragging the long chunk of wood behind me. It wasn't long before I had the beams in place and the outline of the bridge was suddenly visible. Next came the joists which spanned perpendicular over the beams. The circular saw whined in the sunshine as I cut these, one at a time, across the saw horses, laying them in a stack, all exactly the same length, saw-dust piling up fluffy around my feet.

It was late afternoon when I finally got to the part I enjoyed the most: shooting the Paslode nail gun into the floor planks that

I laid perpendicular across the joists. BANG-BANG! Two nails at each joist. The planks were pushed up close to each other—to make a solid deck—and this went on for some time, pairs of syncopated gun-shots, broken only by the silent intervals of reloading.

Then I shot the last nail into the last plank, and the bridge was done. The sun had gone down behind the spiking tops of the forest, the sky draining its light into the black tree canopy. I put away the tools while I could still see, and only then, after I'd stacked the saw-horses under the wood shed, and wrapped the wire around the nail to hold the tool closet door shut, did I give the bridge a thorough testing. I walked across it three or four times, feeling the magic of its solidity at mid-span, directly above the stream. Standing at its edge, above the water, was like flying almost, and I spread my arms and looked up at the sky and felt a momentary vertigo lift me into the air.

It was fully dark when I made my way out of the woods and across to the veranda steps by my father's studio. I'd missed dinner by a long shot. When I opened the door to the camp house I was struck by its empty silence. The gallery night-lights dimly lit the left side wall. The dining room was dark. I could see there was a light on in the river room. I headed down the gallery. Maybe Louise had put out her plate of cookies. But the table under the pool of lamplight was empty.

"You get ambushed by Indians up there?"

I jumped, realizing someone was in the leather chair next to the table.

"Jeez, Maggie! You scared me."

Her legs were curled up under her, a book open on her lap.

"What are you doing here?" I said.

"Someone had to stay up to see if you made it down alive, Mr. Cadwell."

"You were waiting for me?"

"I was reading a book," she said. She held it up for me to see. "Ever heard of it?"

I squinted at the cover.

"Nope," I said.

"I'll loan it to you when I'm finished. You might find it interesting."

"That'd be great. You didn't have to wait for me, though."

"Louise was worried about you. She even sent me up there this afternoon after everyone left—to see if you'd fallen off a log."

"You came up to check on me?"

"I didn't go all the way. I got half-way up the first switchback and heard the gun-battle begin. So I figured either you were being scalped—which I didn't want to have to look at—or you were nailing boards, and likely still alive."

"You should have come up," I said.

"I have plenty to do down here," she said. "There's a plate covered with tin-foil in the kitchen, in case you're hungry. Louise made it for you."

"Great. I'll be right back."

"Take your time," she said. "I'm going on to bed—now that I know we don't have to send out a search party."

I looked at her for a moment, trying to read her mood. The lamp-light was shining on the side of her hair, setting bright fires in the chopped outer strands. But her eyes were in shadow, unreadable.

"You don't want me to bring you something?" I asked.

"I'm tired. I get up pretty early…as you might remember."

She unfolded her legs and stood up, holding the book against her chest.

"Well…" I stumbled for what to say. "Maybe I'll see you in the morning. Maybe we could talk…."

"What did you want to talk about?"

"Well, you know…. We haven't talked much since CM got back…"

"I'm sure I'll see you around." She stepped past the table, out into the gallery, her face in shadow again. "Don't forget your dinner."

She started walking, then stopped and turned.

"Oh, I forgot. Lady Brenda said to tell you goodbye."

She turned again and, this time, kept going.

I went into the kitchen and found the foil-covered plate. I stood at the counter eating and looking at my squiggly-dim reflection in the window above the sink. Definitely, I realized, this was not going to be as easy as I'd hoped.

22

THE FOLLOWING DAYS ESTABLISHED A routine. When I got up for breakfast Maggie had already left, either down to the river with a client or, more often, off on one of her mysterious early morning missions. Sometimes I'd have breakfast with CM and we'd talk about how the unit was coming up on the hill.

"When you get ready to put up the columns for the walls and roof, let me know," CM had said. "I'll come up and help for an afternoon."

"I've been trying to get Maggie to help," I said. "But she seems hard to catch up with these days."

CM gave me a look. "Did you two have an altercation about something?" he asked.

"If we did, I missed my half of it."

He gave a quiet laugh. "She'll come around. Maggie's stubborn. It's one of her endearing features."

In the evenings, after I'd come down from the hill and cleaned up, I'd go out to the cooking deck. Sometimes Maggie would be there, talking with the guests, cooking her vegetables on the grill.

She always gave me a big energetic smile: "Good evening, Mr. Cadwell."

"Good evening Miss Scott," I'd say. I'd begun calling her 'Miss Scott' to turn this stand-off business into a game.

"How is your construction project coming?"

"Really well. I'm up to the tenth floor now. Getting ready for the elevator."

My little jokes would make her eyebrows go up and start the brown specks in her irises swirling.

After dinners Maggie would go into the kitchen to help Louise, and I'd go out to Ben Sprague's unit and read. CM had given me a box of manuscripts to contemplate "in my spare time."

"It might be helpful background stuff," he said. "For the competition."

Every time he mentioned the competition I got that tightening sensation in my chest. I kept hoping this was some kind of fantasy that was never really going to unfold. But CM was continuing to make trips to Seattle every ten days or so, apparently working with a group of students who were building a large model for the presentation.

"Look, CM, I'm still not sure about this competition thing," I said, watching him set the box of manuscripts down on the floor next to my writing desk.

His big smile. "No problem. No commitments, right? Like we agreed? But this stuff might be helpful…. Anyway, I want your opinion about how to organize it into a book later on. That's your expertise, right? Same salary, of course."

I allowed how I could look through it from that perspective.

"Great!" he said. "There's ideas for illustrations in there too, photos of models, slides of a big studio project that Randolph Scott's students did, that kind of stuff. It's a mish-mash. I have a hard time organizing this kind of thing…."

Generally, I'd read through CM's "mish-mash" until late. Then I'd go out on the veranda and sit on one of the benches, my back against a column, and watch the river. It always seemed possible that Maggie might show up and join me. But she never did.

23

CM'S MANUSCRIPTS WERE IN A remarkable state of disorder. They were also repetitive, with three or four versions of each "section" begun but never finished. Then three or four different endings that were never attached to a specific beginning. What looked like a huge volume of writing was actually the accumulation of different attempts at what would have been a fairly slim set of essays. It appeared that on much of this he had collaborated with Randolph Scott, though it was unclear who had written what.

I provide here—as preface to a short but instructive scene that occurred the third week I was at the fish camp—an excerpt that illustrates what seemed to be the main topic of the manuscripts.

> It is too late, now, to save Wild Nature.
> What we can do, if we're lucky, is make enough room for it to save us.

The World City Project
(From The Undelivered Lectures of Charles McCormick and Randolph Scott)

By the year 2030—the year our grandchildren will be graduating from college and beginning their young families and careers—the world population is expected to have nearly doubled to 10 billion souls. It is difficult to imagine this mass of humanity without also imagining a dense, high-rise, urban lifestyle of towering apartment blocks and skyscrapers—nature all but paved over, people living in the sky, traveling back and forth from glass-walled residential towers to brightly illuminated vertical markets and offices without ever touching the ground. The concept of vertical farming has even been seriously introduced! It is a vision in which man's alienation from nature is virtually complete—the natural ecosystems diminished to a few verdant remnants remaining in national parks and preserves which must then be gated against an onslaught of tourists.

A simple calculation, however, puts the necessity for this imagined vertical density in perspective: If the projected population of 10 billion people were theoretically organized into families of three, and if each family were given a five thousand square foot "homestead" on which to subside—more than enough acreage and solar exposure to grow a subsistence diet of food—the entire human diaspora could be accommodated (with land left over for transit corridors, schools, markets and recreation fields) within the boundaries of the U.S. central plateau—the great plain, that is, between the Rocky Mountains and the Mississippi River.

But the most remarkable thing to imagine, were such a "World City" to be built, is that the rest of the earth could then revert to the wild ecosystems of God's original nature: Except for strategic pockets of mining and agriculture, the West and East coasts of the United States, all of Canada, all of South and Central America, the entire continents of Africa, Europe, Asia, Australia, and the archipelagos of Indonesia—all could exist in a state of natural wilderness, without the presence of Man.

The political discipline to create such a "World City", of course, is impossible. Even if it were accomplished, bands of "explorers" would likely escape to colonize and exploit the new wilderness, and one could imagine world history, in an almost comical parody, simply repeating itself. (Except, that is, for one small detail which we'll get to in a moment.) But the notion that there is more than ample room for urban growth to occur at a very low-rise densities, and (if properly conceived and organized) that such a horizontal order could make room for a vast and contiguous replenishment of our wild ecosystems—that notion is suddenly placed there on the table as a viable option for consideration.

But why should we even consider it?

The first reason is social fairness. Vertical architecture was invented by the socialists and communists to efficiently create housing for the masses. It was quickly adopted by the free-market capitalists because of its efficiency in generating profits. In each case, however, the results were unfortunately the same: the greed and corruption of concentrated wealth and, for the common man, the sorry struggle of being existentially homeless.

The second reason is that small detail mentioned earlier: in the year 2030, as it turns out, the post-industrial infrastructure and civilization we will have bequeathed to our grandchildren will begin rapidly to run out of fossil fuel. The great vertical cities we are imagining they will be living in will begin, one by one, to go dark.

Human civilization will irrevocably have begun—after its tumul-
tuous, two hundred year sprint on the adrenaline of fossil-fuels—
an inevitable slide back to the steady-state of Nature herself, the
state that derives its energy for work from the only source there
ever was: the Sun.

The event associated with this passage took place after dinner
one evening. Two of the guests lingered afterwards at the round
table with my father. The others had retired to the river room on
the other side of the stone fireplace to play cribbage. Maggie, as
always, was in the kitchen helping Louise, and Gus had gone
down to equip the drift boats for the next morning's fishing. A
jazz trumpet was playing soulfully up in the shadowed ceiling
rafters. The sun had gone down and the big iron chandelier had
begun to glow over the table.

I typically would have slipped out at this point, but that night
the after-dessert conversation—at the insistence of the couple
remaining at the table—had turned to the architecture of the fish
camp. Curious to see how CM was going to field their questions,
I positioned myself at one of the smaller side tables, pretending to
read a magazine.

The wife of the couple, Grace, had just commented on the
architectural style of the fish camp.

"What's the style?" CM echoed her question. "I suppose we
could call it 'creative survival.'"

"Creative revival?"

"No. Survival."

"But what are you surviving?" the husband, Henry, asked.
"This all seems pretty…comfortable to me."

CM smiled big at this. "I'm glad you think so! So do we."

"In some ways it's almost opulent," said Grace. "I mean, look
at this chandelier."

"That was welded by Randolph Scott, Maggie's father," said
CM. "He was, among many other things, a sculptor."

We all admired the chandelier, the small illuminated bulbs sil-
houetting the swimming and jumping fish as they made their way
perpetually around its perimeter.

"But craft is about a personal survival," said CM. "The fish camp is about a larger effort."

"So like I said, what are you surviving here?" Henry was getting impatient, as if CM were withholding information.

"Have you ever heard of the Olduvai Theorem?" CM asked, giving the lazy Susan a gentle push, sending a dessert plate of dried apricots around to Henry.

"You mean the Olduvai Gorge in Africa? I didn't know it was a theorem." He plucked an apricot from the plate.

"It was just published a few years ago."

"About the archeological excavations?"

"No. It's using Olduvai metaphorically. It's a geologist's calculation of the fact that, within our lifetime, the world is going to begin rapidly running out of fossil energy, and there's nothing, really, to replace it. So the question is, how are we going to respond to the idea of irrevocably sliding back into the Stone Age?"

There was a stunned silence, Henry and Grace staring at CM, he staring back at them, challenging them to accept what he had just said.

"But that's ridiculous," said Henry. "The world's not going to run out of energy."

"Fossil energy," said CM. "Oil and gas and coal. By the year 2030 we're going to be starting to dig out the last of it."

"That can't be true, Henry, can it?" said Grace, looking sideways at her husband.

"They'll find more, I'm sure. They always do."

"I'm afraid not," said CM. "The reserves are pretty well known. Exploration techniques have gotten extremely sophisticated. They know what's left, and where it is, and how much it will cost to get it, and what it will mean if we burn it."

"We'll have nuclear power then," said Henry.

"I'm sure we'll have some of that," said CM. "But it can't replace the fossilized carbons we've been running our machines with for the past hundred and fifty years. There might be some nuclear generated electricity, but ultimately, the world is going back to being powered, basically, by the sun."

"But what about hydroelectric," said Henry. "And wind power? I even read they were developing floating machines that'll make electricity from ocean waves...."

"That's all solar energy," said CM. "That's all there's ever been. Fossil fuels are just solar fuel that by a quirk of fate got concentrated. And now we're getting close to using it up." He gave the lazy susan another push and stopped the plate of apricots in front of Grace. She took one, reluctantly.

"So the question is," CM continued, pulling the apricots around to himself, "how are we going to respond? If we respond with a mad last dash, an insatiable effort to dig and suck the last drops of fossil fuels out of the earth, we're only going to make the situation worse." He selected an apricot and plopped it in his mouth.

"Worse?" said Grace.

"The last of it is going to be the hardest to get, and the most destructive. We could easily end up having to choose between having fuel for our lawn-mower or toxins in our drinking water. Which of those would you rather have, do you think?"

"That's a bit pessimistic," said Henry. "You're being alarmist, I think."

"I actually don't think so," said CM. "Especially when we get to the year 2030, and the world population has nearly doubled. Twice as many people, and the oil and gas industries desperately trying to dig and drill and blast out the last of the reserves. Gas drilling alone uses billions of gallons of fresh water....The same water people are going to be desperately trying to use for irrigation. It's not a pretty sight to contemplate."

CM took another apricot and sent the plate around to Henry, who waved it away with his hand, annoyed, as if he were shooing an insect.

"So...." Grace waved her hand too, a different gesture. "What are we going to do?"

"That's where we started our conversation, right?" CM leaned back in his chair. "That's what the fish camp is about. We decided what made the most sense would be if people started figuring out how to live well again in the stone-age—to see if we could figure out a way to help them do that."

"So that's what this is all about?" said Henry.

"Surely," Grace's eyebrows arched up in surprise, "you don't mean you expect the whole world to live like this?"

As if on cue, a door slammed out in the gallery and Gus stomped in.

"Boats are set for first thing in the morning," he announced. "What time does everyone want to leave?"

Then, seeing our startled expression, he said, "What? Did I interrupt something?"

24

IT WASN'T LONG BEFORE I finished all the floor decks around the chimney box of my unit. CM came up to the clearing to show me how to set the columns. He said he'd bring Maggie to help, but he walked out of the trees and up the sloped, grassy field alone.

"She had to go to Port Angeles for one of her wild-fish meetings," he said. "Are you two still having a dispute about something?"

"Damned if I know," I said.

CM regarded me for a moment. I fidgeted, untangling the cord to the circular saw.

"Well I think in the interest of the Team we need to arrange for a reconciliation, don't you?" He flashed his smile. "We'll have to start Team Practice here pretty soon and it would helpful if everyone was on speaking terms."

Then he stepped up on the floor deck and walked around.

"You've done a terrific job here, Charlie!" he said. "Have you decided how the roofs are going to slope?"

I showed him the model, which I'd brought up and kept, now, on a shelf in the tool cabinet.

"You might want to do it differently," he said.

"How?"

"Well, you have three sheds. I like that. That's nice and simple. But they're all draining away from each other, the rain water is going all over the place."

"What's wrong with that? I'm just trying to keep the inside dry, right?"

"That's the main goal, yes. But if you slope the roofs like this, see?"—he demonstrated with his hands over the model—"you accomplish two things."

His hands were suggesting the roofs drain inward, toward each other, the exact opposite of what I thought should happen.

"But where's all that water going to go?"

"Ah! We'll get to that. But first, if you do it this way you make your outside walls taller, right? And that gives you more sunlight and air inside."

"Okay, I can see that."

"And second, now you can collect all the rain water here in the center, and now you're in control of it."

"But what do I do with it?"

"Well, there's any number of things you could do with it. You could drain it through a pipe to a cistern and store it. Or, you could do something dramatic with it. Like play a water flute."

"Right," I said. But CM's eyes were animated now, and I knew there was some new trick I would eventually have to deal with.

That evening it was just the five of us at the round table for dinner. "Family night," Louise called it. She insisted on telling everyone where to sit. "You sit right here between me and Charlie," she said to Maggie.

Maggie hesitated. She seemed to want to sit somewhere else. I held the chair out for her and she gave me a quick look.

CM started the food platters moving and Gus started naming a laundry list of things to get ready for the next set of guests who'd be arriving the following afternoon. They talked through this topic. Then we were chewing and clinking our silverware in a kind of awkward silence.

"So Maggie," CM said. "Have you been up to see Charlie's unit?"

"It sounds too dangerous to go up there. I'm afraid I might get shot."

Gus laughed. "That nail-gun does make a lot more noise than those other things…what did we used to call them?"

"Hammers?" CM asked.

Gus laughed again, his round face reddening.

"Charlie wouldn't shoot you," said Louise. "Would you Charlie?" She leaned around Maggie and gave me a meaningful look.

"Not on purpose," I said.

"That's encouraging," said Maggie.

"What stage are you at up there, Charlie?" CM asked.

"Well, we got the columns up today, so the main roof beams are next, I guess."

"You're starting to put a roof up already?" said Louise, looking around Maggie again.

"It's not exactly a mansion," I said. "It's not very big."

"You'll probably need some help with those beams," said CM.

"Probably," I said.

"Gus? You have any time tomorrow? I've got to work in the studio."

"Nope. I've got to do patches on two of the pontoon boats."

CM looked at Maggie. "So Miggs, you could probably give Charlie a hand, right? Just to keep him going?"

Maggie was looking at CM, keenly aware of the game he was playing.

"That depends on the pay scale." she said.

"Four dollars an hour," I said. "That's all I can afford."

Maggie laughed and turned her eyes on me for a moment.

"Okay," she said. "I can use the money."

"Maybe you should agree on a time," said CM.

Maggie shot him another glance. "I have to go into Forks in the morning," she said.

"After lunch would be perfect for me," I said quickly.

"Okay," said Maggie. "After lunch then." She gave a big smile around the table. "Is everyone happy?"

"I'm happy," said CM. "Gus? Are you happy?"

"I'm happy," said Gus.

"Lord," said Louise. "You guys are all nut-cakes."

25

THE NEXT MORNING I MEASURED and cut the beams that Maggie would help me set on the columns. One by one I dragged the heaviest pieces from the wood stack and set them up on the saw-horses. Each end of each beam had to be notched to fit onto the top of a column. The skill-saw whined and the saw-dust pile, which had been growing for several weeks now, got a freshly colored coating. Chunks of cut-off beam ends and notches collected in a pile at the edge of the saw-dust pile.

Then the notches had to have a hole drilled in them to match the holes already drilled at the top of the column. When these holes were aligned, round dowels could be tapped through, connecting the beam to the column. It was getting close to lunch as I was drilling the last of the holes. I started glancing down the clearing where the path emerged from the trees. I was thinking Maggie might come early.

But of course she didn't.

I ate Louise's sack lunch sitting on the sunny side of the bridge, my feet dangling over the edge next to the stream. The sun was high and warm. Bright insects and seed-parachutes floated around lazily in the clearing.

I was munching a big red apple when a movement caught my eye. Maggie stepped magically out of the trees at the bottom of the clearing. She was wearing an old pair of Oshkosh suspendered workman's jeans that looked several sizes too large. She came walking up the open field in big floppy strides. I walked out to meet her.

"So this is really a nice place you have here, Mr. Cadwell," she said as she got close.

"Thanks," I said. "I was hoping you'd like it."

"You were?" She stopped, looking up at me, shielding her eyes against the sun.

"Thanks for coming," I said.

"I think you should give me a tour, don't you? How do you get up there anyway? I don't see any steps."

"I guess I haven't gotten around to steps yet," I sprung myself up onto the deck and held out my hand to her. "Just step up on that block of wood down there."

She didn't reach for my hand. She stepped on the block of wood and her arm went up for balance. I grabbed it and pulled her up in one big motion onto the floor.

"Thank you, sir," she said in a formal voice, rubbing her wrist where I'd grabbed it. "Don't you think you should build some steps before you start the roof?"

"We could do that if you want" I said. "Actually, though, now that I think about it, I'm not sure I know how to build steps yet."

She laughed and turned in a circle, looking around. "So you were going to give a tour?"

"Well," I nodded down at our feet. "This is the floor."

"It's very flat!" she said. "I'm impressed."

"And over here is the bridge over the stream."

We walked to the edge of the floor and looked down at the bridge deck.

"That's nice Mr. Cadwell. I like that. Your own little river." She seemed genuinely pleased. She looked around the clearing, up at the sky, then back at the bridge deck over the stream. "So what is it that needs doing?"

I pointed at the stack of beams lying on the ground. "Those need to go up there, across the columns."

"I see." She nodded thoughtfully. "They look pretty heavy."

"I can do the main lifting," I said. "I just need someone to hold the one end so it doesn't fall while I'm lifting the other."

I set up the two stepladders on each side of a column. We carried the first beam over and laid it on the floor. I picked up one end of it and climbed one of the ladders. Maggie climbed the other ladder on the opposite side of the column. I set the notch of the beam in the notch at the top of the column. The other end of the beam was still sitting on the floor deck.

Maggie's face was opposite me, her eyes watching my hands fitting the beam, her eyebrows pinched with concentration above her freckled nose.

"Okay," I said. "Now you hold this here while I put up the other end."

"She glanced at me, then grasped the beam end, focusing her eyes on the task.

I climbed down, moved the ladder over to the opposite column, picked up the other end of the beam and climbed the ladder with it. I set the beam in the notch and adjusted the fit until the drilled holes aligned.

"Are the holes lined up over there?" I asked.

Maggie went down a step on the ladder and eyeballed the connection. "Almost perfect," she said.

"Great!" I said, tapping a dowel through my end with a hammer.

I moved the ladder back to Maggie's column again, climbed up and tapped another dowel through the drilled holes while she held it tight. We let go, and there the beam sat. "Voila!" I said and Maggie laughed.

Repeating this process, we set all the beams except one. Twice the holes didn't align at Maggie's end and I had to drill a new hole while she held the two pieces in place.

There was only the last high beam left. It was still lying across the saw-horses.

I jumped off the deck and turned looking up at Maggie. I held my hands out. "Come on, jump," I said.

"And you're proposing to catch me, Mr. Cadwell?"

"Sure, I'll catch you."

"I think I'll use the steps."

She walked over to where the big block of wood was, sat on the edge of the deck and scooted down onto it. She walked up to the saw-horses, whapping the sawdust off the seat of her Oshkoshes.

"Why don't you call me Charlie anymore?" I said.

She stopped and looked at me steady for a moment.

"I'll consider it."

"But I mean, why don't you? You did at first. The day we went fishing. What's changed?"

She continued looking at me steady.

"Nothing's changed," she said. "I just started thinking of you as Mr. Cadwell. That's all. It seemed to fit."

"Well, I don't think it fits," I said.

"Why?"

"Because my name is Charlie. Everyone else calls me Charlie."

"Okay. I can call you that." She reached out to grab one end of the beam.

"Well?" I said.

"Well what?"

"Are you going to say it?"

"Say what?" She threw out her arms in exasperation.

"Say my name. Say 'Charlie'."

She stared at me. Then she leaned down and picked up a chunk of sawed off beam from the sawdust pile and hefted it in her palm.

"Okay," she said, slowly testing the heft of the wood chunk. "Here, Charlie!" And she threw the piece of wood, with considerable accuracy, at my head.

I ducked.

"What are you trying to do?"

She had another chunk of wood in her hand.

"I'm just practicing...."—she wound up like a pitcher and heaved it—"...saying your name, Charlie!"

"Hey! Stop!" I ducked again.

"I thought you wanted me to say your name!" Now she had picked up multiple chunks of wood from the cutting pile and she began tossing them one after the other—not as hard as the first two but more difficult to avoid. They started bouncing off my shoulders and back as I twisted to avoid them.

I took three big steps toward her, palms out to shield my face against the flying wood chunks.

She leaned down and scooped up a big clump of sawdust from under the saw-horse.

"Stop, Charlie!" she said threateningly, holding the clump of sawdust above her head in both hands. Some of it sprinkled down into her hair.

I took another step toward her and she flung out her hands, filling the air in front of my face with a pink and orange flurry.

I stopped. I could feel the sawdust settling around and over me. I had instinctively closed my eyes and now I opened them. Maggie's eyes were wide in shocked surprise. Her hand went slowly up to her mouth. Bits and flakes floated in the sunlight between us.

Then she burst out laughing.

"I'm sorry, Charlie!" she said. She doubled over laughing, holding her stomach. She looked up, and doubled over again.

I could feel the sawdust going down the back of my neck, dangling from my eyelashes. I took another step toward her.

"Stop," she said, still laughing, holding out a hand to fend me away.

I took another step and she backed up. "Charlie, you stay where you are. I mean it!"

She stepped quickly around the saw-horses. Keeping my eyes on her, I leaned down and dug my fingers into the saw-dust pile.

"Don't you do that," she said, backing up another step. She laughed again. "Don't you even think about it!"

I started around the saw-horse, my hands clutching the biggest clump of sawdust I could hold.

She backed up.

I raised the clump higher and she turned and ran down the hill. The flapping Oshkoshes slowed her down and I closed in from the side in just a couple of strides. She held her hands up and tried to duck away. I took one more step to get in front of her, launching the sawdust and tripping at the same moment on a clump of the tall grass.

She shrieked as the sawdust exploded around our fall. We rolled in a flurried tangle and came to a stop.

Silence. I lay looking straight up at the sky. For a long moment there was something soft under my neck and head, some breathing part of Maggie. Then it moved. My head dropped into the spiky grass, and she rolled away and stood up. Her face appeared in the sky above me, looking down.

"How about a truce, Charlie."

Her hair and face were smattered with sawdust.

"Okay with me."

"Okay then. Truce?"

I sat up and she took a step backwards, looking at me warily.

Then she turned and ran, the blue oshkoshes flapping and billowing, and disappeared into the trees at the bottom of the clearing.

26

WHEN I CAME DOWN FROM the hill that evening, I hurried to shower the sawdust out of my hair and change into clean blue-jeans and my collared shirt. The new guests were due to arrive and I wanted to see Maggie again before they got there.

When I stepped onto the cooking deck, CM was organizing chunks of wood into a small pyramid shape in the middle of the stone cooking grill. He flashed his big smile as I stepped onto the deck.

"Cleaned up and everything!" he said, noting my appearance.

"Well, I figured with the new guests...."

"You don't have to have a reason to get cleaned up!" he said. "It clears the head, I think, every once in a while." Then: "Maggie looked a bit flushed. Did you overwork her?"

"We got all the beams up...except one."

"Excellent!"

"I figured out a strategy for getting the last one up by myself."

Louise pushed open the dining room doors, wiping her hands with her dishtowel. "So Gus never radioed about whether the plane was on-time," she announced.

"It doesn't matter Louise." CM assured her. "They'll get here when they get here."

"Why look at you, Mr. Charlie!" Louise was now focused on me. "All cleaned up." She came over and beamed up at me like she was admiring an apple on a tree branch.

"I washed up just for you," I said. "I thought you'd appreciate not having sawdust on your dinner napkins."

"Matter of fact, Maggie was pretty much sawdusted herself," said Louise. "She comes prancing in the kitchen and I said, 'Maggie get that sawdust out of here!' 'Oh, I've got saw-dust?' she says. 'Looks like you been swimming in it,' I says."

"Yeah, well, we were doing a bit of sawing," I said.

CM was watching me.

"Here, Charlie. Help me put the fire grates back on."

I helped him lift the cleaned grates into place on either side of the pyramid of firewood. Then we set up the bar on top of the stone counter with the wine glasses turned upside down on the folded white towel. Louise wheeled out the cart with the bucket of iced beers and wine. As we set things up, I was searching the various glass doors into the camp house for a sign of Maggie.

But she didn't show up until after Gus arrived with the guests. He brought them directly out onto the cooking deck. There were four: three men and a woman.

"Perfect timing!" said CM. He lit a match with a flourish and held it to the sapwood at the base of the pyramid. Orange flames began to lick the stacked wood. CM brushed his hands on the backs of his trousers and held out his right one to the nearest guest. "Charles McCormick," he said.

The introductions were made while the fire grew and began crackling in earnest. The guests were a husband and wife and a father-son team. The husband was a big, broad man with a deep voice strangely amplified to a grating volume that focused instant and nearly constant attention on itself. Edward Florence.

"You can call me Edders," his voice grated. A quick staccato laugh. "That's what they've called me since I was a pup. This is Helen." Indicating his wife.

"What a dramatic view!" said Helen walking over to the deck railing. "You can see the big rapids from here!"

"I don't think that's the big one, dear."

"Look at the fish-heads, Edders!"

"Where?"

"Not down there. Up. Up." Motioning.

"Indeed! Say, that's quite interesting McCormick."

"You like them?" said CM. "Here's the young lady who can tell you all about them."

Maggie had just stepped out onto the deck, bright and clean in a better fitting pair of jeans than she'd been wearing up on the hill. I caught her eye for just a moment as CM held out his arm, motioning for her to join us. Gus, I noticed, had taken the father and son down for a closer look at the river.

"Let me introduce Maggie Scott," said CM.

Edders' eyes widened. He held out a big hand that seemed swollen.

"Your reputation precedes you Miss Scott," he said, ending with the staccato laugh.

"My what?" said Maggie.

"You're the young lady who knows where the wild fish are," Edders said.

"Where'd you hear that?" said Maggie.

Edders winked.

"We didn't just come here by accident," he said. "We did our research."

"But who told you I could help you catch wild fish?"

"We made inquiries." He winked again with his grating laugh.

"In Port Angeles, dear," said Helen, trying to be helpful. "There's a fly shop there we visited last year."

"I said to them: 'I'd like to do a trip up here and focus on just taking wild fish,'" said Edders. "And the young fellow there in the shop, he said: 'There's only one person I know around here who could help you do that.' 'And who would that be?' I said. 'That would be Maggie Scott up at the fish camp,' he says. So, a year later here we are!"

"Peter Stone," said Maggie. "He's on the hatchery committee with me. I'll have to thank him, won't I?"

"You will, indeed," said Edders. Unexpectedly, he turned his baggy, grey eyes on me. "Are you a guide too?"

"No. Actually, I don't fish," I said.

His eyebrows arched up. "Don't fish?" He turned to CM. "You have somebody here who doesn't fish?" Staccato laugh.

"Charlie has more important things to do," said CM.

This comment elicited a loud chortle from Edders, reddening his face.

"I used to have more important things to do too," he said. "Now that we've branched into forestry, though, I'm up here in the woods so much I forget my priorities."

"Forestry?" said Maggie.

"Yep. You know. Forest products." He waved a big hand around at the trees.

"Really?" said CM. I detected a subtle body movement, a preparation to insert himself in some way between Edders and Maggie.

"And so who is it that's 'branching into forestry', so to speak?" CM asked in a casual tone.

"I-Mart," said Edders, loud and grating. "I'm regional manager. Best business organization in the country. Ever heard of us?" He winked. Then laughed.

"I-Mart's going into the logging business?" said Maggie, her voice rising.

"Well, not directly, of course," said Edders. "But the big-boys decided to expand into home-building stuff—you know, forestry products. So I'm the point man, putting together the suppliers."

"That's interesting," said CM. "Can I get you a glass of wine, by the way? Helen?"

I volunteered to retrieve the drinks. When I returned and passed them out, the conversation topic was still the same.

"Actually, the whole gamut," Edders was saying. "We're figuring pretty much on everything. Our business model, we figure, can take fifty grand out of your average house. We figure that's important. Our contribution to affordable housing."

Gus and the father-son team ascended the top of the stairs, just a few steps away.

"That's a nice river you have here," the father said. The son, I realized, was about my age. I also noted that he was immediately eyeing Maggie, with an occasional glance at me. He was handsome, I thought. Maybe a musician. Soft hands. Secretly, I touched the new calluses on my own, testing them.

"How exactly would you go about reducing lumber prices?" Maggie asked Edders. "I mean the loggers already avoid and talk their way around every habitat protection there is." She was leaning in at him slightly.

Edders ignored Maggie's question and looked at the father and son. He held up his glass of wine. "Fish camp red," he said with his grating laugh. "Highly recommend it. So how's the water look down there?"

Gus started pouring more drinks, and soon Louise rolled out the dolly with plates of meat and a big wooden bowl of sliced zucchini which Maggie, a little later, tossed and flipped on her corner of the grill with the big silver spatula.

Dinner was all polite conversation punctuated by Edders' deep staccato laugh. After Louise brought in the dessert trays, the father and son excused themselves to play a game of chess. Edders poured himself another glass of wine while his wife sipped decaf. There was a brief moment of quiet around the table—only the tiny creak of the lazy-susan as it swung around with a plate of cookies and sliced apples.

CM cleared his throat. "Edders," he said, "would you entertain a question?"

"Shoot."

"In your opinion, how big should an elephant be?"

"Well, I suppose that depends on how big a cage you've got to put it in." Grating laugh.

"Why would you think elephants belong in a cage?" asked Maggie.

"Whoa there ma'am!" Edders holds up his big hands in defense. "I just figured the only reason you'd be worried about how big one was, was if you had to put it in a cage, that's all."

"Not exactly what I meant," said CM. "I was trying to get to the point that maybe there's a natural, appropriate size for things, don't you think? I mean the world gets along just fine with elephants because they're the size of elephants. You know what I mean? What if there was all of a sudden an elephant that was ten stories tall? Or a hundred?"

Edders' baggy eyes regarded CM now with a new part of his attention.

"That would be a big elephant," said Helen.

No one laughed. She sipped her coffee.

"What are you getting at, McCormick?"

"I was just thinking about I-Mart expanding into construction products. I was just wondering what the real consequences of that might be."

"Fifty K out of your average house," Edders repeated. "That's not beans, McCormick."

"That's true. I'm just trying to imagine what the other consequences might be...." CM pondered into his wine glass. "You know. Maybe unintended consequences of creating a bigger than normal elephant."

Edders twirled his wine glass. "Our business model is a proven fact," he said. "We've reduced the living expenses of the average American family by six and a half percent. That's the same as giving every American a six and a half percent raise in salary! Can you visualize that? We've effectively raised the average wage and reduced the cost of living of every person in America. We can apply that same model to anything. We could even apply it to fish!" he said, turning now to Maggie.

"How would you apply it to fish?" she said.

Edders' staccato laugh shot across the table. "Believe it or not, there's actually been discussion. The hatcheries, in our opinion, run at a miserable efficiency. I've seen a technical analysis that says we could reduce the cost of a hatchery fish by fifty percent. You should point that out at your next hatchery meeting."

"I don't meet with the hatchery," Maggie said. "I meet with a group that's trying to close the hatcheries down."

Edders' baggy eyes regarded Maggie, taking this in.

"What's your problem with the hatcheries?" he asked.

"They're killing the wild fish. Did you know that?"

"Well, now I don't think they're intentionally...."

"The government is proposing legislation that says hatchery fish and wild fish are the same. If you're connected with the logging business, I expect you've heard about that?"

"Well, I heard mention of something along those lines. The endangered species act has been mismanaged for so long now..."

"If you count hatchery fish too, then wild steelhead are no longer an endangered species, are they? And that opens all kinds of new areas for clear-cut logging and saves the loggers the big expense of protecting the spawning streams and wetlands. Isn't that right? Isn't that the strategy?"

Edders stared at Maggie, waiting.

"So tell me, Mr. Florence: If they're all the same thing why aren't you just as happy to catch a hatchery fish as a wild one?"

Edders' mouth stretched into a gradual smile.

"You're clever, Miss Scott. I can see how you'd be good at finding wild fish."

"Is that why you want to 'take them', as you say?" said Maggie. "Because you know there's not many left...and soon..."

"Soon...?"

"Soon there's not going to be any left at all?"

"Don't you think that will take a while, little lady? Don't you think you got your hackles up over something that's a long, long way down the road?"

"What does how long have to do with it?"

"And don't you imagine, Miss Scott, there's more interests involved here than simply the interests of some fish species?"

"Whose interests?"

"People's interests. The interests of human beings. Maybe even the interests of the families that depend on logging for their livelihood. Don't they count in your book? If you take a larger view of interests, don't you think the interests of a few thousand wild fish look pretty paltry?...I don't want to lecture here."

"Please don't." Maggie's eyes are flashing now, drilling into Edders.

He senses this, but goes on anyway:

"The world evolves, Miss Scott. We've got to make the best use of it we can to provide for ourselves. The hatcheries can make all the fish we need. The hatcheries can keep the sportsmen happy, the fishing guides in business, the Indian tribes fed. The hatcheries can make enough fish to keep the commercial fisheries going indefinitely. If they're properly run, they can produce more fish than there ever were in the first place. And the loggers, working along side the hatcheries, can pull out more forest product at less cost. Do you know how many houses have to get built in this country alone over the next thirty years? Do you have any idea?"

Maggie's face was flushing with anger. "So I take it," she said, "the plan is to take everything that's real in the world and replace it with something mass-produced by one of I-Mart's manufacturers? And in the meantime the sport of moguls is to catch the few wild fish left to keep as—what? historical trophies?"

"I'd say that's a bit harsh," said Edders.

"Why would you say that?" I interjected, surprising myself.

Maggie looked at me, eyes wide. Then I realized Edders, too, was regarding me under his drooping lids.

"I can see you folks might talk my ears off here," he said with a feigned weariness. Then his deep staccato laugh. "I think I'd rather talk about what time the morning fishing starts."

CM laughed too, and flashed his warmest smile. "Gus usually meets folks down at the drift boats right after breakfast. Breakfast is anywhere between seven and nine."

"And what about you, Miss Scott?" said Edders. "What time do you get started searching for the wild ones?"

"I don't do drift boats," said Maggie. "Gus and one of the boys from town will take you."

Edders' eyebrows arched high in surprise.

"So how do you fish?" he asked.

"Fishing with me requires hiking and bushwhacking, climbing rocks and wading rapids. I'm not sure you could keep up."

Edders was looking at her, a new kind of smile creeping into the corners of his jowels.

"I guess you must not have a whole lot of clients," he said.

"Not many," said Maggie. She pushed back her chair and stood. "I generally help Louise in the kitchen."

I stood up as well and followed. As I caught up to her quick-stepping march toward the kitchen door, a voice interrupted from down the gallery: "Miss Scott…Maggie!"

We stopped and turned. It was the young man of the father-son team. He'd stepped out from the river room and was coming toward us.

"I couldn't help but overhear what you told Mr. Florence," he said, brushing a black wave of hair off his forehead. A white smile of perfect teeth.

"Eavesdropping is only permitted in the dining room," said Maggie.

He laughed, then looked up at me. "I'm not interrupting....?"

"No," said Maggie. "I was just headed into the kitchen to help Louise."

"Well, it's just that I figure I could keep up with you."

"Keep up with me?"

"I mean I can hike and bushwhack, and likely keep up with you. My dad informed me he's a boater all the way. But, if you're not overly scheduled, I'd enjoy doing some adventure fishing. It sounds like fun." Another white smile.

"Okay," said Maggie, smiling back at him. "Sure. I'll meet you right after breakfast."

"Can you join us, Charlie?" the son asked.

"Thanks," I said. "But I've got other things I need to do."

27

PUTTING UP RAFTERS BY YOURSELF, I discovered, is an un-consoling task when you know that somewhere down below, on the river, Maggie is showing a shaggy haired guy where to cross the rapids, her fishing pants, no doubt, rolled up to her hips, her shoulder blades shifting against the loose fabric of her tank top, her bleached hair whipping in the windy sunlight. My most vivid fear was that they would go swimming off the rock, like Maggie had described, diving into the deep water and shooting down with the current, then swimming back along the edge and him stroking up behind her and embracing her watery form, because that's what I wanted to do.

I considered going down, after all, to look for them.

"Oh! Well, my appointments were cancelled," I'd say, "...so I thought I'd find you guys and do some fishing." Which would be a pretty lame statement considering I didn't have a fishing rod. Competing fantasies bounced around in my imagination as I opened the tool box and began setting out the circular saw and nail-gun.

Ultimately, I convinced myself the rafters were more important. "You got that last beam up by yourself?" Maggie would be impressed. "You did all these rafters in one day?" I determined that that was exactly what I was going to do, and I commenced measuring and cutting with as much efficiency as I could muster.

This group of guests stayed two more days, and on each one of them Maggie took the shaggy-haired boy down to the river fishing. He also monopolized her on the cooking deck and sat next to her at the dinner table. CM carefully steered the evening conversations away from anything having to do with hatcheries or forest products, and Maggie, for her part, studiously ignored the florid face and grating voice of Edders. I concentrated on my roofs, starting early and working through the cocktail hour. My plan, of course, was to coax Maggie back up to the clearing as soon as the guests were gone, to extend and consolidate our truce. As things turned out, however, this was accomplished in a completely different and unexpected way.

The morning after the four guests departed, I was having breakfast with CM when Louise bounced in with an agitated energy, a dishtowel twisting in her hands.

"Maggie just called on the radio. She needs help."

"What is it?" CM said.

"Says she has a flat tire."

CM glanced quizzically at me, as if to say, 'a flat tire? Maggie can't handle a flat tire?'

"Where is she?" he asked.

"She's in Forks. Right on Main Street, she says. She needs somebody to help."

"Charlie, you know how to fix a flat tire?" CM asked.

I was already out of my chair.

"Hurry," Louise said, wringing the life out of the towel. "She sounded....upset."

"Did she say where on Main Street?" I called back.

"Stardust Café," Louise yelled after me.

I drove fast across the one lane bridge, and sped up even more when I hit the asphalt on the other side. The alarm I'd seen in Louise's face was new and unexpected. What could Maggie possibly be doing, or have gotten into, that had frightened Louise in such a way? But then Louise seemed to get up about things pretty easily. Maybe it really was just a flat tire.

I slowed down after I crossed the river outside of town. I headed up the long hill into Forks and started searching ahead for the red Cherokee. About half way along the short strip of motels and cafes I saw its red, boxy shape parked on the left side of the road. It was parked directly in front of an old blue-painted building with a fading sign on the flat roof parapet: STARDUST. The

Cherokee was tilted oddly away from the curb and something big and white was flapping up and down from its roof rack.

As I pulled into the side parking lot I saw there were five or six men leaning against the outside wall of the café, looking into the gravel lot where about a dozen pick-up trucks were parked. A police car, olive green with a black star on the side, sat diagonally in the middle of the lot.

The gravel crunched under my feet when I stepped out and slammed the Toyota's door. The white flapping thing on the roof of the Cherokee was some kind of cardboard sign. The wind was lifting it and flopping it back down before I could read the words.

The Cherokee was definitely tilted, as if it had partially sunk in mud. I was half way across to it when the passenger door of the police car opened and Maggie stepped out wearing her jeans and windbreaker.

"So I guess you were the only one around to rescue me?" she said with a twisty expression I couldn't read.

"Are you okay?"

"It's basically the jeep that's got a problem."

The driver's door of the police car opened and an officer stepped out, putting on his cap. He leaned against the roof of the car and peered around the flasher dome at me.

"You a friend of Miss Scott's?"

"I am."

"Maybe you can help her move her car. It's…blocking the view from the restaurant. The owners have asked her to move it."

I looked at Maggie, but she was turned away from me now, looking at the tilted Cherokee.

"Okay," I said. "But what's the problem with it?"

"It's got a tire problem," Maggie said.

"Did you have a flat?"

"Three flats."

"Three? How'd you…"

A sniggering came from the group of men leaning against the café wall. One of them lit a cigarette and flicked the smoking match out into the gravel.

"How'd you get three flat tires?" I said.

Maggie, still looking at the Cherokee, lifted her arms with theatrical exasperation. "It must have been an act of God," she said.

"That may not be far from truth," said the officer. "But what you need to do, Miss Scott, is move the car."

I looked at the officer in disbelief. "Why didn't you guys just get a tow-truck over here, or something, to help out?" I said.

He looked at me blankly, leaning stiff-armed now against the roof of his squad car. "There's been a complaint registered," he said.

"A complaint?"

"The vehicle's blocking the view of the restaurant patrons. The owners have asked that it be removed."

"But it's just parked there," I said. "What's wrong with that? There's parking all up and down the street here...."

"It's parked for a reason other than...parking," said the officer. "So...according to city code, that's illegal."

"What reason?" I asked.

The officer turned his head and gazed at the Cherokee. As if on cue the wind obliged by once more lifting the cardboard sign revealing a glimpse of large block lettering, then flopped it back down against the roof rack.

I looked at Maggie for some explanation but she was still turned away, staring silently at the Cherokee. I could see now, by the language of her shoulders, she was fuming.

I walked across the gravel to where the Cherokee tilted away from the curb. I could feel the eyes of the men leaning against the café wall following me.

The rear two tires were completely flat. I walked around to the street side and saw the right front tire was flat too. A piece of heavy twine was tied to the door latch. Another piece of twine hung down from over the roof rack where the sign lay. I could see the twine had been cut with a knife, the ends frayed out.

I pulled on the twine hanging over the roof rack and the cardboard sign tilted up like a white, rectangular shark-fin. It was hinging on the center of the roof somehow and stiffened on each edge with a narrow wood batten. I read the words, carefully stenciled on it in big black letters:

PLEASE SAVE OUR WILD FISH!
CLOSE DOWN THE HATCHERIES ON THE OLYMPIC PENINSULA!
SIGN THE PETITION for the SECOND WILDERNESS!!!

I let the sign hinge back flat onto the roof of the Cherokee. I crouched down and studied the flat tires on the street side. The valve-cores had been removed. That would deflate a tire pretty quick. Slowly registering what was going on, my heart started speeding up, a tingle of adrenaline shooting into my forearms.

I stood up and walked back around the Cherokee, immediately catching again the stares of the men leaning against the café wall. A couple of them, I noticed, had on tall rubber boots with the tops rolled down. Baseball caps pulled low, eyes peering out from the shadow of the bill.

Neither Maggie nor the police officer had moved. She regarded me defiantly as I came back across the gravel, as if she were expecting a reprimand.

"I can get those fixed," I said as lightly as I could. "All I need is a couple of concrete blocks or something."

I walked past Maggie to where I'd spotted an old retaining wall along one edge of the parking lot that had been clipped by a drunken patron. The impact had knocked off a section of the top row of blocks. I found them on the far side of the wall, lying in the bushes along with miscellaneous beer cans and paper trash.

I carried two of the blocks back toward the Cherokee. Maggie intercepted me.

"What are you going to do?" she said in a lowered voice.

"I'm going to pull those tires off and take them to the gas station down the road and get them filled back up with air. They're not slashed," I said. "Someone's just let the air out. You get the Cherokee's jack. I'll get the one out of the Toyota."

I worked as quickly as I could. Maggie crouched next to me and collected the lug-nuts as I pulled the tires. We worked on the street-side first. I jacked up the rear, removed the wheel, and lowered the frame onto the stacked concrete blocks. Then I jacked up the front, removed that wheel, and left the jack in place.

"Maybe they've all left," I whispered to Maggie as I was pulling the wheel.

"I wouldn't bet on it," she said.

"Okay. You roll these tires over and put them in the back of the Toyota. I'll pull the wheel on the other side."

The spectator party leaning against the café wall had now grown larger—in more ways than one. The leaning men had been joined by a giant dressed in worn, clean dungarees and heavy leather boots. He wore no hat; his big sunburned face emerged from a thatch of thick brown-grey hair that was pulled into a long, tightly braided pony tail. Most remarkable was his full, tobacco stained beard that hung down to his belt where it dwindled improbably into three spindly dreadlocks. He'd been talking to the others and swung around now to watch me as I started on the third wheel. The officer, I noticed, had gotten back in his police car.

Using the second jack I worked under the silent gaze of the spectators. I pulled the tire and rolled it over to the Toyota where Maggie was waiting.

"You coming with me?" I said.

"I'd better stay here. I'll go sit with Jessup."

"With who?"

"Jessup." She nodded at the police car. "The policeman."

"You know him?"

"We went to day-camp together when I was eight."

"Then why is he treating you like this?"

"He's got to put on a show for them I think," she said.

"I'm not getting this," I said.

I climbed into the Toyota, backed around in the gravel, and drove to the service station. I was back in twenty minutes, the valve-cores replaced and the tires inflated. The spectators stood their ground, leaning against the wall, smoking cigarettes.

Maggie climbed out of the police car and helped me set the wheels, handing me the lug-nuts she'd kept in the pocket of her windbreaker.

As I was putting the jacks back in the Cherokee and Toyota the officer emerged from his police car again. He put on his cap and adjusted the brim.

"You two need to get in the patrol car please," he announced loudly.

Maggie got back in the passenger seat. I climbed in the back.

We stared out the windshield at the group of men leaning against the wall, watching us. The giant, who I decided could have no other profession than lumber jack, was rolling a cigarette, pulling on the dainty drawstring of his tobacco pouch with large square teeth. The other men, their ball-caps pulled lower now against the late morning sun, only came up to the beginning of his shoulders.

The officer picked up a clip board and leaned it against the steering wheel. He began writing on it.

"Maggie," he said without looking up from his writing, "you got to stop pressing on these folks like this, okay?"

"We already talked about that Jessup. I'm not pressing on them, okay? I'm just talking to them. Trying to make them see things differently."

"And like I was saying before, they aren't going to see things differently. They're starting to feel threatened. It's their jobs you're talking about here." He continued writing on the clip-board.

"I'm not trying to threaten them or their jobs. I'm just talking to them about another point of view. There's no reason doing things in a more holistic way means there aren't any jobs. There might even be more jobs...."

"They don't see it that way."

"How do you see it, Jessup?"

"It doesn't matter how I see it, damn-it."

He pulled the sheet of paper from the clipboard, made a big point of folding it and handing it to Maggie. He was looking at her now.

"I'm telling you, you got to stop doing this. Folks are starting to get upset about it. They used to think you were just a cute, crazy girl, and your dad was a harmless philosopher. But now, with that group in Port Angeles in the news, they're starting to get upset."

Maggie stared back at the officer, her eyes animated with energy.

"Somebody's got to do something, Jessup," she said. "Ultimately, these people are just destroying their own world."

She pushed open the door and stepped out. I got out too.

Along with the men leaning against the café wall, I watched Maggie walk across the gravel lot, stuffing the folded paper from officer Jessup in the pocket of her jeans.

She climbed into the Cherokee, started it up, did a U-turn out into the street, and headed back out of town, the white sign flapping up and down on the roof-rack.

I followed her in the Toyota. She didn't go far before she pulled over and got out to take the sign off. I stopped to help.

"What the hell was going on back there?" I said untying the twine from one side of the roof-rack. Maggie was working on the other side, the top of her head sometimes visible above the horizontal bar, sometimes her eyes too as she stood on tip-toe to get at the knots.

"I was collecting signatures for the petition," she said.

"You mean you were standing next to the road—collecting signatures?"

"I was in the café. That's where a lot of workers stop for breakfast."

"And what happened?"

"I don't know. I was having a nice conversation in one of the booths. There was a fellow and his daughter in there. She was taking him to the doctor."

The sign became detached and Maggie lifted it from the roof-rack.

"So how long have you been doing this?" I asked as she slid the sign into the cargo area of the Cherokee. "I mean, collecting signatures?"

"A couple years…. Since I got back."

I lowered the cargo door and pushed it closed with a clunk.

"And how many signatures have you got?"

Maggie squinted at me as if I were out of focus. "Five," she said.

"Five signatures, in two years?"

"That's right." She squinted at me even harder, daring me to say something derogatory.

I gave her the biggest smile I could invent. "Jeez, that's pretty damn good," I said. "Given the constituency you've staked out."

She squinted hard at me another second, then her eyes opened wide and she laughed.

"That's a very nice compliment, Charlie," she said. "That's the nicest thing you've ever said."

28

EVEN THOUGH IT NOW APPEARED we were on a first name basis again, it was a couple of weeks before Maggie revisited the clearing. The occasion was my "roofs-up" celebration, as CM called it. He'd helped me with the metal roofing—handing up the long, silver sheets from below while I nailed them to the purlins with umbrella nails, a very descriptive term for an item I never knew existed. I'd framed the roofs as he'd suggested, sloping in toward each other, creating a central slot between their lower eaves, about four feet wide, above the chimney box. CM showed me how to turn that into a shallow metal gutter that would funnel the rain water to one end. When we finished the last section of the gutter, we stood out in the middle of the field, sharing the water canteen, and admiring the roofs. Perched on the columns with their angled braces, they looked like they were about to soar off above the trees.

"It's beautiful," said CM. "I think we should celebrate."

"Don't I need to build some walls before we have a party?"

"The walls can come later—they just fill in between the columns. I can show you how to do that. But the roof's the big accomplishment. From now on it can rain all it wants, and you can work in the dry!"

I could see his point, but I demurred on the idea of a celebration. "I don't think I'm exactly ready for entertaining guests," I said.

This elicited a big smile. "I don't see why we couldn't do it tonight."

"Tonight?" I said, startled.

"There's only the Martins here right now, so that would be seven of us. You could handle seven for dinner, right?"

"You're crazy," I said.

"Let's just make some steps up to the floor deck and....Oh, I almost forgot." He strode up to the edge of the clearing where the small water turbine spun in the stream. There was a grey electrical panel on a short post next to it and he opened the door to the panel and flipped some switches. He came back, his face beaming. "Now we're ready," he said mysteriously.

And so it was, a few hours later, that I found myself dressed in a clean set of clothes, sitting on the edge of my main floor deck, freshly swept, waiting for my six dinner guests to arrive, not having a clue how I was going to entertain them. CM had assured me that would all be taken care of. "Just have the floors clean," he said. "I'll bring everyone up around 6:30."

That time came and went. I was beginning to think there'd been a change of plans when, suddenly, CM emerged from the trees at the bottom of the clearing, holding above his head, like a drum major's baton, a big pair of red tin-snips.

"Ta-Dah!" he announced, pumping the tin-snips. The celebrators followed behind him in single file, first Maggie, carrying a canvas bag over one shoulder, then Louise with a paper grocery bag in her arms, then the Martins with matching long-billed fishing caps, then Gus with a bundle of collapsible camp chairs balanced on his shoulder.

CM stopped at the bottom of the steps we'd just built a few hours earlier. I stood there, looking down at their arrival, shaking my head, making it clear with my expression I was not the one responsible for this.

"We've come to celebrate your roof," said CM as if he were making an official announcement.

I made a formal bow, playing along. "Please come in," I said. "I should warn everyone though, I forgot the wine and cheese."

"Wine and cheese?" said CM stepping up onto the floor. He turned and offered his hand to Maggie. To my surprise, she reached up and took it. "Do we look like we've come to be wined and dined?"

Picking up on CM's gesture, I stepped up and offered my hand to grey-haired Mrs. Martin, who took it with a smile. Then her husband. Then Louise.

"What a nice shirt, Charlie!" Louise said alighting on the floor. "Here, let me straighten your collar."

As Louise fussed at my shirt, Gus stepped by us, his round red face giving me a wink.

"Well, Charlie, I think you should give us a tour," CM announced.

I gave him a futile look.

"But first, let's open the box! You ready Gus?"

"Ready, captain." Gus stepped up holding a box cutter.

Flourishing the red tin-snips, CM began cutting the metal strapping around the chimney-box. Gus followed along beside him with the box-cutter, shiny blade extended, slicing through the white, water-proof wrapping. Big sheets of the wrap began to settle on the floor. Maggie and Louise rolled them into tight bundles and pushed them off the floor deck next to the steps.

Beneath the white paper were plywood panels that I could see had been re-used many times. The panels were held in place with a few oversized screws along each edge. CM started removing these with a ratcheting screwdriver he'd pulled from his pocket.

"We ready?" he asked Gus. "Let's do this one first."

Gus and CM each grasped an opposite end of the plywood panel, lifted it and pulled it away. What was revealed was a fireplace and raised stone hearth beneath a heavy timber mantle built into the stone chimney. Next they pulled away the adjacent panel, revealing a series of open shelves and glass cabinets above a stone countertop. Even more surprising than the cabinetry was the fact that it contained a sparkling set of wine glasses.

"This is my favorite part!" said Mrs. Martin.

I looked at her, surprised. Apparently she had seen this exercise before.

"Other side," said CM. Then to me: "Charlie, go bring up your sawhorses while we finish up."

While I fetched the sawhorses—wondering vaguely if I ought to bring the saw too—CM and Gus continued around the chimney box removing, in turn, the plywood panels from the other faces. Each panel they removed was carried to the edge of the floor and lowered to the ground in a neat stack. They worked all the way around the back of the chimney, around the far end, and finally came to the last panel on the fireplace side, where they'd started. We all stood watching.

"Put the sawhorses right about here," said CM pointing to a spot on the floor. "Little bit further apart. Good....Ready Gus?"

They grasped the last plywood panel, lifted it and pulled it away revealing a built-in wall of bookcases and drawer panels to the left of the stone hearth. They flipped the plywood sheet around and set it on the two sawhorses like a table top.

Maggie and Louise stepped up immediately and flung open a white table-cloth which had appeared miraculously in their hands. They worked efficiently, like a practiced stage crew setting up a scene for the next act. As they smoothed the table-cloth over the plywood rectangle, Gus stepped around from the other side of the stone chimney carrying a silver candelabrum in each hand. He set them on the table with a flourish.

CM had stationed himself in the kitchen space, looking out over the counter-top at us, his big gap-tooth smile radiating.

"What do you think so far, Charlie?" he asked.

"It's amazing!" I said. "I mean, I knew what was in there...but."

"It's been nine years since we did this in Freddie's unit," said Mr. Martin. "It still gives me the goose bumps."

CM reached his hand under the stone counter and lights suddenly came on in the glass cabinets, setting the wine glasses sparkling. Lights hidden under the cabinets came on too, casting round glowing pools on the stone counter itself. I realized the switches he'd flipped earlier in the day up by the water-turbine were the unit's power, and I knew I'd find the under-counter fridge already cold.

"So now," CM said, "give us the tour."

Even though I'd known exactly what was inside that white, water-proof box the whole time I'd been working next to it, the effect of seeing it opened up like this under my roof was startling.

Instantly, my "floor deck" was transformed into a living and dining space. On the other side of the stone counter I now had a kitchen with a sink, a two-burner cook-top and under-counter fridge—which, as I suspected, was not only cold, but contained beer, wine, and a bottle of champagne. Continuing down the backside of the fireplace, a doorway now opened into a compact bathroom with stone shower stall, a small, round sink with running water, and white towels hanging on the towel-bar. Back around to the other side of the stone chimney, a wall of bookshelves and drawers grew upward next to the hearth—exactly like the rest of the units.

CM handed me a box of matches and I discovered a fire had already been carefully laid in the fire-place with two chunks of sap-wood under the kindling. In less than a minute we were all standing around the raised hearth, watching the fire lick up the back of the stone fire-box.

"Do you think that champagne's still good?" CM asked. "It's been in there a bit longer than usual...."

Maggie took down the wine glasses from the sparkling cabinet. I popped the cork of the champagne and it hit the underside of the metal roof with a resounding BONG!

"Oh my!" said Mrs. Martin. And everyone laughed, including me. I poured the champagne and Maggie distributed the glasses, and everyone held their champagne up in the air and gave me a toast.

It turned out to be a very successful party. Gus unfolded the camp chairs and arranged them around the make-shift, but now very elegant, table. Maggie and Louise set out the plates and silverware from the cabinets, and lit the candles in the candelabra. We opened a bottle of wine. Gus and I drank beers and stoked the fire, while Maggie walked around offering a plate of smoked oysters and cracked olives. When the fire died down to coals, CM lowered a cooking grate that hinged from the back of the firebox, and Louise put on the meat. Maggie added three big yellow onions to roast. Another bottle of wine was opened, and we sat around the table, eating and talking and laughing. The grassy field around us, beyond the open walls of my unit, began to grow dark, and the candles grew brighter.

After the plates had been cleared, and Gus had opened a bottle of dessert brandy, CM looked at me and said, "I think we should have some music." I looked at him, puzzled, and he reached into his shirt pocket and pulled out the tape cassette I'd given him the first night we met. He held it up with a faint smile. "Charlie and I want to share this little milestone with someone else, someone who can't be here," he announced. "Is that all right?"

I found the radio and tape-deck in the usual place, behind a sliding panel in the book-case. I pressed the power button and a tiny red light came on. I pushed in the cassette and waited for the sound I knew was coming. A few seconds of scratchy air, then the familiar discordant scraps of a band warming up. I adjusted the volume. The speakers were up in the book shelves. Guitar and drum riffs. Bits of conversation in the background. A whistle from the audience. That familiar fleck of laughter. Then all of it coming together into that chord, that one powerful chord across the guitar strings, then another, and my mother's clear voice into the mike:

"These songs are for a boy I know in Vietnam," she says.

And the base guitar begins its deep syncopated melody accompanied, a moment later, by the rhythmic strokes of that single acoustic guitar....

"It's been years since I heard that song," said Mrs. Martin. "Is that Joni Mitchell?"

"Actually, it's my mother," I said.

"It is?" said Mrs. Martin.

I felt Maggie's eyes and turned my head. She was looking at me as if she'd just realized something new and strange and slightly disturbing.

29

FOR SOME REASON WE STARTED calling them "The Delegation" even before they arrived and we discovered they actually were a delegation. The Chinese, we came to understand, like to travel in groups, with a hierarchy and a leader—mainly, it seemed, for the purpose of determining seating arrangements at the dinner table.

"The Delegation is going to be here in two weeks," Louise announced one day in mid August. "What in the world are we going to feed them?"

"I expect they'll eat the same thing we do," CM replied.

"But shouldn't we have something Chinese for them?" Louise persisted. "We need to make them feel at home."

It was one of those days between guests. We were having "family breakfast" at the big dining table. As we talked, the silver coffee carafe and a dessert plate of orange slices and strawberries swung its way back and forth between us.

"I'll bet the main reason they decided to come here in the first place is to try your famous peninsula cooking," I said.

She eyed me suspiciously.

"I'm sure that's right," CM joined in. "It says it right in our brochure: 'Louise's famous Peninsula Cooking!' I'll bet that's exactly what caught their eye."

Louise looked around at us with a fragile mistrust.

"You guys are full of crap," she said, and Maggie let go a laugh she'd been holding back.

The Chinese delegation had made their reservation nearly a year in advance. From what Gus understood they represented a fly-fishing club in Beijing. Twelve were coming which meant full capacity for the fish camp and tight seating at the dinner table. The day before their arrival, I moved my things up to my project on the hill. Louise cleaned and vacuumed the Ben Sprague unit as I was moving my things, making a big show of shaking out the throw rugs over the veranda railing, cascading clouds of dust down into the river.

"Look, you're going to asphyxiate the fish, Mr. Charlie," she said, shaking and whacking a rug against the railing. "Didn't you ever sweep? Where'd you learn to keep house?"

These were rhetorical questions, since I was coming and going with my moving process as invisibly as possible.

"Lord, I don't think this bed's been made for a month!" I heard her exclaim as I ducked down the end of the veranda with my last box of stuff.

Gus had rented a stretched van and drove off to meet the delegation at the SeaTac airport. CM had made a hand-printed sign in his big slanted-block lettering for Gus to hold up at the gate area. The sign said: "Changbao Fishing Party".

They arrived at the camp long after dark.

I was up on the hill in my unit, lying on the old futon Louise had given me from the camp house storage room, reading by the light of a candle lantern, Gramella's quilt rolled up under my head for a pillow. It was my first night in the place I'd built myself, and I was luxuriating in a warm sense of accomplishment. The light from the lantern cast beautiful, complex shadows on the sloped rafters above my head. The stream chattered in the nearby darkness and the silence of the surrounding forest was immense.

Suddenly this silence included the strident, far-away, sing-song voices of bantering Chinese. I blew out the lantern and snuggled down into Gramella's quilt, glad to be hidden away from what sounded like a chaotic arrival down below.

The next morning I debated skipping breakfast, hoping to avoid having to meet and attempt conversation with twelve Chinese fly-fisherman. Eventually, my empty stomach won the argument and I headed down the clearing. As I came up the steps onto the veranda, I found CM and Gus engaged in animated conversation.

"He's what?" CM was asking.

"That's what he says," said Gus, as if he'd been accused of stretching the truth.

The special interests of the delegate leader, Gus conveyed, had become clear that morning at early breakfast. Xu Changbao (whom we later learned to call "zoo" with a kind mushy "z") had declared he did not want to go fishing that morning, but instead wanted a tour of the fish camp. This was explained, Gus said, through his interpreter Fan. (It turned out Fan—pronounced "Fahn"—like all the other delegates except Xu Changbao himself, could speak surprisingly good English.) Mr. Xu, Gus had just informed my father, was not simply a Chinese fly-fisherman. He was an architect with the Beijing Ministry of Housing.

"Are you sure you understood what he was saying?" CM arched intently over Gus, his eyes bright with energy.

"Course not!" said Gus. "I couldn't understand a goddamn word of it. But according to his interpreter, he's an architect—just like you. He's chief of something in the Ministry of Housing," Gus repeated. "And he wants a tour of the fish camp. That's your department. The rest of 'em want to go fishing. Maggie's taking three down to Zarathustra's pool. Me and the Tommy brothers will float the others. The boats are waiting up at the long bridge. But Mr. Xu, he wants the tour." It was clear from Gus' tone he'd about had it with Mr. Xu.

"I'll be damned," my father said, looking out over the river with a dazed expression. "I'll be goddamned."

Then he looked over at me as if he'd known I was standing there all along.

"Charlie," he said, "I think you need to put on your business suit."

After a rushed breakfast, I sat in my father's studio listening to him shave and brush his teeth. He was talking to me through the open door during intervals of rinsing and gargling.

"Architects," he was saying, "whether they're Chinese or from Mars—are prissy bastards. They have a low tolerance for sloppiness. They try to see everything through a prism of order. Also pompously judgmental....You ever heard the saying, 'You only have one chance to make a first impression?' Well, with an architect you only have a millisecond!"

"For chrissakes CM," I called back through the doorway. "Why are you worried about making an impression?"

CM's head popped around the door jamb, one cheek smathered with white foam, a strand of curly grey hair sticking up like a defective antenna.

"You need to get smart, Charlie", he said. "The whole world is constructed of nothing but impressions. If you want to participate you've got to make one—otherwise you're invisible."

Sounds of razor rinsing and sloshing.

"But why can't you just honestly be yourself? Why isn't that good enough?"

"That's a good question, Charlie. I like that question!"

Sounds of rinsing and face slapping.

"But don't you think that's a bit selfish? I mean to expect the world to love you just the way you are? Don't you think you need to participate a bit? Make an effort to be lovable?"

"That's not exactly what I meant," I said. "I mean, why dress up for god's sake? Why can't someone accept that you work and your shirt gets dirty?"

"Ever picked wild-flowers Charlie?" he asked, still hidden in the bathroom. "Which ones do you pick? Nature goes to extravagant effort to make itself beautiful. Ever notice that? Why do you suppose it does that?"

Wearing wrinkled, pale blue boxer shorts, CM stepped suddenly across the small hallway and disappeared into his sleeping alcove. His legs were surprisingly skinny. Sounds of drawers opening and closing.

"I mean at face value, Charlie, 'just yourself'—with a few notable exceptions among the fair gender—is just a white pudgy bundle of flesh that nobody's much interested in looking at."

Another drawer sliding. Then, a frustrated mumbling to himself: "How the hell did this work?" Then, projected out to me again: "The problem is, Charlie, everyone gets so caught up in the impressions, they forget why they're making an impression...

"So, my philosophy is to strike a balance..."

With these last words, CM steps around the corner of the sleeping alcove, arms open, as if he is about to take a bow on stage. His big smile is shining. His faded fish camp t-shirt has been replaced with a white dress-shirt—slightly rumpled, but clean—and a bright blue, crooked bow-tie. The white shirt sleeves are jauntily rolled up 'for balance'.

"Jesus, CM", I said startled. "Where'd you get that tie?"

In spite of the faded jeans and sandals, I had to admit he looked distinguished. He looked exactly like an architect who'd inexplicably been living and sleeping in the woods for most of his career.

Mr. Xu and Fan were waiting for us on the cooking deck. Mr. Xu was dressed in a khaki-green one-piece leisure suit with permanent creases in the arms and legs. He had a round face and flat head with thousands of tiny erect silver hairs. Fan, much younger, was more informally dressed in shorts and Nikes.

As we approached, Mr. Xu bowed, mumbling a Chinese greeting. Still slightly bowed, he held out a business card with both hands, as if he was going to let you touch it but not have it. CM bowed in response and, to my surprise, pulled a card of his own from the pocket of his dress shirt. Mr. Xu examined CM's card with great appreciation, his bushy eyebrows going up and down.

"Mr. Xu is very appreciative to meet you," said Fan.

"And we're very appreciative to have Mr. Xu and his colleagues as our guests." CM bowed again slightly as he said this.

"This is my...associate—Charles Cadwell," CM put his arm on my shoulder, secretly poking a finger sharply into my trapezoid muscle.

At this prompt I bowed to Mr. Xu, wondering if I should try to shake his hand. I decided to keep my hands behind me.

"Mr. Xu is very curious about the architecture of the fish camp," said Fan. "He believes it is very unusual. He believes it reminds him also of a village he knew as a child."

"We'll be pleased to give Mr. Xu a tour," CM said. "But first, perhaps we should sit and have a coffee. There are explanations I need to make about the process of the architecture which will make a tour more meaningful."

Seeing an opportunity to temporarily escape, I quickly volunteered to retrieve the coffee. Mr. Xu smiled broadly and bowed to me thankfully.

After telling Louise about the request for coffee, I went over to the sink and wetted my hands and ran my fingers through my hair, attempting to straighten out what I knew must be a few disheveled locks.

Louise, standing next to the percolating coffee pot was watching.

"So do you want me to give you a manicure?" she asked.

"Jeez, Louise," I said, "CM's wearing a bow tie!"

"As well he should," Louise responded. "Things get a little too informal around here, if you ask me. You go on out there and I'll bring the coffee.

"Wait!" she said as I started for the door.

She came up and looked me over. She reached up and adjusted the shoulders of my t-shirt. "You know, Charlie," she said, "you could be just about the handsomest man in the world."

When I joined the group on the cooking deck, CM gave me a secret wink without breaking stride in his on-going explanation, which he had obviously warmed into, canting energetically forward in his deck chair, elbows on his knees, hands free and gesturing.

"…So, given that our analysis suggested that horizontal density was going to be important, we asked ourselves: what's going to be the most efficient way to build it? And the answer we came up with is one unit at a time."

Fan stopped interpreting and looked at CM with a surprised expression. "I'm afraid I misunderstood," he said.

"Which part?"

"I heard you say one unit at a time is the most efficient?"

"That's right," said CM, "in which case—"

Fan turned to Xu and translated. Xu's eyebrows arched up, wrinkling his bald forehead.

"So here's the coffee," Louise announced.

CM pulled up a small table amongst our chairs and Louise set down the tray with coffee carafe and cups, cream and sugar. CM poured and handed around the cups. There was a hiatus while Xu and Fan loaded up with sugar.

"So the question that came up then," CM started again, anxious to get his momentum back, "was, if the horizontal density is going to grow incrementally, one small and completely independent project at a time, how is the large scale design going to get organized? In other words, what's going to prevent it from just becoming a sprawling chaos? That's what we started focusing on."

CM stopped and sipped his coffee while Fan translated, Xu listening with his head tilted toward Fan but his eyes on CM. Then Xu spoke something to Fan, who then relayed: "What Mr. Xu doesn't understand is why you would do it that way?" Xu spoke again, and Fan said: "Why would you not build the entire fish camp as a single project? Surely that would be the most efficient!"

"We did that, but only to a point," CM answered. "We designed and built the Enabling Structure all at once, as a single project. That's what establishes the order, do you see?" He was shaping boxes of order now with his long, square fingers. "But then each unit got built within the Enabling Structure separately, in its own way. It was two steps: Step one, the Enabling Structure. Step two, the individual projects that created the units."

Xu spoke immediately to Fan, making his own gestures with hands that were surprisingly delicate.

"Mr. Xu does not understand these words," said Fan. "What is 'Enabling Structure'?"

It took me a moment to realize that Xu was understanding more than he let on, or maybe it was that he understood English but couldn't speak it well, or maybe—this occurred to me later—the process of using a translator gave him a special control of the conversation.

CM picked up on the same thing, for now he started speaking directly to Xu, instead of to Fan. "We call it that because it's something that gets designed and built first and then, because it exists, it enables the individual architectures to happen easier and faster. It 'enables' someone to build something they might not otherwise be capable of building." He gives me a sideways glance, concerned, I could tell, that I might have just been offended.

This elicited a quick smile and nodding of the head from Xu. He spoke again to Fan, his head shaking, now, in the other direction.

"I'm afraid we are not exactly understanding," said Fan.

"Well here's the solution," CM said with a new enthusiasm. "Charlie here, is right now building a unit up on the hill—the last unit actually, that we've planned for. If you wanted to come up and see his project, I think the process I'm talking about will become clear."

Fan translated into Xu's tilted ear.

"Aahh!" Vigorous head nodding from Xu.

"Give me fifteen minutes to get Charlie organized," CM said, "then I'll take you up there."

I was looking at CM now, wondering what he was thinking, what was he getting me into?

30

I WAS FOLLOWING CM'S MARCHING stride down the veranda toward his studio.

"What exactly are you planning to do?" I asked.

"Xu is an architect," he said.

"So?"

"So the only way you can get an architect to agree with you on something is if you give him the chance to have the idea first."

"And?"

We were at the top of the steps down to the studio. CM suddenly stopped and turned. I nearly ran into him. His grey eyes had transformed into an electric blue.

"This is really fun, don't you think, Charlie?"

In the studio he rummaged behind the model table and pulled out a large, black drawing folio. He selected some pencils and started sharpening them.

"You go on up and sweep and put stuff away," he suggested. "I'll bring them up in about fifteen minutes, okay?"

"But what is it you want me to show them?"

"Don't worry about that. Get the stuff out to make us some hot tea."

When I got up to the unit, I swept the floors and rolled up the futon and folded Gramellas quilt on top. I arranged the folding camp chairs around the raised hearth—the table having been dismantled so I could use the saw-horses again—and got out cups and saucers and spoons and a tin of tea-bags. I filled the kettle with water and set it on the cook-top.

"Mr. Cadwell! We have visitors!" From the lower end of the clearing.

Standing at the top of the steps, I watched them emerge from the forest and walk up the clearing, CM in the lead, followed by Mr. Xu, Fan catching up in the rear. CM is carrying the black drawing folio. Mr. Xu, eyes taking in the structure I'm standing in, stumbles as he walks and Fan catches him from behind and helps him regain his balance.

They arrive at the bottom of the steps, CM still in the lead.

"Here we are!" he declares giving me a wink.

Stepping up into the space, Mr. Xu looks around wide-eyed.

Hoping to distract him from a detailed evaluation I held my arms out to the seating arrangement in front of the hearth.

"Anyone like some tea?" I asked.

CM eyed the seating arrangement and gave me another wink. His excitement seemed to generate a multitude of secret winks and nods.

"Yes, please start the tea, Charlie." CM said. "While you're doing that I'll give Mr. Xu a short tour."

I walked around into the little kitchen space and turned on the cook-top—poof! The little blue flame came to life under the tea-kettle.

"This is the Mechanical Core," said CM at my shoulder. Apparently the tour started with me in the kitchen. "This is the heart of the Enabling Structure." CM continues in a professorial tone. "The designer-builder—Charlie in this case—comes to the project with the Core already existing, complete, finished, ready to use. The fact it is here influences what he chooses to do but doesn't totally control it."

Mr. Xu and Fan were standing on the opposite side of the counter, looking over it, watching the flame under the tea kettle.

"Part of our strategy, is that the designer-builder only needs to be focused on creating spaces—not on piping and foundations and electrical wiring. The cores at the fish camp were all hand-built with river stone. But they could just as well be prefabricated with metal or light-wood frames, mass produced by the thousands. While the water's heating up, Charlie, show Mr. Xu the appliances."

Xu and Fan walked around the stone counter.

"So here's the cook-top and oven," I said.

I pulled the stainless oven door open and Xu leaned down and peered inside. "Here's the fridge," Xu looked in that too. "I mostly drink beer," I said, explaining the contents.

Fan translated. Mr. Xu made a comment back and laughed. Then he looked at me, slapped me on the shoulder in a friendly way and laughed again.

"Mr. Xu admires your batchelor cuisine," said Fan.

So I laughed with him, starting to feel more at ease.

"And down here are the bath facilities." They followed me to the compact compartment on the other side of the stone chimney.

Xu ran his hands appreciatively over the little stone counter and stepped into the shower, examining the chrome knobs and shower head. He started to turn the water knob and I quickly reached in and stopped him. "The water's on," I said.

"Chaw-sherr!" Xu exclaimed, jumping out of the shower. He spoke rapidly to Fan, then laughed and shook his head several times.

"Mr. Xu inspects many buildings in Beijing. At this stage of construction it is very odd for the water to be turned on."

"Excellent point," said CM from outside the doorway. "When you come out we'll explain—Tea kettle's ready, Charlie!"

While I was making the tea, CM was pointing out the pattern of stone piers poking up through the wild grass around the floor deck.

"These are part of the Enabling Structure as well," he said. "They establish the potential foundation points and eliminate the need for the designer-builder to perform excavation or concrete work. The piers are completely ready to receive support beams or columns. They have inset tabs to hold the beam or column in place. The beam can go in either direction. All of the piers don't have to be used. They represent possibilities, choices, do you see? Charlie can complete his unit in any of these directions." CM's hands were visualizing surrounding edifices.

Fan interpreted and Xu replied with a question.

"Mr. Xu asks about the unused piers? Are they torn down?"

"No, no! They become part of something else, over time. A garden wall, a trellis, something. The Enabling Structure is a set of potential spaces. All the structure is ultimately used one way or another. But exactly how it's used is up to the designer-builder. The Enabling Structure makes it easy to build, but at the same time, it establishes limits. Builders are not allowed to change the foundation system. That's the only rule. So it's a balance, do you see?—between control and freedom."

I announce the tea is ready.

CM turns and gestures to the sitting area in front of the hearth, giving a slight bow to Xu and Fan. Xu holds his knees together creating a little table for the cup and saucer. He sips then smiles and nods. "Shay-shay", he says.

"Mr. Xu thanks you for your hospitality," Fan interprets.

"It is my honor," I say, nodding, and bowing back. Somehow this formal nodding and bowing has insinuated itself into my body language too.

"So Fan," CM says. "Tell Mr. Xu that Charlie would appreciate his professional and artistic advice on a few things." A discrete wink in my direction while Fan passes this on.

Xu's expression perked up. He puts his cup in the saucer on his knees and regards me with appreciative interest. He speaks at some length.

"Mr. Xu says he is at your service. He compliments you on what you have built so far. He would be most interested to know how you plan to finish."

"Well," I begin searching for what to say. "Please tell Mr. Xu this is a somewhat unusual…assignment. This is to be the sort of 'honeymoon' cottage of the fish camp. That's why it's up here by itself. It's supposed to be…romantic. Its main purpose, actually, is seduction. A place where a man could seduce a woman—or vice-versa, I suppose. Does that make sense?"

Fan interpreted. The muscles around CM's mouth were twitching, working hard, I could tell, at keeping a straight face. Xu's features animated even more as Fan spoke, his bushy eyebrows going up and down. Then a cascade of sing-song words.

"Mr. Xu is very appreciative of this goal. In China the concubine's residence has always been a place of romance and seduction. There is a long history of the art of this."

"Concubine" didn't sound exactly right to me.

"Well, it's not exactly a concubine's residence," I said. "It's sort of a place where the two people are equal, but…"

"In China, concubines are perfectly honorable," CM interrupted. "In China, concubines have to be seduced as well, I believe. It's a matter of honor."

"This is true in a way," said Fan. "Although the old culture is dying away. The party discourages free-sex."

Impatient, Xu speaks to Fan, ending in a question.

"Mr. Xu asks what you plan to build next?"

"Well, it's not a big place," I said. "What I was going to do next is the sleeping alcove. I was thinking of putting it out there." I stood up and walked to the edge of the floor deck and pointed down at my bridge, which was about two feet lower than where I stood. "I was thinking of putting it across there, on the other side…"

CM, Xu and Fan put their cups and saucers on the hearth and joined me. We all looked out at the deck bridging across the stream into the tall ferns under the trees on the other side.

Fan spoke to Xu, pointing.

Xu turned and looked slowly around at everything I'd built. Then he spoke at some length to Fan, gesturing upwards with his arms. He turned and looked down at the stream and spoke again. He pointed at the stream, speaking, and made a big round shape with his arms. Fan asked him a question. Xu answered with emphasis, then turned to me and gave a little bow.

"Mr. Xu says, with all respect, that the sleeping alcove should not be close to the earth like that. That is a mistake, he believes. A woman is full of Yin energy, and the sleeping place should be elevated. It should be up there, he believes." Fan pointed into the air, indicating a direction up the hill. "The sleeping space should be elevated. It should be open to the east. The morning sun should find it first. That is the most romantic time after the seduction, Mr. Xu believes, when the sunlight awakens the sleeping couple."

Mr. Xu, impatient with the translation, spoke again, pointing down at the stream with animation.

"Mr. Xu says he believes the stream is ideal location for a stone bath. Hot-water stone bath. Hot rice-wine and hot-water stone bath increase a woman's Yin, he says. They go very well together before ascending to the sleeping alcove."

Xu nodded to me earnestly as Fan made the translation. He winked and laughed after Fan had finished.

"Let's make some sketches!" CM suggested. He opened the black leather folio he'd brought and pulled out a tablet of paper, pencils and pens. These he carried to the kitchen counter. Obviously, he'd anticipated things getting to this point.

"Ok, so here's a section diagram of what Charlie's built to date," CM said, beginning to draw rapidly in big, bold strokes on the paper tablet.

"This is the fireplace and Mechanical Core, right?" He began adding labels at the ends of long arrows pointing to different parts. "Here's the kitchen space. This is the main room Charlie's already built….As I understand it, Mr. Xu is suggesting the sleeping alcove be up here, on the other side of the bathroom and extending out toward the upper part of the hill. Is that right?"

Fan translated. Mr. Xu answered by pulling a pen from his pocket. It was an old-fashioned fountain pen, shiny black with a gold tip. He uncapped it and CM pushed the paper tablet over closer to him. Xu began to draw over CM's sketch. He drew very precisely with thin lines that squiggled, just perceptibly, with black shiny ink. Then he began adding his own Chinese labels, talking as he did so. Once, his hand touched the ink while still wet and smeared it, but he took no notice.

"This is the morning sun," Fan interpreted. ."It comes in here, so it is logical the roof is like this. We like these roofs that are doing this. This is the first thing we noticed about the camp. It seems illogical at first. But we find it very appealing. We like what it does with the light….And here is the setting sun coming from here. The evening light. This is the place to spend the evening…."

J.D. ALT

Xu was drawing now over the space below the main pavil-ion—the place where the bridge crossed the stream. I watched him draw a watery shape for the stream, draw the floor deck span-ning above it. Then on the other side of the stream he drew a square with a circle in it. His pen was carefully labeling the parts in delicate Chinese calligraphy as he spoke.

"This is the stone bath," Fan interpreted. "The water is made very hot. The bridge becomes a pavilion by which you enter the bath. Here is a little part of the bridge that makes a table for the hot rice-wine. A small cabinet for warm towels. There should be lanterns here and here. They should be lighted early so as the evening light fades, they come alive, like magic."

I watched and listened, fascinated. Mr. Xu was totally immersed in imagining this scene. I glanced up at CM. He was watching, a pensive excitement in his eyes.

Xu put the top back on his pen and slid it into the pocket of his jump-suit. He pushed the paper tablet toward me with a broad smile, saying something quickly.

"Do you like it?" said Fan.

I studied the drawing. "Yes!" I said. "I like it very much!" I looked at Xu and bowed with a sincerity that took me by surprise. "Please thank Mr. Xu very much for his advice. It is a fantastic idea."

Fan translated. Xu beamed and bowed back to me.

"I only have one question," I said. "Please ask Mr. Xu how they heat the water in the stone bath. The stream," I nodded in the direction of its tumbling sound, "is very cold."

Fan passed this on. Mr. Xu listened then spoke rapidly in turn. He made a dropping motion with his hands.

"Mr. Xu says they heat big stones in a fire and drop them in the water. That is why it is called a stone bath."

"Oh!" I said, surprised. "I guess that would work." I was already wondering how I would carry the stones down from the fireplace.

Back on the veranda at the fish camp there were, of course, more bows and smiles. Mr. Xu spoke at some length, ending with what, even in Chinese, I could tell was a succinct statement directed at CM.

"Mr. Xu thanks you for the tour," Fan interpreted. "He understands now about the Enabling Structure, as you call it. This is very interesting he thinks. It makes for a very interesting architecture game. There is only one thing he is uncertain about: The idea that you believe this is the most efficient way to build. With all respect, Mr. Xu believes this is not efficient at all, but— with all respect—it is very inefficient."

The smile faded from CM's face.

Then quickly returned and spread slowly into his big grin.

"I have a presentation that explains that," he said. "It's a bit long and rather boring. But perhaps Mr. Xu would like to see it."

Fan translated.

An equally warm expression spread across Mr. Xu's round face. He nodded forcefully to CM and spoke quickly.

"Mr. Xu would be most appreciative of that. He would like all the delegation to see it as well. We're all in related fields," Fan explained.

"Related fields?" CM asked.

"We all work in the Beijing Ministry of Housing," said Fan. "In various departments."

CM's eyebrows went up high. "In that case," he said, "we should make it a formal presentation. I would be most honored. Would tomorrow night be appropriate?"

Fan translated, Xu smiled and bowed.

Although I didn't know it then, the date had just been established for CM's first and only public lecture.

31

THE NEXT AFTERNOON I HELPED CM arrange the river-room furniture in a grouping facing out into the gallery. He'd brought up from the studio an old Kodak slide projector with a round carousel of 35mm slides. He set the projector up on a side table we located behind the seating arrangement. One by one, CM removed the slides, held each up to the bright window wall, blew dust off it, then held it up again.

"It's been a few years since I put this lecture together," he said. "I wonder if the bulb still works."

He plugged in the projector and flicked the switch. A dim square of light appeared on the gallery wall accompanied by a loud fan noise.

"Loud bugger, isn't it?" CM said. "We need to take those pictures down from the wall—and get some books to raise this up on," he said.

We fiddled for a few minutes with the set up.

"Where was it that you gave this lecture?" I asked.

"I never have given it," he said. "Randolph Scott planned that we'd give it at the University. We put it together for that. But in the end, he decided it wasn't safe. The Dean wanted a full resume and credentials for all guest lecturers. He was a stickler for procedure. That created difficulties, of course. I told Randolph to make the presentation himself. But he didn't think that was right. So we put it on the shelf, waiting for a new Dean, I guess. A pretty dusty shelf, it turns out." He pulled out another slide and blew on it.

"You mean you've never given it at all? Ever?"

"Oh, I've practiced it often enough. Sometimes I'd set it up and give it to myself. There were times that helped me keep going. Helped me feel like what I was doing was part of the world, you know? But that's been a while back. Since the competition announcement, I've stayed pretty focused on that."

"So what exactly is the lecture about?" I asked.

"It's about Brasilia."

"Brasilia?'

"The capital of Brazil—the country. They built it back in the 1950's. It was an experimental city. A utopian city."

"So how exactly is Brasilia applicable to…"

"What we're doing?"

"Right."

"Well," CM smiled. "Just like Mr. Xu yesterday, everyone says, 'I can see what you're doing but I can't see why you'd be doing it that way. That's the reason we put together this presentation. If you understand how Brasilia was created, and what the results were, and what the alternative could have been, you'll understand why we built the fish camp the way we did—what the experiment was all about."

After the projector was set up to CM's satisfaction, we went out on the cooking deck to get things ready for the cook-out. We were laying the firewood in the grill when Louise suddenly emerged on the deck flapping her dishtowel like a distress flag.

"Those durn Chinese have been moving the furniture around!" she said.

"No, no!" CM said. "We did that, Louise. We're having a lecture tonight!"

"A lecture?"

"Yep. Tonight's a special lecture night. Have we got something special for the grill?"

It turned out Louise did have something special, since it was their last night at the fish camp, and it turned out to be quite a dinner party. After the cocktails and the grilling, the delegation, once again, engaged in their elaborate process for assigning seats around the big dining table—a process which depended, initially, on where CM chose to sit. Mr. Xu then took his place to the right of CM. Fan took his place to the left. The others with much chatter, finger pointing and head bows, negotiated the remaining chairs, leaving places for Maggie and me. A handsome fellow with slicked, black wavy hair, a starched white shirt and crisp purple tie, held the back of Maggie's chair. His eyes were all over her as she approached. This, I suspected, had been one of her charges for the day.

The big lazy-susan was filled with the plates of grilled meats and fish and stacks of steaming corn, husked except for the last pale green layer. Louise had added a big, wooden bowl of salad with bright red tomato slices. Gus did the rounds with his white-toweled arm and two wine bottles. CM started the food turning and stopped it with the plates of meat and fish in front of Mr. Xu.

In celebration of their last night at the camp, dinner quickly turned into a Chinese toasting game. If you happened to look up, there was someone at the table waiting to catch your eye, holding up their wine glass in salute. Soon, humorous toasts commenced, the delegation poking fun at each other's fishing and floating exploits.

When Louise put out the plates of strawberry shortcake, Xu arose and formally presented CM with a gift, thanking him for the hospitality of the fish camp. It was a large bottle of clear, Chinese liquor which was quickly opened. Sam distributed high-ball glasses around the table, and another round of toasts began—a formal drinking game, this time, punctuated by the phrase "Gahn-Bai!" and much laughter. Apparently "Gahn-Bai!" meant bottoms-up, since that was what was required each time the phrase was invoked.

It was a raucous crowd that finally made its way into the river room for CM's lecture. They arranged themselves in the chairs, still laughing at each other's toasts and misdeeds. Xu and Fan sat at the front, only slightly more sober. I was wondering whether this was going to work. The mood didn't seem exactly oriented toward a lecture about the architecture of Brasilia.

CM, however, was full of enthusiasm. His eyes were shining with excitement—and also, likely, with the Chinese liquor. Standing next to me he surveyed the group taking their seats.

"They're all drunk, Charlie," he said with amusement. "It may be a blessing." He looked around the room. "Where's Maggie?" he asked.

"I guess in the kitchen."

"Will you get her? I want Maggie to hear the lecture too. It's important."

When I got back to the river room with Maggie, CM was stringing a long cord with a control button on the end from the projector to the front of the room.

He smiled at Maggie. "This is for Randolph," he said. "I wanted you to be here."

Maggie froze for a moment. Then she nodded and walked toward an empty seat near the back. I started after her but CM stopped me.

"Charlie, I need you to sit by the projector in case there's a problem. Okay?"

So I positioned myself at the very back, behind the projector. CM turned off the lights, except for the one that was used to illuminate Louise's cookies. A big glass of water sat on the low table. A few chairs squeaked as people got comfortable.

CM Cleared his throat and took a sip of the water.

"By way of introduction," he began in a voice oddly different than his own, "I was telling Mr. Xu yesterday morning" (a nod toward Xu and Fan) "that my colleague Randolph Scott—Maggie's father (a nod toward Maggie, who's shoulders scrunched up suddenly at his acknowledgement)—who recently passed away, to our great loss—and I have spent the last decade or so building this fish camp as an experiment—a very small, experimental version of a new strategy for building the kind of settlements we believe the future world is going to require.

"Our experiment has been based on the counter-intuitive conclusion that cities must begin to grow with a decidedly horizontal rather than vertical density. There are essentially two reasons for this. The first is the Olduvai Theorem which postulates an irreversible and accelerating decline in fossil fuels starting in the year 2030. This decline will inevitably require human habitation to spread out, so to speak, under the only primary energy source that will remain: the Sun.

"The second reason is socio-economic, and can be illustrated by what transpired in the building of the most ambitious socialist architectural experiment of the twentieth century: Brasilia. This will now be the topic of my presentation. Charlie, can you start the projector?"

I pushed the switch and the projector fan roared to life, sending a white square onto the wall beside CM. He took a sip of water, turned out the light, and pushed the remote button, startling me with a slight rotation and loud KERCHUNK from the projector carousel. The image, large and bright on the wall, was the photo of an enormous, ultra-modern high-rise apartment building. Under it was the title:

BRASILIA: THE FAILED UTOPIA OF THE 20TH CENTURY
BY: RANDOLPH SCOTT & CHARLES McCORMICK

I am able here to give a complete account of the lecture because I'm not just working from memory, but from a manuscript I managed to save with the same title as above. It's open on my desk as I write the following account.

After clearing his throat again, CM launched himself into a professorial voice that seemed to enlarge the darkened frame of his body.

"Brasilia, you will recall, is the modernist utopian city built from scratch on the barren central plain of Brazil in the late 1950's. It was the brainchild of President Juscelino Kubitschek who pledged that the project would thrust Brazil onto the world stage as a leader of modern social-economic development.

"What truly turned out to be remarkable about Brasilia, however, was something entirely unintended by Kubitschek, and unanticipated by his government. What was truly remarkable was not that they succeeded in building the city in only four years," KERCHUNK, "nor the graceful, modernist urban plan by Luis Costa," KERCHUNK, "or the pristine modernist high-rise apartment towers and government offices by Oscar Niemeyer",

KERCHUNK, KERCHUNK, "—though these were, in fact, much remarked upon, and endlessly photographed at the city's inauguration in April, 1960."

The audible participation of the old Kodak projector was almost like a percussion accompaniment to the presentation. Even so, I thought I detected someone already snoring in the midst of the delegation. What this presentation needed, I was thinking, was music, something to keep people awake.

"What was, in fact, remarkable about Brasilia," CM continued, "was what transpired during the last twelve months or so leading up to that inauguration." KERCHUNK. (Here the projected image was of something that, on first impression, looked like a trash-heap, until you realized there were people sitting on chairs inside it.)

"But first, a short history. To achieve the ambitious construction schedule, the Brazilian government engaged a very large work force." KERCHUNK. "These workers came from the unemployed masses of the cities and rural countryside. They were attracted to Brasília by high wages, long work hours, a chance to start out as laborers and quickly ascend to skilled technicians making ten, twenty or a hundred times what they could ever have dreamed of previously. This workforce proudly referred to themselves as 'Candangos'—pioneers. At the height of construction, this community of labor peaked at something over 40,000 workers.

"These tens of thousands of workers were initially housed in carefully managed tent camps where the government provided meals and bath facilities. A special area, known as the Free Zone, was established for non-government entrepreneurs to set up businesses to serve the workers. Bars and brothels and clothiers set up shop," KERCHUNK "and later, the workers families began to arrive, swelling the Free Zone with boarding houses and tenements." KERCHUNK, KERCHUNK. "As the utopian city churned toward completion, its population of construction-worker families and Free Zone entrepreneurs grew to exceed a hundred thousand people."

CM took a sip of water. I snuck a glance at Maggie. She seemed to be sitting forward in her chair, tense, frozen in place.

KERCHUNK. We're looking at the image of a lake.

"This is a current view of Brasilia's Free Zone. You'll note that it's under water. Eighteen months or so before the scheduled inauguration, the Free Zone entrepreneurs were reminded by the government that their leases stipulated they would pack up and leave three months prior to the ceremonial opening of the city. This dismantling was rendered unavoidable by the fact that the Free Zone had been intentionally located in the bed of what was to be the city's recreational lake.

"An inevitable and unsettling comprehension began to coalesce in the minds of the entrepreneurial and Candango workers and their families: Brasilia was being built for someone other than them! They were not going to move into the pristine apartment towers with the running hot and cold water, the tiled showers and electric refrigerators. They were not going to drive down the wide boulevards, and shop in the modernist commissaries or play bocce in the green parks. They were not going to set up shops and restaurants along the commercial avenue. What they had spent the past three and a half years slavishly building, in fact, was for someone else. What was for them was a slow rise of lake water around their ankles and knees until they were forced to pack up and go back to the slums or tilled fields they'd come from. It was not a question of fairness. It was a question of Utopia.

"And then a strange thing happened." KERCHUNK.

"Illegal settlements began to appear overnight, scattered around the pristine city like mushrooms sprouting after a heavy rain." KERCHUNK..... KERCHUNK. "Before the government knew what was happening, these settlements quickly connected and coalesced into sprawling, chaotic flavellas. They were constructed of discarded materials from Brasilia itself: broken boards and pilfered plywood forms, torn tar-paper, chipped blocks of concrete, rejected bricks, slabs of bent corrugated metal…combined with mud and stones from the land. The determined and creative ingenuity of the workers in acquiring and adapting these materials to create shelter was remarkable."

KERCHUNK...KERCHUNK...A series of slides, in silence, documenting CM's last statement. A wall made of 55 gallon drums cut in half lengthwise. A roof made of discarded plywood concrete forms. A window—embellished with a stained-glass Madonna—framed in the shell of a broken, pre-cast concrete manhole.

"Of course, this creative energy was not appreciated by the Brazilian government. They were mortified—terrified in fact—at the prospect of inaugurating their new socio-economic utopia, and having the international press drive through miles of sprawling, chaotic, impoverished slums to arrive at the event. Imagine it!"

CM pauses, letting everyone imagine this. He takes a long drink of water.

"The irony here, of course, is that Kubishchek and Costa and Niemeyer all missed a huge opportunity—and the modernist movement of architecture, obviously, misunderstood what really is the essential ingredient of a human utopia."

A hand suddenly shoots up from the middle of the delegation.

"Mr. McCormick! May I ask a question please?"

CM was as startled as I was. He stared out against the glare of the projector, shielding his eyes.

"It is Lui Yan, sir." He stands up.

"Yes, of course, Mr. Yan… Please feel free to ask questions at any time...I forgot to say that at the beginning."

"What is the opportunity you are suggesting they missed?"

CM smiles. "I was getting to that," he says. "But let's just jump right to it! Think of it like this: Here's a hundred thousand people who desperately want to build a community to live in. They've got skills, they've got energy, they're highly motivated. Just look at what they did, in fact, accomplish with essentially nothing—no real building materials, no real tools to speak of, no financing, no help or assistance whatsoever. Now, just imagine what they might have been able to build if Kubichek and Costa and Neimeyer had just given them...how shall I introduce the idea? A framework to build within…. What we call an 'Enabling Structure.'"

"But Mr. McCormick," Yan is still standing. "In Beijing there are thirteen million people. We have been building housing 24 hours a day since I can remember. Every night Beijing looks like the 4th of July in America. Are we shooting fireworks? No. We are welding steel. Thousands of welders, thirty stories in the night sky, welding sparks in the darkness. We cannot build housing fast enough! We need 48 hours in every day. So, with all respect, if you are suggesting that the people of Beijing should just start building their own housing....Well, that would be catastrophic! It would be chaos! It could not begin to achieve the efficiency of the modernist construction machine."

"I understand what you are saying," CM replied. "Charlie, can you turn off the projector please?"

I hit the switch and the room went dark. CM turned on a lamp next to his water glass, and here we all were again, sitting together in the camp room—except for Yan, who looks around now and self-consciously sits down.

"I appreciate what you are saying," CM says, nodding in Yan's direction. "But we have come to the conclusion there is a middle way to building high-density—a horizontal way—and there is a way to do it that is very efficient, much more efficient, in fact, than vertical development. All of that welding is happening because you are building upward—as you say, thirty, forty stories in the air. All of that steel and enormous concrete work is happening because you are carrying huge point loads down to the earth. If you build only two or three stories high, you do not need welded steel frames. You can build lightly. You can build with simplicity."

Another hand shoots up. CM fields the question with a gesture like a talk-show moderator.

"Mr. McCormick, sir, with all due respect. Isn't horizontal sprawl precisely what we are trying to avoid? It uses up the land and destroys the fields for agriculture."

"Yes, good!" CM is starting to get energized by the give and take of the questions. "These are exactly the points I want to address now. If you will bear with me...."

Fan stands now in front and turns toward the delegation. "Mr. Xu requests that Mr. McCormick be allowed to finish his presentation."

"No, no!" CM objects. "I appreciate the questions! Please ask any questions….Are there any more?" CM looks around the room. There are no more questions. This slightly deflates his energy. I'm thinking I should ask a question, to keep him going, but can't think of what to ask.

"There is a difference," CM is trying to transition now back to his presentation voice, "a very big difference, between what we think of as sprawl and the kind horizontal density we are suggesting. That is what I would like to share with you now—what Randolph Scott's students so aptly demonstrated could have happened in Brazilia. Charlie? The projector?"

KERCHUNK. The room goes dark again, the delegation's heads are silhouettes against the bright image on the wall. Then a loud POP! And the wall goes black.

"Charlie?" The lamp comes on again next to CM's water glass.

"I think the bulb popped," I said, pushing the projector switch up and down.

CM looks at me in dismay, his mouth open slightly as if he's about to speak.

"I think it's gone," I said. I could smell the burned bulb now.

Maggie was turned, looking at me. I lifted my hands in futility.

"Isn't there a spare?" she whispers.

I rummaged through the old cardboard box we'd taken the projector out of. No bulb.

"Well," CM is saying, "we have to apologize here…. I guess I'll have to conclude as best I can."

Fan stands again. "Mr. Xu says there is no need to apologize. We are very appreciative of what you have shown us."

"Thank you," CM bowed toward Fan. "What I was going to show you next specifically answered, I think, the question of efficiency…."

But the presentation was over. People started scooting their chairs, standing, a few coming over and peering down into the slide projector, shaking their heads, as if viewing an accident. Xu and Fan were talking with CM whose smile was valiantly trying to maintain its energy. But I could see the disappointment in his shoulders, in the slack way his hands hung at his side. And Maggie, in the midst of the confusion, had somehow vanished completely.

32

IT TOOK A FEW DAYS for CM to get his energy level back, but it arrived with renewed force and determination. And the first result was that I learned how a water-flute works. CM, with mischievous and mysterious excitement, presented me with what he said was the "essential accoutrement" for my unit: one of the fish-head sculptures I'd first noticed on Maggie's initial tour—the junk-metal gargoyles, made by her father, that she'd called "Zarathustra".

"This was actually the first one he made," CM said. "It was the experimental model. He refurbished it just before he got sick."

It was about six feet long and surprisingly light—mostly hollow. A welded cage of metal bars formed the head structure, with junk-metal sheets forming the skin and the details of the fins and gills. The oversized welded-washer eyes gave it a surprised, staring expression.

Inside the cage were a series of black plastic plumbing pipes joined together with plastic pipe elbows and tees. Dried globs of glue hung from some of the joints. One end of a plastic pipe—maybe three inches in diameter—ended just inside the edge of the of upturned, pooching fish-mouth. Another open end—much larger in diameter—protruded out the back. Where the fish's side fins would be, heavy welded bars protruded—a handle on each side so two people could carry it easily between them.

"Let's take it down to the beach," said CM. "The only way to get it to the chute is by drift boat."

"The chute?"

"It has to be tuned before you put it up on your roof." He gave me a wink. "Maggie will have to help you do it. Randolph Scott always gave her the assignment."

I anticipated, of course, the usual push-back from Maggie at the prospect of helping me do anything with my unit. But she surprised me.

"You what?" she asked, her voice rising.

"I need you to help me tune my fish-head."

"Where'd you get a fish-head?"

"CM gave it to me."

She became animated with excitement. "Let me see it. Where is it?"

I took her down to the beach where CM and I had leaned the sculpture against one of the pontoon drift boats. Its protruding eye-balls seemed to be watching us as we approached. Maggie reached out and touched it with reverence.

"I remember this one," she said. "That was a long time ago. I wondered what happened to it."

As Maggie explained it, the principle of the water-flute is simple: Water rushes through a tube, its motion sucking in air to accompany it —a venturi effect. The water is pushing air out in front of it and so has to pull air in behind to replace the air it's pushing out. If you can direct this incoming replacement air over the aperture of an air chamber—like blowing across a beer-bottle—you can cause that chamber of air to resonate. Thus, the mindless movement of rapidly flowing water can be made to simulate the lungs of a jug-band player.

Even more interesting, as Maggie's father discovered, you can split the air over a second resonating aperture, creating a double note. If you adjust the size of the apertures, you can "tune" this pair of notes. And if you were musically inclined, you could even create a harmonic—two notes that resonated in complement—creating a complex "super-note" that could be heard for a great distance over, say, the sound of a rushing white-water river.

"We have to take it to Zarathustra's Pool to tune it," she said. "That's where the tuning chute is."

"So what is this chute thing?"

"You'll see," said Maggie. "You're going to like this Charlie. You're going to really like this!"

Thus I found myself, the next morning, helping Maggie drag one of the drift boats out to the edge of the river. The boat was essentially two inflated banana-shaped pontoons, dark blue, with a tube-metal frame strapped on top. The metal frame supported a webbed floor and three sitting stations. The seats at the front and the rear were raised, and could swivel. These were for the fishermen, high and swiveling so they could turn and cast in different directions. The middle seat was low and fixed. This is where the guide sat, who rowed or, more accurately, steered the boat through the running river with oars that pivoted on the metal frame.

Maggie and I lashed the fish-head against the rear seat with the boat's anchor line, tying multiple knots to secure it in place.

Maggie reached into the boat and tossed out a pair of felt bottomed canvas shoes.

"I brought the waders too," she said. "Do you want those?"

"I'm fine like this, aren't' I?" I said. "We're going to be in the boat, right?"

"Hopefully," she laughed. "But you'll at least need the shoes when we get to the pool."

While I tied on the shoes, Maggie repeated the odd ceremony of unzipping the inseam of her khaki nylon pants—this time only partially—rolling them up to her knees.

We pushed into the water and I climbed into the forward seat. Maggie took the middle position and the oars. She turned us down river with the current.

"I thought you didn't do drift boats!" I said back over my shoulder.

"I don't do them," she said. "But I know how to do them. You can't help but pick it up, even if you don't want to fish that way."

"But this is great!" I shouted back.

And it was. Being in the middle of the river, flowing along with it, was completely different from slogging along the trails on the bank. It was like being the kite instead of just holding the string.

"You're telling me you don't think this is great?" I said, turning to look over my shoulder.

She flashed a smile. "It's not the boats I disapprove of," she said. "Get ready, here comes the first rapids!"

I turned around and observed that we were being carried slightly sideways now towards a rocky patch where the river sluiced in different paths around and through a series of large boulders. One path was particularly turbulent, with standing white waves splashing in the sunlight. I could feel Maggie tugging at the oars, turning the boat, pushing it across the current, across the mouth of the turbulent section. We glanced off a rock and my stomach tightened up. Her oar banged on another rock, and we glided smoothly into a peaceful section that slid around the left side of the turbulent white-water. That wasn't so bad, I thought. Ahead was a placid section of the river, a fluttering green-yellow wall of trees on either side of a blue slice of sky.

"You did that really nice," I said, looking over my shoulder.

"Just remember, Charlie. I forgot to tell you. If you go in, for any reason, even if for fun, go downstream feet first. Use your hands and elbows under you to keep your head up. Fend off the rocks with your feet."

"Okay," I said, but there was something about this advice that began filling a secret compartment just under my diaphragm with alarm. I tried to focus my eyes on the green shore-line, just above the water.

"This is where we practiced casting when you first came, remember?"

I looked around, but it seemed unfamiliar.

"We're coming up to where we caught the disciple."

I searched ahead. Yes. There was the huge fallen log I'd hidden behind. I recognized it! And here we came, the strengthening current sluicing us sideways again, making my stomach twist as if it were trying to steer the boat, and Maggie cranked across with the oars to the rapids at the head of the pool. The boat bounced, once, twice, like a rocking horse, and we slid into the pool itself where the fish had jumped, and I'd gone under. My grip on the tube frame was tightening.

"How much farther?" I asked over my shoulder.

"Just a couple of bends. And a class three before the chute."

"What's a class three?" I asked over my shoulder. The river was making a wide, slow turn to the left. I tried to focus my attention on the wall of forest to the right.

"They rank them," said Maggie. "Sort of like hurricanes. Class one is what we did a few minutes ago."

The chamber of dread under my diaphragm began to blossom and balloon. "So, what's a class three?"

"It's just a bit trickier. A bit bumpier. You might get a splash in your face, Charlie!"

I looked over my shoulder. Maggie was smiling intently, anticipating something, looking ahead. She'd dropped her sunglasses over her eyes.

"So maybe we should stop and kind of…?"

The sound arrived just in the middle of my question. The rushing white noise of a big rapids. I turned forward. The river was beginning to turn back to the right now and up ahead I could see a chaos of boulders and foamy water.

Maggie began pushing us over to the right of the standing white-water. I could see a clear undulating ribbon of the river that ducked behind a large boulder. A sudden current caught the boat and twisted it sharply sideways. I glanced over my left shoulder, expecting us to slide backwards into the maelstrom, my hands tugging at the sides of the seat frame, pulling instinctively to the right. Maggie pushed hard, and hard again with her left oar and we nosed around, sweeping with the clear current now, going with it wherever it was going to take us into the rushing noise. I stuck my feet out on the nose of the raft, preparing to collide with the boulder that was coming at me like an asteroid through sun-sparkling spray.

Swhoosh! It was literally that sound. Bang!-the slap of Maggie's oar against another rock on the right, and the boulder flashed by my left shoulder as we dropped, shooting into the pool below like a landing sea-plane.

"So that's a three," said Maggie.

I stared straight ahead, daring not to turn around, my heart racing in my head, my stomach frozen in a twisted knot.

"You okay, Charlie?"

I didn't answer. I was filling up with something, an anger that I couldn't fathom.

"Charlie?"

I rotated in the seat and faced her. "You did that on purpose," I said.

She looked up at me, grinning. Tried to turn her grin downward. Then broke out laughing.

"You guys are all nuts," I said, swerving my chair back to face the front. "I swear, you're all nuts."

We drifted aimlessly in the slow pool.

"Hey, Charlie? I'm sorry. I guess I could have…"

"Could have what?"

"Well, I mean, usually, I suppose, Gus…"

"Gus what?"

"Sort of gets people ready…you know?"

"Ready for what?" I said.

"Well, ready to go around that boulder like that. I mean it's really pretty safe. A lot safer than it seems, I suppose, if you know what's coming."

"Okay," I said. "That's good."

"Charlie?"

I heard her dip the oars into the water and the boat nosed out into the current again. The slow, easy current. Ahead, the river was almost like a mirror. The wall of green-yellow trees and the blue slice of sky—with a recently arrived puffy cloud—all were reflected upside down on the watery surface, floating like a chalk-painting on a wide, mirrored sidewalk.

"I'm sorry, Charlie," Maggie said again. "I really am….Forgive me?'

"Forgive you for what?"

She was rowing now, moving the pontoons forward through the painted liquid of the water. Then the current picked up again, and the chalk painting dissipated with a rippling restlessness.

Maggie steered over to the left as the current picked up speed, and soon the white rush of another rapids could be heard.

"We don't classify the chute," she said. "We walk around it. Only kayakers can do it."

"Well don't hesitate on my behalf," I said, puzzled by the knot still tied inside my chest. I really wanted to get past this, but my mouth somehow wouldn't give it up. "Didn't we bring a kayak?"

33

WE PULLED THE FRONT OF the drift boat up on the rocky beach and untied the fish-head from its perch on the rear seat. Maggie pulled a fair-sized, rusty crescent wrench from a small tool box in the boat. "Will this fit in your pocket?" she asked.

"What's it for?"

"You'll see."

"Why is everything a mystery?" I said. "Why are you always setting me up to laugh at?"

She looked at me in surprise, lifting her sunglasses into her hair. "I'm not laughing at you."

"You've been laughing at me ever since we got in the boat."

"Charlie! You can't believe I'm laughing at you?"

"What're you doing then?"

"I'm just enjoying you." She lifted the small anchor out of the boat and carried it up the beach until the line was taught. She wedged the anchor into the rocks.

"I enjoy you, Charlie. You bring me joy," she said, looking at me. Then she dropped her sunglasses back onto her nose.

We toted the fish-head down a path through the white-barked Alder trees, and I was trying to remember, trying to understand, what it was she'd just said. The sound of the water was intense, and just before the path descended steeply, we cut off to the right. A formation of large boulders jumbled together here, splitting the river into separate, rushing slews, and we climbed carefully toward the formation, each of us holding one of the iron bars of the sculpture, its weight balancing easily between us. Off to our left, the cascading crash of the water dropping into the pool was loud and pulsing. At the base of the rock formation, we stopped and rested. Parts of the river were sliding all around and under us, but a big section of water was being steered through the chute.

Maggie climbed up first. I lifted the fish-head up to her then climbed up beside her. The chute was about four feet wide, between the relatively flat tops of two enormous slabs of rock. The water is churning through this slot, then shooting out and free-falling into a large and almost perfectly round pool about ten or twelve feet below. The pool is a transparent blue-green with sunlight and shadows rippling around in its depth. Huge, ancient fir trees, shaggy and silent, lean out high above it. Then I notice, through the down-river opening in the trees, a distant bridge with heavy X-shaped timbers, spanning the water.

"I'm seeing a bridge," I said.

"That's the bridge across to the trail-head," said Maggie. "It's the one we drive across to get to the fish camp. It's where we pull out."

"Pull out?"

"Well, Charlie," she looked at me, trying carefully to control her amusement, "How do you think we're going to get back? Row?"

I was stunned to realize I hadn't even given this particular detail any thought.

"So how are we going to get back?"

"We carry the boat around the chute, float down to the bridge, and pull out. Gus will have dropped off a vehicle this morning on the way to his put-in spot—probably the Cherokee, since it's me. It's like clock-work! This is basically what the fish camp does up and down the rivers every day."

I absorbed this obvious idea, understanding suddenly the entire logistics of river fishing.

"So you ready, Charlie?"

"Okay," I said. "Show me how this works."

"One of us has to be on each side of the chute," Maggie said.

"So we're going to put this in the water?"

"That's why we're here. We've got to get the water going through the pipes."

"But how can we hold it?" I was gauging the force of the water as it swept between the rocks.

"Look," she nodded down at the rock. "This is the spot my dad made for doing this. It's where they all got tuned."

Deep slots had been chiseled into the rock on each side of the chute. I could see the iron bars we'd been using as handles on each side of the fish-head would fit into these slots—holding the head in a suspended position within the rushing water.

"I'll go across," said Maggie. Without hesitation or calculation, she sprang across the wide slot, landing nimbly and balanced on the other side.

"Okay, reach the other handle across to me," she said.

I stepped toward the edge, holding the fish-head in both arms, and extended it across to her outstretched hands. She grabbed the handle on her side.

"So, we're going to lower it slowly," she said. "But don't let it touch the water. The water will grab it fast, right? And take it. So we lower it slowly above the notches—just a few inches back, behind the notches, right? Then when I say 'drop', we just drop it, okay? The water will catch it, and push it right into the notches."

"Jeez, Maggie! This seems…tenuous."

"We've never lost one. It works perfect."

"But, I mean, what if…."

"Are you ready? Just lower it slowly to a place about three inches back…close to the water, closer…. Back a little more. Now, when I say drop just let go. Okay?"

"Okay."

"Drop!"

And the fish-head fell into the chute and lurched to a sudden stop, its metal bar handles embedded deep in the chiseled slots, just as Maggie had predicted.

The next event caught me by surprise even though I was expecting it: The fish-head began spewing a white arc of water far out over the pool, like a fire-hose.

"Now I need the wrench," Maggie said.

On her knees, one hand on the sculpture's dorsal fin for balance, she reached into the metal cage of the fish-head, and started turning something. Very subtly at first, a sound began to rise eerily above the pool. It didn't seem to be emanating from the fish-head, but from all around—from the air itself. It grew louder and higher.

Maggie leaned deeper beside the fish-head, cranking the crescent wrench in the foaming water, adjusting her knees to keep her balance. Suddenly, the airy voice of the first sound was joined by another lower one. Maggie cranked some more and the lower sound wavered and disappeared. The higher note continued on alone.

She cranked the crescent wrench again and the second note came back, sliding upward like a ghost—and the two sounds linked, combined into a single voice, and suddenly it was like someone had spun the volume control all the way over. Completely detached from the shooting display of water, the air above and all around us was resonating and pulsating with a pure, hovering complex musical note—as if the sky itself had begun to hum a deep mantra.

Maggie sat back on her side of the chute, and put the crescent wrench against her cheek, listening. I watched her in amazement. Then I saw that tears were flowing down her cheeks. But she wasn't crying. She was listening.

After a while, she wiped her cheeks with her fingers and smiled strangely at me. "What do you think, Charlie?" she said, raising her voice above the humming air. "The first time I heard that, I was ten years old."

We listened a few more minutes, then Maggie said we should pull it out.

"We do it on the count of three," she said. "Pull it straight up all at once. Ready? One. Two. Three!"

And up we stood, the fish-head between us above the chute, as if we'd just caught a world record, the air instantly going quiet again, only the sound of the chute free-falling into the pool. Maggie leaned toward me, and I took the weight of it to my side, and she let go. I set it down on the top of the boulder.

She sprang back across to my side, landing slightly off balance, and I grabbed her arm to steady her. She looked up at me, startled. Then she's looking over my shoulder, her eyes registering something with alarm.

I turned to see what she's looking at.

Sitting on the distant bridge, supported above the very center of the heavy timber X-bracing, is a long black sedan with dark reflective windows, the bright noon sunlight glinting dully on its roof.

"That's the strangest car I've ever seen here," said Maggie.

We stared at it. And the blank windows seemed to stare back at us. Then, as if it had seen what it came for, the slinky black length of it rolled slowly across the bridge toward the main road and disappeared.

34

I'D BEGUN HOPING THE DESIGN competition had just been a bizarre ploy to get me to stay at the fish camp. July and August had passed and CM had never directly mentioned the competition again. Only his occasional, cryptic references to "The Team" kept the topic in the back of my mind.

Other than his Seattle visits, to which he often carried rolls of drawings and returned with boxes of building model parts, there was little indication CM was working on anything at all. He seemed to float through the days without purpose, sometimes visiting me up on the hill, sometimes holed up in his studio with the door closed, sometimes sitting on the veranda, sketching and writing in his little black books. At dinner, on the cooking deck, he seemed to wake-up, engaging the guests in conversation and argument. Then, after dark, he'd often disappear again down into his studio.

For me, the late summer had fallen into a relaxed routine. I worked in the mornings, when it was cool, at the special project by my little bridge. This was not my favorite work: it involved digging and laying stone and mortar instead of shooting nails with the Paslode gun. It involved piping and some valves, none of which I knew much about, but CM sketched out the basics of what I needed, and even showed me how to fit the parts together. He alluded to the fact that what I was doing was illegal in terms of the fish camp building strategy—people building with an Enabling Structure weren't supposed to be doing any digging or piping, they were only supposed to be building spaces—but that he'd allow it under the special circumstances. I'd stopped trying to attract or coerce Maggie's assistance; in fact, I did not want her to see what I was doing until it was finished. She seemed to be gone more often now anyway: there were hearings taking place in Port Angeles about the State Hatchery policies, and she was stalking the venues with her petition.

I was reminded of Maggie's extracurricular activities one afternoon when I drove into Forks to get some umbrella nails for the last section of metal roofing I was putting up over the sleep-loft. I seldom had any reason to go into town. I'd been up in the deep forest of the fish camp long enough now that I was actually surprised when the asphalt road, winding down the mountain, began encountering signs of civilization. The clear-cut logging areas came first. When I hit the main highway, there was a saw-mill operation off to the left I hadn't noticed before. Then came the motels leading into the main street of Forks.

As I rolled past the Stardust Café, I glanced to my left half expecting to see the surly group of sullen men still leaning against the blue wall, flicking their burning matches and cigarette butts into the gravel parking lot. This premonition was fulfilled when I pushed open the door to the hardware store and saw the clerk, standing behind the counter like a Paul Bunyan monument: He was the same bearded giant who'd joined them to watch me change that last tire on Maggie's Cherokee.

He watched me come in and I knew he recognized me right away. He leaned forward stiff-armed on the counter, his huge shoulders bunching up, glaring at me.

I nodded to him and he nodded back.

"I'm looking for some umbrella nails," I said.

He tilted his head to the side, toward the back of the store. "Nails in the back."

"Thanks," I said, and walked down the nearest aisle. Against the back wall I found a long shelf with boxes of nails. It took me a while to find the umbrella nails.

I followed a different aisle back out to the front. The giant clerk hadn't moved. Still leaning stiff-armed against the counter-top, watching me. I put two boxes of nails on the counter and pulled out my wallet. He still didn't move.

"You're the fish-girl's boyfriend," he said.

"I'm sorry. What?"

"You changed her tires for her."

Even though he was hunched over I had to look up at him.

"She's a friend," I said.

"Where're you from? Not around here."

"Actually, I'm from North Carolina."

"What are you doing up here, then?"

Involuntarily, I glanced out to the street expecting maybe to see someone crouching down around the Toyota letting the air out of the tires.

"I'm...just visiting for a while."

I pushed one of the boxes of nails a little bit toward him, hoping he'd pick it up and read the price. He didn't move.

"We like visitors here," he said.

"I'm glad to hear that."

"You know why?"

"Why you like visitors?"

"Because when it's time to go, they leave," he said.

"Well, that makes sense," I said. "Otherwise, I guess...."

His stare was flat, expressionless.

I pushed the box of umbrella nails a little closer to him and pulled some bills out of my wallet. He still didn't move.

"So," I said, pushing the second box of nails up close to the first, "are these nails here for sale?"

He straightened up like a mountainous statue suddenly finding motion. A huge paw of a hand with strangely calloused knuckles reached out and grasped the nearest box.

"You building something?" he said, poking the product code into the register.

"Just some repair work," I said. "Just keeping the water out, you know?"

"It'll start raining here before long," he said. "You ever seen it rain here?"

"I guess I've been visiting during the dry season."

He looked up from the register, a smile twitching the corners of his mouth.

"That's when visitors generally leave," he said, poking back at the register. "When it starts raining."

"I'll bet," I said.

I paid him and he gave me change, his thick fingers dispensing the bills and coins with surprising dexterity—even delicacy.

I stacked the boxes of nails against my arm and turned to go.

He spoke into my back, forcing me to stop and listen.

"The rest of us stay up here and make a living in the rain," he said. "That's what the rest of us do."

35

TO MY DISMAY, IT WAS not long after this encounter that I found myself standing in CM's studio reading aloud from a typed page that's balanced on the edge of the work table so that my hands are free to make appropriate and important gestures.

"Picture, if you will, the world's tallest building," I say, "and then imagine tipping it over and laying it on its side." I gesture with my hands as if I'm holding something very tall, grasping it at its bottom and top, and then rotating it gently, so it is now horizontal. "So now each floor of the building has one edge lying against the ground, right?" I do short karate chops indicating the floors. "Next, imagine slicing down the middle of this building lengthwise and folding those floors out to each side—exactly like you'd filet a fish." I slice and pull open, and spread out. "So now you have a wide, flat skyscraper, lying horizontal on the ground, with the floor spaces of the apartments and offices spread out on each side, and down the middle you have the long back-bone of its elevator shafts."

CM is sitting on one of the stools, elbow on the knee of his crossed leg, chin on his knuckles, eyes watching me over the tops of his wire-framed glasses. Maggie is standing next to a long, three-piece architectural model of New Hope, Iowa, which is supported on six folding trestles like an oversized, long-legged insect marching almost the entire length of the studio.

"Next we grab each end of this horizontal skyscraper and stretch it, just slightly—"

"Demonstrate," said CM.

"What?"

"Demonstrate, like this." He pulls his hands apart like he's stretching a sock.

"So we stretch it, just slightly," I say, mimicking his gesture.

"You know," Maggie interrupts, "I think there might be a better way to do this."

The previous day, CM had surprised us by returning from one of his trips to Seattle in a newly excited and energized state, with a tarp carefully secured over the bed of his old blue pick-up. We helped him unload the three sections of the model, carrying them one at a time down to the studio.

The model, I had to admit, was quite a beautiful and impressive thing. It was made of a combination of light-colored basswood and creamy-smooth, white cardboard. But its dominant colors, overall, were blue and green: the blue a complex and repetitive pattern of what were clearly solar collectors, and the green what were neatly organized gardens (tiny painted sponges in the model) interspersed, and integrated into the wood and cardboard forms of a mosaic of walls and columns.

CM explained that we were going to be presenting three very simple ideas—"none of which has anything to do with architecture," he emphasized, trying to give me a reassuring look. Maggie was watching this exchange with amusement, and I realized she was unaware of her intended role in this. I attempted to give her some warning signals with my eyebrows, but she seemed oblivious. I was amazed this was actually happening, that CM was going forward with this bizarre intention, and even more amazed to find myself participating.

"So when is the presentation?" Maggie asked.

CM gave her his big smile. "Three weeks," he said. "We have just enough time to get ourselves prepared and drive out there. You'll help, won't you Miggs? You can take some time off, can't you?"

Maggie still didn't seem to get it. "Sure, CM," she said. "I'll help. Of course! Tell me how I can help."

CM, turned his big smile on me, confirming this little victory.

At our first "Team Meeting", as CM insisted on calling it, he gave a brief outline of the three major ideas we'd be presenting.

The first idea was that the proposed new city was to be built as a "horizontal skyscraper." The backbone of this "skyscraper" was a horizontal elevator system which he called the "ZIPPER". This was an electric streetcar system that was powered by three hydrogen fuel cell generators—one at each end of the skyscraper, and one at the halfway point. The hydrogen, in turn, was generated from water using a cluster of solar cells rising in a vertical array above each generator.

The idea of the Horizontal Skyscraper was that people could drive cars to and from the city—just like they drive cars to and from a building—but once they were there, the cars remained parked, and people moved around in the city either by walking, biking, or by riding the ZIPPER. This was very convenient, CM pointed out, since no point in the Horizontal Skyscraper was more than 1200 feet from the backbone of the horizontal people-mover corridor, and a ZIPPER was available for boarding—going in either direction—every two minutes.

"It functions, literally, like a horizontal elevator," CM emphasized. "If you understand how people move around in a sky-scraper, you understand exactly how they'll get around in New Hope, Iowa. And," he added with emphasis, "you'll understand that the city, itself, will require no gasoline. That's important."

Idea number two was that the city was to be developed in two distinct phases—just like the fish camp. The first phase would construct an Enabling Structure that defined and organized the form of the Horizontal Skyscraper. The Enabling Structure for New Hope was unique in that each "building slot" within it would be equipped not only with the necessary foundation system for up to four levels of floor-space, but also an adjacent slot of garden space, which could, if desired, be trellised and terraced. Each slot also included, in addition to the hot-water panels and a photo-voltaic array, an integral rain-storage cistern with a small, solar-powered pump that fed a drip irrigation system.

The second phase of construction would consist of a piece-meal design-build process which would be undertaken by a multitude of New Hope individuals and small-business entrepreneurs. A new bank would be formed—THE NEW

HOPE CREDIT UNION—specifically to finance this piece-meal construction process.

"In essence, Charlie." CM observed, "each of these projects would be similar to what you're doing, right now, up on the hill. Right? So you should be able to present this with the voice of experience!" Big smile. I'm sure I returned this with a blank stare, since I recall feeling more or less numb the first time he went through all this.

The third idea was that the I-Mart was to be physically broken into twelve small, "sales units"—each dedicated to a specific category of merchandise—and these were to be interspersed with other business spaces along the commercial spine of the ZIPPER.

"I-Mart?" says Maggie with sudden interest. "What's I-Mart got to do with it?"

"Well… there's a few details I haven't gotten around to yet," CM says. He fidgets uncomfortably now and proposes we have some lunch over which the 'details' can be discussed.

So the "Team", as he's calling us now at every opportunity, adjourns to one of the small tables in the camp-house dining room. Louise brings in some sandwiches and CM starts going over the 'details'. There are basically two: The first is that one of the requirements of the competition is that the new city of New Hope should include, at a conspicuously central location in its business district, an I-Mart store. This had been presented as if the citizens of Hope had requested it. CM said he had his doubts about that.

"Maybe they did, though" said Maggie. "I would guess I-Mart's pretty popular in Iowa."

"That might be," said CM, "but there's another reason for this, I think." He looked at me, and I could tell there was something coming. The second detail was going to be something I didn't want to hear.

"I didn't know this when I entered the competition," CM said. He was explaining now to Maggie, his body language trying somehow to embrace her. "I supposed you knew, maybe, about why I came here to the river and stayed all these years? That Randolph told you?"

"Told me what?"

Maggie was staring at CM, trying to shift gears. "I only knew there was…some reason."

"I've told Charlie."

Maggie looked over at me, quick, then back to CM. I'm trying to grasp how we got on this topic.

"The FBI's been looking for me for twenty two years," CM said, flatly.

Maggie sucked in her breath and blinked. She stared at him, frozen for a moment.

"Jesus, CM," she said, and she pushed sudden tears out of the corners of her eyes, looking at me, confused.

"It had to do with the Vietnam war," CM said. "I won't go into it now—"

"Wait a minute," I said. "Why are we even talking about this?"

"Because what I've suddenly found out, to my great surprise, is that the congressional sponsor for this competition is Congressman Abe Pikeman."

"Who?" Why was this name familiar?

"Pikeman," CM said. "Remember? The FBI agent who tracked me to Idaho. He's a congressman now. From Iowa. And it turns out he's the one who got the competition sponsored by FEMA. He's the driving force behind the whole show. Whoever gets to build this town is going to make a lot of money. And it's pretty clear to me he's setting this up as a shoo-in deal for I-Mart."

"What about that guy Edders?" Maggie asked, suddenly. "Wasn't he from I-Mart? The guy who wanted me to help him catch wild fish?"

CM took off his glasses and rubbed his eyes. "Our competitors, no doubt, have been checking us out," he said.

"What do you mean our competitors?" I asked.

"One of the short-listed winners is a group called Patriot Homes," he said. "I looked them up. They're owned by….guess who?"

"Pikeman?"

"I-Mart," said Maggie. And I could tell by the way she said it that she was in. She was energized now, the specks in her eyes swirling.

36

SO, OF COURSE, I WAS in too.

There was not much time to prepare. We had to plan for a three day drive to Iowa, finalize and practice the presentation, and "make ourselves presentable", as CM vaguely put it.

At our next Team Meeting, CM drilled us on two things: First, in order to succeed in our mission, all we had to do was make the presentation. The idea of expecting—or even trying—to win was unnecessary. "I don't know what we'd do if we actually did win," he said. "We're not exactly in a position to follow through—so don't try too hard." He winked at me, saying this. Our goal, he said, was just to get the three ideas out there, to get them into the public debate. That would at least partially accomplish what he and Randolph Scott had worked toward all those years. In any event, he was convinced the project would be awarded to Patriot Homes, to I-Mart.

"But we can't let that happen!" Maggie complained. "We've at least got to try!"

"The best we can do is just make the presentation," CM said. "Just people knowing about these ideas might make a difference. That's all we need to accomplish. Even if you guys end up just reading it from the script."

Which is exactly what we ended up doing. We practiced once a day, modifying it as we went, experimenting with different ways to divide the talking points between me and Maggie, noting the strategic moments where we'd point at the appropriate features of the model.

We added a section, presented first by Maggie, in which she emphasized how the strategy of building with Enabling Structures would spread the economic benefits of the construction process over a wide spectrum of the New Hope population—lots of people would make a profit creating, owning and renting small-scale buildings, many people would participate as suppliers, contractors and subcontractors. I immediately followed, pointing out that our competitors were using a different model entirely: They would come in with their own big contractors, their own supply chains, and they'd build the new city all at once, with themselves in charge, and then they'd sell it, or lease it, to the citizens of New Hope, exporting the profits to offshore bank accounts.

Initially, I challenged CM on this. "How do we know that's going to be true?"

"Believe me," he said. "It's going to be true. It's how they're going to make their money. And it's what they're going to do with their money. Do you think anyone from the inner circle of Patriot Homes and I-Mart is going to settle down and buy a house in New Hope?"

"So how are we going to make our money?"

CM found this question amusing: "Charlie!" he said. "I'm shocked! You want to become rich or something?"

"No!" I defended myself. "It's just that I was wondering...."

CM watched me struggling to say whatever I was going to come up with. Then something clicked behind his eyes, his lips pursing together for a moment, and suddenly he spills out this remarkable and impassioned speech, as if he'd been programmed and someone had just hit the remote control button:

"The Vietnam war cost the United States two hundred and fifty billion dollars," he began. "And what did we get for that investment? South Vietnam still became a communist country—an eventuality that our leaders somehow convinced themselves would be absolutely catastrophic. Was it catastrophic? No, it was not. The world went on. The United States went on—albeit without the lives of sixty thousand of my high-school and college compatriots. Vietnam even went on—and now I read that it's starting to experiment with market economies and becoming a U.S. trading partner.

"So what might have been a better investment for that quarter of a trillion dollars? According to my calculations, the Enabling Structure we're looking at right here for New Hope will cost two hundred million. That means the U.S. government could have built a thousand Enabling Structures like this—habitat for three million people—for what it cost to wage the Vietnam War. And, while the money spent in Vietnam just went down the toilet with nothing to show for it but defoliated jungles and burned out villages, building a thousand Enabling Structures like this one might have demonstrated to the communists and the socialists alike there might be a better way to organize society and generate an economy everyone can participate in. If we'd been enlightened instead of trigger-happy and greedy, we might have won the war in a completely different way than we lost it."

This speech spilled out of CM so seamlessly and formally, it was obvious he'd been practicing some version of it in his head for weeks, months—maybe even years. And as he gave it, a strong emotion built up in his voice, and his cheek-bones flushed, and when he finished he looked at us for a startled moment, then stalked outside and down the steps to the stone beach, and he continued stalking down the river, where he was gone until the evening cocktail hour.

37

WE STILL HAD GUESTS—FALL was actually the busiest time at the fish camp—and when we weren't practicing the presentation, Maggie, more often than not, was out guiding some fisherman in the misty rains that were coming more frequently now. The heavy rains, which CM said would begin in early November, hadn't yet arrived. With that in mind, I spent my time up in the clearing preparing for them as best I could.

I'd basically finished everything. The siding was still just plywood, but the roof of the sleep loft was now complete, sloping its run-off into the central trough above what had been the chimney box. My tuned Zarathustra fish-head was mounted at the end of the trough, ready to receive the rush of rain-water the roofs would produce, its welded-washer eyeballs staring out over the doorway like a sentry. Instead of glass in the windows, I had plywood shutters that hinged out like small roofs above the openings. I held them up with a simple wooden rod, cut to length, and in that position they sheltered the interior nicely against even a moderate rain. For the heavy rains, I'd hinge them down over the openings, and that would do until I got around to putting in the glass.

"The Team" had the presentation finalized and reading smoothly, but it turned out, there was a final, last-minute adventure to be gotten through before we left for Iowa—something unexpected: As the final days before our departure approached, the last thing I anticipated was that I would be participating in a drift-boat fishing excursion down the white water river, with Maggie guiding one of the boats and my father another. Yet things conspired to make this improbable event come to pass.

"We've lost our guide help for day after tomorrow," Gus announced to CM and me as we were getting the grill ready for the evening cookout. A light rain was falling. Maggie and Louise were in the kitchen; the guests were playing cards in the river room.

"You mean the brothers grim?" asked CM. It was an old joke apparently.

"Both of 'em," said Gus. "They got a thing at the elementary school. Volunteer day or something."

"Jesus," said CM, annoyed. I could tell he didn't want to think about this. As the presentation drew closer he'd become obsessively preoccupied, spending less time with the guests, sometimes not even appearing for dinner till after the food had been grilled.

"The folks already paid for the day, too," said Gus.

"We could give them a refund," said CM.

"True," said Gus. "But we're a bit short this month, you know—what with only five guests this week. And you taking Maggie off all next week. I was thinking…maybe we could just do it. Make it a short float, but at least get 'em out on the river that last day."

"What do you mean 'we'?" asked CM.

"Ourselves," said Gus. "You and me and Maggie. You and Maggie can each do a boat. You've done it before, you know. We've only got the five of them to take."

CM considered this.

"Okay, why not," he said. "Charlie can come too. He can ride behind me in case I need some extra paddling."

Gus laughed. "Charlie," he said. "You might save your dad's ass."

"One thing," CM said to Gus.

"What?"

"You've got to convince Maggie to go drift-boat fishing. Not me."

"You always give me the shit work, don't you." Gus laughed again and shook his head.

It turned out Maggie complained only briefly, and even the guests thought it was a fine solution. "So we're finally going to get the experts," one of them commented gamely. The plan we laid out was to get everything ready for Iowa before the river float. We'd leave for Seattle the day after, spend some time there getting "presentable", and then head for Iowa. After dinner, we loaded the three sections of the model into the back of my Toyota camper and covered it with blankets. I also pushed in next to it the box of CM's drawings and manuscripts, thinking there might be something there we'd need.

The next day it continued to rain lightly but steadily, and I headed up to my unit on the hill to close things up. I stacked a load of dry firewood next to the hearth, and another stack down under the shelter of my bridge pavilion. I brought up canned goods Louise gave me and stocked up the pantry. I filled the fridge with bottles of beer and wine, and turned the temperature up to a modest setting, so more of the water turbine could go toward keeping the batteries topped off. I stacked rows of candles in the kitchen drawer and put boxes of matches, and the two candle lanterns on the fireplace mantle. In the sleep loft, I rolled up my futon and quilt and pulled down the window shutters and secured them tight from the inside. I planned to sleep in Ben Sprague's unit that night, down at the fish camp, to be ready for the early morning fishing expedition. I closed the rest of the window shutters too, and secured everything tight from the inside. Thinking there might be wind while we were gone, I decided to partially nail the temporary plywood doors—the one at the front entry under the fish-head, and the one at the back, going out to the bridge-deck—to their frames. When I finished, I put the hammer on a rock, under the floor, next to the steps.

It was getting dark when I walked down the clearing. I stopped at the edge of the woods and looked up the grassy slope, contemplating for a good while the angled roof shapes silhouetted against the rainy evening sky. It was, I thought, the most beautiful thing I'd ever seen, and I was anxious to get back and live through the winter in it, coaxing Maggie closer and closer to the secret I'd built on the other side of the bridge-deck.

I slept that night under the steady drum-beat of rain on the metal roof. The next morning it was still drumming steadily and

I slid further into the comforter, hoping desperately the fishing would be called off due to inclement weather. I was just about to drift into sleep again when there was a sharp knocking on the door.

"Up and at 'em!" CM's energetic voice. "You awake Charlie? Breakfast in fifteen minutes!"

Resigned to the inevitable, I got up and dressed in the paraphernalia I discovered in the duffle Maggie had given me the night before. The floppy, chest-high waders again. I put these on over sweatpants. A sweatshirt from my laundry bag and a zippered fleece from the duffle. The canvas, felt-bottomed wading shoes were larger than I remembered. Even with an extra pair of socks over the waders, my feet slid around in them. Since I was going to be sitting in a boat all day, I decided it didn't matter.

The last things I pulled out of the duffle were an olive green rain parka and a rain cap with two bills—one in front and one in back. After three months of almost pure sunshine, it seemed now we were getting ready to do battle with the elements.

Outside, the veranda was soggy and wet. Not from the steady drizzle that encapsulated the surrounding darkness, but from a misty thickness clinging to the air itself. The felt-soled boots gave the odd impression I was walking on wet moon-dust. The unfamiliar feeling of the waders across my upper chest added to the impression that I was dressed for some strange—and likely dangerous—mission.

The camp-house was lit up like an over-sized, fog-bound lantern. I pushed open the heavy doors and clomped in, already feeling drenched after the short walk along the veranda and cooking deck.

"Welcome to the fray, Charlie!" CM's voice.

There was a big fire going in the stone hearth. Everyone was already seated around the table under the glowing chandelier: CM, Gus, Maggie, and the five guests. Steaming plates of eggs and sausage were revolving around the lazy susan.

Everyone had peeled off their upper coats and sweaters. Lopsided bundles of outerwear lay on the floor behind each chair. A curly white haired man with freshly shaved cheeks and his wife sat on either side of Maggie. Mr. and Mrs. Wilson, I remembered. Mrs. Wilson was wearing what appeared to be a bright red shower hat.

I mumbled a good morning, removed my hat, jacket and fleece, and took a seat next to Gus. CM guided the platter of eggs over to the front of my plate.

"Dig in Charlie!" he said. He was in exuberant spirits. "Fill 'er up! The rainy season has finally begun!"

"So I noticed," I said. My spirits weren't quite equal to CM's.

"Do you think the rain will have raised the river much?" Mrs. Wilson asked.

CM scratched in his curly grey hair. "This time of year is tricky," he said. "The river comes from way up there." Rolling his eyes toward the North. "What it's doing up there I haven't a clue. Down here, this is just a little drizzle. Typically, we'd go sunbathing in this."

Mrs. Wilson laughed, although not with complete comfort. "In Florida we reserve that for days when the sun is actually visible," she said.

A little hum of laughter. The sound of silverware on china.

"What I'm trying to ask," Mrs. Wilson persisted, "is do you think the river is still going to be safe today?"

"What do you think, Gus?" CM asked turning his grin on Gus's round red cheeks.

"It might be up a tad," said Gus. "But it shouldn't be that much different than what you've already done."

"There was that one rapids we did the day before yesterday with Johnny. What was it? The Coolee?" Mrs. Wilson looked at her husband for confirmation. He nodded. "It wouldn't be so great if that rapids were even bigger."

"I've heard sometimes more water makes it go easier," said one of the other guests. "Fewer rocks to bump into."

"There's truth in that," said Gus. "Plus, we're not doing the Coolee today."

"Have you ever lost a boat?" Mrs. Wilson asked, adjusting her red shower cap.

"Nope. Never lost a boat," CM said. "Lost a couple passengers once. But never a boat." He winked at me across the table, eyes as alive and happy as I'd ever seen them.

"CM, that's a ridiculous thing to say!" said Maggie, genuinely alarmed. "We've never lost even a water bottle," she added to Mrs. Wilson. "I don't know what CM's drinking in his coffee this morning."

"But I heard you don't even go drift-boating," said one of the other guests. "Why's that?"

"It's not how I like to fish," said Maggie. "Not because it isn't safe."

"So here's the sack-lunches," Louise announced, entering with a flurry of paper bags, the dishtowel thrown over her shoulder.

"Morning Charlie!" She put the bags down on the side table and came over beside my chair. "Did you get your orange juice?"

"Morning Louise. I'm all set."

"Well, you try to stay dry today," she said, patting me on the shoulder. "CM, you take good care of my boy, here. You understand?"

"The plan was he'd take care of me," said CM.

Gus stood up and started gathering the sack-lunches. "Okay folks. Sun's up," he announced.

Down on the beach, in a thick, grey illumination that barely qualified as daylight, the three pontoon drift-boats were lined up in a row. The river flowed by smooth and dark, strangely quiet in the steady drizzle. I realized the water was indeed higher, deeper.

Gus put a cooler of sack-lunches and bottled water in each rowing cockpit, strapping it down with a bungee cord.

"Okay," he said, and outlined his ideas on who should go in which boat and what the general plan was. Afterwards he pulled CM and me aside: "Just keep the raft going the speed of the current. Stay generally on the shallow side so Mr. Chandler can shoot his line over to the deep side. If we come to a nice pool, Charlie, you throw out the anchor and Mr. Chandler can work the pool. We'll try to stay in sight, but it's helpful if we spread out some, you know? Oh, and don't forget, we gotta walk around the chute."

"Ok Gus!" CM said. "We're ready! I reckon we'll out-catch the lot of you. Any bets?"

"I'll put ten bucks on that," said Mr. Wilson, his pink shaved chin already dripping with water.

We climbed into the rafts and pushed off, paddling out into the current. Gus had given me an old wooden canoe paddle to wield from my aft seat in the boat. I paddled a couple of strokes but couldn't see it made much difference. CM, sitting ahead and below me in the rowing cockpit, seemed to control the raft easily.

Mr. Chandler selected a fluffy, reddish-purple fly from a little box in his vest and spent some time attaching it to his line. His droopy mustache dripped slow drops of water as he concentrated. Then he began a few warm up casts. The raft gained speed and headed toward the first bend in the river. The rain drops got bigger, prickling the river surface. I pulled my hat down tighter. Mr. Chandler shot his line across the river perpendicular to the boat and followed it down stream with the tip of his rod. Then he retrieved it slowly and cast again. We drifted in the chatty silence of the current.

The other boats were ahead of us. Gus had just disappeared around the bend. Mr. and Mrs. Wilson were casting in tandem from Maggie's raft, shooting their lines like a choreographed ballet. Then they drifted around the bend too.

"I think I need to add a sinker," said Mr. Chandler. "Don't think I'm getting deep enough." He hunched over and worked on the end of his fly line as we began to follow the others around the bend.

The sound of the first rapids approached. CM did a couple experimental strokes with the oars and peered down river.

"I have time for a couple casts," said Mr. Chandler, flaying his long rod in the air and shooting his line back out across the water.

CM was watching which side of the rocks Maggie was taking. He steered gradually in that direction. We started to pick up speed.

"Better pull it in," CM said.

Mr. Chandler reeled in his line and held his rod straight up in the air. We headed toward the rushing sound of the white-water on the right hand side of the rocks. The current began to turn the boat sideways and CM rowed hard, twisting us back in line. We accelerated into the rapid, the boat bucking smoothly, the big rocks sliding by quickly.

"Eee-Hah!" CM shouted, and we slid into the pool.

Maggie's raft was at the far end, sitting peacefully, the Wilsons already casting their lines.

"Toss out the anchor," CM said. "We'll stay up here till they leave."

Mr. Chandler began working the opposite bank with his fishing line. He was a good caster. I started making mental notes on his technique, thinking how I might surprise Maggie one day with an elegant shooting cast.

A sudden shout from the other end of the pool. Mr. Wilson is standing, his fly-rod arching deeply. A fish breaks the surface and rolls. The rain subsides and his taut, angled line becomes visible as it cuts through the surface of the river. We watch him play the fish. Maggie has the handle of a big fishnet in her hand. Soon she leans and dips it into the water beneath the arching fly-rod and scoops out the fish. Mr. Wilson holds it up for us to see.

"Nice Coho," said Mr. Chandler quietly. "Looks like maybe a twelve pounder." Then he went back to his casting. "Maybe there's another one of those buggers in here."

There wasn't. But in the next pool Mr. Chandler connected. As he worked the fish CM picked up the big net. When the sudden silver shape appeared in the clear dark water next to the pontoon, I remembered vividly Maggie's disciple earlier that summer: its red gills pumping like the nostrils of a racehorse. CM scooped the fish up in the net and flopped it into the bottom of the boat. Mr. Chandler leaned over and removed the hook from its jaw. He lifted the fish with both hands for us to see, its mouth and gills still working.

"Another Coho!" he said, his smile almost visible beneath his dripping mustache.

As he put the fish back in the water the rain swept down again from behind us. This time harder.

When we drifted around the next bend Maggie's raft appeared against the far bank, hanging on its anchor line. I could hear the sound of the rapids ahead and remembered this must be the class three. As we swung around with the increasing current, Maggie pulled up her anchor and steered out to intercept us.

"How're you doing?" she smiled at us, rain dripping off the brim of her hat.

"Fine," said CM. "Stimulating!"

Maggie's raft was starting to accelerate ahead of us.

"Follow me," she called back to CM.

The sound of the white water grew. Then through the rain, the rock formation emerged and I recognized the big rock that I'd experienced as a flying meteor.

Maggie steered across the current and CM followed. I lifted the canoe paddle, thinking I might fend off with it. The boat began to buck and bounce as we approached the heavy ribbon of clear water right behind Maggie. She gave a hard twist with her oars, lining the boat up. CM made the same move and we lined up too.

"Eee-Haaw!" shouted CM as we shot by the rock and skidded down through the white water into the quieter pool. It seemed easier this time.

Maggie turned around in her boat and gave us a thumbs-up. I waved the canoe paddle at her.

Even in the rain, the sound of the chute and falls at Zarathustra's Pool was louder than I remembered. CM steered the raft over to the stone beach, and we got out and carried it down the path to the pool.

"Lovely day isn't it?" said CM halfway down.

"You have to pay a lot of money to have this much fun," said Mr. Chandler.

It started raining harder.

We put in at the pool and soon were approaching the narrow bridge with the big wooden X braces. A sudden image of the long black sedan that had been up there a month earlier flashed in my memory. The bridge was empty now. As we swept under it, I looked up, appreciating the momentary shelter from the belting rain drops.

Later, we rounded a bend and saw that Maggie and Gus had pulled their boats up together against the bank. Gus waved his arm and CM pulled the oars to steer us over toward them.

"How've you been doing?" asked Gus.

"We got a nice Coho back a ways," said Mr. Chandler.

"That's about what we've done," said one of Gus's riders.

"We was thinking about lunch," said Gus, glancing up into the rain. "The hatchery's just a mile or so down river. There's that old storage shed on the bank where we could get some shelter. It's Saturday. There shouldn't be nobody there."

"Let's do it," said CM. "That okay with you, Maggie?"

She hesitated. "I wouldn't normally go within three miles of that place," she said. "But I think Mrs. Wilson might appreciate a dry sandwich."

"Bless you," said Mrs. Wilson. "And some warm tea."

We stayed together now and soon swept around a bend to a narrow part of the river where the high fir trees, leaning in from each bank, nearly touched over the water. A concrete damn-like structure jutted into the river, going nearly halfway across. The current swirled swiftly to the left to go around it. A series of tall wire-mesh stalls stood out of the water along the other side of this bulkhead. We steered to the right and pulled up to the river bank not far away.

"What's that all about?" asked Mr. Wilson as we carried the coolers up the bank toward an open shed tucked back under the trees.

"It's a fish trap," said Gus. "It's where they catch the breeder stock for the hatchery."

The back and one side of the shed were enclosed with rough horizontal boards. A few rusted steel drums lined up against the back wall. The floor was sawdust and wood chips, damp and spongy, but comparatively dry. The rain picked up harder as we ducked under the shelter, drumming suddenly so loud on the roof you could hardly talk, hissing and splashing on the ground out-side.

We stood around while Gus and Maggie opened the coolers and laid out lunch. Mr. Wilson was staring out at the fish trap with interest. It was pleasant to be out of the rain, relieved of the constant rapping pressure of it on your shoulders and head.

"Here's some hot tea." Maggie poured from a thermos and handed Mrs. Wilson a steaming tin mug.

Mrs. Wilson grasped it thankfully in both hands and put it against her cheek.

We sat in a circle around the sandwiches and apples and cookies laid out on top of the coolers. Everyone helped themselves.

"So how does that work?" asked Mr. Wilson, nodding out toward the concrete bulkhead.

"Not very well," said Maggie.

"Don't get her started, please," said CM.

"I mean just an overview," said Mr. Wilson.

"When they close the gates, the fish coming up river to spawn have to swim into the holding tanks," said Maggie. She was looking out at the wire-mesh stalls as she explained. "They sort the fish. The wild ones they let go so they can go on up river to spawn. The ones born at the hatchery they keep. They don't really have any place to return to for spawning anyway. They keep them in the holding areas until they're ready. Then they take them out and strip them of their eggs and sperm..."

"Oh!" said Mrs. Wilson, startled.

"Yes," said Maggie. "It's not a pretty affair." She'd stopped eating her sandwich.

"Here, have a cookie," CM said, trying to distract her.

She munched the cookie, staring intently out into the rain. I could see now she was watching something, like a cat watches an unseen bird in a bush.

She stopped munching.

I peered out in the direction she was looking, but saw nothing except the sheeting rain, like a curtain against the trees where the fish-trap met the river bank.

Then I saw a movement.

A figure stepped out from the trees carrying a large white bucket. The man—I assumed it was a man from the broadness of his shoulders—was wearing an orange raincoat flapping open at the front, and high, yellow boots. Long black hair swooped down from under a ball-cap.

The figure looked our way for a moment, hesitating because he could see we were watching, then walked out onto the bulkhead carrying the bucket. I glanced at Maggie. Her eyes were following the orange raincoat. Mr. Wilson was watching too.

The figure stopped at the end of the bulkhead where the wire cages stuck up out of the river. He leaned down and picked something up: A large fishnet on a long handle. His back turned to us, he peered down into one of the wire-mesh stalls. Walked to another. Peered down again. Then, seeing what he wanted, he slowly reached the long-handled net down into the stall. With a swift, sudden motion he pulled the net up with a wildly twisting silver fish. There was a faint flash of neon red.

"What's he doing?" said Maggie to no one in particular.

She stood up and walked to the edge of the shelter.

The orange-clad figure was down on its knees, struggling with the fish.

"He's supposed to let that fish go," said Maggie. "That's wild."

She hesitated, just inside the dripping roof of the shed.

The orange raincoat was partially obscuring the flapping silver fish.

"What's he doing!" Maggie yelled suddenly, and bolted into the rain.

"Go get her, Charlie!" said CM. "Fast!"

I jumped up and nearly fell as I tried to launch a sprint in the floppy waders, trying to run, cursing the oversized boots.

The orange, black-haired figure had put the fish in the white bucket. Its thrashing tail stuck out the top. He was walking back down the bulkhead. Maggie was running at an angle across the rocky grass to intercept him.

"What are you doing?" she shouted again into the rain.

The orange figure continued to walk along the bulkhead toward the bank, head turned, watching Maggie approach. I was stumbling and pushing hard to catch up. Then he stopped and his high yellow boots stepped off the concrete bulkhead onto the river bank.

"What are you doing?" Maggie shouted for a third time. She slowed and stopped, about ten feet away. The man's orange rain coat was flopped open showing white, chest-high waders.

"That's a wild fish," said Maggie. "What're you going to do with it?"

I came up slowly behind her, trying to catch my breath.

The man was staring at Maggie with dark, dull eyes, a heavy growth of whiskers on his cheeks, water dripping from his chin. He ignored my approach, focusing specifically on Maggie, regarding her.

Unhurriedly, he set the bucket down on the ground. He grasped the fish's tail and pulled out its big silver form and clasped its still struggling body hard against his side with one arm.

"What are you doing?" said Maggie again. She took a step toward him.

He reached his free hand inside the orange open coat.

Out flashed, in slow motion, a long knife blade, shining bright in the dull light.

"No!" Maggie screamed and lunged forward.

I tackled her from behind just before she reached him.

The ground was mud and rocks and grass. I climbed quickly over her back, lying on top of her, struggling to hold her down.

Something slapped loud in a muddy puddle a few inches from my face.

It was a bloody fish-head, mouth still gasping for oxygen, a big, round silver eye staring rapidly at nothing.

Maggie screamed and lurched forward under my weight toward the mud spattered yellow boots. I held her down, gripping her shoulders, pushing all my weight onto her squirming energy.

Then she went slack, her face straight down into muddy gravel. She began to cry, big heaving cries. I held her, trying to spread out over her, and closed my eyes. My cheek pressed against the back of her wet hair, my ear directly connected with her choking, heaving lungs.

I sensed a movement. I opened my eyes and flinched at the sight of boots next to my face. I twisted upward. It was CM. He was holding the fish-head in the palms of his two hands, trying to wipe the blood away from the muddy ground with the toe of his boot.

"I'll be back in a minute, Charlie," he said quietly. "Take Maggie over to the boats. We're leaving."

We pushed the boats back into the river and waited for CM. He came out of the trees wiping dirt-covered hands on the legs of his waders.

"You take Maggie's boat," he said to me. "She can ride in the front of mine."

Maggie didn't say a word. She was staring into the trees, mud smeared on her cheeks and the front of her rain gear. She climbed into the front chair of CM's boat. The Wilsons gave me two weak smiles as I stepped into the rowing position Maggie had vacated. Mrs. Wilson, who was in the forward seat, leaned back and patted me on the shoulder. "You'll do fine," she said.

"It's only a couple miles to the pull-out," said Gus. "You stay behind me, Charlie. Just follow right behind. CM will bring up the rear."

"Okay Gus," I said grabbing the handles of the oars. My heart was still pumping wildly, the adrenaline still burning in my muscles.

"There's no bad water at all from here on," Gus said over his shoulder. "Just a couple of easy riffles. You ready?"

I nodded. We pushed off and swung into the current. I realized I wasn't even worried about handling the boat. My mind was still clamped on the sound of Maggie's screams, as if they were still ringing in the air. I was watching the back of Gus's boat like my eyes were glued there, but all I kept seeing was a bloody fish head staring up from the mud.

I don't even remember the river or the riffles. We got to the pull-out and dragged the boats up onto the stone beach. Gus climbed up a steep gravel road to get the van and boat trailer. It continued to rain hard. I went over and stood next to Maggie, but she was lifeless. She was staring up the road to where Gus had disappeared. Except for a couple of streaks, the rain had washed most of the mud from her cheeks.

After we loaded the boats on the trailer, we drove in silence, packed wet and rubbery in the clammy interior. The windshield wipers slapped back and forth against the rain. The smells of fish and mud and wet hair hung amongst us. Maggie sat ahead of me between CM and Mrs. Wilson. It seemed a long drive.

When we got to the put-in we climbed back out into the rain and Gus backed the van and the trailer down to the river again. This was beginning to feel senseless to me.

"Why don't we just drive them back to the camp?" I asked CM.

"No place there to put them in," he said. "Makes the next day longer. The camp's just around the bend. We'll be there in less than fifteen minutes."

The rain continued unabated as we pulled the rafts from the trailer. Gus drove the van back up to the road, the tires spinning for a moment in the mud. When he returned we all climbed in the rafts as before and pushed off.

Gus looked back over his shoulder. "Stay right behind me again, Charlie," he shouted. "It's just a ways around the corner now." The current caught the rafts as he said this and we swept out away from the bank.

My mind had achieved a numbness, partly from continually replaying the scene back at the hatchery, and partly from the drumming texture of the rain on my head. Suddenly the rain came even harder, the slot of sky above the river turning almost to night, the downpour hammering and slicing us in thick, sweeping silvery sheets.

The shape of Gus's raft disappeared behind a rain-veil. A worm of panic twisted in my diaphragm as I momentarily lost my sense of direction. Then Gus appeared again, just off to the right. I pumped my left oar trying to get closer to him.

We were starting around a bend to the right and I realized the air around us was behaving strangely. It was pumping somehow, pulsating. I pulled the oars out of the water, listening. The sound disappeared. Then it came again—a pulsating hum above the driving slash of the rain.

CM's raft had come up nearly along side us. Maggie was sitting up straight in the bow, leaning forward, gripping the sides of the seat frame in a trance. The boats slid into the enveloping sound as it began to multiply and divide in a hovering, chaotic harmony.

"What is it?" asked Mrs. Wilson, turning back to me, frightened. "What is that?"

Before I could think how to answer, the outline of the tree-spiked river bank on our right peeled away, revealing the fish camp. The big sloping windows of the river-room glowed like a lop-sided light-house through the blurry, slanting rain shroud. Next to it, the dimmer shapes of the veranda and the sloping complex of silver roofs jutted high along the dark embankment. And from this curving architectural wall, six bright jets of water were shooting out into the river, shooting through the slanting rain in perfect, silver arcs of song.

38

EVERYONE TURNED IN EARLY THAT night, after a somber dinner without much conversation. The occasional attempts by CM to cheer up Maggie had failed and, finally it seemed, everyone just wanted to make the day end. We were still scheduled to leave the next morning for Seattle. CM offered to put it off a day. "No, I'll be ready," Maggie answered with a grim determination. "I'll definitely be ready."

Back in Ben Sprague's unit, I sat for a long time in the same deep-cushioned chair I'd sat in the very first night I'd arrived at the camp. The harmonics of the water-flutes, muted now by the drumming of the rain on the metal roof, continued to rise and fall intermittently outside in the darkness. I was trying to grasp the events that had just transpired. I was trying to process and package them into something that seemed normal and safe. With difficulty. For one thing, the chair I sat in mysteriously rocked and bumped imperceptibly, as if I were still on the drift boat in the river. For another, the slapping sound of the fish head in the mud and its staring eyeball kept jumping into my mind. But most of all, it was Maggie's screams and the choked cries in her lungs I couldn't get rid of.

Finally I went to bed. I crawled under the comforter in the sleeping alcove and tried to close my eyes against the swirling thoughts, my knees pulled up against my chest. Why hadn't I lunged past Maggie and knocked the knife out of that bastard's hand? Why hadn't I hammered his scraggly chin with my fist and grabbed the fish and rushed it down to the water?

The rain drummed on the metal roof close above my head.

Later, I pushed my shoulder back against something prodding at me. Pushed back against it again.

"Charlie?"

Adrenaline shot through me. I twisted around and bolted upright in one motion.

A dark silhouette in front of me.

"It's only me. It's okay."

"Maggie?"

"Will you just hold me?"

The dark form leaned down and folded itself into the bed, wriggling under the comforter. An arm reached back and found my hand. She pulled my arm around her, backing close against me, pulling the comforter around us.

"Just hold me, okay?" She squeezed my hand again and pulled my arm tighter around her, fitting her backside into the shape of my thighs and chest.

"Okay," I said.

She was wearing something made of flannel. I was afraid to breathe. I could feel her chest expanding and contracting with her breath, could smell the fragrance of her skin and hair just an inch from my nostrils. I tried to match my breathing with hers. Imperceptibly, without realizing it, I pulled her tight against me and listened to the sound of the rain on the roof, and wondered how, now that I had her, I was ever going to let her go.

When I awoke, she was already gone.

PART III

The Horizontal Skyscraper

39

IT HAD BEEN FIVE MONTHS since I'd taken the ferry from Seattle to Bainbridge Island on my marathon drive from North Carolina. Now, taking the ride in reverse, watching the Seattle skyline materialize from a cloudy mist beyond the passenger deck railing, it was like looking at another person's memory.

Maggie was sandwiched between CM and me, the three of us leaning against the steel bulkhead of the big green and white ship, its unheard engines vibrating beneath our feet, our collars turned up against the chilled, cloudy air. Since leaving the fish camp early that morning, Maggie's energy had gradually normalized. There was no acknowledgement, in any way, of the fact she'd slept next to me—for how long I didn't know. She'd grown playful as we did our last-minute loading of the trucks. She seemed to have put the murder of the fish into a compartment somewhere and closed the door tight. Driving to Bainbridge, following CM's dented blue pick-up, we'd fought over the radio station, finally settling on a country and western station, and Maggie sang happily along in a startlingly off-key voice. But now, watching the massive and intimidating array of skyscrapers sliding inevitably towards us, we'd all grown quiet and introspective.

Maggie finally broke the awkward silence that had enveloped us. "CM? Is this really going to work?" she asked. "I mean, do you think they're really going to believe we're architecture associates or whatever it is we're supposed to be?"

I was shocked to hear her vocalize so precisely what I had been dreading since my father had first broached the topic of the competition.

"Course they will, Miggs," he answered without hesitation, but I sensed a slight doubt even in his voice.

"But look at us!" Maggie said. She held out her arms and looked down at her jeans and river boots.

This declaration energized CM in a new way: "I'm glad you brought that up!" he said quickly, reaching into his pocket and pulling out a folded piece of paper. "I was trying to think how to...introduce the subject."

The vibration of the ferry made a subtle change. The city was looming close now, cars and buses gliding along the elevated freeway above the waterfront.

"We'll have to go down to the trucks in a minute," he said, handing the folded paper to Maggie. "Here's a couple of appointments I made for you guys. The first one's at noon. That's in about—" he looks at his watch, "forty-five minutes."

"But what is it?" asked Maggie, peering suspiciously at CM's bold, slanting letters.

"It's a very exclusive hair salon," CM answered matter-of-factly.

"A what?" said Maggie.

"A place where they put your hair in order," he said. "Ever hear of one of those?"

"But—"

"As a matter of fact, Miggs," he said, his big smile breaking out now, "you will be an inspiration to them! They'll probably take photos and add your hair-style to their catalog! Their big challenge, I'm afraid, is going to be Charlie."

"What do you mean me?" I said. "I'm not going to a hair salon."

CM laughed, shaking his head in dismay. He took his glasses off and rubbed his eye lids.

"That's what I've liked about you from the very beginning, Charlie. You're a resistor. You resist anything and everything. It's a good trait to have, too. Especially when your better judgment takes over in the end."

"No way I'm going to a hair salon."

"You might like it," said Maggie.

"Are you guys crazy?"

"But Charlie," said CM. "You're going to be representing a very sophisticated company, right? The McCormick Planning Group! And you know what they say about the messenger, right? It's nothing personal here, believe me. I like your hair just the way it is. It's very…rustic. Unfortunately, it just doesn't fit the role. You know what I mean?"

This insight inspired him to a new level of enthusiasm. "Think of it as if you guys are movie stars," he said, eyes glittering now behind his wire-frames. "And you're getting ready to shoot a big scene!"

"Wait a minute," said Maggie. "I thought you were saying I was going to stay pretty much as me."

"Guys," said CM, suddenly serious. "It's time to get real. It's like the cameras are going to start rolling here. What's the audience going to see, right? We have to transform ourselves into the McCormick Planning Group. Sorry, but if we're going forward, this is the only way it's going to work."

We drove off the ferry in our separate vehicles. CM first in his old blue pick-up, Maggie and I following in the Toyota. As arranged, CM turned left and we turned right heading into the heavy traffic.

"I cannot believe we are doing this." I kept repeating these words.

"A little hair-cut's not going to hurt you," Maggie says, interrupting my mantra. "I cut my hair myself, see? And I'm fine."

"Yes, I can see that," I said. "Maybe they can make an improvement."

She gave me a pointed look. Her energy was definitely back.

On schedule we entered Salon Frederique, overwhelmed suddenly by the sweet floating fragrance of shampoo and hairspray. A short, aging, fuzzy-haired man waddled over to us with a radiant toothy smile.

"Bonjour! Welcome! I'm Frederique!"—bowing—"and I already know who you are." He winked. His buggy brown eyes rolled over Maggie's chopped hair, took in her figure, skipped over to me and came to a sudden stop just above my eyebrows.

"Follow me!" Frederique turned with business-like abruptness and waddled into a maze of mirrored cubicles.

"You dear, are here," he said to Maggie, tapping the back of a rotating salon chair. "And for Monsieur Charles, my own private chamber!" He waved his arm dramatically toward a translucent chartreuse curtain.

My heels stuck to the floor.

"Frederique," I said. "I think Maggie should go with you. Beauty deserves the best, I think."

Frederique, already half-way to his chartreuse curtain, stopped and turned. He tilted his wild fuzzy head, regarding us. He pressed the end of his nose in thought, his eyes searching first Maggie, then me, then Maggie again.

"Oui!" he said. "Of course, you are right!"

Maggie shot me another deadly look.

"Mademoiselle," Fredrique gestured grandly toward his curtain. "I will be honored! Please!"

I began backing away, aiming in the direction I remembered the entrance to be. Then, as if his big round eyes could see through the back of his fuzzy head, Frederique turned suddenly: "Guzzo!" he said. "There you are! You will do the Monsieur!"

"Oui!" said a deep voice immediately behind me.

I turned and looked up. Guzzo was literally seven feet tall, with a head as bald and shiny as a light-bulb.

When Guzzo finished his initial foray with the scissors, he was wading in the deep brown curls of my hair. He swung me around to face the mirror and I was appalled to see the face of someone who, from my perspective, looked about sixteen.

Guzzo met my eyes in the mirror: "It will all grow back my young friend. Then, when you get old, it will all fall out, like mine!" He laughed.

When I emerged light-headed from Guzzo's mirrored cubicle, Maggie was sitting with an unnatural primness in one of the black leather and chrome chairs in the reception area. Her hair was even shorter, but most startling it was slicked back on the sides, revealing the full outline of her ear. I'd never noticed her ear before. The soft-hard, translucent pink shape was immediately mesmerizing, mysteriously attractive.

She hadn't seen me yet. She seemed to be waiting, apprehensively, for something to happen.

"Here we are!" Frederique waddled in carrying something aloft in his hands.

He stood in front of her and delicately placed behind her newly revealed ears the straight black temples of a pair of glasses, which he then rotated gently down to rest on the bridge of her nose.

He stepped back and observed the affect.

"Beautiful! Perfeccion!" he exclaimed.

Maggie just looked up at him through the black, sharply rectangular frames.

"Jesus!" I said, and Maggie's head turned abruptly in my direction. The affect of the glasses and her flashing eyes, each now framed in a sleek black rectangle, was startling.

"Maggie!" I said. "You look...fantastic! I'm amazed! I mean, you always looked great, but...."

"Monsieur Charles," said Frederique, "I can see compliments come naturally to you. What he is trying to say, Mademoiselle, is that you are a beautiful woman. But more, your brains are in your head!" Frederique sighed. "It is an intriguing combination. It will make a big scare to any man who ever tries to seduce you."

Maggie just looked at us—first at Frederique. Then at me. Then at Frederique. Then she stood up and walked out the door, slicked back hair and glasses in the lead.

"Oui! Charlie! Are you in love with this girl?"

"Am I what?"

"I think she's pretty hot, Charlie." He mumbled something in hasty French and crossed himself.

The next appointment on CM's list was at Nordstrom's. It took us a while to find it. "I never did much shopping here," Maggie explained. "I don't know where Nordstrom's is."

"How could we have an appointment at a department store?" I said.

"I don't know, but when we get there, go for the Armani," Maggie advised.

"What's Armani?"

"He's a fashion designer. He's what you want."

"I'm not sure I'm going to know what to get."

"I'll help you."

But this turned out to be unnecessary. As we crossed the street in front of the entry canopy to Nordstroms, two familiar faces appeared amidst the milling pedestrians and street people on the sidewalk: Frederique's fuzzy head and Guzzo's towering baldness, each searching in opposite directions with frowns of concern.

Maggie grabbed my hand and squeezed it, sending a sharp sensation through my arm.

"Our fashion advisors," she said. "Are you ready?"

I was not ready, of course, for anything. Squeezing my hand harder Maggie pulled me onward.

"Cheri! Look who is here, Guzzo!" said Frederique, waddling out to meet us.

Three hours later Maggie and I emerged from Nordstrom's with plastic sheathed wardrobe hangers over our shoulders. It was nearly dark. Behind us, Frederique and Guzzo carried bags of shoes, shirts, ties, belts, necklaces, earrings, socks and under-wear—and two wardrobe suit-cases with soft side-pouches. Frederique had paid for everything, and half way through the shopping spree I'd realized, suddenly, who he was: The gay French attaché whose life CM had somehow saved in Vietnam.

A taxi pulled up to the curb in front of us. The driver jumped out and opened the trunk. The bags and boxes, wardrobe hang-ers and suit-cases were carefully stowed in the trunk under the fussy supervision of Frederique. Guzzo solemnly held the rear cab door open as Maggie slid in, then me. He poked his head in the window and winked.

"Remember, Monsieur," he said. "It will all grow back!"

"And you!" came Frederique's voice from the other side of the cab. I glanced across Maggie and saw that CM was sitting in the far corner of the back seat, slouching down slightly with Fred-erique wagging a finger in his face. "If you ever come to Seattle again and don't take me to dinner, I will cross you off my list!—Fsst!" Frederique slashed his finger across his neck.

CM's big, square hand reached up from the shadows and clasped Frederique's in an upside down handshake that I recognized, somehow, as being the salutation of two comrades-in-arms.

The electric window slid up as the driver pulled away from the curb into the stop and go evening traffic.

40

THIRTY MINUTES LATER THE CAB turned down a narrow street decorated with the neon names of restaurants and bars. We stopped in front of The Italian Parrot.

"Wait for us, okay?" CM handed the driver a folded bill. "We'll be about an hour, I imagine."

The restaurant was dark and small with a low ceiling. We passed through a bar with four or five patrons staring at a blinking television suspended above the cash-register. In a back room we slid into a high-backed booth with a red-checkered table cloth. CM sat across from Maggie and me. He looked from one of us to the other.

"You guys look fantastic," he said, grinning wide. "The McCormick Planning Group is looking very nice, I think."

Maggie tipped her glasses down on the end of her nose and peered over the black rectangles.

"It's been really a fun day, CM," she said sardonically. "I feel like I've finally discovered the real me."

"So what's the next big surprise?" I said.

"Well I had to get you here, didn't I? Like I said earlier, you're a resistor, Charlie. And Maggie...you're..."

"I'm what?"

"You're just as stubborn as Charlie."

"Can I get you drinks?"

An astonishingly beautiful girl, hair pulled back in a black pony tail, appeared next to our table.

CM smiled up at her, his eyes widening momentarily, taking her in. "Yes! Great!" he said. My eyes widened too, and I could feel Maggie bristling next to me.

The waitress took our orders, writing them studiously on a pad, then she hesitated a moment, looking at me. "You aren't Leonardo DiCaprio, are you?"

"Who me?"

"You look just like him. Are you him?"

"Yes, this is Leo," said Maggie, grabbing my arm and leaning into me affectionately with her shoulder.

The waitress's eyes widened at Maggie, then looked at me again. "Well," she said, unsure now, "it's nice to meet you."

"It's nice to meet you too," I said, and gave a little bow with my head.

CM's smile stretched across his face as he looked at us, shaking his head slowly. "I think this is going to be a big success," he said.

The rest of dinner CM basically reassured us and gave a few last-minute instructions. He reminded us that all we needed to do was read the scripts and then leave. The model would stay there.

"What if somebody asks a question?" I asked.

"That's likely," said CM. "Just answer it as best you can. Don't make something up. If you don't know a reasonable answer, say you'll be happy to defer the question to the design team."

Then he gave me a thick envelope with hundred dollar bills in it. "This is for your expenses," he said. "Remember, we got a big chunk of money for being short-listed, so don't go cheap. Stay in nice places on the drive out. Eat good food. Your rooms at the Buchanan Hilton are already paid for."

Then he said, "I think we should get going. I think you should drive to Cle Elum tonight. I'll leave in the morning. But we won't see each other again until we get back to the fish camp, right? If anything goes wrong, or if you need anything on an emergency basis, here's a number to call." He handed a folded paper to Maggie.

"What could go wrong?" I asked. Though I could think of at least a thousand things on my own, I wanted to hear what he thought could go wrong.

"I don't think anything's going to go wrong," he said. He was getting nervous. "This is going to go just fine," he said. "Just play your roles, read your script, and have fun."

Outside the restaurant, he gave Maggie a hug. Then he shook my hand and clasped his arm around my shoulder. "Thanks for doing this, Charlie," he said. "I'll always be grateful…."

"Look," I objected, "I'm happy—" but he was already opening the taxi door, Maggie already getting in, sensing some urgency. "I'm glad I could do it," I said, sliding in next to her. He closed the door, then tapped on the window.

"Don't forget the stuff in the trunk," his voice was muffled by the glass.

As the taxi started off, the driver turned on his windshield wipers.

41

THE DRIVE TO CLE ELUM was mostly in silence, the Toyota's windshield wipers keeping time with the stripes of white centerline flying at us in the headlights. The sudden transition of the send-off back at the restaurant had created a hurried time compression that had somehow numbed my perceptions. But now, encapsulated by the rushing darkness, the reality of what was unfolding began to re-establish itself. Maggie seemed lost in her own thoughts, the lights from the dashboard casting dim shadows above her cheekbone. She was still wearing the fake glasses.

"What are you thinking about?" I finally asked.

"You really want to know?"

"Yes."

"I was thinking about how much you really liked that waitress back there."

"What do you mean?"

"I mean how much you were attracted to her. You can't deny it, right?"

"She was pretty, okay? But—"

"No, I mean you were really attracted to her. I could feel it."

"Jeeze, Maggie. Are you crazy?"

"I don't think so."

Now we were driving in a strange silence, and these old feelings are coming back, catching me completely off guard, and I'm thinking, why is this happening? Why is this happening now? Then I said it: it just popped out after being suppressed the entire summer:

"You're still mad about Lady Brenda, aren't you?"

"Lady who?"

"You know who," I said.

"Why would I be mad about Lady Brenda?"

Silence again. The windshield wipers whacking their cadence.

"But you didn't have to fuck her so many times, did you?" She said this in a very matter-of-fact way, as if it's just a casual observation.

"What are you talking about?"

"Lady Brenda told me I really had something to look forward to, that's all." Casual and matter-of-fact again.

"And you believed her?"

"About which?"

Silence again, as I was trying to figure out how to untangle all the twists this conversation was having, where it was going.

"Look," I said, "I didn't really even do it once. She came into my room. I was asleep…. Women seem to be doing that recently," I stupidly added, and could feel Maggie give me a look.

"Well," and she stretched this out icily, "it's not something— if I were you Charlie—that I'd start counting on."

Silence again. Windshield wipers slapping.

The first motels outside of Cle Elum start to appear, their neon signs smeared by the rain, and suddenly I understood three things. First, I understood what this whole conversation had been about. Second, I understood, in no uncertain terms, what the sleeping arrangements were going to be for the remainder of the trip—something, I realized now, that I'd been vaguely thinking about in the back of my mind. And third, I understood how profoundly I wanted to possess and wrap myself around Maggie Scott and her fish-scale tattoo.

42

THE NEXT MORNING MAGGIE WAS her cheerful self again, a mood that was matched by a bright sun that came out as we headed into the Columbia River valley. We fought over the radio station, and I let her win her country and western song, to which she hummed off-key accompaniment, her black rectangular glasses pushed up in the hair on her forehead. After half an hour of singing, she turned down the volume, and asked me to tell her about my mother.

"I know less about her than about my father," I said.

"But you have that tape of her singing."

"That's about all I have," I said.

"Do you remember her?"

"She died when I was one."

"How did she die?"

"She drowned…in a river," I added, meaningfully, suddenly making a connection I hadn't made before. Maggie thought I was ribbing her somehow.

"Seriously," she said.

"I am serious. I have the newspaper clipping. It was at a music festival in North Carolina. She had a band. They traveled around in a bus. She had a boyfriend named Kurtz. They went swimming after an evening performance, a bunch of them. It was in the French Broad River. It took them three days to find her."

Now Maggie became silent again, and I was remembering the nightmares after Gramella had shown me the article, the vivid watery searches for my mother, and I could picture, very clearly, the exact shape and color my closet door had assumed in the small illumination of my adolescent night-light.

By the time we got to Sioux Falls, Iowa on our third night, we'd talked about our mothers and our high-schools, and almost everything in between. We'd settled into a comfortable rapport, even agreeing to an intricate game for rotating between radio stations. I was careful not to upset the mood. I was hoping that Maggie was secretly reprocessing the truth about Lady Brenda, was readjusting her vision of what had transpired so soon after we'd met. She seemed to be getting there.

Driving into Iowa visibly changed our energy. The topic of the presentation didn't come up directly, but I found myself gripping the steering wheel tighter, scrunching and shrugging the tension out of my shoulders more often, testing the worm of apprehension that seemed to have been growing secretly in my intestines. Maggie became more decisive, business-like. She pulled the rectangular glasses back onto her nose.

"Let's fill up with gas in Sioux City," she decided, studying the roadmap in her lap. "It's about a four hour drive from there tomorrow. We're supposed to have the model in the courthouse before the end of the day."

The word "courthouse" did not sit well with my worm; it lurched and started squirming with alarm. We ate at McDonalds and retired early to our respective motel rooms. I took in with me the box of CM's manuscripts. I was suddenly focused on the prospect of somebody asking a question. It was this probability that filled me with dread. And, somehow, I intuitively knew exactly what question they were going to ask. It was going to be the same question Xu had asked, the question everyone seemed to ask when they heard CM start to explain his theory: They were going to ask, "Why?" Why build in a way that's so intentionally inefficient? It was the question CM had just been getting ready to answer when the projector bulb blew out. I was determined to have an answer for it. To have memorized a succinct explanation that would quell any doubts that Enabling Structures were, in fact, the most sensible way to build cities. It was to be an answer that, when I got the opportunity to deliver it, would astonish Maggie, win her warmest admiration and perhaps, I fantasized, even save the day.

I thought I knew where the answer was. I'd been perusing CM's manuscripts off and on all summer, and now I remembered one in particular that seemed to address this topic. I put the box on the bed and started spreading out the stapled bundles of pages until I found what I was looking for.

Here's the passage I spent half that night trying to commit to memory:

It's true that vertical architecture appears to be much more efficient. If we build a thousand units vertically, each unit only uses a tiny fraction of ground area. Moreover, verticality almost requires the extreme efficiency of mass-production and repetition—the builder gets the maximum amount of architectural product with the least materials and effort. The builder doesn't buy a front door a thousand times, he buys a thousand front doors—and doing that, he gets a big discount from the door supplier. He doesn't hire a thousand door installers, he hires a single installer to hang a thousand front doors. And he gets a big discount there as well. The vertical builder thus maximizes his profits and the cash-flow from rents. And because he controls so many units from such a small piece of ground, his profits and their cash flows are multiplied exponentially. Vertical architecture doesn't create wealth; it creates a small group of wealthy builders.

But our strategy is the opposite. We design and build the horizontal Enabling Structure so that each architectural unit within it is built as a separate project, one at a time, by small design-builders and craftsmen. Our strategy doesn't buy a thousand front doors, it buys a front door a thousand times. Our process doesn't hire a single door installer, it hires a thousand door installers. The Enabling Structure empowers thousands, or tens of thousands of small business entrepreneurs—designers, builders, tradesmen, artisans—to participate in creating a tightly organized human settlement. It's true that, from one perspective, this is very inefficient. But from another perspective, this inefficiency is a virtue. Our strategy doesn't create an elite class of wealthy developers, it creates wealth itself. And the very inefficiency of it distributes and shares that wealth in the most efficient way possible.

43

THE NEXT MORNING I OVERSLEPT and Maggie was knocking on the door.

"You in there, Charlie? You awake?"

I pulled on my jeans and opened the door. The air was chilly and I wrapped my arms around my bare torso. Maggie's eyes widened in surprise.

"Come on. We gotta get going," she said. Then she looked me over again. "Did you not sleep, or what?"

She walked across the street and got coffee and bagels while I dressed. I packed the manuscripts back in the box, leaving the page I'd memorized paper-clipped and on top, where I could find it again. We ate the bagels in the front seat of the Toyota with the engine warming up, and then started off for Buchanan, the worm in my stomach expanding like a balloon.

I spent the first hour of the drive practicing the Answer in my head. There were a couple of parts I knew I was ad-libbing now, and I was going to have to look those up again, but for the most part I had it down. This exercise helped somewhat to deflate my worm, though it continued glowing and squirming in my gut.

Then Maggie, for no apparent reason, started laughing.

"What?" I said.

"Look at us." She said.

I looked at her. I held my arm up and looked at my arm.

"What about us?" I said again.

"Look at what we're wearing!"

It was true, I realized. We were still wearing our fish camp clothes. The outfits from Nordstrom's were in the suitcases in the back of the truck.

"I think we're going to have to stop for a costume change," Maggie said.

I volunteered to watch for a gas station, which gave Maggie another laughing fit.

"You think I'm going to put on those clothes Frederique picked out in a gas station?"

"So what do you want to do?" I said.

"We're going to have to stop at a motel."

"But we just left a motel."

"We're going to have to stop again. You need to shave, too."

I touched my chin. Sure enough there was emerging stubble there that surprised me.

"We've got to get ready to make our appearance," Maggie said.

"This is such a waste," I said. "We just paid for two rooms. Now we're going to pay for two more, just to change our clothes?"

"Let's just get one cheap one," Maggie said, matter-of-factly. "We can take turns in the bathroom."

So now I started thinking about how this might unfold, and I discovered that I couldn't remember anymore the opening sentence of my Answer.

Shortly before noon we pulled into a Super Economy Inn and got some raised eyebrows and knowing looks from the overweight desk clerk. I pulled the suitcases out of the back of the camper and we went into the room, which was small, with a single king-size bed occupying virtually the entire floor space.

We each took a side of the bed and opened our suitcases out on the bedspread. Maggie immediately began to select items and organize them next to her suitcase. I just stared into mine, dumbfounded. Suit and shoes and sports coat, shirts and ties and underwear and socks. I hadn't worn socks all summer. I was trying to remember if I'd ever worn a suit—other than the tuxedo I'd put on for the prom.

"What is it?" Maggie was looking at me, some folded silky fabric in her hand.

"I'm not sure where to start here," I said.

THE ARCHITECT WHO COULDN'T SING

"I think we've kept you up on the river too long," she says.

"No, I mean, should I be putting on the suit or the sport coat?"

"Let me see what you have."

She came around to my side of the bed, and started sorting through my suitcase, still holding the folded up silk in one hand.

"This doesn't look like Armani," she commented as she rummaged. "But it's nice. Guzzo did a good job for a basketball player."

"I don't think he's a basketball player."

"Oh, this is nice," Maggie holds up a tie. "This goes great with the suit, see?"

"So is that what I'm supposed to put on? The suit?"

"Save that for tomorrow. You're traveling, right? So you're casual. Just slacks and a shirt. Maybe the sports coat." She's sorting stuff on the bed, working with one hand, the other still holding the folded silk, which I can see now has some straps folded up with it. "Do you want me to pick out your socks?"

"I can manage that," I said.

"Surely there was a time when you functioned in civilization, right?"

"Okay. Okay. I can do this now. Thanks for your…assistance."

"You want to go first?" Maggie nodded at the bathroom.

"You go ahead."

"Okay." And she walks into the bathroom and closes the door almost all the way. The sound of water coming on, filling the sink. The door moves slightly more closed, but not quite closed. The worm in my intestines is starting to move again. The toilet flushes. I sit down on the bed between the piles of clothes next to the suitcases and put my head between my knees. I'm starting to feel nauseous, starting to taste the morning bagel again in the back of my mouth. I try to recite my Answer, but I still can't remember the first line and the rest is a meaningless jumble.

The bathroom door swings open. I look up to see Maggie stepping out into the room completely naked—or so I think—all arms and legs and skin, but then I realize she's wearing the silk underwear she'd been holding, but it was so skin-colored and sheer it almost didn't look like it was there, and I immediately see the tattoo of fish-scales around her upper thigh, for the second time now, but this time its even more startling because of its contrast with all the rest of her.

"Victoria's Secret," she says, making a little pirouette so I can see it all.

"Jesus, Maggie," I manage to say. I'm standing up now, looking at her. "What are you doing?"

"I'm getting dressed," she said. "Your turn in the bathroom." Business-like, she lifts a pair of black slacks from the suitcase and, turning her back to me—as if to create some privacy—she steps into them, one long leg at a time, and scooches them up over the round, silk shapes of her buttocks.

"What are you doing back there, Charlie?" Without turning, she demurely reaches behind and picks up a chartreuse-green blouse she'd laid out.

"I'm watching you," I said.

"Well, you're supposed to be in the bathroom. It's your turn." She's pushed her arms and shoulders into the blouse and is now working on the buttons, the brightly colored collar up around her neck. "What are you waiting for?"

She turns around, buttoning the last button, and gives me a long, hard look.

"I want to win the competition," she says.

"I know that."

"I want to win it for Randolph Scott."

"I understand."

She picked up the rectangular glasses from the suitcase and slid them onto her nose. "I want to see our mister Edders crawl out of I-Mart on his hands and knees."

I went into the bathroom, closed the door, turned on the water in the sink, turned on the shower as well, and then regurgitated my breakfast bagel into the toilet. After that, I felt a lot better.

44

SOMEHOW WE MANAGED TO GET lost on our way to Buchanan and it was late afternoon before we arrived. We dropped the model off at the courthouse—a brooding, grey-stone building with frosted windows—where two uniformed guards carried the three sections, one at a time, up to the rotunda. The other models were already there, set up on their tables, but in spite of our curiosity, we weren't allowed to linger over them. The courthouse was closing.

We found the Wapsi River Hilton, parked at the covered drop-off and walked in together. I held the glass door for Maggie and she stepped through ahead of me, her chartreuse blouse announcing the arrival of something to be contended with, her high-heels suddenly clacking on the tile floor of the lobby. I stepped up beside her at the reception desk. The clerk looked up, his eyes widening as he took in Maggie's slicked back hair and glasses.

"McCormick Planning Group," I said. "I believe we have reservations."

The clerk typed on his key-board and stared bug-eyed at a screen we couldn't see.

"Yes! Cadwell and Scott." He looked up at us.

"This is Miss Scott," I said.

He looked at Maggie again and his smile animated.

He went back to his screen and typed some more.

"Miss Scott is in room 203. You're Mr. Cadwell? Room 303. Do you need help with your luggage?"

"We can manage it," I said, instinctively.

"Of course we do," Maggie countered, giving me a slight knee in my thigh. "And can you tell us where the lounge is?"

So the performance had begun. The lounge was a dark, windowless alcove adjacent to the hotel restaurant. We slid into a booth with our brief cases, ordered glasses of wine, and had a short planning session.

As we understood the agenda, the presentations were scheduled to begin the following morning, and continue for three days. The morning of day one was assigned to jury orientation and review of the models on display in the courthouse rotunda. That afternoon each team was assigned a one hour slot for their "Qualification Session". CM had written a script for this which Maggie and I had practiced a dozen times. It was surprisingly short. We wouldn't need anywhere close to an hour. The McCormick Planning Group was scheduled to go first, at one o'clock.

Days two and three were given entirely to the main presentations. Each team was allotted a two hour time slot. ZForm was scheduled to go first, in the morning of the second day; Patriot Homes were to go second that afternoon. McCormick Planning Group was scheduled for the morning of the third day. The afternoon of day three was to be an open question & answer session, with all three Teams present. That evening, a gala dinner would close the event. The Jury's decision was to be announced the following week.

We had dinner in the restaurant and retired early to our rooms. I undressed and practiced my Answer a few times. Then I decided I wanted a beer, but realized I was going to have to get dressed up again to go down to the lounge. This business of having to be in costume all the time was tedious. I got out the suit I was going to wear the next day and practiced putting it on, tying and untying the tie several times before I could get it to hang at the right length. The suit felt nice, and I angled the bathroom door with its full length mirror so I could see my side reflection in the mirror above the sink. It was like looking at a stranger, and I looked at him from as many different angles as I could manage. It seemed odd that when I moved my arm, or lifted my hand, he moved his arm or lifted his hand in exactly the same way.

45

THE NEXT MORNING I PUT the suit back on and met Maggie in the hotel restaurant for breakfast. We had a window table that looked out on a grey and drizzly street.

"Are you feeling pretty ready?" I asked her.

"Yep." She squinted at me through her rectangular glasses, mocking a helpless near-sightedness. "I think it's going to go perfectly. How about you?"

"I don't know," I said, looking out at the drizzle.

"You'll do fine, Charlie," she said. "Remember, you're the expert on Enabling Structures. Nobody else knows anything about them."

The waitress delivered our breakfast plates.

"Do you think we should go down there early?" I said. "Kind of check out where it's all going to happen?"

"I think that would look iffy," Maggie said. "I think we should just march in at 12:55 and ask them where we're supposed to be. I don't think we want to be hanging around peeking in doors. Do you want my toast? I can't possibly eat all this toast."

I looked around the hotel dining room. It was nearly full. Several tables were occupied by men and women who appeared to my eye suspiciously like architects.

"Do you suppose any of these guys are the other teams?" I asked.

Maggie surveyed the room over the tops of her glasses with a cool nonchalance.

"I think those guys over there in the corner are," she said. "They've got rolls of drawings sticking out of their brief-cases."

I followed her look. Three men and two women were huddled around a table for four. One of the men had pulled up an extra chair. The carpet around their feet was thick with black leather brief-cases. They were having an intense conversation, leaning into the middle of the table. One man and woman were older, the man with wavy hair and a large gold wristwatch that sparkled. These were people, it was obvious to me, who knew what they were doing.

At 12:30 we parked the Toyota on a side street about a block from the courthouse. We started down the sidewalk, but Maggie stopped and put down her briefcase.

"Here. Let me fix your tie," she said. "You feeling okay?" She pulled the knot tighter and yanked on it.

"Actually I'm psyched," I said. "I'm ready to do this."

And, oddly enough, I was. The crisp draping of the suit around my shoulders and hips gave me an unexpected exhilaration. My mind felt clear: the opening line of the Answer, which I'd rehearsed a dozen times in my morning shower, was there now each time I reached for it. The soft, black leather brief case, hanging solid and supple from my left hand, held the typed scripts for the various parts of our presentation—scripts that I'd underlined and highlighted where there should be emphasis in my voice—scripts that I merely had to read, verbatim, to accomplish our goal. I actually felt like this was going to work.

We walked into the courthouse at 12:45. Once again, when Maggie's high heels hit the marble floor, a mean, echoing staccato rose up around us. This time my stride seemed to naturally extend, keeping time next to her.

"McCormick Planning Group," Maggie says to a guard standing by a doorway. "Is this the Hope Relocation presentation room?"

"Down there at the end," he nods. "Main courtroom."

Tall wood-paneled doors were open. Groups of people milled around just outside. We entered and walked down a center aisle between rows of fixed bench seats under a balcony. A scattering of occupants turned and looked at us. Beyond the seats the room opened up, tall and harshly lit. It smelled old.

There was a buzz of light conversation. To our left was a long table covered with overlapping white table cloths, microphones, water glasses, water pitchers and little wooden blocks holding name plates. Behind this table, a few men and women were grouped in conversations.

Straight ahead, just in front of the raised platform where I assumed the judge would normally sit, a large projection screen had been set up. On the right, opposite the long table with the name plates, was a shorter table, also covered with a white table cloth, water pitcher and glasses—and a single microphone.

Maggie walked directly to the smaller table and set her brief-case on it. I did the same. We opened our briefcases and began extracting our scripts.

A voice came from behind us. "McCormick Planning Group?"

A middle-aged woman held out her hand with a friendly smile. "I'm Dr. Albright," she said. "Celene. Chair of the evaluation committee." Half-rimmed reading glasses hung down against the front of her black turtle-neck. She looked like a school-teacher.

We introduced ourselves.

"It's very nice to meet you," said Dr. Albright. "I'm concerned about Mr. McCormick's illness. The committee was looking forward to meeting him."

"He's resting comfortably," I said. "We'll do the best we can…in his absence."

"I'm sure you'll do fine," she smiled. "Are we ready to start? Come, you should meet the rest of the committee."

She led us over to the long table. The others broke off their conversations and took positions behind their chairs. Dr. Albright marched us down the length of the table, like a military officer making introductions to the troops. Friendly smiles. Concerned inquiries about Mr. McCormick's recovery. It was an odd group—a mixture of business suits and khaki pants, striped ties and crew-neck sweaters. I found I was more comfortable with most of them than I had anticipated. Dr. Albright, especially, I immediately trusted.

Maggie and I returned to our table and sat down.

"Can we close the doors, please?" Dr. Albright asked the uniformed attendant.

People were still coming in, taking seats. I glanced up at the balcony. There were fifteen or twenty people in little groups. They all seemed to be local. working people, dressed in street-clothes and overalls.

Maggie spoke into the microphone, bringing my attention back to where we sat. "Does everyone have a copy of our technical specification? Or do I need to hand out copies?"

"I believe we all have copies, right?" Dr. Albright looks down the table for confirmation. She glanced at the guard who was closing the doors. Then she begins the proceedings in a formal voice:

"I'd like to welcome, on behalf of the committee, the McCormick Planning Group. As you know, the purpose of this session is to substantiate the technical qualifications of your design proposal…." She glanced up at the balcony, and added in explanation: "Whether or not the proposed town plan meets the stipulated program requirements—and the qualifications of the participants to deliver the project. This session, then, is not about the merits of the design, but simply about the nuts and bolts reality of it. Are we all in agreement about our purpose?" She looked down the table. Nods and shuffling of papers.

"Then I believe we can proceed. Mr. Cadwell? Ms. Scott?"

There was a disruption over by the doors, which the guard had opened again. A group of men entered: a wide man with short grey hair and a dark, elegant suit surrounded by four smaller men whose thin-collared suit jackets were buttoned up tightly. They marched and shuffled to an open space in the center of the second row of bench seats, the grey-haired man flashing metal cufflinks as he adjusted his sleeves.

Ms. Albright observed this and waited, I could sense, with a hidden impatience.

She made eye contact with the guard after the doors were closed again—willing him to keep them actually closed this time. Then she turned and looked at Maggie and me again.

"I believe we were in the process of beginning," she said.

Maggie gave me a little nudge and pushed the typed script over in front of me.

"Okay," I said, surprised at the sound of my voice. Was that my voice? Or had someone else said that? "Do you want us to just go through this from the top? Or are there specific questions you have? How would you like us to do this?"

"Can you speak into the microphone?" said Dr. Albright.

"Sorry," I said, pulling the skinny, metal wand closer to my face. I'd never spoken into a microphone before. It looked absurdly ineffective.

"Is this better?" I asked doubtfully—instantly hearing the difference myself.

"That's fine," said Dr. Albright. "Why don't you go through your specification once," she said. "And we'll follow along. The committee," she glanced down the table again, "will be free to ask for clarifications at any time."

The committee looked at us expectantly. They seemed friendly.

I cleared my throat. Maggie poured me a glass of water and set it next to the script.

"You'll have noted," I began too forcefully, "that our proposal for the New Hope Relocation can't exactly be quantified as stipulated in the specifications request. This is because our proposed development method can't predict exactly how many units of this or that type will be constructed. We therefore have listed what we call 'capabilities'. By this we mean what the town-plan and Enabling Structure are capable of supporting."

In speaking these first sentences my mouth unexpectedly became so dry I had difficulty getting out the words "capable of supporting." They sounded to me more like "cable of sporting." I reached for the water glass and was surprised to discover my hand shaking so badly I was afraid I'd spill it. Pretending to look at my watch, I grabbed the wrist of the hand holding the water glass, as if it belonged to someone else, and steadily raised it to my lips. Under the white tablecloth, Maggie grabbed my knee and squeezed it, hard.

"We also are unable to provide exact unit costs," I forged ahead, willing my attention onto the typed words of the script. "Again, because each unit—each dwelling, each store, each office suite—is a separate project which ultimately will be controlled by someone other than ourselves...."

"May I ask a question, Mr. Cadwell?"

I looked up. "Yes?" Maggie grabbed my knee again.

A friendly Mr. Wellington, according to his name plate, was addressing me, adjusting his microphone as he did so.

"The committee is familiar with the unusual nature of your proposal. I for one am willing to accept the proposition that the numbers you have provided in your specifications are approximations. My question, however, is this: How does your method, your..." he picked up a stapled sheaf of papers and looked at it momentarily. "Your Enabling Structure, as you call it—how does that process guarantee that we're going to end up even close to your projections?"

"Well, sir, I believe the answer to that is a central part of our main presentation which will be given the day after tomorrow. I'm afraid if I try to answer now, we'll run out of time."

Maggie leaned over and spoke into the microphone, pushing her shoulder against mine as she moved. "I think we could give a short answer," she said. "A preview."

She pulled the microphone over to her side of the table, and thumbed open the script at a deeper tab, turned a page, quickly looking for what she was going to say, adjusting the rectangular glasses, business like, on her nose.

"You'll have noticed in our model—I assume everyone has had time to at least give it an initial study?" (she adlibs this part, looking up over the top of her glasses for a brief moment) "—there are only three complete architectural projects: a two story project, a three story and a four story project. These are provided to illustrate the range of structural possibilities that can be vertically supported within each building slot. Also, each example project utilizes different proportions of its ground area for outdoor space, garden or veranda. A single building slot makes a small project. Combining two or three building slots makes a bigger project. Each design-builder—whether utilizing single or multiple slots—is free to choose within this range of indoor-outdoor and vertical possibilities. A single-slot, two story project might be two apartment flats or a single-family town-house; a three-slot, four story project might be a restaurant with offices above." Here Maggie took off her glasses and spoke directly to the jury: "The numbers we've provided are an average range of what the total New Hope build-out might be. What we tried to show is that this average is within the stipulated program requirements."

Mr. Wellington smiled. "Thank you Miss Scott. That's helpful, I think." He glanced up and down the table at the other committee members. "Can we agree to accept this as meeting the program requirements? Is there a consensus on that?"

Several heads nodded.

"So perhaps," Mr. Wellington said, "we should just proceed to the qualifications part. Who the development team members are that will be responsible for the actual implementation of the project."

I pulled the microphone toward me.

"Miss Scott will address that topic," I said, following the script as we'd planned. I pushed the microphone back to her, realizing how ridiculous that little interjection had just been.

Maggie adjusted the glasses on her nose, thumbing back to the front of the script.

"The composition of our development team is quite simple," she read. "The project components shown in our model—the Enabling Structure –will be engineered and constructed under the management of any qualified civil engineer in the State of Iowa."

She paused and looked up, making sure this statement had registered.

"The remainder of our development team," she continued, "are the citizens of New Hope themselves—and the local design-builders and contractors and subcontractors and craftsmen they choose to help them build the projects they decide to build."

An expectant silence starts building. The selection committee is looking at us, waiting for more.

"Miss Scott."

Another voice. I looked to see who had spoken. A small balding man formally dressed with suit and vest and bright blue tie. Rimless glasses. A Mr. Silberman, according to the name-plate in front of his microphone.

"May I ask, Miss Scott, was your father a professor of architecture at the University of Oregon?"

I could feel Maggie tense up next to me.

She hesitated. "Yes."

"I remember him well," said Mr. Silberman, smiling in a friendly way. "A brilliant teacher and theorist. A communist too, as I recall."

"Excuse me? What did you say?" said Maggie

"I was recalling that your father was a communist, wasn't he?"

"You're saying my father was a communist?"

"Well, only recently I stumbled across an article he wrote in 1973." Mr. Silberman waved a sheaf of clipped magazine pages in the air.

"And what do you call yourself?" Maggie shot back.

"I'm sorry?"

"If you call my father a communist, what do you call yourself?"

"Why, I'm an American, Miss Scott." A confident smile.

"By virtue of what? That you were born here? My father was too."

"Are you denying your father was a communist?"

The sound of a gavel came banging forcefully into the middle of this exchange. Except there was no gavel. Dr. Albright had taken off her shoe, pulled back the white tablecloth, and was pounding her spiked heel onto the bare table-top.

"What is this?" Dr. Albright demanded. "What is this about, Mr. Silberman?"

"I only wish to establish the roots of this team's proposal," he answered. "This country has fought two wars, sacrificed tens of thousands of its sons to rip these communist roots out of the earth....And here we confront them again. Here they're held up to us again, disguised as some higher set of ideals when, in fact, they represent the lowest undermining of our democratic freedoms."

His words seemed to stun the air into silence. The other committee members seemed frozen.

Dr. Albright banged her shoe again. "Mr. Silberman, this is completely out of line. We're here to discuss design solutions not political ideology."

"Design, I must remind you, is not apolitical," he replied. "This team's proposal is blatantly un-American. It undermines the way we do business! It undermines our economic principles! I call for a committee vote to eliminate this team and their proposals from the competition. For reasons of being anti-American."

Mr. Wellington, who had spoken before, leaned his crewneck sweater up to his microphone. "Madame Chair," he said calmly, "how can we vote without even hearing the presentation? I for one would like to draw my own conclusions and assign my own labels."

Ignoring Mr. Wellington's comments, Mr. Silberman huffed himself up. "Madame Chair, I have a motion on the floor...."

"This is not City Council, Mr. Silberman," said Dr. Albright. "We're a design evaluation committee, remember? In the end, we each have a vote on the Town Plan proposals we're reviewing. Remember how it's supposed to work?"

"Dr. Albright," Mr. Silberman replied indignantly, "the U.S. government is investing over a hundred million dollars in this project. I respectfully submit it is anti-American to even allow consideration of a Communist inspired proposal."

Bang! Dr. Albright hit the table again with the heel of her shoe. "I'm calling this session to a close," she announced. "We're not going to make this into a political circus."

She looked at Maggie and me sitting across at our table.

"Miss Scott, Mr. Cadwell, you are excused," she said. "Thank you for coming. We look forward to your full presentation Friday morning."

She looked out at the spectators. The grey-haired man who'd arrived late sat with his arms across his chest, his cuff-links sparkling, a sour expression on his lips.

"I'm shifting today's schedule forward thirty minutes," Dr. Albright announced. "The next session will be at 2:30. In the meantime, I'd like the guard to vacate the spectators." She looked at her committee. "I want us to stay here and establish a few rules about how we're going to proceed."

"I'm afraid I have to object," said Mr. Silberman into his microphone.

Dr. Albright caught the arm of the guard as he walked by to herd out the spectators. She leaned up to him with her hand covering the microphone, and I distinctly saw her say the words: "Please bring me a fucking gavel!"

We followed the last of the spectators—the wide man surrounded by what I now decided looked and behaved like bodyguards—down the aisle. Instinctively I wanted to keep my distance from this group. I slowed down and walked behind Maggie, looking over the top of her slicked-back hair at their backs.

They passed through the doors and turned left. Maggie turned right. I stepped forward quickly to catch up—and nearly collided into her back. She'd stopped in her tracks.

A few feet in front of us stood a dark complexioned, handsome man in his late twenties, early thirties maybe—with slick black hair and a dark shadow of afternoon whiskers. He was looking at Maggie with an open, very straight-tooth smile.

"Hi Mag," he said.

"What are you doing here?" she said.

"How could I not come? I've been reading about this in Architectural Record for the past six months." A deep melodic voice. "But look at you, Mags! You're more beautiful than ever!"

"But I thought you were in…"

"New York? No. I'm in Portland now."

"Portland?"

"I'm sorry I haven't kept in touch." He held up his hands innocently.

"But what are you *doing* here, Benjamin?"

"I read about the McCormick Group being short-listed. How could I not come…and help, maybe? Where's CM?" His eyes wandered up to mine for a moment. Then back to Maggie.

"He's—Ben, look." Maggie whirled around, looking for me, nearly whacking me with her swirling briefcase.

"This is Charlie Cadwell!" she said. "He's...." Maggie's cheek bones were flushing pink, her eyes panicky behind the rectangular frames of her glasses. "Charlie, this is Ben Sprague."

I just looked at him, numb.

Ben Sprague stepped forward holding out his hand. Dazed, I took it and he squeezed hard. "Nice to meet you, Charlie."

"Let's go somewhere we can talk," said Maggie. "Let's get out of this building."

I followed the two of them down the long corridor, out the exterior doors and down the sidewalk. They were talking rapidly, Maggie gesturing with her hands.

Then she suddenly stopped and turned around, looking for me.

"Where are we going?" she said.

"My car is right over there," said Ben Sprague. He pointed to a new blue-grey BMW parked against the curb across the street.

"You guy's go ahead," I said. "I'll get the truck."

Maggie looked at me, her eyes searching for a moment, trying to detect something.

"Okay, Charlie," she said. "Meet us at the hotel. In the dining room. We can talk there."

46

I WATCHED THEM CROSS THE street. Ben Sprague opened the passenger door in the sleek, polished car and Maggie stooped in without looking back.

I walked on to the Toyota and slid in behind the steering wheel, staring out the windshield at the car parked in front of me, trying, for some reason, to visualize what Ben Sprague had been wearing. Had he been wearing a suit? Or was it a sports coat and jeans? I sat for a while, waiting for some feeling to flow again.

The hotel dining room looked empty when I walked in. Then I saw them in a corner booth, heads leaning into their conversation, elbows on the table. I hesitated, watching, noting it was a sports coat. Grey-brown tweed with leather patches on the elbows.

After a moment, Maggie's head turned and her rectangular glasses focused straight on me. She straightened up and waved, gesturing for me to come over, smiling insistently.

"What took you so long?" she asked.

I wasn't sure which side of the booth to get in on. I didn't want to sit next to Ben. But it suddenly seemed presumptuous to slide in next to Maggie. I hesitated.

"What took you so long?" she asked again, patting the booth seat next to her, telling me with her eyes to sit there.

"I had to get some gas," I said.

"We were worried about you," said Ben. "Thought maybe the anti-communist enforcers had picked you up." Deep melodic voice again. Very square chin with its dark shadow of beard. Long black eyelashes. Intense blue eyes.

I gave a short laugh. He was smiling at me. He seemed friendly and open.

"They were pretty rough back there, weren't they?" he said.

"Who was that guy?" I said to Maggie. "Did he know your father?"

"That was a ploy, I'm certain," said Ben. "I noticed Pikeman was enjoying it immensely—in the beginning, anyway. They probably fed that guy the article."

"Who did you say?"

"Congressman Pikeman."

"He was there? Today?"

"In the second row," said Ben. "He's hard to miss."

Details of the elegant, grey-haired man and his buttoned up companions began piecing themselves together in my mind, and the worm re-awakened for a moment, squirming in my lower stomach.

"The Chair was on your side, though, "said Ben. "She's Dean of the School of Architecture at Michigan. Look," he said, glancing down at his neatly manicured hands, "Maggie's told me you guys are doing this on your own. It's pretty amazing, actually. CM picked a great moment for gall bladder surgery."

Maggie gave me a nudge with her knee under the table.

"Yes," I said. "It's…a bit awkward."

"So," Ben lifted his hands and clasped them under his chin, "can I do anything to help?"

"Help?" I looked at Maggie. "Did you ask for help?"

"No," she said, nudging me with her shoulder. "Ben just offered. I didn't say anything."

"Do you think we need help?" I asked her.

"He's just offering, Charlie. I don't know. What do you think?"

"I have a fair amount of experience making presentations now," said Ben with what was obviously a very smooth, presentation voice. "I'd be happy to help out any way I can. I know the song and dance about Enabling Structures forward and back." His blue eyes gave Maggie a confirming little smile across the table.

There was a part of my thinking that immediately wanted to grab onto this tossed life-preserver, wanted to transfer all the dread and stress to this competent guy who, no doubt, could make the presentation much better than me. Maggie had said she wanted to win. Obviously, it seemed to me, she'd have a much better chance at that with Ben Sprague than with me. But what would CM think? He'd made such a production of the fact we only needed to make the presentation, read the script. That was all he wanted. And then, if I backed out, what would I think of myself?

"Thanks for the offer," I said, forcing the words out. "But I think it's pretty much scripted, how CM wants it to go. Maggie and I can do it." I said this last part with all the conviction and confidence I could muster, avoiding a glancing look at Maggie to see if she agreed.

Ben gave a friendly smile. "Fine," he said. "I'm sure you guys will do great. I'll just be here for moral support then. Anything I can do to assist—coffee runs, chauffeuring, let me know."

"Moral support will be perfect," said Maggie, and Ben's smile and his blue eyes shifted back to her and stayed there.

By the time we agreed to go out to dinner, I had come to understand several things. First, I understood what Maggie had told Ben, and what she hadn't. He knew I was building the last unit of the fish camp up on the hill behind CM's Studio, and he was interested to know about it. He didn't know I was an English major and not an architecture student, and he seemed to accept me as a comrade in the trade which, in spite of myself, I found to my liking. He knew CM was my father, but didn't know I'd met CM for the first time in June. Another thing I understood was that the real reason Ben had come to Iowa was to lay claim to Maggie, to court her back again. This was crystal clear to me each time he looked at her, and I realized Maggie's revelations on the flat rock by the river, still vivid in my memory, had stopped short of her telling me why she'd split with this guy, why she'd stayed at the fish camp after returning for her father's service—why she was still there, guiding fishermen and gathering signatures for the hatchery petition.

At dinner, after a couple of beers—while Maggie and Ben shared a bottle of wine—I began to warm up to the situation. Ben was friendly and funny—I would have liked him under any circumstances—and full of stories about the various architectural firms and restaurants he'd worked at in New York City. Even more warming was Maggie's newly acquired and unexpected habit of touching me, squeezing my wrist, or poking me affectionately in the shoulder, at every reasonable prompt in the conversation. This was clearly for Ben's benefit, and though I didn't completely trust her motivation—how could she prefer me over this obviously beautiful and successful guy who she'd been passionately in love with—I was happy to play along at the small round table where we sat, her chair, I noted with pleasure, pulled intentionally closer to mine than his.

Back at the hotel, we discovered that Ben's room was on the same floor as Maggie's, an eventuality that caused some awkwardness as they got off the elevator together. Maggie found it necessary to reach out to touch my arm again, giving me a look over the tops of her rectangular glasses, touching me and squeezing above my elbow for just a moment, her eyes drilling into me, saying that everything was okay. She was still looking at me like that as the elevator doors slid closed.

47

THE NEXT MORNING THE THREE of us arrived at the courthouse late because Ben had insisted on driving the BMW, and his fastidiousness about finding a safe parking spot took a few extra minutes, and required a longer walk than we'd anticipated. The guard was starting to close the doors as we hurried down the hall. The staccato of Maggie's heels caught his attention and he held them for us.

The seats on both sides of the aisle were nearly filled. We filed into the back row causing some consternation as we went. Maggie entered first, her slicked back hair catching the courtroom lights, then Ben in his sport coat with the elbow patches, then me. It was just how we walked in, but I ended up sitting next to Ben with Maggie on the other side. Dr. Albright was already speaking as we settled into the seats. I looked around, noting immediately that Pikeman and his body-guards occupied the same row they had the day before.

"…We'll reserve our questions until the completion of the presentation. As agreed, we'll take a short break then have an hour for questions. So," Dr. Albright looked at her watch, "Zform, you have our undivided attention until 10:30."

"Thank you, madam chair."

It was the man with the wavy hair and bright gold watch, from the previous morning in the dining room, who now stood up. He approached a large and brightly faceted architectural model which had been moved from the rotunda and set up on two square pedestals about knee high in front of the jury table. He telescoped out a silver pointer about two feet long, as if he'd drawn a fencing foil from an invisible scabbard.

"Psst. Charlie." Maggie was leaning in front of Ben, looking over at me.

"What?" I whispered.

"We need to get one of those pointer things," she whispered back.

Ben leaned over to me. "I have one in the Bimmer," he said.

"What we'd like to show you today," said the man, flourishing the pointer, "is a glimpse of New Hope, Iowa as a visionary town for the twenty-first century. A town that celebrates the self-reliant spirit of America to be sure, but also the technological prowess of America's creative ingenuity."

What fascinated me most, although the message itself seemed logically compelling, was the way his gold watchband flashed as he articulated and gestured his arguments—like a hypnotist's swinging bobble. His topic was glass. Structural glass. Digital glass. Electrified glass. The building material of the twenty-first century. Here was glass you could walk on; glass that was transparent one minute and opaque at the flick of a switch; glass that allowed sunlight to penetrate or, at the passing of a cloud, reflected it back into outer space; glass that generated electricity and stored heat in phase-changing chemicals; glass that accumulated information about the weather and swiveled out to catch prevailing breezes, glass that cupped itself in gutters to catch the rain and then transmitted messages of its storage capacity to other glass. Glass, that could be curved or straight or organically molded to capture any aesthetic expression. Glass that formed a shimmering array of tall apartment blocks and condominiums, that housed vertical slabs of green gardens, that cradled blue reflecting pools of water. Glass that formed a syncopated sawtooth building form that was a futuristic I-Mart, the central structure of the model.

By the time he was finished dangling and waving his gold-linked watch band, flourishing the foil of his telescoping pointer at this feature and that feature of the model, it was clear, to me at least, his design was head and shoulders beyond what we were proposing. Our model, I realized, didn't really even have an actual building in it. Only parts and pieces of what would become buildings. There was a small corner in my thinking that began to deflate with the realization that what my father had designed was inferior—seemed suddenly almost naïve and childish. Looking at the slick, pristine geometries of Zform's glass buildings, the image that foundered in my imagination was of the nailed plywood siding and rough, recycled beams and joists of my unit up on the hill.

48

BEING IN THE BACK ROW, we were the first to escape the courtroom for the lunch break between presentations. Outside, we started down the steps at the front of the courthouse, headed for a café up the street. I was still preoccupied with the glaring contrast between what we'd just seen and the primitive tin roof I'd recently finished nailing back at the fish camp.

"Miss Scott!" someone called.

A young man, with a bow-tie and open sports coat, was approaching us, quick-stepping along the sidewalk.

"Miss Scott?" He held out his hand, catching his breath. "Oley Franks. I'm with the Register and Tribune," he said. "Can I ask you some questions?"

Maggie hesitated, then turned and started walking again.

"We're on our way to lunch," she said.

The young man walked along beside us.

"Is it true your father was a communist?" he asked.

Maggie stopped and turned on him. "No," she answered.

She turned and started walking again. I was on her left. Ben stepped up on her other side, separating her from the reporter.

"But is it true," he persisted, trying to talk around the obstruction of Ben's square physique, "that he wrote an article proposing the common ownership of land in cities?"

"Look," said Ben. "Why don't you join us for lunch?"

"What?" I said, stepping out in front of Maggie.

We all came to a jostling halt.

Ben looked at me. "Why not?" he said. "Why not let's get the story straight, right?"

I glanced at Maggie. She was undecided, bordering on angry. "Okay," I said. "That's actually a good idea I think. Let's do that."

Her eyes widened for just a moment. Then, without saying anything, she started walking again..

The four of us entered the café and got a table in the far corner. Maggie immediately excused herself to the ladies room.

"She's a bit touchy about her father," I told the reporter. "He died suddenly a couple of years ago. They were really close." I glanced up at Ben when I said this, wondering if this registered with him in some way. But he was reading the menu.

"I'm sorry," the reporter said. "I had no idea about that."

"So is this a big story with the papers?" Ben said, putting the menu down. "Architecture doesn't usually get much attention—unless something collapses."

"It's just second page stuff," the reporter said. "But there's a lot of interest. The IMF is here observing this—international interest. It's been in and out of the news for a while now. My editor thought maybe this communism angle could move it to the front page. This is a pretty conservative region, you know. The idea of building a communist inspired city in the middle of the state of Iowa would obviously generate some attention."

"So what do you want?" I said. "Do you want the truth? Or do you want to sell newspapers with some half-baked story about…"

"Please! Charles Cadwell, right?" The reporter held out his hand. I shook it. He gave a friendly smile. He and I were about the same age. "I'm a reporter, right?" he said. "I don't make up the news. Or at least I try not to."

The thought occurred to me that if I'd left the fish camp when I first understood CM's plans, I might now be a reporter just like him. For some reason this made me trust him.

"Okay," I said. "I believe that."

Maggie came up to the table and Ben stood immediately to pull out her chair.

"Thanks," she said. "Have you guys ordered yet?"

"No," said Ben, looking around for a waiter.

"So," said Maggie, regarding the reporter over the tops of her glasses, "Mister…?"

"Franks," he said again. "Oley Franks."

"Okay, Oley," she said. "Can we be friendly about this?"

"Yes, of course!" he said, smiling. "I think we're getting along pretty good here," he added, looking at me.

"I think we can trust him," I said to Maggie.

"You should stop saying that," said Ben. "Otherwise he'll start thinking there's some big secret we're trying to hide."

"Are you?" asked the reporter straight out, all business. He pulled a small notebook from the inside pocket of his sports coat. It reminded me of the black notebooks CM was always writing in.

"Of course we're not trying to hide anything." Maggie said.

"You folks ready to order?" A blonde-haired waitress in a pink dress and white apron stood next to our table, writing pad in hand. The café, I noticed, was beginning to fill up. Two of Abe Pikeman's group—what was it that made them so instantly distinctive to me?—had walked in. Their buttoned up suit coats? Or was it the way they were always looking around, as if they expected someone to be hiding behind the curtains, or spying down from the light fixtures.

We quickly picked up our menus and ordered.

"My editor pointed out to me," said Oley Franks, "that your town plan for New Hope, in fact, includes the idea of all the property being commonly owned. Is that right?"

"Not exactly," said Maggie in a tone that clipped off any willingness to explain. She clearly was not warming up to this.

"What she means," I interjected, "is that the land area is owned by a non-profit entity that builds what we call the Enabling Structure. After that, building spaces within the Enabling Structure are assigned—"

"I wouldn't use the word 'assigned'," said Ben.

"Right," I said. "What I meant—"

"I think a better word," said Ben, "would be leased. Just like property is normally leased. No different."

"Are you part of the McCormick Team as well?" Oley Franks asked, referring to some earlier notes in his little book. "I didn't catch your name."

"Ben Sprague, AIA," Ben said, smiling smoothly with the melodic syllables. "I'm sort of an adjunct member of the team."

"I see." The reporter was writing in his notebook. Then to Ben: "But what is the purpose of this Enabling Structure? Why put in this extra step before the property is privately owned?"

"Well," said Ben, warming up to being in the spotlight, "the Enabling Structure is perpetually owned by the non-profit community—only the architecture is privately owned. The Enabling Structure is the community skeleton, if you will, and everyone owns that together."

"The what?" said Oley Franks.

"I don't think…" I began to say, but Ben turned on his presentation voice and started to roll.

"That's how I think of it, anyway," he continued. "The town first designs and builds its skeleton. The structure that holds everything up, holds everything together, you see?" He was making a shape with his hands, which the reporter was observing doubtfully.

"It's like this," said Ben, grabbing the salt and pepper shakers from the middle of the table. He quickly made an arbitrary arrangement of the shakers and his knife, fork and spoon on the paper place mat in front of him. Then he grabbed Oley's silverware too, and expanded the arrangement. "Let's just say this is the skeleton," he said. "This is owned by the whole community, right? It's built all at once—one big, centrally managed project."

"Okay," said Oley Franks.

"So this is the skeleton," Ben continued. "And from here to here is the part of the skeleton you lease from the community. And from here to here, is the part that I lease. And from here to here is the part that Maggie leases—except the rent for her lease is cut in half because she's a single mom, right? And this last part of the skeleton, here, is transferred to Charlie there on a deferred lease basis—meaning he doesn't have to pay any rent for his piece of the skeleton for ten years because he's going to build something the community really wants—a day-care center, say. There's lots of ways the leases can be set up. Are you with me?"

"Sort of, I guess," said Oley Franks, studying the odd assemblage of condiments and silverware.

"So now," Ben reached and pulled out a handful of the flat sugar packets from their holder in the center of the table. "I build something around my part of the skeleton." He began leaning sugar packets against the shakers and silverware, like little tents. "In other words, I create the actual living and work spaces I need for my project. I use the Enabling Structure to help me do that. Right? I make it become complete architecture. And you do the same over here with your section." More sugar packets. "And Maggie does it here. And Charlie over here. See? The skeleton gets enclosed and incorporated into all these little projects. And I own my project, and you own yours. You can sell your project, for a profit hopefully, and whoever buys it takes over paying the rent on the skeleton. And what we have as a result is this community, or this town, that's been organized by the Enabling Structure."

"I think I sort of get it," said Oley Franks, staring down at the little village of sugar packets. "But why do it that way?"

"Who had the ham and cheese?" The waitress has arrived, our lunch plates balanced on her arms.

Ben quickly and deftly dismantles his village and redistributes the silverware while the waitress serves the lunch plates. Now Ben is looking at Maggie's plate.

"I thought you ordered Bleu Cheese dressing." he said.

"It doesn't matter," said Maggie. "This is fine."

We ate for a while in silence.

"So, Mr. Sprague," Oley Franks said. "You were going to tell me why."

"Why?" Ben had just taken an aggressive bite of cheeseburger.

"Why build a town that way? Why build New Hope the way you just described."

"I can answer that," I said, glancing sideways at Maggie, reaching into my memory for the Answer that I knew so perfectly.

Oley Franks turned his attention to me, and suddenly I had no idea what I was going to say. The practiced sentences I had been about to pronounce with such confidence seemed completely erased, as if someone had yanked the power cord to my brain stem. I just stared at him, my face going numb.

"It's simple," said Ben, putting his hamburger down. "We do it that way because it creates an economy. Doing it the other way—for example that glass city of Oz we just saw presented—that way just creates buildings. We don't just create buildings. We create an economy. Do you see the difference?" He had a french fry in his fingers now, and was pointing with it at the collapsed sugar-packs he'd slid to the center of the table.

"The process we're talking about is very inefficient, messy, chaotic even," he continued. "It's all these little separate projects, all these individual purchases and efforts—and that creates an economic engine. It spreads the economic opportunity over the largest number of people. To a certain extent it's unpredictable. But the Enabling Structure organizes all of that unpredictability into a very tight urban order—and that order has been carefully thought out and designed beforehand."

I was still staring at Ben's french fry, trying to reconnect with my memory. Then Maggie's hand was squeezing my knee. "So I guess we've convinced you," she was interjecting to Oley Franks, "that we're not communists, right?"

"I think I can see that," he said.

"That's all we have time for now, I'm afraid." Maggie said. She looked at her watch. "We've got to be getting back."

"Okay," said Oley Franks. "Look, I'll get lunch, okay? I appreciate you giving me the interview. Maybe after tomorrow…"

"Maybe we could arrange something," said Maggie, standing up.

"Are you in a hurry, Mag?" Ben asked, picking up his cheeseburger again.

"I want to have better seats for the afternoon presentation," she said. "Come on Charlie. Ben, you can catch up with us."

Outside, Maggie put her arm through mine and pulled me against her shoulder as we walked down the sidewalk. "You okay, Charlie?" she asked quietly.

"I don't know," I said. My mind still felt numb. "I don't know if I'm going to be able to do this."

She squeezed my arm. "You can do it."

"Ben could do it better."

"If CM had wanted Ben to do it he would have asked him."

"But…"

"Remember that."

"That doesn't change the fact that Ben could do it better."

"I don't want Ben to do it."

"I appreciate that."

"I'm serious, Charlie. I don't. And CM doesn't either. And as a matter of fact, I don't think Ben could do it better. You just didn't have your script with you, that's all. You just drew a blank. That could happen to anybody."

But it was more than just forgetting that was bothering me. I was shocked to realize how quickly I'd been swayed by the other presentation, by the "land of Oz" city, as Ben had so accurately labeled it. No one knew this but me. But I knew it, and I decided now, no matter what else happened, I was going to perform flawlessly the next day. I was going to do whatever it took to make that happen.

49

IF THE MORNING PRESENTATION WAS about glass, the afternoon session was about porches. This was the Patriot Homes team, the one owned by I-Mart, the entry which, according to CM, was in the back pocket of Congressman Pikeman. I noticed, oddly, that the Congressman wasn't even there. Three of his buttoned-up body-guards studiously occupied the center of the second row, but his wide, elegant form was absent. Half way through the presentation I figured out why: He'd probably heard it before, and saw no reason to spend such a boring two hours again. Suffice it to say, if Patriot Homes got the deal, the people of New Hope were going to get a lovely suburban town, with quaint front porches, two car garages, five floor plans to choose from, and an I-Mart approximately the size of an airport terminal.

When we returned to the Wapsi Hilton late that afternoon, I carried the box of CM's manuscripts up to my room. I spread them out on the bed and began to organize them, for the first time, in what I thought was a sequential logic. I reread my Answer page twice, then a third time, then recited it to the mirror with my eyes closed. I tried to think of some mnemonic device to irrevocably attach the opening sentence to my most accessible brain cells.

Next, I practiced the presentation itself, reading the script—both my parts and Maggie's—pacing the room, pointing at the imagined model with the telescoping pointer Ben had given me from the glove compartment of his BMW. Then I stood listening for the question:

"Mr. Cadwell?"

"Yes?"

"Can you please tell us why this Enabling Structure isn't just an extra step? Why should we build a city in such an awkward and inefficient manner?"

"It's true that vertical architecture appears to be much more efficient," I would begin.

Suddenly I felt an overwhelming tiredness. I plopped in the chair by the through-wall air-conditioner and closed my eyes. If I could just get a good night's sleep, tomorrow it would be over. I just needed to relax and calm down, let things unfold, do what I'd promised to do: read the script, drive back to the fish camp, finish my unit, learn to fly-fish....

The phone rang.

"You ready for dinner?" Maggie asked.

"I think I'm going to skip it," I said. "I'm just going to stay here, go over the script a couple of times, have a couple of beers and go to bed."

"You're not coming with us?" She sounded concerned. "Are you okay?"

"I'm fine," I said. "You guys go ahead. It'll give you a chance to catch-up."

"We don't need to catch up, Charlie."

"Well, I didn't mean it that way," I said. "I just meant—"

"Okay," she said with hesitation. "We'll check on you when we get back."

"I think I'm going to turn in early," I said. "I want to get a good night's sleep."

"I'll give you a wake-up call then. Bright and early, right?"

"I'll be ready."

I hung up the phone and closed my eyes again. When I opened them, the room was dark and quiet, but I was too tired to even get out of the chair and crawl to the bed.

When I opened my eyes again, someone was knocking on the door.

I wondered, why they would they come back so soon from dinner? I turned on the desk light and hopped over to the door in my stocking feet.

"Mr. Cadwell?"

I was confused. Two men in dark buttoned up suits stood at the door, one tall, one short. Absurdly, I looked for Maggie and Ben behind them. They stepped inside and pressed the door closed.

"Can I help you?" I said.

The taller one stood by the door. The short one stepped into the room and did a circle, looking at things. He ended up looking at me as if he was gauging what size box I'd fit in.

"I'm Mr. Jones," he said. "We're here to give you a ride. Are you ready?" He looked doubtfully at my feet. "You'll probably want some shoes."

"Where are we going?" I asked.

"To visit the Congressman," he said. "The Congressman would like to have a little conversation, that's all. He asked us to swing by and give you a lift."

"The Congressman?"

"The honorable Abe Pikeman," said the man by the door.

"Abe Pikeman? Wants to talk to me?"

"Pretty flattering, huh?" said Mr. Jones.

"Why does he want to talk to me?"

"Hey, we're only the chauffeurs, Mr. Cadwell. These your shoes over here?" He walked over by the bed, craning his head to read the papers spread out there.

"That's personal stuff," I said.

"I was just getting your shoes," he said. He kicked them in my direction, one at a time. "The Congressman likes his visitors to wear shoes."

"Look," I said. "I'll be happy to have a conversation with the Congressman. But I can drive myself." I slipped my feet into the shoes, leaning down to pull the heels on. "I have some errands I need to run anyway."

"Now that's silly," said Mr. Jones, smiling suddenly. "The Congressman always likes to provide transportation for his guests."

I picked up my sports coat from the back of a chair and put it on, checking the side pocket for the keys to the Toyota. "I can follow you guys," I said.

"Don't panic here, Mr. Cadwell," said Mr. Jones. "We'll have you back in an hour. Why panic? A United States Congressman wants to have a conversation and you look like you want to jump out the window."

"I'm not panicking. I just have some errands I remember now...."

"We can stop off anywhere you want on the way." He smiles again. "Shall we go?"

"Look," I said, trying to make my voice calm and reasonable and entirely cooperative. "I really prefer..."

He put his arm through mine and locked it there with a muscle I could feel through his coat sleeve. "The Congressman really insists," he said.

The tall guy opened the door. "It would be a shame to disappoint the Congressman," he said as we walked through.

I recognized the car immediately. A vivid memory: That day on the river—Maggie and I standing at the top of the chute, my hand grasping her arm to help her regain her balance, the pulsing water shooting past behind her, the alarmed expression in her eyes looking over my shoulder, the long, black sedan with black reflective windows, sitting on the bridge above the X-braces.

My stomach began squeezing into a knot, my mind racing, trying to connect things together. Mr. Jones opened the rear black door with his free hand. I held back, looking across the parking lot where I could see the Toyota. The impulse to run built up in my reflexes. His muscular arm tightened again around mine.

"It's just a visit with a Congressman," he whispered. "Relax."

He shouldered me, almost gently, into the back seat and closed the door.

The tall guy got in the driver's side. Mr. Jones slid into the passenger seat and turned to look at me. A small perceptible clunk as the doors locked.

"Comfy?" he asked.

"How far do we have to go?"

"Oh, it's not far. Just out in the country a bit."

"Why is the Congressman out in the country?" I'd seen enough movies to begin playing out in my imagination what was going to take place.

"The Congressman likes to relax," said Mr. Jones. "He doesn't like the city congestion."

We drove in silence for about ten minutes. At the edge of town we passed the restaurant where Maggie and Ben and I had eaten the night before. A great longing welled up in me to be in there again, and I twisted around and watched the neon sign disappear as we turned a corner and swung up onto the interstate—the same interchange with the big green and white sign Maggie and I had arrived on. I found myself trying to push back time. To be back then driving along with her beside me. I knew what was now could not actually be happening. Time had gotten out of sync somehow—disconnected.

In a calm center of my thinking, I determined, definitely, that as soon as they opened the door I was going to run. I didn't think past that. I simply decided it would be stupid not to run—and in the end, less painful. I did not want pain. I wanted to just run, to explode with adrenaline. If they tried to grab me, I'd kick them in the face or groin and run like hell. I wouldn't let my mind go beyond that. I began to focus entirely on this plan: To run.

The car exited the interstate. We turned onto a two lane country road. There were a few lonely lighted farmhouses out in the fields: Distant refuges of normality—families watching the late night news, unaware of our fateful passing. Then we slowed—my stomach became rigid—and turned left onto a narrow asphalt driveway with big cedar trees lined up formally on each side. The driveway ascended slowly, the headlights reaching stiffly out in the dark, catching the gnarly edges of the cedar trunks.

Suddenly, a large house looms up straight ahead. White columns. A mansion. Tall lighted windows. A circular drive, around which we slowed to a stop.

"Here we are," said Mr. Jones.

"Whose house is this?" I asked, surprised, trying to recalculate what was happening. Somehow I'd been expecting that we'd be pulling into an empty field, dark and remote.

"A friend of the Congressman. An associate."

I relaxed slightly. Maybe I really was going to be meeting someone. The idea of running suddenly didn't seem to fit anymore.

The tall driver got out and opened my door. Mr. Jones climbed out the other side. The driver motioned with his hand for me to go in front of him. Mr. Jones and I climbed the steps to the front door side by side, the driver behind us. Mr. Jones pressed the doorbell.

The door was opened by a man dressed like a servant—an elderly man.

"The Congressman's guest," Mr. Jones announced.

The servant nodded and stepped aside. I walked in and the servant closed the door behind me. I looked back, surprised the others hadn't followed.

"This way, if you please," the servant said.

I followed him through the tall foyer, glancing up at a crystal chandelier hanging over us like a colossal electrified spider. We walked single file down a high corridor with illuminated, heavy-framed paintings on either side. At the end of the corridor is a gilded, cut-glass mirror reflecting our approaching figures.

The servant stopped abruptly and turned, motioning with his arm for me enter a room to the left. I stepped in and could feel the door being closed behind me.

It was a library and reading room: two floor-to-ceiling walls of bookshelves on either side of a large bay window. The room was dimly illuminated by table lamps. The glass window panes reflected back the shapes and colors of the book shelves. Between where I stood and the sitting area was a large bronze statue of a horse rearing up on a marble pedestal, its uplifted nostrils nearly touching the ceiling.

I hesitated, listening, looking.

"Please come in Mr. Cadwell." A deep, lazy drawling voice. "Don't be shy."

I stepped around the statue and confronted Abe Pikeman, U.S. Congressman, short grey hair neatly combed, immersed in a deep leather chair with his black-stocking feet up on a puffy leather ottoman. He was balancing a hi-ball glass on the starched white stomach of his dress shirt. The shirt collar was open to a thatch of grey chest hair. His cufflinks, I could see now, were made from polished bullet casings.

"Excuse me if I don't get up," he said without moving. "It's been a long day."

I stood, looking at him, remembering what my father had told me happened in Idaho, trying to imagine this man standing in my father's doorway, flipping an FBI badge at him.

He made a little grin, as if he was offering to be friendly.

"Help yourself to a drink, Mr. Cadwell." He nodded toward a side table set up with a tray of glasses and decanters.

"Just some water," I said.

There was an iced metal pitcher on the tray. I poured a glass and drank it down quickly. Then poured another.

"You were thirsty," the Congressman observed.

I turned around and looked at him. He grinned again.

"Have a seat." He nodded, indicating a chair opposite his own. Except for these little directional movements with his forehead, he seemed immobile. Then he surprised me and took a sip from his hi-ball glass, the ice sliding and tinkling.

I sat in the deep leather chair he'd indicated.

He regarded me in silence. I took another sip from my glass of water and looked for a place to set it down. The chair I was in was so wide the nearest side table was beyond reach. I leaned forward, crouched out of the chair and reached the glass out onto the low table that separated us.

"I appreciate your coming to visit, Mr. Cadwell." His way of speech was deep and slow and relaxed.

"Well, I..."

"I'm a great admirer of your team's project. Your town plan."
"You are?"

"Indeed I am, Mr. Cadwell. Indeed I am. It is very inventive. Ingenious, I'd say."

I knew I couldn't trust him. I had to say as little as possible. What could this possibly be about?

He took another sip of his high-ball, the ice sliding and tinkling, then held the glass up to the light and eyed it.

"Would you mind giving me a refill?" he asked. "It's been a long day. It's the Chevis Regal—on the right. Have you ever had a long day?"

I retrieved the decanter and approached his nearly recumbent form. He lifted the glass off his stomach and held it out, eyes watching me from beneath bushy grey eyebrows.

"That's very hospitable of you," he said.

I returned the decanter and sat down again.

"As I was saying, Mr. Cadwell. I have great interest in the McCormick town plan. More than you might guess."

I nodded, my heart skipping at the way he said this. I knew suddenly this was not going well.

"It's because I appreciate it so much," the little grin again, "that I genuinely regret having to ask you to withdraw it."

"What?"

"I'm asking you to withdraw it, Mr. Cadwell. From the competition."

"But.... Why would you want us to do that?"

"Because it's not what we're looking for," he said. "It's not what we want."

"Who's we?"

His eyebrows went up. He took a little sip of his Chevis Regal.

"Is it always your custom to cross-examine a U.S. congressmen, Mr. Cadwell?"

"I didn't mean to cross-examine, sir. I just wondered who you meant by 'we'. I mean, what about the committee?"

"What about them?"

"Well, what if they like our plan?"

"That's exactly the point, don't you think, Mr. Cadwell?" The little grin.

"I don't think I understand."

He stared at me, blankly, waiting.

"What?" I said. "You mean you think we might win?"

"Your winning is not one of the options on the table, Mr. Cadwell. That's the little point we're here to come to agreement on."

There was an old pendulum clock on the side table, next to the tray of decanters, and it began a scratchy wind-up noise that led to a soft, single chime. I looked over at it. 9:30. How long had I been here?

"Mr. Cadwell, have you ever heard of Dow Chemical?"

"Who?" One side of my thinking went numb.

"The Dow Chemical Corporation."

"I've heard of them, I guess."

"Were you aware they have a manufacturing plant in Torrance, California? A plant that used to make something called napalm?"

I hesitated. "No."

"Did you know this plant was attacked by anti-war saboteurs in 1973? An explosion set off?"

"...No."

"Were you aware, Mr. Cadwell, that a Dow worker was killed in that explosion?"

"That's not true," I said.

His eyebrows arched up. He made his little grin, and took a sip of the Chevis Regal.

"Wasn't killed immediately is probably what you meant to say. Right, Mr. Cadwell?"

"What are you saying?" My heart was banging in my ears.

"I mean the worker recovered, of course. Even went back to his job." The little grin. "Six years later, though, he fell down dead for no apparent reason."

The Congressman shook his head with mock sadness.

"They did an autopsy, of course. You know what they found?"

I stared at him, my face now completely numb.

"They found a little piece of metal that had penetrated his chest during the explosion. Gotten up under his left ventricle, and slowly worked its way in....He died instantly. It was—how would you put it—a kind of delayed homicide."

I was staring at the hi-ball glass he still balanced on his starched white stomach, daintily held between his thick thumb and forefinger.

"We'd already caught the saboteurs, of course. Two of them at least. A third one escaped, disappeared...fshht!" He made a startling swat into the air with his free hand, causing the hi-ball glass to jostle, but not spill. "Did you know that, Mr. Cadwell?"

I stared at his face, trying to make sense out of the shapes of his cheeks and nose and lips. I was certain if I'd tried to speak my voice wouldn't make any sound.

"There's an envelope on the table there," he nodded again with his forehead. "You might be interested in what's inside."

"Actually, I don't think I am," I said, my voice squeaky. I could not even force my eyes to look at the table. My gaze had returned to the high-ball glass rising and falling on the white starchy stomach of his shirt.

"I think you should look, Mr. Cadwell," he said with genuine concern.

I looked down at the table. Next to my water glass was a page-sized manilla envelope I'd failed to notice earlier. I leaned forward, crouched out of my chair again and retrieved it. Inside were four 8X10 photos, glossy black and white. I looked at the first two, bewildered.

The photos were of an elderly man in work overalls, a thick scruffy beard and a stocking hat. He was sitting in the balcony of the presentation courtroom. I recognized the molding pattern above his head where the balcony wall met the high ceiling. He looked like an Iowa farmhand come into town for the presentation—or an auto-mechanic. I'd known an auto-mechanic once who wore a stocking hat like that—even in the summer.

I looked up at the Congressman with a blank expression.

"Look at all of them," Pikeman said. "Sometimes cameras have a hard time capturing the essence of a person."

The pictures captured the man looking in different directions. My confusion was beginning to be replaced with a new dread. I looked at the last photo a long time, my heart pounding again in my ears. The man was talking to an elderly lady sitting next to him. She was knitting, and had said something to him that had caused him to smile. A big, gap-tooth smile, that I instantly recognized.

I slid the photos back into the envelope. I stared at it in my hands, wanting it not to be there but not wanting to let it go.

"Looks like a charming fellow, don't you think?" said Pikeman.

I looked up at him. He'd moved. He'd taken his feet off the ottoman and now sat with one leg crossed over the other, one black-stocking foot bouncing just slightly in the air in a steady rhythm. This position made him taller, and I realized how big he was in the shoulders.

"Of course, we could have taken him in at any time since you've been here. But what would that accomplish? There might be a certain…sympathy for him in some minds. Certain people might rally around these ideas of horizontal skyscrapers and Enabling Structures. People are like that. And the sentiment of the press is so unreliable." He shook his head sadly about the dependability of the press. "We decided it would be preferable if he just quietly disappeared…along with the ideas. Do you see our perspective, Mr. Cadwell?"

"How long have you been following me?" I asked.

A little smile, as if he were going to enjoy telling me. "Oh, we've been following you ever since a pot-head guitar player made a visit to your father in Idaho. Ever since your mama drowned. Boys will generally find lost fathers, if they're findable. It's just a matter of time."

I shook my head slowly in disbelief, trying to think back if I'd ever seen anything like these buttoned-up guys in dark sedans in my high-school or college days.

"So I can assume, I believe, that we have an agreement?" Pikeman said.

"An agreement?" I said, trying to think through the numbness throbbing in my head.

Pikeman gave me a patronizing smile.

"It's very simple, Mr. Cadwell: If you were to go through with your presentation tomorrow, it might start some minor controversy in the press that we view as…unnecessary."

I stared at him.

"Don't you agree—how unnecessary that would be?"

I tested my tongue around in my mouth and swallowed.

"So, what we suggest is that you withdraw the McCormick plan before the presentation. Unforeseen circumstances." He smiled slyly. "Maybe Mr. McCormick's emergency surgery hasn't gone well? Maybe he's taken a sudden turn for the worse?"

"And then what? You'll let him go? You'll leave him alone?"

The little grin formed itself slowly on his lips. "Them, Mr. Cadwell. Them."

"Them?"

"Charles Robert—your father. And Margaret Scott."

"Maggie?"

"Harboring and aiding a wanted felon is a felony itself, Mr. Cadwell. Surely you were aware of that?"

"But she didn't even know...."

Pikeman shook his head with empathy.

A fluttering panic was trapped in my chest. I took a deep breath.

"How do I know you'll...keep your end of the deal?"

"Mr. Cadwell." He pretended shock. "I'm a U.S. Congressman. Besides, if you think it over, you don't really have any choice, do you? Can you see that, Mr. Cadwell? Can you see that you really have no choice whatsoever?"

My mind was trying to work, trying to understand this.

Pikeman watched me, his little grin relaxing into pleasure.

"Oh...one other thing," he said.

"What?"

"This conversation is our little secret, right? Not for anybody's ears but yours and mine. Not your father's. Not Miss Scott's. Not anybody's. Not ever."

His momentary pleasure was gone. He was staring at me with a steely harshness that emphasized, without a doubt, what he was capable of doing.

50

THE PHONE RANG SHRILLY, WAKING me. I squirmed on the bed-spread, realizing I was still fully dressed—even wearing my shoes. The bedside table light is on, illuminating CM's manuscripts spread out beside me. I lurched over to the phone.

"Wake-up call!" Maggie's perky voice. "You awake?"

"Yeah," I said, but then had to clear my throat and say it again. "Yeah, I'm up."

"You okay?" A note of concern.

"I'm fine." I had to clear my throat again to get my voice to resonate. "I'm fine."

"I've been up since 4:30," she said. "I almost called you earlier…to talk.

"Talk about what?"

"Nothing. Just talk."

"Okay."

"I decided you needed your beauty-sleep for today."

Today? My thinking is starting to operate now. Today?

"You need to wake-up, Charlie," she said. "Go take a cold shower. Do you want me to bring you a coffee?"

"No…. I'm fine," I said. "Let's meet downstairs. What time is it anyway?"

"Seven o:clock. Wake-up call. Remember?"

"How about seven thirty in the dining room. Okay?"

"All right. I'll be there sooner if you want to come down. Ben probably won't show up till later. He had a few too many glasses of wine last night. You sure you don't want me to bring you a coffee?" She was really revved up. "Help you get started? I've been up since 4:30!"

A vivid flash of Pikeman's grin materialized in front of my face. Panic was starting to expand and flutter under my ribs. How was this going to happen? How the hell was this going to work?

I stepped into the shower with the water running cold and gritted my teeth, imagining the coursing frigidity was a pain I had to endure, a pain I deserved. After less than a minute I started shivering and turned the faucet to hot and let the water hammer on the back of my neck, let the sound of it blot out my thinking.

I'd just lathered up my face to shave when the phone rang again.

"Do you need help bringing anything down?" said Maggie.

"No. I'm fine," I said. "I'm just getting out of the shower. I'll be a couple minutes late."

"Okay," she said, with a long hesitation in her voice.

After I dressed, I stacked the manuscript papers back into their box and slid the presentation script, and the silver telescoping pointer, into the soft black briefcase. The first line of my Answer unaccountably popped into my mind as I closed the latch. "It's true that vertical architecture appears to be much more efficient." There was a full length mirror on the closet door. I observed my suited figure and carefully straightened my tie before I left the room.

I found Maggie at the same table where we'd sat the first morning. She was staring out the window, elbow on the paper placemat, chin resting in her palm. She didn't hear me approach, so I stopped a few feet away and watched her. She was already dressed for the presentation, too. Her hair seemed slicked back more severely than before, making the bone of her cheek more pronounced, her pink, curlicue ear more naked below the black temple of her glasses.

"Whatcha thinking about?" I asked.

"Oh, Charlie!" she turned around, surprised. "I was thinking about—I was thinking about the fish camp." She adjusted her glasses.

"I think you're starting to like those glasses," I said, taking a seat and looking out the window. Avoiding eye contact was going to be tricky, I realized. I tried to calm myself into inscrutable neutrality. I knew she could read me like a book. "Have you seen the waitress?" I said, glancing now around the room.

"Is something wrong, Charlie?"

"No. I just need some breakfast here." I saw a waitress come out of the kitchen doors, and tried to flag her with my arm.

"Look at me, Charlie."

I glanced at Maggie quickly as the waitress came over.

"You ready to order?" she asked.

I looked down at the menu. "What are you going to have?" I said. I could feel Maggie's eyes working on me

"I'll just have oatmeal and wheat toast," she said.

I ordered the Swedish pancakes. The waitress started to clear away the extra place settings.

"You can leave one of those," said Maggie. "We're waiting for another person."

"You want me to wait on your orders?"

"I'll take mine now," I said. "And coffee too, please."

"I'll have some hot tea," said Maggie.

When the waitress turned to leave, I looked out the window again.

"Looks like it might snow or something," I said. "It looks cold out there. Have you been out?"

"I went for a walk early."

"And...?"

"It wasn't that bad. It didn't feel like rain to me...or snow."

"I wonder if it snows a lot here," I pondered.

"Charlie?"

"What?"

"Why are we talking about the weather?"

"The weather?" I glanced at her, then back out the window. "I was just wondering if it was cold out there, that's all. Whether I needed to put on my long underwear." I gave her a quick silly smile.

"I think your Tommy Hilfiger will be adequate," she said.

I stared out the window, ignoring this little joke, feeling my cheeks flush.

"So did you…practice last night?" asked Maggie.

"I went over it a couple of times," I said. "I…"

"What?" she asked.

"I got it to where I think I can do it really well," I said.

"You don't seem very…up, Charlie. Why won't you look at me?"

I looked at her. "You know what I just realized I forgot?" I said.

"What?"

"I forgot the pointer that Ben loaned me."

I stood up and reached down for the briefcase.

"We can get that after breakfast," said Maggie.

"I want to get it while I'm thinking about it," I said. "I'll be right back."

I flung the strap of the briefcase over my shoulder and walked quickly out of the dining room. I headed for the elevator lobby. My heart was beating as if I'd just run a sprint.

When I got to my room I flung the briefcase on the bed and began pacing the floor. How was this going to work? There were nearly two hours before the presentation was scheduled to begin. How the fuck was this going to work?

I picked up the phone and called Ben Sprague's room. He answered, sleepy-sounding on the third ring. We exchanged good-mornings.

"How soon can you come down to the dining room?" I said. "I've got some questions you can help with."

"Ah! Questions!" he perked up. "How about ten minutes," he said. "I can come back and get dressed after breakfast."

"Great. See you in ten minutes."

I paced the floor for five minutes, then grabbed the briefcase again and went down to the dining room. Coffee cups and a plastic coffee carafe were on the table, but Maggie was gone.

I sat down and sipped the coffee and looked out the window. Where had she gone? Had she followed me? Had she gone up to Ben's room? How was all this going to happen?

"We're front page," said Maggie excitedly, sliding abruptly into her chair.

She was reading a folded newspaper.

"We're what?"

"It's by that reporter we had lunch with. Oley Franks. Listen." And she read in her newspaper-reading voice, looking over the tops of her rectangular glasses.

I found myself staring at her hands holding the newspaper. The words she was reading made no sense; they were just background sounds accompanying the twitches of her fingers as they clutched the edges of the newsprint.

"Pancakes?" The waitress had arrived with our breakfast.

Maggie continued reading out loud, shifting how she held the newspaper to make room for her bowl of oatmeal. Then she put the folded paper down next to her bowl, looking at me with excitement. "So what do you think?" she asked.

Things seemed like they were happening now in a disconnected dream.

I poured syrup on my pancakes, an activity that helped me avoid Maggie's look.

"Charlie?"

"Well, well, the early risers!" Ben walked up to the table wearing jeans and a heavy, prickly shadow of black beard.

Maggie handed him the paper as he sat down.

"We're front page," she said, bristling with energy.

Ben read in silence.

"Wow," he said, looking up for a moment. Then he continued reading.

"Coffee?" asked the waitress, appearing suddenly next to Ben.

I took a bite of the pancakes. Maggie fiddled with her oatmeal.

"I guess he was paying attention to my little demonstration!" said Ben.

I could feel Maggie watching me. I was trying to figure out how to get away from the table.

"So Charlie, what was the question you had?" Ben asked.

I ignored Maggie's surprised look.

"I was wondering," I said, searching for what I'd thought I was going to ask him. "…Whether you thought we should tip the model up so the committee could see it better. You know, put something under it on one side."

"That's your question?"

I started talking fast now. "Yeah. I mean I was noticing yesterday that the committee really couldn't see down on the models very well from where they sat. They were just kind of looking at the side. You know what I mean? What do you think?" I took a bite of pancake and chewed rapidly, looking at Ben.

Ben was watching me chew. "I guess it wouldn't hurt," he said. "I guess we could do that...."

"That's exactly what I was thinking," I said, already starting to get up. I was slurping coffee and pushing back my chair at the same time. "I'm going on over there early and see what I can set up. I've got some pieces of wood in the back of the Toyota..." I was rising out the chair and trying to put my coffee cup back into the center of the little saucer in the same motion. I noticed an odd-shaped splotch of coffee on the white table cloth.

"Charlie? Where are you going?" said Maggie.

I got the cup right-side up in the middle of the saucer and picked up the strap of the briefcase.

"I'll meet you guys there," I said. "I'm going to see if I can get the model tipped up before everyone gets there."

"Don't you want some help?" said Maggie as I turned to go.

I stopped and looked back at her. I'd spent the whole summer trying to get Maggie to help me.

"I'll be fine," I said, meeting her gaze for the smallest fraction of a second I could manage. "I'll meet you there."

I walked through the lobby and out to the parking lot as fast as I could without running. The whole way I was expecting to hear Maggie calling out for me to stop, calling out for me to explain my behavior. As I got close to the Toyota, my strides lengthened. I jumped in and started it up without looking back.

I drove to the courthouse, circled it a couple of times, then parked on a side street. I sat looking out the windshield for a few minutes, my heart pounding. Forty-five minutes until people would begin filing into the presentation room. I realized, suddenly, I was going to need to park closer to the courthouse.

51

I WAS THE FIRST ONE to arrive at the court room. The guard who opened the door for me smiled and nodded his head.

"Good morning, Mr. Cadwell," he said.

I realized it was one of the guards who'd helped carry the model into the courthouse the day we arrived. I looked at him, surprised, knowing I should say something—but I couldn't focus on what that might be. I tried to nod my head at him in a friendly way.

"The model's already set up," he said, shooting his arm out to indicate its presence in the center of the courtroom.

"Good! Good," I managed to say. "Thanks."

I walked into the empty silence of the big room and put my briefcase on the presenter's table. The white table cloth under the microphone was the same. Now there were a few coffee stains and wrinkles. I took the presentation script out of the briefcase and put it on the table.

I went over to the model and looked down at it, imagining all the work that had gone into it. An image floated across my mind of the work desk in CM's studio with the cutting knife and cardboard chips and bottle of glue. The three section model was stretched out just as it was supposed to be—beautiful, but in a fundamental way incomprehensible—waiting for the script to illuminate what it meant, how a city would take form within and around that intricate mosaic of gardens and walls and columns. The miniature streetcars of the horizontal Zipper were distributed up and down the central pedestrian spine. The small fragments of the de-integrated I-Mart were identified and distributed as small, red box-shapes, each with a white "I" on its roof. The long arrays of solar collectors caught the courtroom lights, like tiny mirrors. I studied for a moment the three example projects which had been completed in the model, each with its garden planters and rain catchments and collector array. I imagined, for a moment, my unit up on the hill at the fish camp being built right there, in miniature in the model, and I suddenly wanted more than anything to be back at the river, back where everything was safe.

I sat down at the presentation table and waited. There was a round white clock centered in one of the wooden wall panels behind the committee table. No matter how much I willed it to stand still, the second hand continued to rotate, and the minute hand—just as I was convinced it would stay where it was—would jump to the next black tick-mark on the clock-face.

Committee members started entering, usually in pairs. They nodded my way and I nodded back, careful not to hold their eyes.

Dr. Albright came in briskly, her high-heels clicking. At first I'd thought it was Maggie and my heart clenched in a knot. She came over to the table and I stood.

"Good morning, Mr. Cadwell." A friendly smile.

"Good morning."

"I'm looking forward to your presentation," she said.

"I...am too," I said, glancing down at the typed script.

She joined the other committee members in an impromptu meeting off in the corner.

Spectators began to arrive and take seats on the lower level. I could hear people moving and talking above me in the balcony as well, but I didn't dare look up.

Clicking heels again. This time there was no doubt. Maggie and Ben appear, moving rapidly down the center aisle. Ben has added a tie to his tweed coat. He looks classically like an architect. Maggie's black suit makes her sun-bleached, slicked back hair seem luminous. She is, I notice, way more beautiful than anyone or anything in the courtroom. They walk side by side over to the table.

"You mind if I sit with you guys?" asked Ben.

"No!" I said. "I mean, I assumed you would."

"Maggie, you sit in the middle," Ben instructed, pulling another chair over to the table.

She slid into the chair next to me, adjusting her glasses.

"Charlie, are you okay?" she whispered at me.

"I'm fine."

Ben leaned forward and looked around Maggie. "Couldn't get the model tilted up?" he whispered.

"No. It wouldn't work," I whispered back. "I decided its fine the way it is."

The committee was taking their seats behind the long table. Silberman studiously avoided looking our way. He adjusted his microphone with a sour twisted expression. A sudden rustling and whispering rolled through the spectator area. Abe Pikeman was taking his seat in the middle of the second row, two of his assistants, buttoned up suits, on each side of him. I looked instantly away when his head turned in my direction, my cheek burning as if he'd slapped it. My heart commenced thumping as if it were operating with pistons.

"Charlie?" Maggie leaned the weight of her shoulder into mine.

"Will the guard please close the door?" Dr. Albright said into her microphone.

It was all beginning. I could feel the events beginning to slide down on me.

"This morning we are pleased to hear from the McCormick Group. Are you ready, Mr. Cadwell? Miss Scott?"

I cleared my throat and licked my lips.

"Miss Albright...Madame chair, I mean," I said into the microphone. "We have something to say...an announcement."

"Yes?"

I stood now, feeling suddenly exposed. I could feel Maggie's surprise next to me. I tilted the microphone up.

"Miss Albright. Dr. Albright, I mean... I regret to inform you that we've just received news that requires us to...withdraw from the competition."

"Excuse me, Mr. Cadwell?"

"Charlie?" Maggie is pulling on my sleeve.

"We have to withdraw our entry." I said. Then more decisively, my voice rising: "We have to leave immediately for the West Coast."

A muffled commotion in the balcony above me.

Dr. Albright bangs her gavel, looking up above my head. "Quiet! Can we please have quiet!...." Then she looks back at me: "...Mr. Cadwell?"

But I've already thrown the script back into the briefcase and slung it over my shoulder.

"What's happening, Charlie?" Maggie's voice is panicky.

"We have to leave," I say to her, more harshly than I intend. I reached down and grab her arm, but she pulls it away. "We have to go, Maggie! Now!"

I walked quickly toward the doors, keeping my eyes straight ahead. For a moment I thought the guard—I recognized him again with surprise—was going to block my way. But as I neared he pushed the door open for me.

I met his eyes for a moment, then headed rapidly down the corridor.

There were footsteps behind me, coming fast. A complicated rapid staccato on the marble floor. Maggie was coming. I got to the outside doors and held them open. Maggie and Ben were nearly running. Behind them, down the corridor, people were spilling out of the courtroom in a loud buzz of conversation.

Out on the sidewalk, Maggie grabbed my arm trying to stop me.

"Charlie! What are you doing? What's happening?"

"I can't tell you," I said.

Maggie looked at me, uncomprehending.

"What do you mean you can't tell us?" said Ben, stepping up beside her. "What's going on here?"

"Look," I said. "Let's get away from here before they're all over us asking questions. Okay? I'll meet you at the hotel."

"But Charlie..." Maggie started to say.

"Just go!" I shouted at her, and I pushed past Ben Sprague, clipping his shoulder with mine.

People were starting to come out on the sidewalk. I walked quickly away across the grass, toward the side door parking space where I'd left the Toyota. I was hoping that Maggie and Ben would have no choice but to leave as well.

When I got to my hotel room I pulled out my suitcase, opened it on the bed and started flinging clothes in it. The phone rang.

"Charlie, we have to talk," said Maggie in a breathless voice. "What are you doing?"

"I'm packing."

"Charlie, what's wrong? What's happened…?"

"I can't explain it to you right now," I said. "But I know we have to leave. You need to start packing Maggie. Please. Believe me."

"Charlie, I want you to come down here right now and tell us what's going on."

"Look, damn-it. There's nothing to tell. Its just over, that's all. Okay? It wasn't meant to happen. We have to pack-up and leave."

She hung up.

I went in the bathroom and swept stuff off the counter top into a plastic bag.

The phone rang again.

"Ben has offered to drive," Maggie said coldly. "I'm going with him." She was angry now.

"Okay."

"Where are you going?"

"I'm going back."

"Back to the fish camp?"

"Oh, Jesus," I said. "Where do you think…?"

"What am I supposed to think, Charlie?"

"Just try not to be angry," I said. "I'm sorry, Miggs. I'm really sorry…"

Silence. I knew what she must be thinking.

"Maggie?"

"Charlie, this is really bad," she said, and hung up.

When I pulled out of the hotel parking lot Ben's BMW was still there. I drove around the block and parked where I could watch it. I wanted to make sure Maggie left, that nothing happened. I was worried about the commotion up in the balcony. What had that been about? I was half expecting to see Pikeman's associates drive up to the hotel in their buttoned up suits. I was still pumped with adrenaline. Ready to fight now. I imagined gunning the Toyota over the curb and driving through the bushes to run them down before they could get to the hotel entrance. I could see picking them off, one by one, on the front grill....

Then Maggie and Ben appeared, walking quickly toward the BMW. The trunk popped open before they got to it and Ben slung in their luggage. Maggie stood by watching him. She seemed slumped, wilted. He took her arm and guided her around to the passenger side and opened the door. It seemed like he had to push her in.

I realized I was going to follow them.

I managed to keep the blue-grey BMW in sight for the rest of the afternoon, staying five or six cars behind on the interstate. They stopped in the early afternoon and checked into a Hampton Inn. I parked in an I-Mart parking lot next door and fell asleep, sitting behind the steering wheel trying to keep watch on the BMW. When I woke it was nearly dark. Ben's car was still there, glinting under the sickly sodium lights in the parking lot.

Later, Ben came out alone and drove off. He returned with a boxed pizza and a paper bag twisted tight around the neck of a bottle. Wine, I assumed from the shape of it. I watched him walk back into the motel with his big confident strides.

I stared a long time at the lighted Hampton Inn windows, wondering which one they were behind. Imagining what they were talking about. Imagining their little meal of pizza and wine. Imagining how they were getting ready for bed.

I got out of the Toyota and walked a long ways up behind the I-Mart to find a tree I could pee behind. I walked back to the Toyota and climbed into the back of the camper. I rolled up in my old familiar smelling quilt. The one we'd used as the main cushion for the model of New Hope. When I climbed out of the camper the next morning, the BMW was gone.

52

I COMPLETED THE DRIVE BACK to Washington much as I'd made my original journey there, stopping only for gas and food, and to roll-up for a couple of hours in the quilt in the back of the camper. I wouldn't let myself think about the commotion in the balcony—about the vision I had in the back of my mind of Pikeman's men manhandling CM into handcuffs and secreting him away. That couldn't have happened, I thought. Pikeman's buttoned-up suit men were all sitting down below on either side of the Congressman himself. The commotion in the balcony had come too quickly. I replayed it over and over as I drove. Also, Pikeman had given his word. I'd done what he'd asked. More likely, I decided, the commotion had been CM's rapid exit when he realized what was happening. He would have been the first one out of the courthouse. He would probably get back to the fish camp before any of us. Or he might lay low in Seattle for a while. I decided I'd wait three days before I'd let myself even begin to worry.

At first I was surprised to realize CM had been there, up in the balcony, disguised like a migrant worker, listening to all the presentations in the courtroom, looking down at Abe Pikeman's entrances and exits. But then I understood he'd planned this from the beginning, and there was no place else he could have been. It was not possible that he wasn't going to be there when the thing he'd worked on for so many years was going to be presented to the world.

I skipped Port Townsend. Some part of me felt it would be good luck to repeat my initial route, my initial steps. Perhaps CM would be at the Blue Moose having a cup of coffee, waiting for me, knowing I'd stop there. But I knew that was fantasy. I headed straight for Port Angeles and drove through it without stopping.

In Forks, I stopped for gas and had a quick dinner. It was dark and drizzling. I was sure I'd be at least a day ahead of Maggie and Ben. They must have spent another night at a motel. Maybe even two. I'd started considering the possibility they wouldn't show up at all. Maybe Maggie would send me a postcard from Portland— or wherever it was Ben had said he lived. Maybe this was the thing that would get them back together. Ben had wanted that, I knew. I wasn't sure about Maggie. Imagining what she must think of me made my heart ache with shame. I decided I was going to have to tell her. Why hadn't I already told her? How could Pikeman ever know? Maybe there was a different way I could have handled it back in Iowa. Even so, I didn't trust Pikeman an inch. He was deadly. My mind was such a chaos of thoughts and feelings I had difficulty focusing on my chicken-fried steak. I hardly touched it.

I drove out of Forks and down the long hill, my headlights reaching feebly into the drizzle, the windshield wipers slapping. I turned left off the main highway and began ascending the narrow winding asphalt, my headlights catching the broad bases of the big fir trees on either side. The drizzle had subsided leaving a thick misty darkness that seemed to absorb the Toyota's headlights. I drove faster than I should, anxious to get to there.

The road seemed to go on longer than I remembered. Finally the asphalt changed to the gravel two-track. And abruptly, ahead of me, illuminated in my headlights was the blue-grey BMW.

How could they have gotten ahead of me? What had happened? They were pulled off to the side, leaning slightly. As I approached the driver's door opened. Ben got out holding his hand out against the glare of my headlights.

I stopped and turned the lights off, momentarily blinded in the darkness.

"Jesus, is that you Charlie?" Ben's voice approaching. I got out.

"What are you guys doing here?" I said, trying to force my eyes to adjust to the dark. "Where's Maggie?"

"I'm here." I made out a figure standing on the other side of the BMW.

"This is luck," said Ben. "We'd just decided to start walking."

"But why are you stopped?"

"It started overheating outside of Forks," said Ben in a low-ered voice. "We've been driving like maniacs. Maggie wanted to get back here like her life depended on it. I don't have a flash-light."

It was cold. Our talk came out in white puffs.

"Let me throw some stuff in the camper," I said. "You guys can squeeze in with me. We can come back and check it out in the morning."

I grabbed an armful of maps and sweatshirts and peanut wrap-pers from the front seat. Ben opened the back of the camper for me.

When I climbed into the driver's seat, the passenger door opened and Maggie looked in at me. Her black rectangular glasses were gone. The greenish light from the dashboard made her cheeks look sunken.

"Hi Charlie."

"Come on. Get in." I said, "It's cold out there."

She stepped in and slid over toward me. Ben got in, his bulk forcing Maggie over against my shoulder. This sudden touch was like an electric shock, almost painful. Ben reached out and pulled the door closed, pushing Maggie against me again. She was rigid.

I switched on the headlights and pulled around the BMW. The drizzle had started again. I turned on the wipers. We drove in silence, Maggie's shoulder bumping mine with its strange, painful sparks.

Soon we crossed the one-lane bridge. After the bridge, the headlights bounced stiffly into the muddy darkness ahead, catch-ing glimpses of big trunks and branches on either side of the road ruts. Then the blue rock lit up, bright in the headlights, and next to it the big shaggy tree trunk flashing strangely now with sparkling, iridescent silver shapes.

Maggie caught her breath.

Instinctively, I slammed on the brakes. I stared without comprehension at the scene illuminated before us. A dozen or more severed fish-heads were nailed to the broad side of the tree trunk, big spike nails hammered straight through each eye, the mouths gaping, the severed necks dripping.

"Oh God," Maggie choked. She put her hands over her eyes. "Oh, Jesus!"

My stomach clutched tight.

"What the hell?" said Ben softly.

I squeezed the steering wheel and edged the Toyota forward, past the grizzly scene of the tree. I turned at the blue rock and we bounced slowly down the familiar little hill and came out under the dripping branches. The headlights reached stiffly ahead into the darkness. I hit the high-beams and they extended brightly out across the rocky meadow. I edged forward and the blackness seemed to grow deeper the further the high-beams reached.

Then I realized what was gnawing at my stomach: it was the smell, growing stronger, of wet charred wood. Maggie suddenly was reaching across Ben, pushing on the door latch, her body a panic of motion. I stopped the truck and killed the blinding lights that were illuminating nothing. The door flung open and Ben tried to climb out with Maggie crawling over him at the same time. She went down on the ground, then was up again, running ahead with a harsh scream into the dark: "Louise!"

I stepped out into the cold drizzle, squinting into the darkness. Maggie's black shape was running ahead. Unfamiliar, low, bulky forms were materializing in the grainy murk. The wet burned smell was intense.

A dark figure stepped out from a boulder and merged into Maggie as she ran. They grappled. Then became frozen together, unmoving.

I ran forward, adrenaline surging, then stopped. Maggie and the other figure were crouched ahead, twisted oddly together. I stepped up cautiously.

CM had his arms around her. They were on their knees. Maggie's face was buried against him, her shuddering cries muffled by his heavy coat. His head was up looking over her, past her, out at the black shapes where the Fish Camp had been. I could see now there were twisted metal roofing sheets, tangled in the blackness.

I stepped around CM and Maggie and started forward.

"Don't Charlie," CM said. "Don't go over there."

I turned around and looked back at him. Maggie was still clutched into his chest like a broken shape of clothes.

"What happened?" I said.

"They burned us out."

"But what about…Louise and Gus? Where are they?"

"They got out. I've seen them. They're okay…"

"But who…?"

"It doesn't matter, Charlie…."

Ben walked past us like a ghost.

"Don't go down there," CM said again. "It's dangerous in the dark."

Ben stopped. I looked past him, my eyes seeing more and more in the grey darkness. It looked like an airplane crash. The silver roof slabs were twisted and broken and charred like fragments of giant wings.

My head turned up toward the hill.

"It's all gone," said CM. "I've looked. Everything is gone."

In the graying light I could see the heavy smudge of smoke hanging like a shroud draped over the trees on the hill.

Maggie had separated herself now and was on her knees, head down, hands over her ears.

"We have to go," said CM. "We have to leave here now."

Maggie was shaking her head from side to side.

CM grasped her shoulders and helped her stand. "We have to leave," he said again. "You come with me, Miggs."

"My car's broke down," said Ben.

CM regarded him as if he was wondering, for a moment, who he was.

"You ride with Charlie. I'm taking Maggie to where Gus and Louise are staying. You can follow me. Keep your lights off till I turn mine on."

CM's pick-up was parked behind some boulders up near the edge of the trees. Ben and I got in the Toyota. I backed around and waited for CM to pull out ahead.

We drove slowly in single file, lights off. As we eased by the black hulk of the giant tree, the fish-heads sparkled ghostly pale.

"What the fuck has been going on here?" said Ben.

"I'm…not really sure," I said.

We crept along in the dark. We passed the BMW.

CM kept his lights off until we reached the asphalt. Then he illuminated the road and sped up. I did the same. We drove into Forks. The restaurants were closed. Only the motels were lighted as we drove by. CM turned onto a side road and we followed his dented blue tailgate into a neighborhood of little houses. He stopped in front of one. A single bare bulb illuminated a brick stoop. Maggie's red Cherokee was parked in the drive.

We got out and stood in a little group, looking at the house.

"This is where Louise and Gus are staying," CM said quietly. "They're probably asleep—but they'll be happy for you to wake them up."

Ben had put his arm around Maggie. She seemed to be shivering.

"Where are you going?" I asked CM.

"I'm going…Look, let's talk a minute, Charlie." He pulled me off to the side.

"Where are you going?" I asked again.

"I'm going to Canada," he said. "I've got it set up. You don't have to worry about it."

"I'm going with you," I said.

"No, Charlie, there's no reason…"

"There is a reason," I said. "I'm going with you."

He looked at me, the wrinkles around his eyes etched deeply by the distant harsh light bulb.

"You should stay with Maggie," he said.

"She doesn't need me. She's got Louise and Gus. And Ben."

"Look, I don't know what went wrong back in Iowa, but…."

"It doesn't have anything to do with that," I said.

"Okay," he said. "We can take your truck and leave Gus mine. After I get settled, you can come back down and check on things for me."

"Oh Lord!" came a familiar voice from the brick stoop.

Louise had come out of the door wringing the front of her bathrobe in her hands, Gus behind her. Maggie broke away from Ben and ran across the yard towards them.

53

IT WAS STILL THE MIDDLE of night when CM and I drove through Seattle, headed north on the Interstate. I marveled again at the huge scale of the skyline, lit up now like immense transparent crystals in the darkness, bright and clean—and completely empty, it seemed, of life.

"Don't speed," said CM.

"Okay."

North of Seattle CM started writing in his little black note-book, using a small pen-light to see with. He carefully tore out the page, folded it, and wedged it into the ashtray with the dimes and quarters I kept there.

"That's where I'll meet you," he said.

"What do you mean?" A wiggle of panic in my stomach.

"I'm not driving across the border with you."

"Why not?" I said. "You have a driver's license, right?"

"Yes. But I don't trust the situation right now," he said.

"What do you mean?"

He was silent for a moment. The headlights were clicking off the white dashed stripes of the interstate.

"Pikeman got to you, didn't he Charlie."

I squeezed the steering wheel, my stomach clenching.

"You can tell me. There's no reason not to now."

"Maybe there is, CM….I don't know."

Silence again.

"I'm sorry, Charlie," he said. "I didn't know I was putting you in that position. Do you believe me?"

"Yes."

"I wish I'd created a way for you to contact me. We could have talked it through. I could have slipped away…"

"It wasn't just you, CM."

Silence.

"That son-of-a-bitch," CM said quietly. He turned his head and looked out the passenger window, pounding softly on his knee with his fist. Then he turned again.

"You did the right thing. You have to believe that."

We drove a few miles in silence again.

"Did you tell Maggie?"

"No."

"What does she think?"

"I don't know what she thinks."

"She needs to understand, Charlie."

"I promised not to tell her. It was part of…the deal."

Silence.

"After I get to Canada, you can come back down and tell her," he said.

"Okay."

"Take the second Bellingham exit," CM said. "I'll tell you the turns. After you drop me off, go straight back to the interstate and up to the border. I'll meet you at the place on that piece of paper."

"But how are you going to get there?"

"Fredrique has a friend with a boat," he said. "I'll probably get there even before you do."

54

I STAYED WITH CM INITIALLY for a month. His accommodations were a small trailer sitting up on concrete blocks at the end of a dirt road, not far from Chilliwack, near the Fraser River. The land was flat and weedy. But when it wasn't cloudy and raining, snowy mountain ranges appeared in the distance, levitating like mirages.

The furnishings were sparse. There was a wooden deck on the front of the trailer with a 2X4 railing and steps going down to the weedy yard. We stacked the deck with firewood. I'd drive into town for supplies when we needed them, and in the evenings we'd cook on the small propane stove and talk by the old cast-iron wood heater.

One day we went into Chilliwack together and CM paid cash for an old, Ford pick-up truck that had good tires and large rips in the upholstery. "So I can have my own transportation when you go back to Forks," he smiled.

What cheered CM momentarily was his discovery that I'd taken so many of his manuscripts and drawings and slides with me to Iowa—and still had them in the back of the Toyota.

"Jesus, Charlie!" he said, eyes wide as I carried in the box. "This is a miracle. I thought this stuff was gone."

He opened the box and started pulling out stapled chunks of typed pages, reading the first pages like they were satisfying a thirst.

Then he stopped. He put it all back in the box and tucked the flaps closed. He pushed the box over against the wall with his foot and sat in his chair by the heater.

"What is it?" I asked.

He waved his hand. "Never mind Charlie."

"What is it? I asked again.

"It's too late for all that," he said. "It would have been better, I think, if it had just burned up with everything else."

That was the beginning of his depression.

I took to going into Chilliwack in the mornings where I'd sit in the library and read the newspapers. Each township along the Fraser River had its own thin paper. There were a lot of jobs. Fishing boats. Lumber mills. Real-estate sales. Brick mason. Carpenter. I could be a carpenter, I thought. I had experience.

But I didn't call any of the numbers. I started reading a couple of books in the library stacks where I hid them on the wrong shelf so no one would check them out between my visits. There was a stuffed reading chair next to a window, and if I got there before ten o'clock it was usually empty. The librarian was a pretty brunette who wore short dresses and ballet leg-warmers. From the stuffed reading chair I could observe her comings and goings around the check-out counter, her ballet legs crisscrossing back and forth.

After several weeks of rain a bout of bright sunny weather cheered CM up. He had bought an old fly-rod in Chilliwack and began practicing with it out behind the trailer. He set up targets on the ground and paced off distances from which he'd try to cast a short piece of red yarn tied to the leader. He found a trail that led through some fields and woodlands down to a creek that fed into the Fraser River.

"There's trout in there," he told me. "I've seen them."

"Yeah? Really?"

"When you go back down to see Maggie tell her I've finally taken up fly-fishing. That'll make her happy. She'll feel like she had a positive influence on me after all." He flashed his big smile, the first time I'd seen it in Canada.

"I'll do that," I said. "I'll tell her."

"I'm fine now, Charlie," he said. "I think this is a good time for you to go. You can come back if you want. You need to start thinking about what you're going to do."

"There's lots of things to do around here," I said. "I've been reading the papers. I sort of like it here."

"That's fine," he said. "But go settle things with Maggie. I want to know she's all right."

It was snowing when I drove up to the small house with the brick stoop in Forks. The driveway was empty but there was a light on inside. I knocked twice. I was turning away when the door creaked open behind me.

"Lord have mercy! Is that my Charlie?"

Louise seemed a lot smaller than I'd remembered. She gave me a bear hug but she was a tiny bear, the top of her head barely making it up to my chest.

"Lord, let me look at you," she said, pulling me inside and closing the door. "Charlie! I believe you're still growing!"

"I don't think that's possible," I said. I was glancing around the small living room, looking for clues.

"Come on back to the kitchen," said Louise. "I was making some tea. You want a beer? I think Gus has some in the back of the fridge."

The kitchen was bigger than the living room. It had a small table and chairs under a hanging light with flowers painted on the shade. A kettle was steaming on the stove. There were familiar smells of Louise's cooking.

She was rummaging in the fridge, the door half closed on her.

"How are you, Louise?"

"I'm fine," she said, producing a green Heineken bottle with a grin.

"How's Gus?"

"He's fine too. He's still guiding. He works out of the lodge on Lake Crescent. They call him when there's work."

She poured hot water in a cup and dipped in a tea-bag. We sat at the table. She dipped her teabag up and down in the cup, looking at me. "Lord have mercy," she said again slowly, under her breath. Then: "You look tired, Charlie."

"I've been driving."

"Is CM...settled somewhere good?"

"Yeah. It's okay," I said.

"How is CM?"

"I don't know," I said. "He's different. Sometimes he's the same. I think he's depressed a bit."

"Stands to reason a man would be depressed," said Louise.

"Yeah. I guess we're still kind of taking it all in."

"If you can take in something like that," said Louise with an undertone of anger. Her face flushed. She sipped her tea.

"So how is Maggie?" I finally asked.

Louise looked away from me, out the window into the back yard where the snow was falling harder now, starting to lay down a white carpet.

"She's down in Portland."

"I thought that's were she might go."

"She really couldn't take it here." Louise looked at me, tears welling up. She pushed them away with a swollen red knuckle. "We went up to the camp one day. Gus had pulled down all those fish-heads and buried them. Pulled out all the nails too. But Maggie took one look at the holes left in the tree bark and she broke down. She wouldn't even go in to see…to look for anything. We just put a chain across the road with a padlock and came on back….Gus and the boys went down again one time. They pulled stuff up out of the river. No one's gone back since."

"Was there any insurance?"

"Maggie said no."

"Did they…was there an investigation?"

"It was an accident, is what the newspaper reported."

"Do you think it was an accident?"

"It weren't no accident, Charlie." Louise's eyes narrowed and she made a red fist on the table. "Whoever it was, they came in the middle of the night. Gus got me out after the first explosion. It wasn't overly loud. It was a poof. When we got outside we could see everything had gone up together—at the same time. There wasn't time to get nothing except ourselves." Tears welled up again. This time Louise just let them slide down her cheeks, looking at me.

Gus came later and we had dinner. I spent the night and left the next morning.

Louise had given me a piece of paper with a phone number and address for Maggie in Portland. I got in the Toyota, drove a couple of blocks then stopped. I unfolded the paper and read the address. I was trying to remember if I'd ever seen anything with Ben Sprague's address on it. But I realized that was impossible.

Portland was only a three hour drive to the south. But when I hit the Interstate I turned north without even hesitating. There was no reason to go see Maggie, to drag out the awkward pain of seeing her and Ben. North of Seattle, I exited the Interstate and found a post office where I purchased a pre-stamped envelope. I went out and sat in the Toyota and composed a letter:

> Dear Maggie,
> I came down to visit and Louise gave me your address. I hope you are doing well. CM is settled in a nice spot. He told me to tell you he's taken up fly-fishing and has started to perfect a really nice roll-cast. I expect to find work nearby. There's lots of interesting jobs I've been seeing in the newspaper. I'll try to keep in touch. There's a P.O. Box written below where you can contact CM if you need to. He asked me to give it to you. He loves you a lot. He wanted to make sure you're okay. And, in Portland, I'm sure you will be.
> Maggie, I'm sorry the way things turned out.
> I can't explain what happened in a letter. But I hope someday I can explain it, and that you'll forgive me.... There was a reason.
> Lots of love, Me. Charlie

55

A FEW WEEKS LATER, A post-card came with a picture of Mount Hood behind the Portland skyline. "Thanks for the letter, Charlie", it said. "I'm fine. All my love to CM."

CM still had some of the money left over from being short-listed in the competition. But I could tell by the way he'd fold it out to pay for things that it was starting to run low. I got a job writing for a small paper near Chilliwack to help pay for things. I wrote local interest stories. Someone would call the editor and say so and so was doing this or having a tragic time with that, and the editor would send me out with a name and address to do an interview. I also took classified ads over the phone and did cold-calls to regional merchants trying to sell ad space.

In the spring CM and I built a small addition to the trailer with used lumber and windows we got at a salvage dealer. I called it the studio but CM refused to call it that. He called it "the salvage room." It had big north-facing windows that looked out at the mountain range when the weather was good. Below the windows we built a work table and set out CM's drawings and manuscripts. For a few days he was energized, going through the materials and organizing them into stacks. Then he lost interest again.

He spent most of the summer and fall practicing with the old fly rod out behind the trailer and taking long walks down to the creek. In the evenings he mostly occupied an old easy chair by the cast-iron heater, tying flies. He'd set up a low table in front of the chair and he'd sit through the evening, leaning forward with thick magnifying glasses on the end of his nose, winding colored threads around tiny feathers and patches of fur held in a miniature vice.

He'd started listening to a tape on an old boom-box we'd bought at a second hand store: The Three Tenors. Operatic arias that drove me crazy at first, but slowly grew on me. There was one in particular, Nessun Dorma, that he would re-wind back to and play two or three times in a row, sometimes with a long, inward stare across the room or out the dark window.

One evening, with the arias playing in the background, I tried to coax CM out of his shell with an idea that I'd been thinking about for several weeks.

"What if we put together a book about the competition," I said during the applause after one of the arias. "You know, document what our entry would have been if…we'd presented it."

"Why do you want to do that Charlie?" he said, glancing at me over the tops of his magnifying glasses. He was positioning a fluff of yellow feather, the spool of thread he was winding with stopped mid-air.

"You said we didn't need to win," I said. "You said all we needed to do was make the presentation. A book would do that too, right?"

He held my gaze, considering this argument.

"Maybe," he said.

"Also, I think people would be interested," I said.

"I think what people are interested in is getting a set of tires for half price."

"Why be cynical?" I said. "You're just thinking yourself into a hole here. It's not like you. It's painful to watch, CM."

He set down the spool of thread and sat back in his chair and regarded me.

"It's painful to be in the hole, too," he said.

"Well, then let's get out of it."

"What are we going to do, Charlie?" He poured himself another glass of the cheap red wine he'd taken to drinking after dinner.

"Let's put together a book about Enabling Structures. About the competition. All that stuff is in there on the table. The slides. The drawings. All your manuscripts. Pikeman can't keep us from doing that…can he? What can he do now?"

CM sipped his wine, looking at me under drooping eyelids.

My question hung in the air. I thought about Maggie. Maybe there was something Pikeman still could do—or would. I wasn't sure.

"Maybe we could just get it ready," I said. "Maybe Pikeman will get hit by a bus."

"I don't know if I have the energy for it," CM said.

"I'll help you! Remember? That's what you hired me for."

He gave a little smile.

"On second thought, maybe it's not energy I don't have."

"What then?"

"Maybe I don't believe in it anymore."

"You what?"

"It just doesn't seem real anymore, Charlie. It doesn't seem important."

"What's important, then?"

His gapped-tooth smile stretched in a feeble effort. "Maybe nothing's important. Maybe that's what you finally come to realize…."

"Jesus, CM," I said.

He set down his wine glass and leaned closer to the little clump of feathers in the vice. He started winding thread again.

"Well then," I said, "do you mind if I do it?"

Another glance over the tops of the magnifying glasses.

"Do what, Charlie?"

"Do you mind if I go through your stuff and organize it? Do you mind if I put it together for a book? Do you mind if I get it published and cram it down Abe Pikeman's fucking throat?"

I stood up and kicked open the door and walked out into the warm night. I got in the Toyota and went for a long drive through the open, empty flat-lands of the Frazer valley. When I returned, CM was asleep in his chair by the cast-iron heater, a water glass with an inch of red wine was perched on his stomach, held there by his big, square sleeping hands.

I began working evenings in the salvage room-studio while CM tied his flies, sipping his wine and listening to his arias. I created an outline for the book, and began transcribing sections of

CM's manuscripts with an old electric typewriter I'd found at a Good-Will store in Chilliwack. I also found a photo lab that processed the 35mm slides into prints. I converted one wall of the studio into a story board, and began to pin up an outline of the book, including the photo prints and drawings that would illustrate it.

Sometimes CM would wander in and stand in front of the story board wall. His standing frame seemed to be shrinking and tilting. His curly hair had grown long and the beard he'd allowed to flourish was mostly white. One evening, as he slouched and tilted in front of the pinned up photos and drawings, I realized with a shock that I hardly recognized him.

"CM," I said, turning around from where I sat at the typewriter. "Tomorrow, lets work on this together. There's drawings that I'm thinking you could do…"

"I don't know, Charlie," he said looking down at the hand that wasn't holding his glass of wine. "It's been a while since I've drawn anything."

"But that's the point," I said. "You need to get back involved with this. I'm going to need your help."

"We'll see," he said and shuffled back into the trailer.

56

THE LAST DAY OF SEPTEMBER was a Saturday. I drove into Chilliwack for groceries and stopped at the library to read the news. The librarian, in her short skirt and ballet leg-warmers, handed me a folded newspaper as I settled into the reading chair by the window.

"I saved you *The New York Times* from yesterday," she said. "There's an article you'd like, I think."

"Thanks, Sally," I said. "What's it about?"

"It's about why J.D. Salinger quit publishing his work. I thought you'd be interested, since you seem to be hiding his books all over the library."

I gave her a quick look, but she just smiled, and spun around and went back to her desk.

I opened the paper, which she had folded so the Salinger article was facing out, and began to read. But there was a headline just under the Salinger article that kept drawing my eyes downward:

"America's Cities only Half Complete," said the headline.

After a moment, I abandoned the Salinger story and began reading the other one:

> By 2020 America is going to need 44% more building space than currently exists today, according to a new study by the Brookings Institution. The study, expected to be released today, estimates that only about half of the total 427 billion square feet that will be needed for residential and other uses in 2020 is currently standing.
>
> "Given that nearly half of the space needed in the next 30 years has yet to be built,' said Arthur C. Nelson, the report's

author, "it's not too late to change our built environment to make things better—or even a lot better than they are now."

I read this last sentence three times.

Then I got up and walked quickly to the front desk.

"What is it?" Sally asked, surprised.

"Can I borrow this paper?" I said.

"I saved it for you," she said in a hushed voice. "Go ahead and take it."

I went through the grocery aisles more quickly than usual. I piled the three bulging paper bags onto the passenger seat of the Toyota, next to the folded newspaper, and drove back to the trailer.

I carried one bag of groceries and the newspaper inside. CM was taking a cat-nap in his chair, a spool of fly-tying thread loose in his hand. He woke up when I put the bag of groceries down on the counter.

"Charlie," he said. "Back so soon?"

"Read this," I said, thrusting the folded newspaper into his lap.

"Which?"

"Read the one right there," I said pointing at the article. "I have to get the rest of the groceries."

I went out and retrieved the other two bags. When I came back into the trailer CM was sitting up straight, holding the paper in both hands, reading intently. I put the grocery bags on the counter next to the first one and began pulling things out, putting them away. I watched CM as I was doing this. He was sitting rigid.

He dropped the paper to his lap for a moment, staring straight ahead. Then he picked it up again and read. Then he folded the newspaper and slapped it hard on the arm of his chair.

He sprang up, his gap-toothed smile shining suddenly in his white whiskers. "It's not too late, Charlie!" he said. "Did you read this?"

"I read it," I said.

"It's not too late!" he said, slapping the newspaper again on the arm of his chair.

His body expanded in some way, filling out his old drapy jeans and shirt with an electric energy.

He spun suddenly and stepped to the door of the trailer, pushing it open. He strode with a big step out into the sunshine, looking up at the sky. With some great purpose, he started down the steps, his motion cascading oddly into a crumpling fall—as if someone had played a joke and pulled the steps out from under him.

Instinctively I shouted his name and bolted for the door.

At first, I thought he had fallen. But he lay crumpled too oddly and too still on the ground. When I turned him over, his forehead and cheeks were already blotching white, his eyes already looking far beyond the space I existed in.

57

ON THE THIRD RING, SHE answered.

"Hello?"

"Hi… Maggie?"

"…Charlie? What's the matter?"

"Maggie?"

"Charlie? Is that you?"

"Can I call you back?" I said.

"What is it?…."

"…In a minute. I'll call you back."

I hung up. I thought I'd had it under control.

I stepped out of the phone booth and sucked in some deep breaths. The sudden sound of Maggie's voice had caught me by surprise.

Another deep breath.

I rehearsed what I was going to say, what I'd decided to do. I went back in and called again.

"Charlie?" she said right away.

"Yes, it's me."

"Something's wrong. I can tell."

"It's CM," I said, already fading from my planned statement.

"Is he okay?"

"No."

"Is he sick?"

"No."

"Charlie…?"

"He died, Maggie."

Silence.

"Maggie…?"

"I'm here." Small voice.

"He had a heart attack. I thought he fell down the steps, but he...had a heart attack."

"Oh, Charlie..."

"...Maggie?"

"...Yes?"

"He's going to be cremated."

"Okay."

"I've decided...where he would have wanted to be. Where to spread his ashes."

"...Okay."

"I want to go to Zarathustra's pool."

"...Yes."

"Will you come with me?"

"Yes."

"In a few days," I said. "I'll call you."

"Okay."

"...And Maggie?"

"Yes?"

"I know Ben might want to come. But...would it be all right if he didn't come? I mean...."

"Oh, Charlie..."

"I'm sorry. I didn't mean...It's just that..."

"...Ben's not here, Charlie."

Silence.

"Okay," I said. "I'll call you in a couple of days."

"All right.....Take care of yourself, okay?"

"Okay."

I was concerned there might be complications with CM's identity. But I gave them his driver's license, and made up a story, and in the end they gave me CM's ashes in a brown paper bag sealed with packing tape. They'd tried to sell me an urn to carry them in but I told them it wasn't necessary. CM wasn't big on formalities like that, I explained. He'd be happy with a paper bag for a short period of time.

Maggie and I decided to meet in Port Townsend at the Blue Moose Café and drive up together in the Toyota. I got there early and parked next to a big sailboat standing on its keel, a ladder leaning against its hull. I was trying to remember if the same boat had been there on my first visit, before I even knew what CM's voice sounded like. But that was impossible. The boats must come and go.

The plan was to meet at the cafe at nine o'clock, then drive straight to the river. It would be a forty minute walk down to Zarathustra's pool. That would give us time to do the ceremony and get back to Forks before dark. We were going to stop and tell Gus and Louise on the way back. Maybe take them to dinner. They'd understand. Louise couldn't have walked to the pool anyway.

It was half-an-hour before our meeting time. I went into the café anyway and sat in a booth by the window. A waitress brought me a menu.

"I'll just have some coffee," I said.

She brought a steaming coffee mug and set it down, smiling.

"Can I ask you a question?" I said.

"Sure."

"Did a man by the name of Charles McCormick ever used to come in here?"

She considered a moment. "No, I don't recall that name."

"Thanks," I said. "It was a long-shot."

"Was he a boat worker?"

"A long time ago."

"I've only been here a year," she said. "Cream and sugar's on the table."

I sipped the coffee and gazed out the window. Was Ben just out of town, I was wondering, on a business trip? Is that what Maggie meant? Or had she meant something else? The little worm started twisting around in my gut as I stared out the window at the boat with the ladder leaning against it.

"Hi, Charlie."

My heart clamped tight. She was just suddenly there next to the booth.

"Where'd you come from?" I asked

She laughed. "I just walked in. And here you were."

"Jeez," I said, and slid out of the booth, banging my knees under the table, making the coffee cup jiggle out a little spill. I gave her a hug, and she hugged me back.

"You look great," I said. Her hair was different. Pulled back and knotted somehow so it fell behind her neck. "Your hair's gotten long," I said.

A shy laugh, her hand reaching back to as if to verify this fact for herself.

"I just stopped cutting it," she said.

"Wow, Maggie. It's great to see you." I couldn't stop staring at her.

"You too, Charlie."

I realized I was looking at her cheeks and nose and mouth and forehead…everywhere but her eyes. I was not looking into her eyes. I was afraid to look directly in there.

"You want some coffee?" I said, indicating we might sit in the booth.

"No, let's just go," she said. "Let's get started."

Outside, the old red Cherokee was parked next to the Toyota. She opened the rear door and pulled out a duffel bag.

"Looks like it might rain," she said. "So I brought some contingency stuff."

I glanced up at the sky. What had begun as a sunny morning was clouding over, though the early October air was still warm.

We drove out of Port Townsend and headed for Port Angeles, making small talk. It was profoundly strange being in the Toyota with her again, driving down the highway.

"So how have you been doing, Charlie?" she said after a while. It was the first real question. I could sense she was looking at me. My right cheek began to warm from her gaze.

"I've been okay," I said.

"What do you suppose you'll do…now?"

"I hadn't really thought about it."

"Did you meet some interesting people in Canada?"

"I had a job. For a newspaper."

"Really? You must have liked that."

"It was okay. It was strange living with CM. He was...he wasn't himself. He was depressed, I think."

"I'm sorry."

"I tried to get him to work on a book. To make a book out of his manuscripts and drawings. I'd saved almost all of them, you know. They were in the back of the camper. I wanted to tell the story about the competition...."

"Did he want to do that?"

"No. I did."

"What was the story, Charlie?"

I glanced at her. She was looking at me steadily.

"Maggie, there's stuff I have to talk to you about. Tell you."

"Okay."

"But not now. I'd rather wait till afterwards."

"That's okay too."

We drove in silence for a while. After Port Angeles the road climbed, then descended into the long, winding, picturesque curves along the edge of Lake Crescent. The snowcapped mountains were dark and ominous now, the wide expanse of water grey and cold looking, reflecting the sky. The wind whipped marching white caps along its surface.

The silence in the Toyota began to feel uncomfortable, so I plunged in:

"So tell me about you. How've you been?"

"I've been fine....It was hard at first, but I'm fine now."

"And how's Portland? Do you like it there?"

"Portland's nice. I live downtown in an apartment. There's lots of things going on. Lots of people....I've gotten to like that."

"....So, what's Ben doing?"

"Ben moved back to New York City."

"He did?... I figured you guys were going to..."

"Going to what, Charlie?"

"You know."

"I thought about it."

"...What happened?"

"It wasn't any better the second time than it was the first."

The lake was behind us now. As my mind worked on what Maggie had just said, I glanced at the side mirror, at the post-card image of the mountains above the lake, the ribbon of highway unspooling back into the photo.

"So what have you been doing?" I asked. "In Portland."

"I work for the Sierra Club."

"Wow. That sounds perfect."

"It's nice," she said. "The people are nice. I help do research."

A splattering of rain began to hit the windshield.

"Looks like you were right about the rain," I said. "Do you want to stop in Forks for lunch? Maybe it'll pass over."

"Let's just go ahead. I've got some granola bars here in my bag."

We drove through Forks without stopping, Maggie looking out the window, immersed in an introspective silence.

58

BY THE TIME WE GOT to the two-track portion of the road to the camp, it had begun to rain steadily. The Toyota's wipers clattered back and forth. We crossed the one-lane bridge, and both of us glanced to the right, up river toward where—except for the veil of the rain—we could have glimpsed Zarathustra's pool. I took the opportunity to briefly study the back of Maggie's head, the highlights of her woven hair.

The painted blue rock looked smaller than I remembered. The paint was peeling away from its surface in large, scaly chunks. The shaggy fir tree next to it seemed to have grown larger and wider. I didn't want to look at it closely but I did. A few nail-hole scars still puckered in the bark, with sap dribbling down. The two-track down to the meadow was barred with a heavy chain and padlock.

"Do we have a key?" I asked, looking at the padlock through the clacking windshield wipers.

Maggie rummaged in her bag. "Gus sent me one in case I ever needed it," she said.

I hopped out of the truck, opened the back of the camper and pulled out my rain-gear and a floppy, wide-brimmed hat that would keep the water out of my eyes. The big padlock clicked open and the chain slipped to the ground. I glanced down the little hill, but we were still too high to see into the meadow. I climbed back in the driver's seat.

"I like your hat," Maggie said.

"Thanks," I said. "Are you ready?"

"Okay." She put her hand out on the dashboard, as if preparing for some impact.

The Toyota bounced at the bottom of the little hill and rolled out onto the rocky meadow. Weeds and bushes had grown up in the driveway. We drove slowly forward, winding around them. The wreckage began to appear through the steady drizzle. I drove up to the edge of it and stopped. The wipers clacked back and forth, pushing the collecting rivulets of water aside, and we sat in silence for a moment, looking out at the ruins of the camp.

It was a flattened, scattered heap of metal sheets and charred timbers. Here and there, parts of river-rock walls and pilings stood up a few feet into the air. The metal roofing sheets that weren't blackened, glistened wet and dull in the overcast light.

"Jesus," I said softly.

Maggie was still holding the dashboard, bracing against it.

I killed the engine and the wipers stopped, mid-swipe. The scene blurred as the rivulets of water thickened and ran together on the windshield.

"Are you okay?" I said. "Do you...think we can do this?"

She was still looking straight ahead, her hand braced on the dashboard.

"I want to do it," she said. She looked at me quickly, her eyes wet and bright. "I'm okay Charlie." A quick smile, and she pushed on the door latch and stepped out.

I lifted the door of the camper and pulled down the tail gate. Under the protection of the raised door, Maggie opened her duffle and pulled out her waders and rain gear.

"Did you bring waders?" she asked.

"Yeah, I got some on the way down."

We pulled on our outfits and sat next to each other on the tailgate tying the laces to our boots.

"Okay," Maggie said, standing up and squinting into the drizzle. The waders and boots seemed to have brightened her mood.

I reached into the camper and brought out the paper bag of ashes.

"Is that...it?" she said.

I nodded.

She reached out and touched it.

"We should put it in something, to keep it from getting wet," she said. She rummaged in her duffle again and pulled out a plastic sleeping bag cover with a draw-string. "This'll work," she said.

We walked in a wide sweep around the edge of the wreckage. The rushing sound of the river called up from below, but we couldn't see it. The semblance of a path opened alongside a broken river-stone wall. I was trying to visualize which wall this had been. The ends of three charred timbers still lay across one end of it. Then we could see the river, the water swirling white and bubbly through its obstacle course. The boulders and rocks were larger than I remembered, more numerous.

"Water's really low," said Maggie. "It was a dry summer."

On the opposite bank, the wall of alder trees shimmered in the dull rainy light. We stood for a minute and watched the river.

"How are we going to get down?" I said.

The bank was steep where we stood. A series of rock pilings stood along the edge, a jagged, blackened timber protruding upward from each. This had been the veranda, I realized.

Maggie began making her way along the edge of the bank, stepping carefully over half-burned timbers and broken stone piers.

"We can get down here," she said at a spot where the bank dipped lower. "I'll go first, then you hand me the bag."

She stepped over the bank, taking hold of the gnarly trunk of a bush that had taken root in the rocky soil. She reached up from below and I lowered the plastic bag by its drawstring into her hands. Then I grabbed the same gnarly trunk, pulled on it to test its strength, and backed myself down to the stony beach. Maggie handed me back the ashes.

We headed down the beach and as we passed the last of the stone pilings I looked for the opening in the trees that would lead to the path up the hill to my unit. I'd thought about going up there on the way back, to see what was left. But now, where I thought the opening should be, there was only a thick wall of alder branches and undergrowth. I was beginning to doubt if I wanted to make the effort.

We followed the edge of the river bank, Maggie walking ahead. After a ways, she cut up into the trees. The old river path had overgrown with waist-high ferns, completely hiding, in some cases, the big windfalls we had to navigate. As before, Maggie somehow floated over them. After a ways we stepped back out onto the beach. We walked along the edge of the river again, balancing from rock to rock.

I was trying to remember if this was the place Maggie had given me the fly-casting lesson. She'd gotten ahead of me, and now had stopped to wait.

"You okay, Charlie?" she asked.

"I'm keeping up," I said.

"Keep your eyes on where you're stepping."

"I remember," I said.

The drizzle had subsided now, but the clouds seemed lower and darker. In places the river looked almost black. Clear, translucent black.

We climbed back up into the trees again to get past a big rapids. I should remember this place, I thought. But it looked foreign, the rocks bigger. The sound though was familiar: the throbbing engine-sound of the rushing water.

We descended to the water again, stepping onto the gravel bank from between the trunks of two enormous, moss-covered trees.

"This is where we should cross," said Maggie. "The pool is just around this bend. Can you hear it?"

I listened. A wind had come up and I could only detect the sound of the alder leaves clattering on the opposite bank.

"Not yet," I said.

"Follow my steps," said Maggie. "The water shouldn't be too far over our knees."

I followed Maggie out into the flowing current. The water was cold and pushed hard against my legs. I slipped and nearly went down, holding the bag of ashes above my head for balance.

When we got to the opposite bank the steady drizzle started again. We climbed into the restive, clattering alder trees and found another overgrown path. Soon, we came out above the gravelly beach where I remembered we'd landed the drift-boats. From there we found the path down to the pool.

I was struck by how beautiful a place it was—more than I remembered. Under the darkening sky, the large green room created by the pool and the sound of the rushing falls embraced us. The water was dark and clear and deep. The rocks on the bottom seemed illuminated by an inner light. Above, to our right, the falls shot out between the big boulders with a pulsing urgency, then relaxed into a lazy, arching free fall.

"I'm going up there," I said. "You stay here, Okay?"

She nodded.

I walked a ways back up the path and then cut over to the rocks that led up to the chute. I looped the draw-string of the plastic bag around my neck so I could use two hands to climb. The rocks were slippery and cold. When I got to the top, I stood over the chute and looked down at Maggie. She gave me a little wave.

I got down on a knee—startled for a moment to see the two deep grooves in the rock that had held the welded fish-head in place so long before—and removed the paper package from the plastic bag. I broke the tape seal with my fingers, and pried it open. A white puff of dust, like smoke, fluffed from the opening, surprising me. I stood up, holding the bag in both hands.

I had thought I was going to say something, a tribute. But I hadn't rehearsed anything and, at that moment, I realized nothing I could say would make any sense. Nothing seemed to make sense anymore.

I knelt again next to the notches in the stone, and tipped the bag toward the shooting water. The ashes tumbled out, a fine white powder clumped together in places by the moist air. A breeze came up and some of the powder fluffed onto the knee of my waders. I poured, and the urgent water sucked the powder into its flow, and carried it away over the edge.

When the bag was empty I folded it and climbed back down to the pool. I walked up to Maggie and stood in front of her. She reached out and we hugged. I walked over to a flat rock and sat down. She sat beside me. We were silent for a long time, listening as the drizzle thickened into rain.

Maggie broke the silence. "What was it you were going to tell me, Charlie?"

I swallowed and took a breath.

"I was going to explain…what happened in Iowa. CM wanted you to know."

Silence.

"I know what you think…I know you must have thought that I…decided I couldn't do it."

"I didn't think that, Charlie. I didn't know what to think."

The rain grew stronger, pocking the surface of the pool.

"The night you and Ben went out to dinner…remember? I stayed in my room to practice."

"I remember."

"They came and got me."

"Who?" A faint note of alarm.

"Pikeman."

"The Congressman?"

"His men."

Maggie took a deep breath.

"They took me out in their car. They…I thought they were going to kill me. They sort of pretended like that."

"Charlie…"

"But they weren't after me, Maggie."

Silence.

"They took me out into the country, to a big estate. They took me to a room where Pikeman was waiting. They left me there alone with him. He was drinking bourbon. He showed me photos they'd taken of CM in his disguise. CM was up in the balcony the whole time, did you know that?"

Silence.

"They'd been following him. They'd been following all of us, I think."

I remembered something suddenly, and turned my head and looked down the river. Far down, beyond the tail-out of the pool, I could see the dim, rain-blurry outline of the bridge.

"Do you remember that long black car we saw that day?" I said.

Maggie looked at me then followed my gaze toward the bridge.

"Yes."

"That was the car they took me in."

Maggie looked back at me, startled.

"They were going to arrest you both," I said.

Her eyes widened in surprise. "Me?"

"Aiding a wanted felon, Pikeman told me….I believed him."

Her eyes widened further, the green irises swirling.

I looked away.

"Pulling out of the competition was the condition, the deal he offered….I didn't know what else to do. It seemed like the only thing I could do."

The rain suddenly became intense. We watched as it turned the pool into white froth, mixing its sound with the shooting water. We sat in the deluge and watched.

After a while, Maggie said: "I wish you'd told me, Charlie."

"I do too," I said.

Silence again.

"And then…I assumed you and Ben…"

"I got your letter," she said.

The sound of the rain and the shooting water enveloped us, wrapping tightly around our hunched forms like a fuzzy, watery cocoon. Yet I could feel our energies drifting apart.

"Are you going to stay in Portland?" I asked.

"I don't know," she said. "I think I'd like to go away."

"Away?"

"Someplace away… someplace far away."

I watched the white frothy surface of the pool through the slanting downpour, my mind slowly going numb.

"I think we should go back," Maggie said, standing suddenly. The rain was now obscuring the opposite bank of the pool, and when she stepped away she nearly disappeared.

I followed up the slippery path, trying to keep her in sight. We crossed the river again and climbed up under the trees. It was quieter under the forest canopy, the thick branches high above absorbing and cushioning the sound of the rainfall. Maggie got ahead of me, sometimes disappearing entirely in the ferns and undergrowth that enveloped the path and it began to feel like I was just watching her walk away—that our parting was simply this: her walking farther and farther ahead until she was gone. I stopped trying to keep up. Just staying on the overgrown path seemed to require all my concentration.

The trail descended down to the river again, and I stepped out once more into the slanting rain-curtain, wondering if I was going to be able to find my way now. Then, in the distance, I saw her. At first I thought she was waiting for me. But she wasn't. She was standing on the rocky beach at the edge of the water, her back to me. I walked up behind her.

She didn't move.

"What is it?" I said.

She raised her hand for me to be quiet. "…Listen."

I listened.

The rain was driving hard against the river and the rocks. Inside the rain sound was the engine throb of the white water. Then I heard it. Faint. High in the air above our heads. As if carried by the wind, it grew louder: A deep, thrumming, harmonic note.

A tingling electric sensation ran up the back of my neck. I stepped around Maggie as if to get closer and the blood rushed into my legs, hot and rubbery. The sound faded, and came back again stronger, humming and throbbing in the rain-rushing air.

"It can't be," Maggie whispered behind me. "Where is it?"

But I knew.

I began running and stumbling as fast as I could up river, slipping and sliding on the rocks, the undulating call beckoning and urging me forward.

I came to the first stone pilings and stopped, momentarily visualizing where CM's studio had stood. Then I walked straight toward the solid wall of alder branches and underbrush, arms ahead of me like a prow, and stepped into it. The branches slapped my face and stripped my rain hat, and I pushed forward.

Then I stepped onto the path. I heard Maggie pushing into the trees behind me. I held back the last branches and she stepped through. The switch-back trail up the steep hill was overgrown with ferns, but faintly visible. The thrumming harmonic of the fish-head called out again and we began to run.

We came out into the clearing and looked up in amazement. At the top of the hill, the jutting silver roof slabs of my unit stood clear and strong against the slanting veil of the sky, and the fish-head gargoyle—thrusting out from the juncture of the roofs—was spewing a long white arc of water into the air, singing its disembodied song as if celebrating that we'd finally returned.

59

I WAS ASTONISHED. EVERYTHING APPEARED to be exactly as I'd left it. Why had I assumed it had been destroyed? Why had CM made that assumption as well? Or had he? Had I just misunderstood?

I walked up the field and checked that the water turbine was still turning in the stream. The hammer was under the steps, exactly where I'd left it. I quickly extracted the nails holding the plywood door, and we pushed on it and stepped inside. The rain drummed loud on the metal roof above our heads. It was dark— the window openings still shuttered with the plywood covers I'd fastened closed from the inside. Behind us the doorway cast a rectangle of grey-rainy light across the floor. The inside air smelled of wood and old, dry sawdust.

"See if the lights work," said Maggie.

I found the switch next to the kitchen counter and flipped it. Amazingly, the two white spots above the counter flickered on, illuminating the stone counter.

"I don't believe this," I said.

Without speaking, we pulled off our waders and rain-gear and hung them on wooden pegs next to the doorway, as if we'd just returned from a day of fishing. I unlatched the plywood shutters over the windows and, one by one, we pushed them open, propping each one up with its notched stick. The rain had slackened now, and with each new window opening, more of the soggy afternoon light flowed into the space.

"Charlie, it's different than I remember." Maggie said, turning in a circle. "You did a lot of work since the last time I was here....what's up there?"

"That's the sleeping loft," I said. "Come on, I'll show you."

She followed me up the steep ships-ladder next to the book cases. The space at first seemed cramped and dark.

"Help me open it up," I said.

The loft window openings were large, and when we pushed out the shutters, the space opened and filled with the soft wet light. It felt like we were standing high in the trees.

"This is so wonderful!" Maggie said. She turned around slowly, taking in details of the roof rafters and wall framing. She studied the poster of Van Gogh's Starry Night, that I'd nailed to the wall with a silver, galvanized umbrella nail at each corner. Then she leaned out a window and touched the dripping branch of a tree.

"I love being in the trees like this," she said. "It must be what it's like to be a bird."

"A bird?" I laughed.

She laughed too. "It's just like a nest, Charlie!"

She leaned out the open window frame again, and I marveled to see her there, delicate fabric shoulders framing her woven, gleaming hair. *What magic door in the universe have we just walked through?* But I didn't really think that; I can only imagine now that I might have thought it—or should have.

"Show me the rest!" She turned and started for the stair-ladder.

"There's only one other part that you haven't seen," I said.

"Show me!"

I used the hammer again to pry the nails out of the other plywood door, and it swung out to the short set up steps down to the deck over the stream. This deck was now partially covered with a roof as well, making a pavilion across the tumbling water. On the other side of the stream, the deck stepped up again to a raised platform under the trees. Around the edge of this platform, spaced about every three feet, were round, cantaloupe-sized river stones.

We crossed the stream and stepped up on the raised platform, and I watched Maggie explore all the parts and pieces with her eyes.

"What is this?" she said.

There were two circular holes in the platform, each with a raised river-stone edge you could sit on. One hole was about four feet in diameter and eighteen inches deep. This was a fire-pit, I explained.

"And what's this one?"

"That," I said, "is a Chinese stone bath."

She looked at me doubtfully, then stepped up and peered into the hole. It was about six feet in diameter and it was deep, and dark.

"So how does it work?"

I explained to her how I'd dug down as far as I could, then built the sides with river stones and mortar—exactly like she'd help build the piers for the fish camp. When I got it the right depth, I built the raised deck around it. I explained how a pipe from a higher water level upstream, would fill the bath when I opened the valve, and it would fill to same height as the upstream end of the pipe.

"Here, I'll demonstrate," I said. "The valve is right down here." I jumped off between two of the round stones, reached under the deck and opened the valve.

"There's water coming in!" said Maggie.

I climbed back up and we stood together, peering down into the dark stone hole, listening to the water rushing in. Then we could see the surface dimly reflecting the patch of grey sky and tree limbs above us, and we watched this quavering reflection rise up against the sides of the river-stone walls.

"This was Mr. Xu's idea," I said.

Maggie looked at me with surprise.

"You remember him?"

"You mean the Chinese delegation?"

"We brought him up here. CM and I. To consult...."

"Consult about what?"

"Consult...on certain ideas...about the unit here. CM wanted him to see it. He was using it as a way to explain his theory. He wanted to get Mr. Xu to participate....It worked, actually."

Maggie looked back into the bath. The water was about half way up.

"But that water's frigid," she said. "What was this supposed to be? Some kind of Chinese torture Mr. Xu was recommending?"

I looked at her, surprised and started laughing.

"What is it Charlie?"

I sat on the edge of the fire-pit holding my head, laughing harder than I can ever remember laughing, and then there were tears coming out between my fingers and running salty into the corners of my mouth, and I wasn't laughing any more.

Maggie sat next to me and put her arms around my shoulders.

"I'm sorry," I said, trying to stop.

"Go ahead," she said. "You need to."

And I could feel that she was crying too, and we kind of crumpled together for a minute. I reached around her with my arm, and for a moment she fell into my embrace.

Then she twisted away slightly, keeping her arm still around my shoulder, but pulling away.

I pushed the tears out of my eyes and off my cheeks with my fingers.

"Jeez, Maggie," I said, still shuddering for breath. "It's just that CM would have thought…that was so funny," I said, regaining my breathing.

"What was funny?" Maggie separated and stood up.

"Mr. Xu's Chinese torture chamber." I wiped my cheeks dry with the backs of my hands.

Maggie peered down into the bath again. "Well," she said, "it looks pretty frigid to me."

"That's what I thought too!" I said, standing up. "But wait till you see how it works!"

I walked over to the firewood I'd carefully stacked so long before, filled the crook of my arm with five or six wood chunks and carried them over to the fire-pit. Repeating this, I arranged a big fire-stack in the middle of the pit while Maggie watched in doubtful silence. I strategically slid the chunks of resin-wood starters into the fire-stack.

"And now for the stones," I said with dramatic flourish.

I hefted up one of the big round stones lining the edge of the raised deck, and carried it to the fire pit. Then I hefted another, arranging a dozen of them around the edge of the fire-stack. All the while, Maggie watched, too dubious to help.

I struck a match with a silly magician's gesture and held it to each of the resin-wood chunks. They lit up brightly, casting orange light and sudden shadows up through the firewood. Soon, flames were licking into the air, illuminating the underside of the metal roof of the pavilion. We stood back and watched. The drizzly grey, late afternoon light visibly faded around us as the fire brightened.

"So I assume," said Maggie, looking down into the bath, which was now filled and undulating, "you're planning on putting those big hot stones in the water, thinking—I assume again—that strategy is going to actually heat it up?"

"You're quick," I said. "I'm really impressed."

"And you think this is actually going to work."

"Mr. Xu assured me it would. He said it was an ancient Chinese method."

"And how did the ancient Chinese get the hot rocks out of the fire? Ancient hot-pads or something?"

"You think I haven't thought of that?" I said.

"I'm certain you've thought of just about everything."

"Just wait and see," I said. I stacked some more wood on the fire. "We need to get a big bed of coals to heat the rocks. Maybe we should make something to eat."

"Dinner would be lovely," said Maggie, a familiar playful voice slipping out. "What have you planned?"

"I thought we'd begin with vegetarian chili," I said, crossing the bridge deck over the stream. When I stepped up through the doorway into the unit, I turned and was surprised to find Maggie so close behind, she nearly ran into me. "Then artichoke hearts with almonds," I said, into her face.

And she laughed, and pushed me out of the doorway.

We went into the little kitchen space and started opening cabinet doors. I pulled down a big can of chili.

"I can guess what else is in here," said Maggie. She started opening cupboards too. "Look! Here's a can of cheese ravioli. Have you ever had ravioli-chili?"

"I doubt that's ever been made before."

"Well, I think that's why we should make it," she said, still going through the cupboards.

We built a fire in the raised hearth of the main room and pulled the primitive table I'd built to write on over close to it. The white table cloth and silver candelabra were still in the storage compartment next to the bookshelves. Two folding canvas chairs quickly completed the dining room.

By now the darkness outside the open windows was complete. The damp air had grown chilly, and I dropped the awnings over the windows. We lowered the steel cooking grate over the fire and set out pans and pots on the counter. We arranged the canned foods we'd chosen in order: The vegetarian chili and cheese ravioli next to each other—symbolizing their soon-to-be gourmet intermingling. A small space, then the can of artichoke hearts. Another small space and the canned pair of plum-cake pudding and condensed milk. We opened a bottle of white and a bottle of red wine and set them on the stone hearth near the table. We set out folded, cream-colored napkins and plates and silverware and wine glasses. We lit the candles in the candelabra and the facets of all these shapes and surfaces began to glisten and dance to the rhythm of the candle flames and fireplace.

I went out to the bridge pavilion and put more wood on the fire-pit and used the poker to pull and spread the growing mound of coals over and around the stones. When I came back up, Maggie had put a pot of water on the fire-grate. "For tea, later on," she said.

I went into the kitchen, pulled open a drawer and found a can-opener.

"Dinner's begun," I announced, holding the can-opener for her to see.

We poured ourselves big glasses of wine, and I opened the paired cans of chili and ravioli and handed them to Maggie's outstretched hands. She lifted them with graceful formality and dumped their contents into the large pot.

We sat on the stone hearth, sipping our wine, Maggie peering into the pot on the cooking grate, stirring occasionally with a spoon. I watched the firelight reflecting warm and bright against the side of her face. She was concentrating, her lips parted slightly, the same concentrating expression I remembered when she was slowly retrieving her fly-line.

"Okay. This is ready," she said.

We worked quickly, like a choreographed pair of chefs. Maggie tipped the pot from the grate, and I held white crockery bowls for her to spoon the chili-ravioli into. She pushed the pot off to the side of the grate to keep warm and I put the bowls on the table. I slid out her canvas camp chair and stood behind it.

"Madame," I said, bowing slightly.

She looked at me, surprised, and a sudden shadow of doubt crossed her eyes.

I nodded quickly at the steaming bowls. "We have to eat while it's hot," I said.

The shadow passed and she smiled hesitantly. She sat down and I scooted her chair in toward the table.

After the chili-ravioli, we took the candle lantern from the mantle and went down to check on the stones. The fire-pit had died down to a glowing heap, casting the deck in a dull red light.

"They seem to be cooking nicely," said Maggie.

"I think we should put them in before we start dessert," I said.

"And how do we do that?"

"By an ingenious method, of course," I said. "Here, hold the lamp for me."

In the side of the fire-pit closest to the round bath, I had left one of the masonry stones loose. Using the steel poker I pushed this loose stone into the firepit and off to the side, creating an opening.

"Okay. Now bring the light over here," I said.

I reached down, under the edge of the raised deck, and pulled up a length of board that had smaller boards nailed to each side, creating a shallow chute.

"Ah!" said Maggie with mock admiration. "What else do you keep hidden under your floor?"

"You will notice," I said, as I set the chute as a bridge from the edge of the fire-pit to the bath, "that the fire-pit has been ingeniously configured to be just slightly higher than the bath."

Maggie lifted the candle lantern up to illuminate what I was doing, its light shimmering on the dark, tight surface of the bath water.

"You know, Charlie," she said. "You may have hidden talents after all…. I'm serious."

Using the bent end of the steel poker, I coaxed the first stone out of the coals and edged it toward the gap in the fire-pit. At the top of the chute, I gave it a nudge. It rolled smoothly down the board with a bowling ball sound and chunked into the bath with an angry hiss. The reflecting water surface undulated—a small wispy cloud of steam the only hint of what it had just swallowed.

One after the other, the stones rolled down and chunked with sizzling hisses into the bath.

I removed the chute, slid it back under the deck, pulled the masonry stone back in place in the fire pit, and stacked new firewood on the coals. Flames quickly began to lick and wag into the darkness again, casting a shimmering orange light that brightened Maggie's face.

I knelt down and put my hand in the water.

"Heating up fast?" she said.

"Yep. It's almost ready," I said.

"Let me feel." She knelt and thrust her hand into the water. "Charlie! It's freezing!"

"Give it a little time" I protested, wondering if this was really going to work. "This is a very ancient method."

We crossed back over bridge and stepped up into the main room. I moved the chili dishes to the kitchen counter while Maggie heated the plum-cake pudding in a pan on the fire grate. She added the can of condensed milk and stood looking down at the concoction as it began to cook.

"My father used to heat condensed milk and make cocoa with it," she said. "It was the best cocoa you can imagine."

When Maggie announced it was hot, we put the pudding in a big white bowl and set it in the center of the table to share. I refilled our wine glasses, and we reached in with our spoons from opposite sides.

"It's good," Maggie said, stabbing her spoon into the bowl again with relish. "Isn't it?"

"It really is," I said.

Maggie was spooning the pudding into her mouth like a seven-year-old at a birthday party.

"So, I have a confession to make," I said, leaning back in my chair.

"A confession?" A big bite of pudding was bulging her cheeks.

"Yeah. Promise you won't be angry?"

"Angry?" She partially swallowed.

"Or laugh? I mean it. Will you promise?"

"Okay, Charlie." She looked at me, leaning forward with a tentative concern, her empty spoon poised above the white bowl of pudding, the candelabra light flickering over her face.

"Well…" I immediately faltered.

"What, Charlie?"

"…The reason this unit got built was so I could seduce you."

Her eyes widened. "What did you say?"

"It was actually CM's idea…"

"CM?"

"I mean, not that I seduce you….That was my own idea….I mean, it wasn't like we discussed it or anything. What I'm trying to say is that it was my interpretation of CM's idea….Do you see what I mean?"

She leaned her face closer, searching my face intently. Then her lips pursed tight together. Her cheeks began to bulge slightly, the muscles trying to hold them flat. In spite of these efforts, her laugh popped out—with a few flying specks of pudding.

"I'm sorry, Charlie," she said, still laughing. "I'm not laughing at you. I…didn't mean to spit on you either."

She reached across the table with her napkin and tried to wipe my cheek.

"Who are you laughing at, then?"

"It's just that…." She calmed herself. She looked up at the ceiling, like she was trying to cure hiccoughs. She put her spoon down and took a long sip of wine.

"It's just that—what?" I said.

"Would you say that again?" she asked, looking up at the ceiling again. "I mean, say that whole thing again."

"Well...." I organized my thoughts. "What I was trying to say was that the reason I built this unit was, basically...so I could seduce you."

"That's what I thought you said."

"Okay, then."

She stared at me and I glared back.

"But what was the part about CM?"

"Well, I was trying to explain that. When CM wanted me to do this, I didn't really want to do it. I resisted. I told him I didn't know how to start. I'm not an architecture student, I said. How the hell am I supposed to know how to design a building? 'How am I supposed to know what it's supposed to be like?' I said. 'You're trying to make me do something that I don't know how to do,' I said."

"And what did CM say?"

"CM said...." But my throat unexpectedly swelled up. I hid this with a big gulp of wine. "CM said that he had a secret. He said I just had to think erotically. He said all I had to do to design my unit was to imagine.... Imagine the most beautiful girl I could imagine. And then imagine...imagine how I would seduce her....How it would happen, you know....Where we'd sit...and drink wine. How we'd cook dinner...where we'd...." I stopped.

Maggie was looking at me—no, into me. Her eyes had become strangely calm. She was looking past, I could tell, my eyes and mouth and nose and cow-licked hair, examining something way deep inside. What was she looking at? What was she seeing, that I couldn't even feel myself?

"So...I just wanted you to know that," I said.

"But you never tried to seduce me, did you Charlie?"

"Well, I never got around to that part," I said.

"Why?"

"Well, you were always too busy, for one thing."

Maggie's lips pursed together again, her cheek muscles flexing, holding in another laugh.

"You were!" I said. "I could never even get you to come up here!"

"I can see how that would make it difficult," she said.

"Good, then. That's settled."

Maggie leaned back in her chair, still looking at me intently. Then she reached for her wine glass and took a long sip.

"Don't we have any music, Charlie?"

"I don't know."

"Go check. Some music would be nice, I think."

I got up and went over to the bookcase next to the fireplace. I pulled down the hinged door concealing the tape player, remembering how I'd done this exact same thing at my roofs-up party. I turned on the player, watching the little blinking lights come on—and out popped the cassette. I hadn't played it since that night.

I pushed the cassette back in and pressed the play button.

The speakers in the top of the bookcase crackled with static. Then the background sounds of the band tuning up. A couple of drum strokes: Tada—Tadum. I leaned my head against the bookshelves, listening, remembering. The random sounds began coalescing like they always did—like the backwards running movie of a broken wine glass leaping off the floor onto a table-top, the pieces and shards of guitar and drum, and drops of conversation and laughter, colliding backward-seeming into that first powerful chord—then another that made everything hush.

"These songs are for a boy I know in Vietnam," my mother says, and the base guitar begins its deep, syncopated melody—joined a moment later by the up-rhythm strokes of her strident, hand-swept acoustic guitar....And then her clear, bell-like voice:

"...I came upon a child of God...." leaning against the grille of an old Mercedes Benz. "He was walkin' along the road....And I asked him, where are you going ...."

When I turned around Maggie was gone.

I walked around the table and into the little kitchen. I looked down the short passage to the bathroom. But the door was open, the room dark. I walked back around the kitchen and stuck my head out the entry door, searching into the chilly darkness. I walked back around the table and fireplace. I glanced up the stair-ladder into the sleeping loft. Then I heard a sound out on the bridge pavilion.

I descended the steps slowly, and walked half-way across the bridge, the song growing fainter behind me.

Maggie was standing with her back to me, tossing chunks of wood into the fire-pit, stoking the fire back into bright, high flames. I could feel the heat reaching across the cold, damp air.

She leaned the poker against the side of the fire pit. She reached down and pulled off her wool socks. She turned around facing me, but not looking at me. The bright flames cast her partially in silhouette. She began to unbuckle her belt.

"What are you doing?" I said.

"That's why I always loved you, Charlie," she said, looking at me now. "From that very first day: You're a beginner. You're always learning the beginning of things...."

She removed the belt and dropped it on the floor boards of the deck.

"Everyone else wants to be the expert. But you're the only person I've ever known who was always at the beginning...."

Maggie slid the baggy, khaki pants down her legs onto the deck and stepped out of them. The fire light instantly began exploring her suddenly naked thighs and hips, and the fish-scale tattoo was iridescent in the orange brightness.

In one swift motion, she pulled her shirt and vest over the top of her head—the orange flames highlighting and shadowing her ribs and belly as her arms stretched upward. She reached behind, holding my eyes with hers, and unclasped her bra, holding it against her breasts as she lifted the straps over her shoulders, then held it out and let it drop. She slipped off her underpants and flicked them lightly with her toe onto the growing pile of clothes. She stepped up to the stone bath, the fire light licking all the shapes of her nakedness.

She stopped and stood there, looking straight at me.

"I think you succeeded, Mr. Cadwell," she said. And without hesitating, she stepped up on the edge of the stone bath and dropped into the water.

60

THERE'S AN ENTRY IN MY mother's diary that I didn't pay a lot of attention to the first time I read it. It's one of the few that she wrote before my father left for Vietnam, and I associate it closely with the black and white photo of them standing on either side of the Mercedes Benz. The entry stands out today because I realize it reports the planting of a seed that was going to grow into an idea that would entangle and transform my life in ways I can only now begin to appreciate.

> 72-11-16
>
> Strange argument with Charlie last night. I don't know how we got onto the topic, since he ships out next week, and this was supposed to be our first "last night"—champagne dinners at the best restaurants we can afford in Charleston (except we have to bring our own champagne because of the dumb brown-bag rule!) It was supposed to be fun and celebratory, but I could tell right away we were celebrating the beginning of a dreaded inevitability that had been creeping up on Charlie these past few months of special training.
>
> We were into our second bottle of champagne when somehow the topic of conversation became my music. Not that we'd never discussed this before. Charlie was always appreciative and supportive of my music. He's the least musical person I've ever known—he can't even dance, let alone carry a tune. But I always knew he enjoyed, my singing, my music. The fact that he was so different, that he expressed himself so differently, attracted me. Music seems so easy. What Charlie does seems so hard, so complicated....
>
> But suddenly he said something that hurt. It just came out of the blue, out of the conversation somehow, and it jammed into me like a hot poker:

Here's the thing, he says. You sing this beautiful music, these great songs and lyrics, and strum through these great chords and riffs, and the whole world is in rapture about it. They think you're the most profound messiah they've ever experienced. But in reality, what do you give them? In REALITY what do you create? NOTHING!! (He said this with real vengeance!)

Me, on the other hand, he says, I can give them something that will literally change their lives, something that can actually CHANGE the world they live and walk around in. And yet, they could care less. You sing—and you're up on everyone's pedestal. I draw a better world people can actually LIVE in—and I'm invisible.

I asked him, so what am I supposed to do?

He shrugged me off. This anger was something I'd never seen before, not all the time we dated at Clemson, not once since we've been living together here in Charleston.

In defense, I told him I thought the reason people responded the way they did to music was because the music was really in THEM—like they're the musical instruments and all I'm doing, really, is helping them strum the strings inside their own heads, sing the words in their own hearts. And so even though they're listening to ME, THEY are making the music themselves somehow, and that gives them a sense of power, a feeling of expression, it makes them feel alive and living and creative....

He stared at me a long time after I said that. It was a flat kind of distant stare that I wasn't used to. At first, I thought he was getting even more angry, and I started dreading what was coming next. Then, all of sudden, he smiles—his CHESHIRE SMILE—as I call it—and his eyes started going off like Chinese sparklers.

Laurie, he says, I can't explain it now. But what you just said is going to change my life. And he lifted his champagne glass to me in a toast, his smile beaming as big as I'd ever seen it, and it ended up being the best night we've ever had....Way, way the very best.

And what's amazing to me, even now, is that's exactly the kind of night I was about to have with Maggie Scott: The best. Way, way, the very best. Because half way through it we realized and understood we were not just going to be lovers, we were going to be revolutionaries.

###

Author Bio

J.D. ALT started out intending to be a novelist, but became an architect and urban designer instead. He holds two U.S. patents for a single-lane downtown people mover system, has lectured on the form of urban communites at various national and international conferences, and was invited to present his urban transit concepts in Beijing, China. Most recently, he completed two experimental "affordable" houses built around a prototype prefab core module he calls a "HOUSEED." The housing market collapse in 2009 put further development of the prototype on hold, and gave him the free time to finally sit down and complete the novel he has long been contemplating. He lives with his wife in Annapolis, Maryland.

CPSIA information can be obtained at www.ICGtesting.com
Printed in the USA
LVOW072009141211

259457LV00001B/9/P